STAR TREK

THE NEXT GENERATION

TERRA INCOGNITA

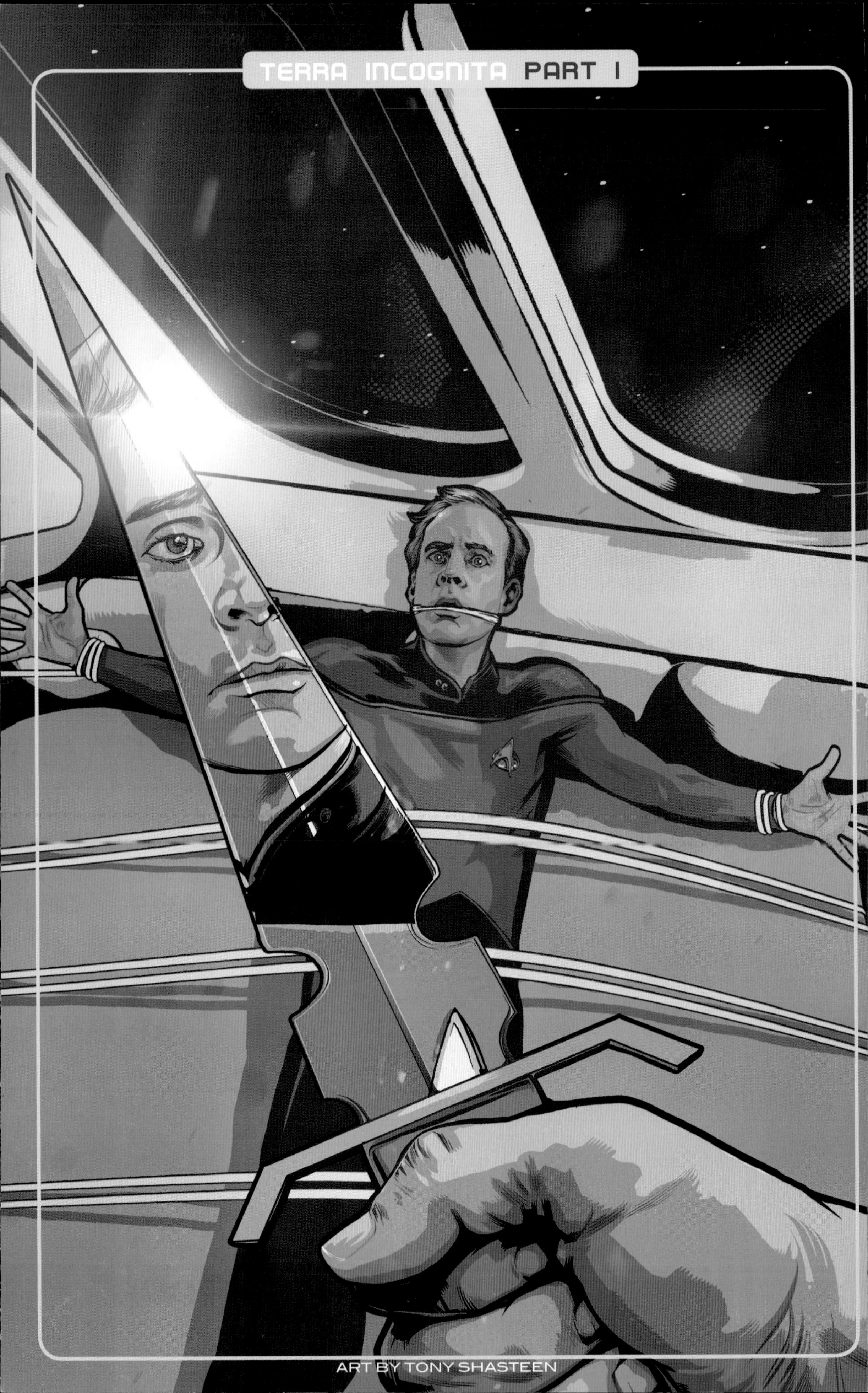
TERRA INCOGNITA PART I

ART BY TONY SHASTEEN

STAR TREK
THE NEXT GENERATION
TERRA INCOGNITA

WRITTEN BY
SCOTT TIPTON & DAVID TIPTON

ART BY
TONY SHASTEEN (#1),
CARLOS NIETO (#2 & 6),
ANGEL HERNANDEZ (#3-5)

COLORS BY
JD METTLER (#1),
FRAN GAMBOA (#2 & 6),
MARK ROBERTS (#3-5)

LETTERS BY
NEIL UYETAKE

SERIES EDITS BY
CHASE MAROTZ AND DENTON J. TIPTON

STAR TREK CREATED BY
GENE RODDENBERRY

Facebook: facebook.com/idwpublishing
Twitter: @idwpublishing
YouTube: youtube.com/idwpublishing
Tumblr: tumblr.idwpublishing.com
Instagram: instagram.com/idwpublishing

ISBN: 978-1-68405-429-9   22 21 20 19   1 2 3 4

Cover Art By
J.K. Woodward

Collection Edits By
Justin Eisinger And
Alonzo Simon

Collection Design By
Ron Estevez

Publisher
Chris Ryall

Originally published as STAR TREK: THE NEXT GENERATION –
TERRA INCOGNITA issues #1–6.

Chris Ryall, President, Publisher, & CCO
John Barber, Editor-In-Chief
Robbie Robbins, EVP/Sr. Art Director
Cara Morrison, Chief Financial Officer
Matt Ruzicka, Chief Accounting Officer
Anita Frazier, SVP of Sales and Marketing
David Hedgecock, Associate Publisher
Jerry Bennington, VP of New Product Development
Lorelei Bunjes, VP of Digital Services
Justin Eisinger, Editorial Director, Graphic Novels & Collections
Eric Moss, Senior Director, Licensing and Business Development

Ted Adams, Founder

Special thanks to Risa Kessler, Marian Cordry, and John Van Citters
of CBS Consumer Products for their invaluable assistance.

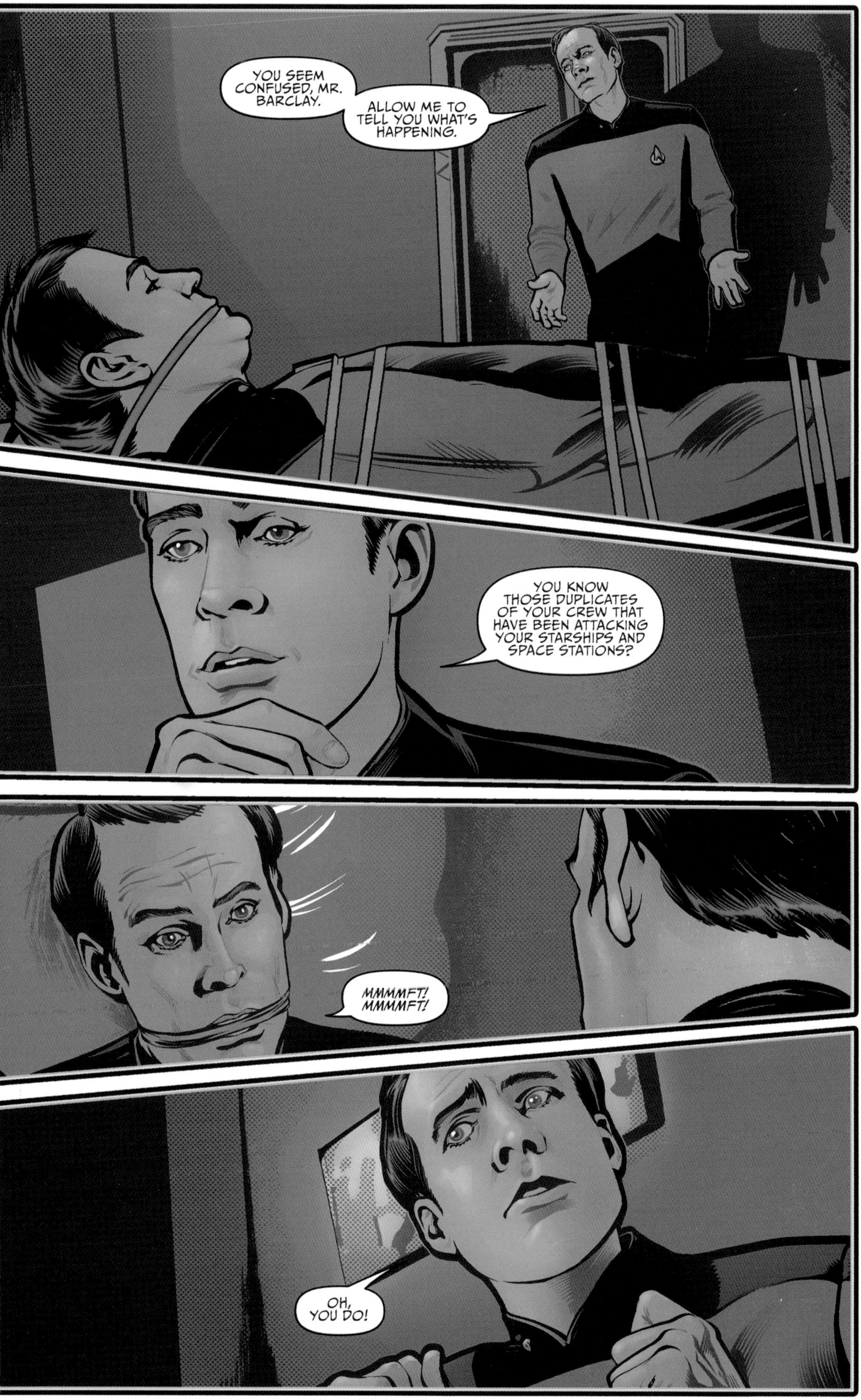
YOU SEEM CONFUSED, MR. BARCLAY.
ALLOW ME TO TELL YOU WHAT'S HAPPENING.
YOU KNOW THOSE DUPLICATES OF YOUR CREW THAT HAVE BEEN ATTACKING YOUR STARSHIPS AND SPACE STATIONS?
MMMMFT! MMMMFT!
OH, YOU DO!

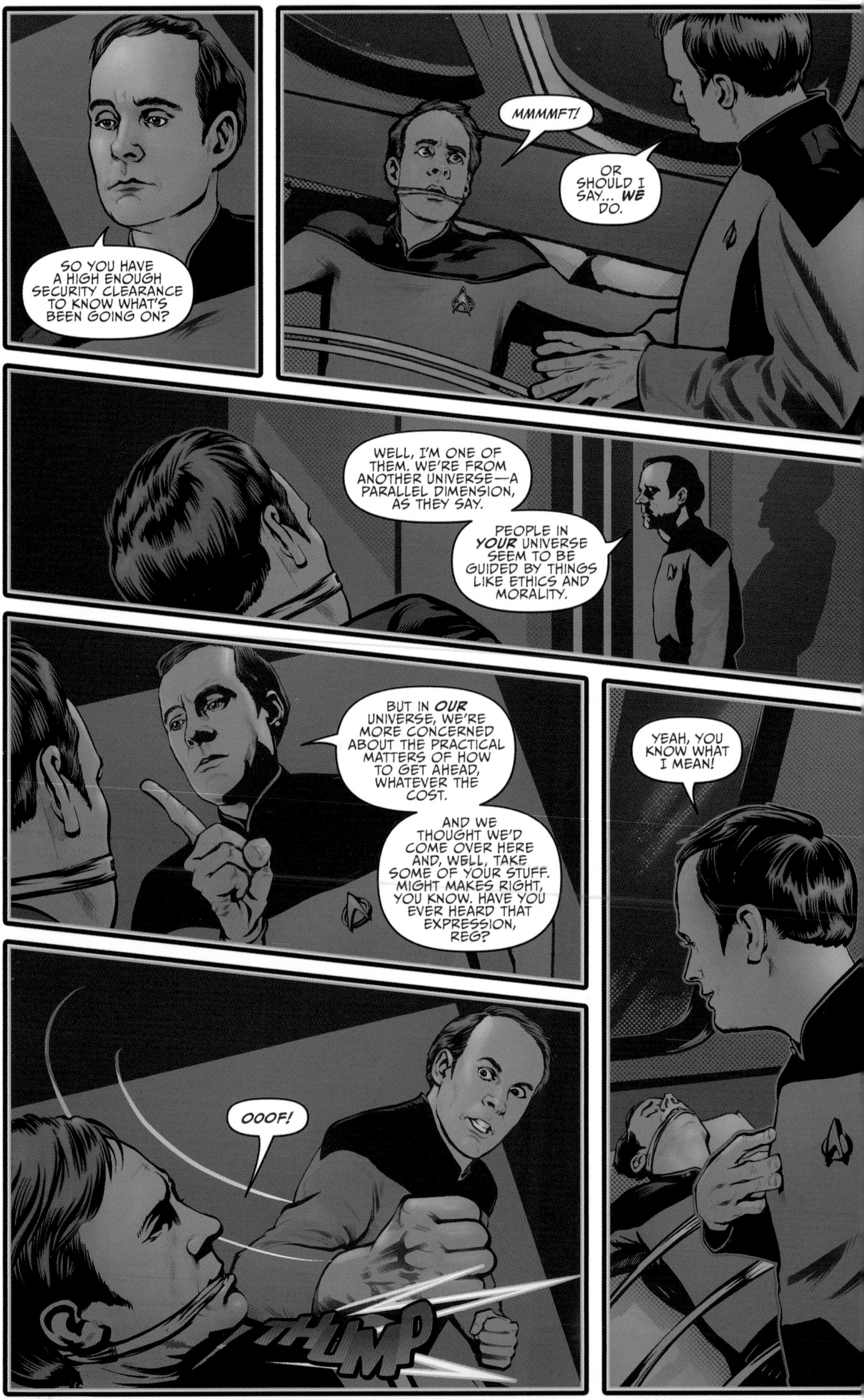
SO YOU HAVE A HIGH ENOUGH SECURITY CLEARANCE TO KNOW WHAT'S BEEN GOING ON?
MMMMFT!
OR SHOULD I SAY... **WE** DO.
WELL, I'M ONE OF THEM. WE'RE FROM ANOTHER UNIVERSE—A PARALLEL DIMENSION, AS THEY SAY.
PEOPLE IN ***YOUR*** UNIVERSE SEEM TO BE GUIDED BY THINGS LIKE ETHICS AND MORALITY.
BUT IN ***OUR*** UNIVERSE, WE'RE MORE CONCERNED ABOUT THE PRACTICAL MATTERS OF HOW TO GET AHEAD, WHATEVER THE COST.
AND WE THOUGHT WE'D COME OVER HERE AND, WELL, TAKE SOME OF YOUR STUFF. MIGHT MAKES RIGHT, YOU KNOW. HAVE YOU EVER HEARD THAT EXPRESSION, REG?
YEAH, YOU KNOW WHAT I MEAN!
OOOF!
THUMP

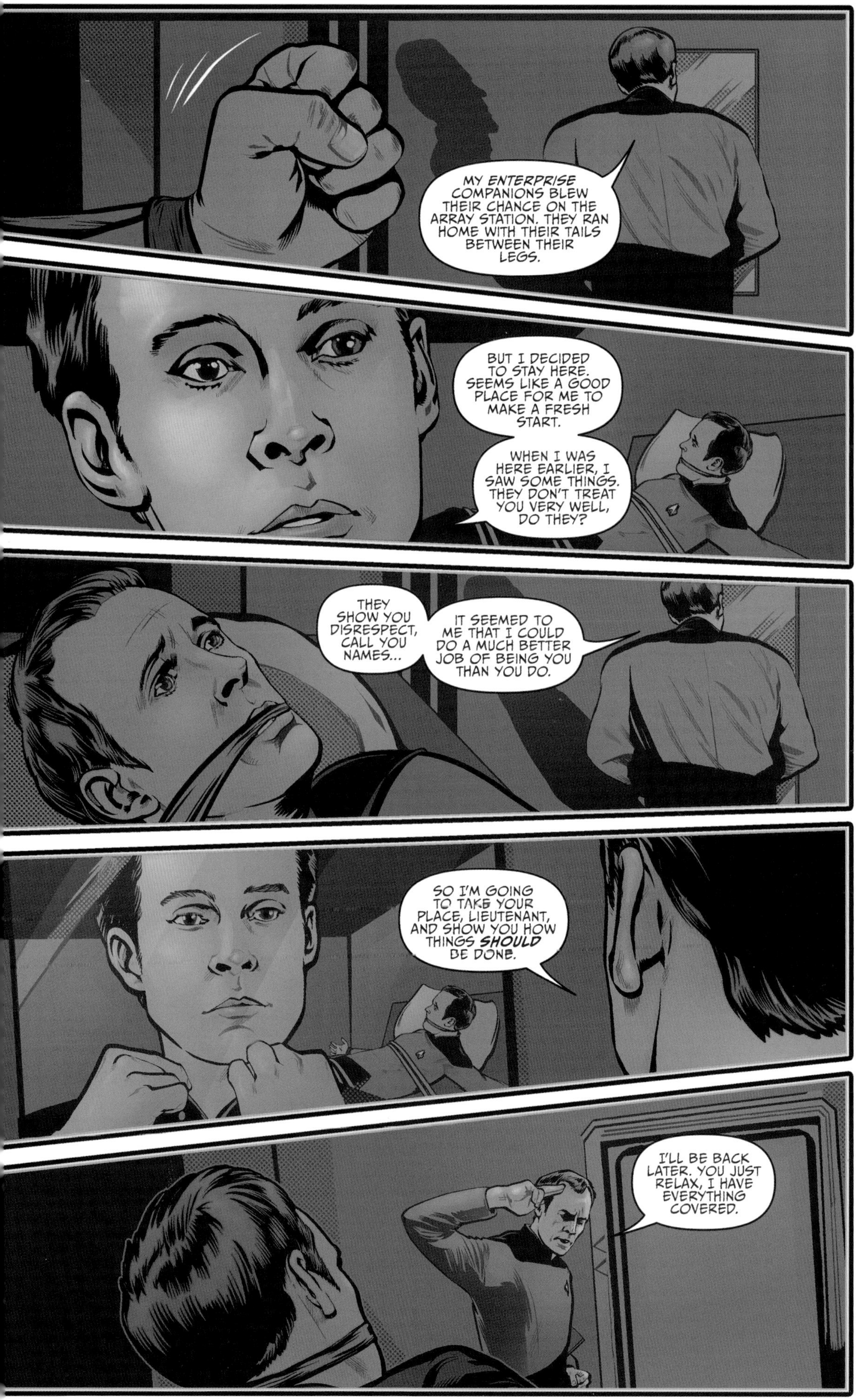
MY *ENTERPRISE* COMPANIONS BLEW THEIR CHANCE ON THE ARRAY STATION. THEY RAN HOME WITH THEIR TAILS BETWEEN THEIR LEGS.
BUT I DECIDED TO STAY HERE. SEEMS LIKE A GOOD PLACE FOR ME TO MAKE A FRESH START.
WHEN I WAS HERE EARLIER, I SAW SOME THINGS. THEY DON'T TREAT YOU VERY WELL, DO THEY?
THEY SHOW YOU DISRESPECT, CALL YOU NAMES...
IT SEEMED TO ME THAT I COULD DO A MUCH BETTER JOB OF BEING YOU THAN YOU DO.
SO I'M GOING TO TAKE YOUR PLACE, LIEUTENANT, AND SHOW YOU HOW THINGS ***SHOULD*** BE DONE.
I'LL BE BACK LATER. YOU JUST RELAX, I HAVE EVERYTHING COVERED.

MY ALTER EGO WILL BE OKAY TIED UP IN THERE FOR NOW. BUT EVENTUALLY, IF THIS IS GOING TO WORK, I MUST ELIMINATE HIM. NOT REALLY LOOKING FORWARD TO IT, BUT THAT'S A PROBLEM FOR LATER.

FIRST THINGS FIRST, I NEED TO FIGURE OUT HIS DUTY ROSTER. AH, GOOD; HE'S OFF DUTY. BUT HE HAS A NOTE HERE TO VISIT DATA'S QUARTERS "TO FEED SPOT."

DATA'S CAT? THAT SABERTOOTHED MONSTROSITY MIGHT TEAR MY HEAD OFF. I BETTER FIGURE THIS OUT, BEFORE THE ANDROID COMES BOTHERING ME ABOUT IT.

SPOT?

HM, YOU'RE NOT AT ALL WHAT I WAS EXPECTING.

PURR PURR PURR

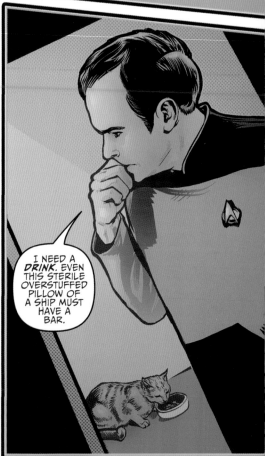

I NEED A *DRINK*. EVEN THIS STERILE OVERSTUFFED PILLOW OF A SHIP MUST HAVE A BAR.

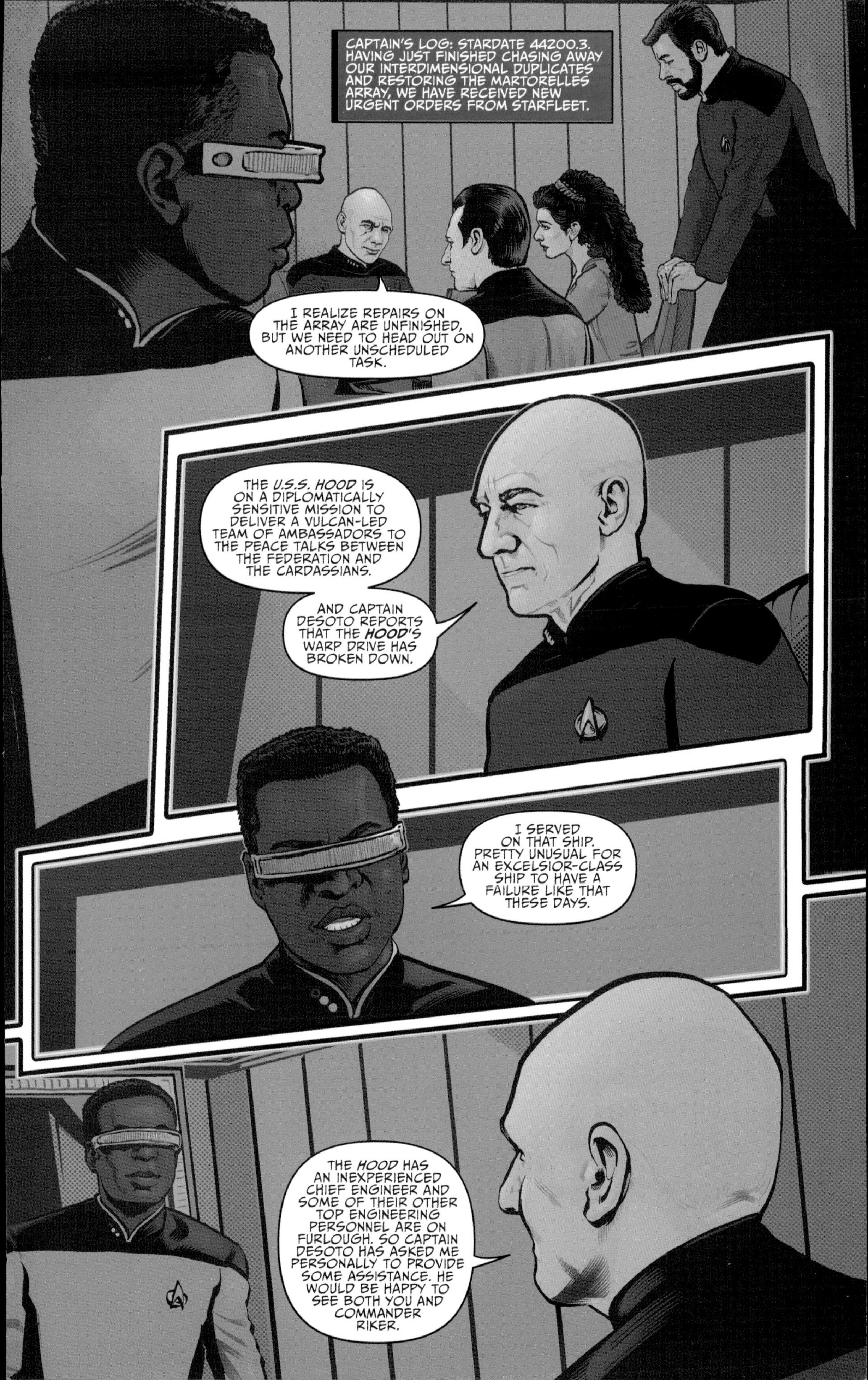
CAPTAIN'S LOG: STARDATE 44200.3. HAVING JUST FINISHED CHASING AWAY OUR INTERDIMENSIONAL DUPLICATES AND RESTORING THE MARTORELLES ARRAY, WE HAVE RECEIVED NEW URGENT ORDERS FROM STARFLEET.
I REALIZE REPAIRS ON THE ARRAY ARE UNFINISHED, BUT WE NEED TO HEAD OUT ON ANOTHER UNSCHEDULED TASK.
THE *U.S.S. HOOD* IS ON A DIPLOMATICALLY SENSITIVE MISSION TO DELIVER A VULCAN-LED TEAM OF AMBASSADORS TO THE PEACE TALKS BETWEEN THE FEDERATION AND THE CARDASSIANS.
AND CAPTAIN DESOTO REPORTS THAT THE *HOOD'S* WARP DRIVE HAS BROKEN DOWN.
I SERVED ON THAT SHIP. PRETTY UNUSUAL FOR AN EXCELSIOR-CLASS SHIP TO HAVE A FAILURE LIKE THAT THESE DAYS.
THE *HOOD* HAS AN INEXPERIENCED CHIEF ENGINEER AND SOME OF THEIR OTHER TOP ENGINEERING PERSONNEL ARE ON FURLOUGH. SO CAPTAIN DESOTO HAS ASKED ME PERSONALLY TO PROVIDE SOME ASSISTANCE. HE WOULD BE HAPPY TO SEE BOTH YOU AND COMMANDER RIKER.

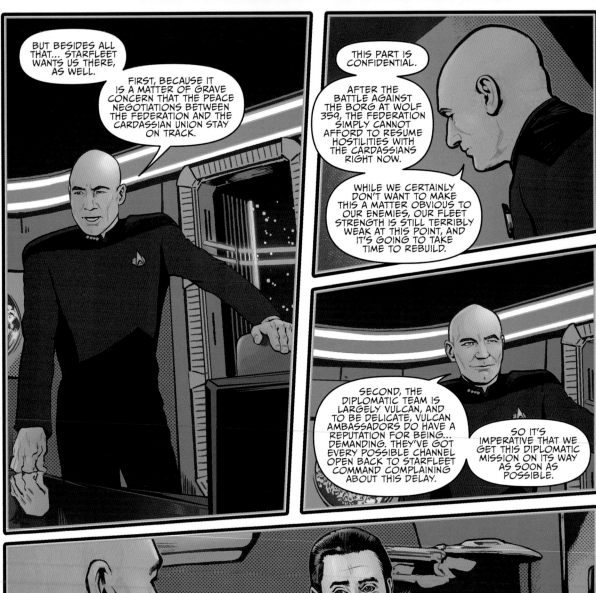

BUT BESIDES ALL THAT... STARFLEET WANTS US THERE, AS WELL.

FIRST, BECAUSE IT IS A MATTER OF GRAVE CONCERN THAT THE PEACE NEGOTIATIONS BETWEEN THE FEDERATION AND THE CARDASSIAN UNION STAY ON TRACK.

THIS PART IS CONFIDENTIAL.

AFTER THE BATTLE AGAINST THE BORG AT WOLF 359, THE FEDERATION SIMPLY CANNOT AFFORD TO RESUME HOSTILITIES WITH THE CARDASSIANS RIGHT NOW.

WHILE WE CERTAINLY DON'T WANT TO MAKE THIS A MATTER OBVIOUS TO OUR ENEMIES, OUR FLEET STRENGTH IS STILL TERRIBLY WEAK AT THIS POINT, AND IT'S GOING TO TAKE TIME TO REBUILD.

SECOND, THE DIPLOMATIC TEAM IS LARGELY VULCAN, AND TO BE DELICATE, VULCAN AMBASSADORS DO HAVE A REPUTATION FOR BEING... DEMANDING. THEY'VE GOT EVERY POSSIBLE CHANNEL OPEN BACK TO STARFLEET COMMAND COMPLAINING ABOUT THIS DELAY.

SO IT'S IMPERATIVE THAT WE GET THIS DIPLOMATIC MISSION ON ITS WAY AS SOON AS POSSIBLE.

DATA, HOW QUICKLY CAN WE GET TO THE *HOOD* BASED ON THE COORDINATES I FORWARDED YOU EARLIER?

AT TOP SPEED, LESS THAN FOUR HOURS, SIR.

I'LL TAKE CARE OF EVERYTHING, CAPTAIN.

AND I'LL GET AN ENGINEERING TEAM PREPARED TO BEAM OVER TO THE *HOOD*, CAPTAIN.

THANK YOU BOTH. LET'S GET THIS TAKEN CARE OF QUICKLY AND MAYBE WE CAN GET SOME WELL-DESERVED REST.

AND SOME TIME TO THINK ABOUT HOW TO KEEP OUR DUPLICATE TORMENTORS FROM TROUBLING US AGAIN.

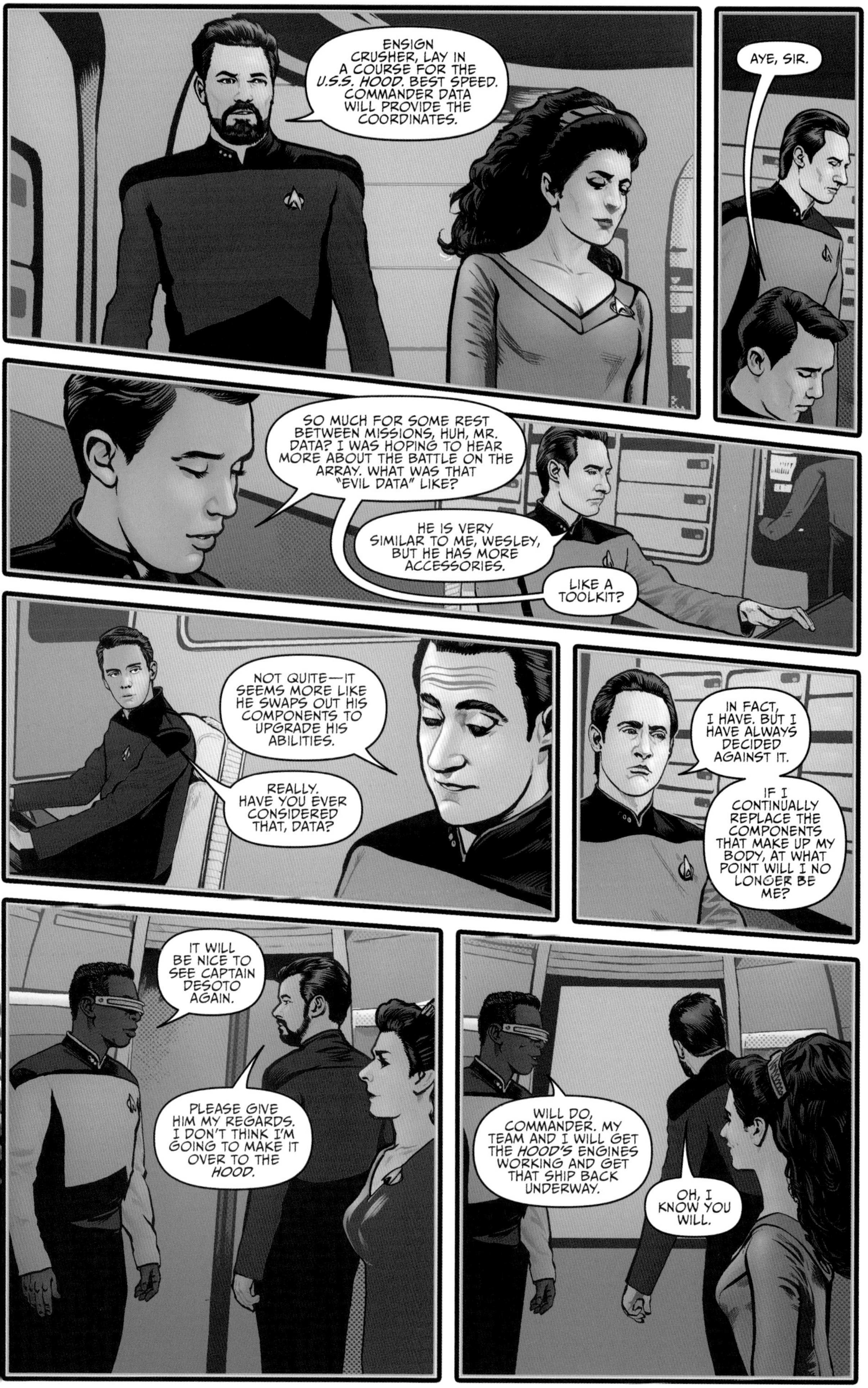
ENSIGN CRUSHER, LAY IN A COURSE FOR THE U.S.S. HOOD. BEST SPEED. COMMANDER DATA WILL PROVIDE THE COORDINATES.
AYE, SIR.
SO MUCH FOR SOME REST BETWEEN MISSIONS, HUH, MR. DATA? I WAS HOPING TO HEAR MORE ABOUT THE BATTLE ON THE ARRAY. WHAT WAS THAT "EVIL DATA" LIKE?
HE IS VERY SIMILAR TO ME, WESLEY, BUT HE HAS MORE ACCESSORIES.
LIKE A TOOLKIT?
NOT QUITE—IT SEEMS MORE LIKE HE SWAPS OUT HIS COMPONENTS TO UPGRADE HIS ABILITIES.
REALLY. HAVE YOU EVER CONSIDERED THAT, DATA?
IN FACT, I HAVE. BUT I HAVE ALWAYS DECIDED AGAINST IT.
IF I CONTINUALLY REPLACE THE COMPONENTS THAT MAKE UP MY BODY, AT WHAT POINT WILL I NO LONGER BE ME?
IT WILL BE NICE TO SEE CAPTAIN DESOTO AGAIN.
PLEASE GIVE HIM MY REGARDS. I DON'T THINK I'M GOING TO MAKE IT OVER TO THE HOOD.
WILL DO, COMMANDER. MY TEAM AND I WILL GET THE HOOD'S ENGINES WORKING AND GET THAT SHIP BACK UNDERWAY.
OH, I KNOW YOU WILL.

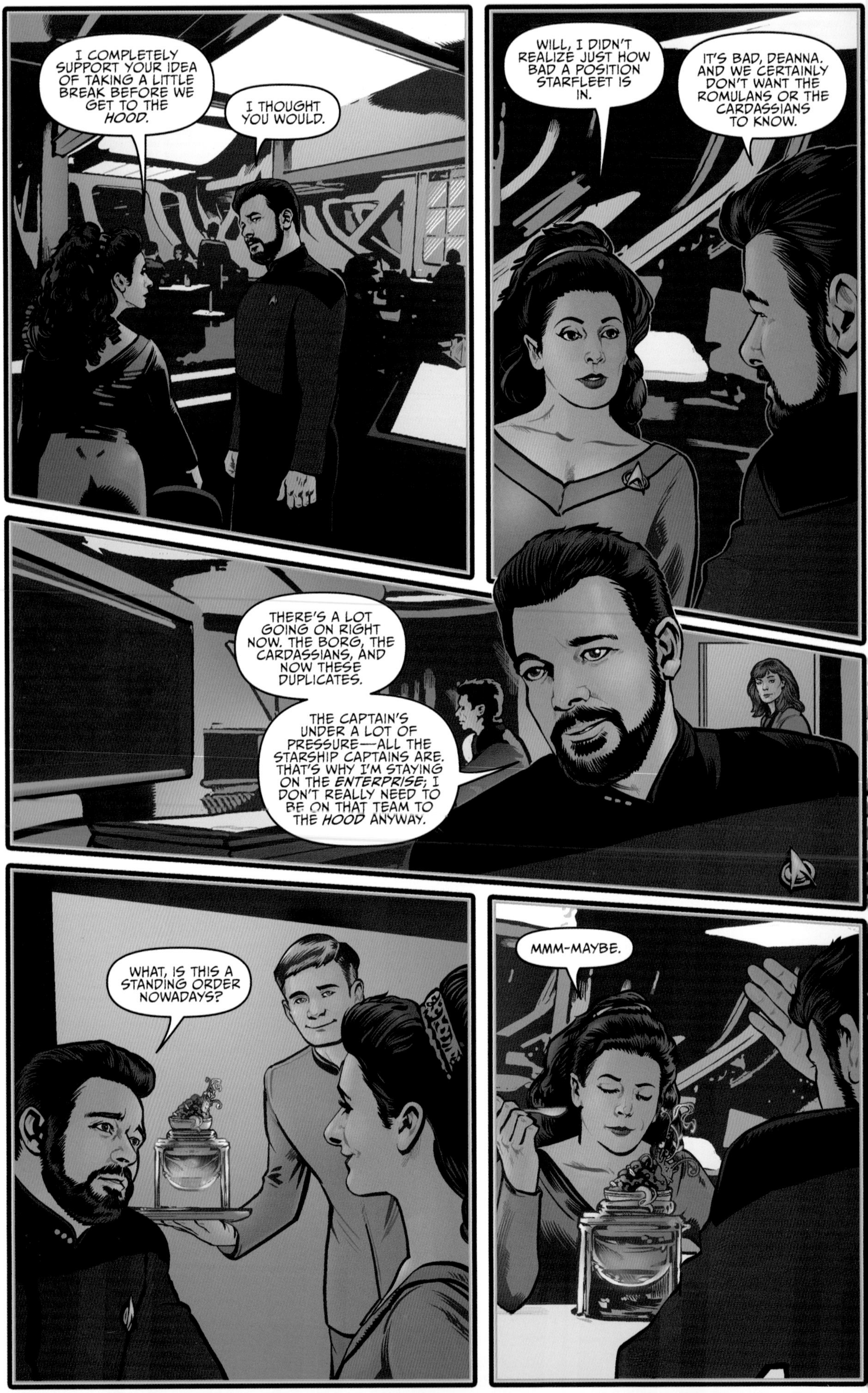
I COMPLETELY SUPPORT YOUR IDEA OF TAKING A LITTLE BREAK BEFORE WE GET TO THE *HOOD*.
I THOUGHT YOU WOULD.
WILL, I DIDN'T REALIZE JUST HOW BAD A POSITION STARFLEET IS IN.
IT'S BAD, DEANNA. AND WE CERTAINLY DON'T WANT THE ROMULANS OR THE CARDASSIANS TO KNOW.
THERE'S A LOT GOING ON RIGHT NOW. THE BORG, THE CARDASSIANS, AND NOW THESE DUPLICATES.
THE CAPTAIN'S UNDER A LOT OF PRESSURE—ALL THE STARSHIP CAPTAINS ARE. THAT'S WHY I'M STAYING ON THE *ENTERPRISE*; I DON'T REALLY NEED TO BE ON THAT TEAM TO THE *HOOD* ANYWAY.
WHAT, IS THIS A STANDING ORDER NOWADAYS?
MMM-MAYBE.

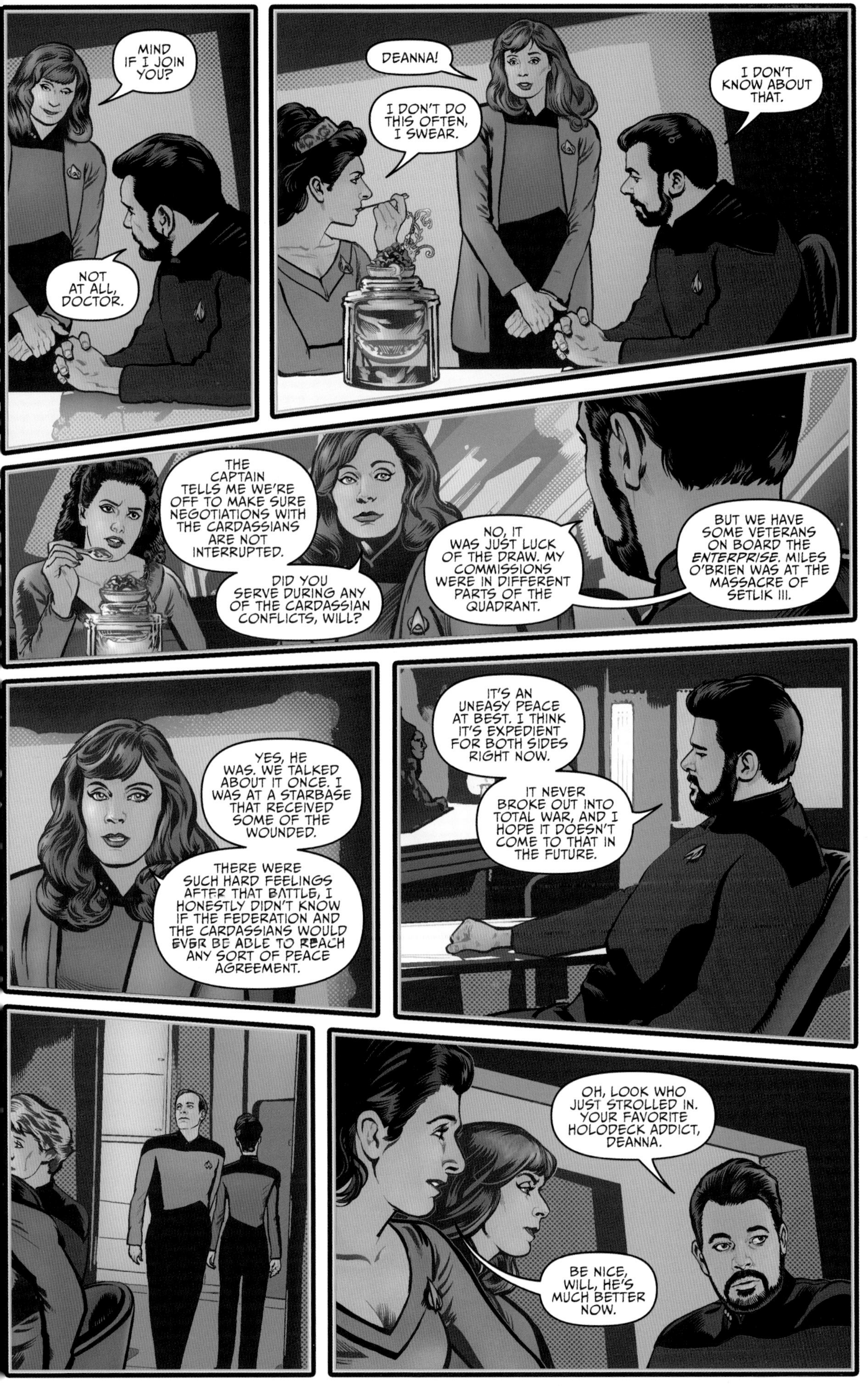
MIND IF I JOIN YOU?
NOT AT ALL, DOCTOR.
DEANNA!
I DON'T DO THIS OFTEN, I SWEAR.
I DON'T KNOW ABOUT THAT.
THE CAPTAIN TELLS ME WE'RE OFF TO MAKE SURE NEGOTIATIONS WITH THE CARDASSIANS ARE NOT INTERRUPTED.
DID YOU SERVE DURING ANY OF THE CARDASSIAN CONFLICTS, WILL?
NO, IT WAS JUST LUCK OF THE DRAW. MY COMMISSIONS WERE IN DIFFERENT PARTS OF THE QUADRANT.
BUT WE HAVE SOME VETERANS ON BOARD THE *ENTERPRISE*. MILES O'BRIEN WAS AT THE MASSACRE OF SETLIK III.
YES, HE WAS. WE TALKED ABOUT IT ONCE. I WAS AT A STARBASE THAT RECEIVED SOME OF THE WOUNDED.
THERE WERE SUCH HARD FEELINGS AFTER THAT BATTLE, I HONESTLY DIDN'T KNOW IF THE FEDERATION AND THE CARDASSIANS WOULD EVER BE ABLE TO REACH ANY SORT OF PEACE AGREEMENT.
IT'S AN UNEASY PEACE AT BEST. I THINK IT'S EXPEDIENT FOR BOTH SIDES RIGHT NOW.
IT NEVER BROKE OUT INTO TOTAL WAR, AND I HOPE IT DOESN'T COME TO THAT IN THE FUTURE.
OH, LOOK WHO JUST STROLLED IN. YOUR FAVORITE HOLODECK ADDICT, DEANNA.
BE NICE, WILL, HE'S MUCH BETTER NOW.

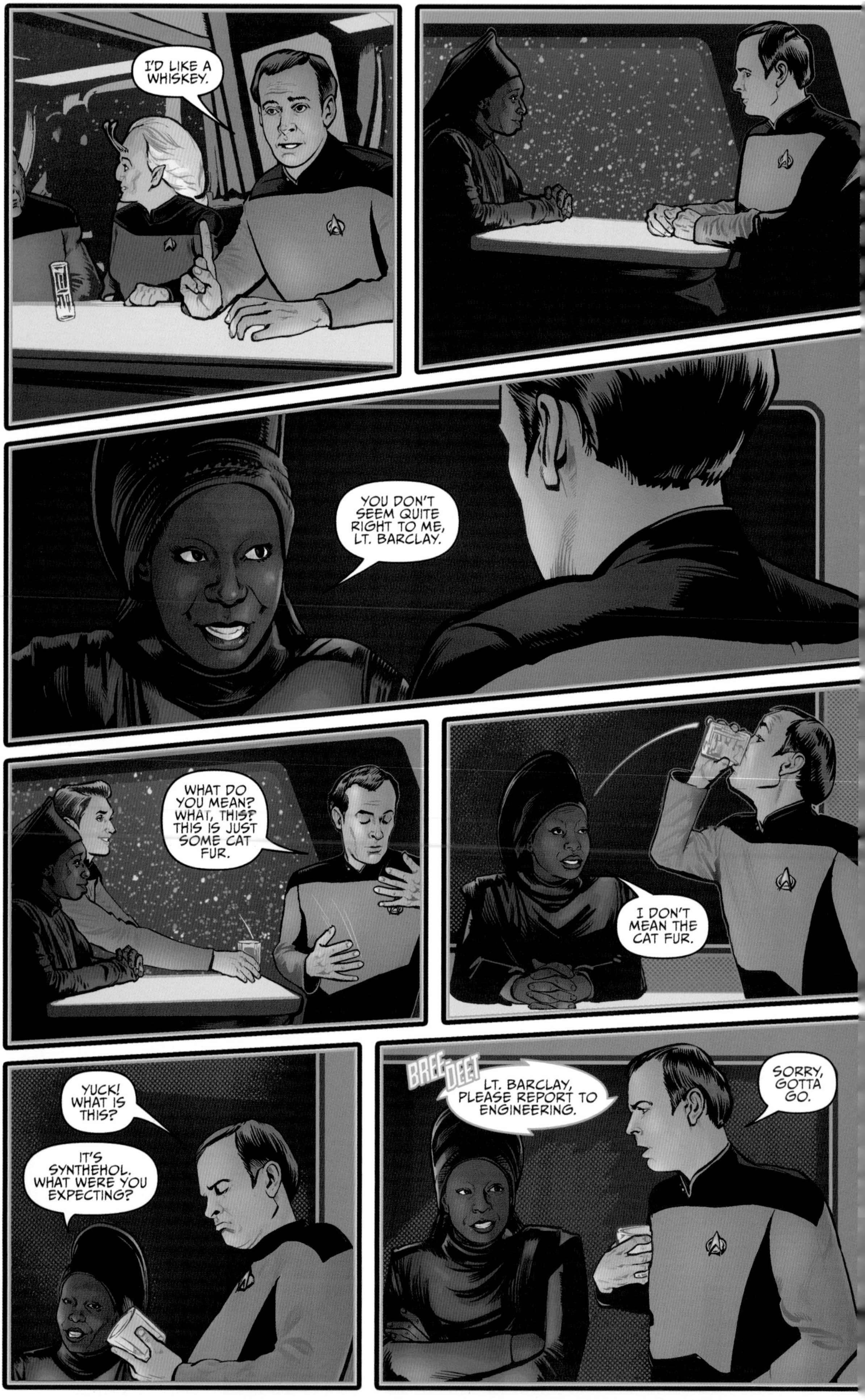
I'D LIKE A WHISKEY.
YOU DON'T SEEM QUITE RIGHT TO ME, LT. BARCLAY.
WHAT DO YOU MEAN? WHAT, THIS? THIS IS JUST SOME CAT FUR.
I DON'T MEAN THE CAT FUR.
YUCK! WHAT IS THIS?
IT'S SYNTHEHOL. WHAT WERE YOU EXPECTING?
BREE-DEET
LT. BARCLAY, PLEASE REPORT TO ENGINEERING.
SORRY, GOTTA GO.

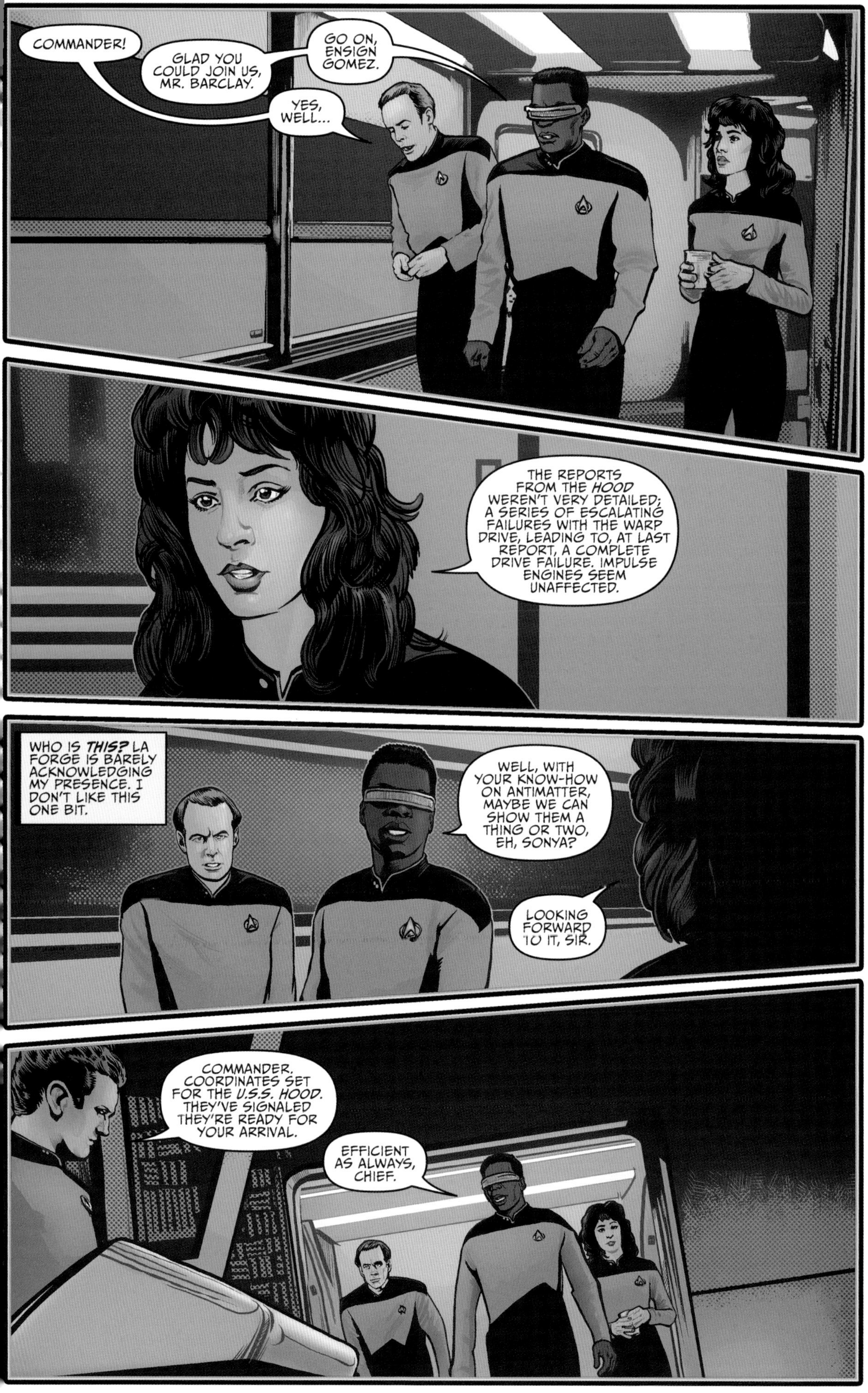
COMMANDER!
GLAD YOU COULD JOIN US, MR. BARCLAY.
GO ON, ENSIGN GOMEZ.
YES, WELL...
THE REPORTS FROM THE *HOOD* WEREN'T VERY DETAILED; A SERIES OF ESCALATING FAILURES WITH THE WARP DRIVE, LEADING TO, AT LAST REPORT, A COMPLETE DRIVE FAILURE. IMPULSE ENGINES SEEM UNAFFECTED.
WHO IS ***THIS?*** LA FORGE IS BARELY ACKNOWLEDGING MY PRESENCE. I DON'T LIKE THIS ONE BIT.
WELL, WITH YOUR KNOW-HOW ON ANTIMATTER, MAYBE WE CAN SHOW THEM A THING OR TWO, EH, SONYA?
LOOKING FORWARD TO IT, SIR.
COMMANDER. COORDINATES SET FOR THE *U.S.S. HOOD*. THEY'VE SIGNALED THEY'RE READY FOR YOUR ARRIVAL.
EFFICIENT AS ALWAYS, CHIEF.

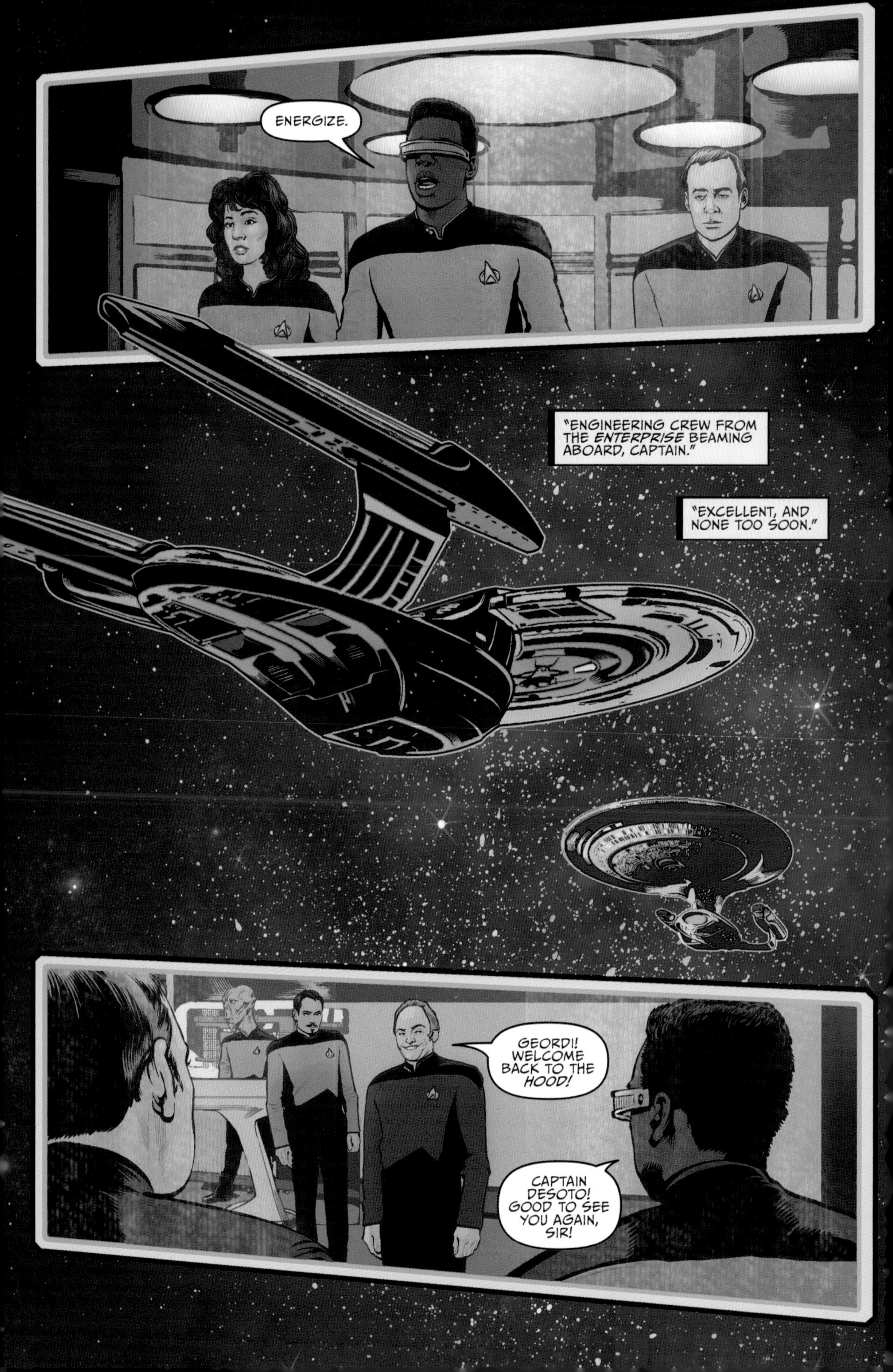
ENERGIZE.
"ENGINEERING CREW FROM THE *ENTERPRISE* BEAMING ABOARD, CAPTAIN."
"EXCELLENT, AND NONE TOO SOON."
GEORDI! WELCOME BACK TO THE *HOOD*!
CAPTAIN DESOTO! GOOD TO SEE YOU AGAIN, SIR!

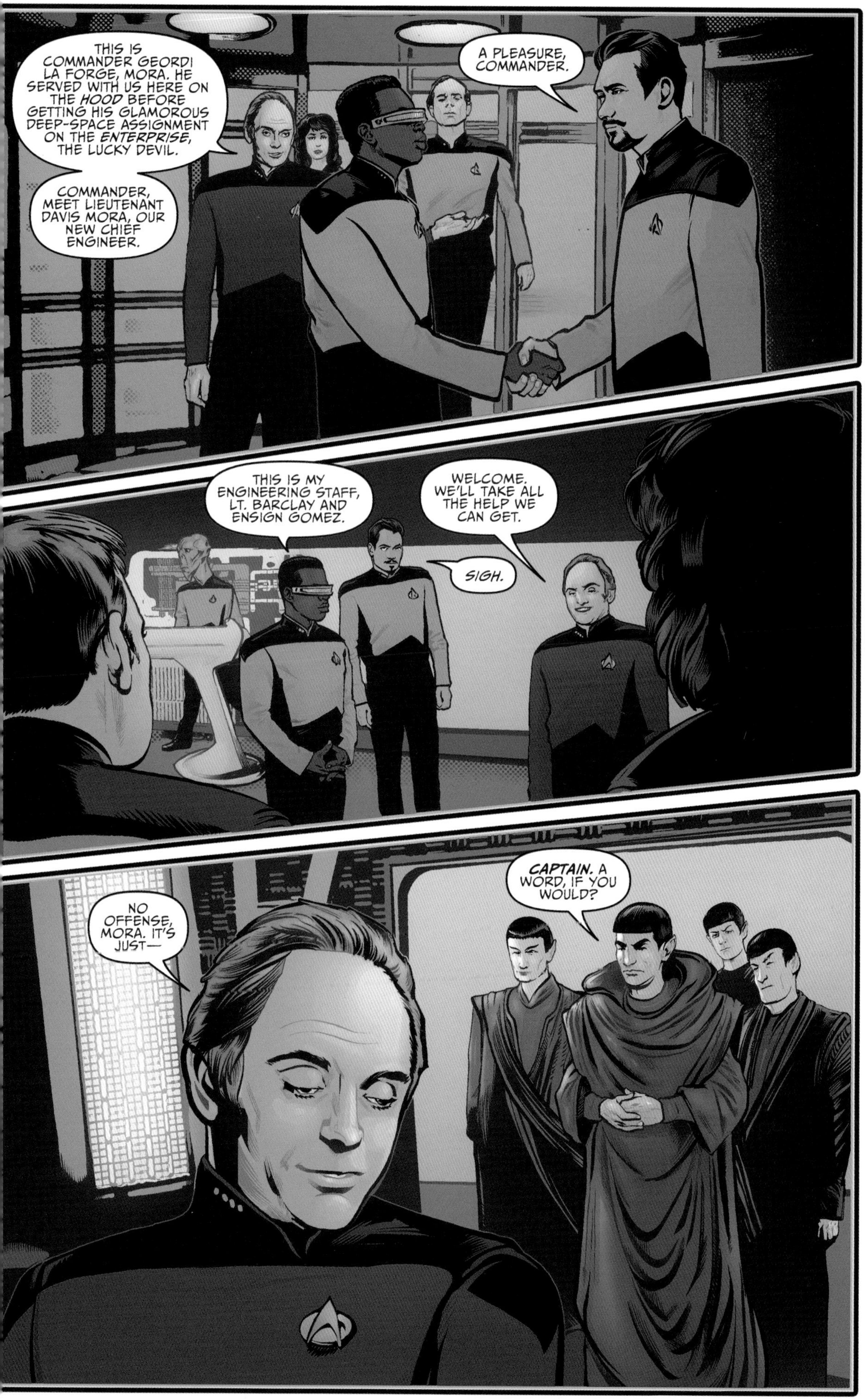
THIS IS COMMANDER GEORDI LA FORGE, MORA. HE SERVED WITH US HERE ON THE *HOOD* BEFORE GETTING HIS GLAMOROUS DEEP-SPACE ASSIGNMENT ON THE *ENTERPRISE*, THE LUCKY DEVIL.
COMMANDER, MEET LIEUTENANT DAVIS MORA, OUR NEW CHIEF ENGINEER.
A PLEASURE, COMMANDER.
THIS IS MY ENGINEERING STAFF, LT. BARCLAY AND ENSIGN GOMEZ.
WELCOME. WE'LL TAKE ALL THE HELP WE CAN GET.
SIGH.
NO OFFENSE, MORA. IT'S JUST—
CAPTAIN. A WORD, IF YOU WOULD?

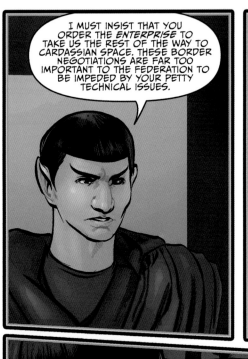

I MUST INSIST THAT YOU ORDER THE *ENTERPRISE* TO TAKE US THE REST OF THE WAY TO CARDASSIAN SPACE. THESE BORDER NEGOTIATIONS ARE FAR TOO IMPORTANT TO THE FEDERATION TO BE IMPEDED BY YOUR PETTY TECHNICAL ISSUES.

MY ORDERS ARE TO GET YOU TO THOSE NEGOTIATIONS, AMBASSADOR HENDRYK, AND THAT IS PRECISELY WHAT I INTEND TO DO.

I AM NOT EMPOWERED TO COMMAND OTHER CAPTAINS TO TAKE OVER MY RESPONSIBILITIES, NOR WOULD I BE INCLINED TO DO SO IF I WERE.

IT IS NOT LOGICAL FOR US TO REMAIN ON A CRIPPLED SHIP WHEN A FUNCTIONAL ONE IS NEARBY—

CRIPPLED?!

LET'S ALL TAKE A BREATH HERE! WE HAVEN'T EVEN GOTTEN A CHANCE TO TAKE A LOOK AT THINGS! I'M SURE WE'LL HAVE YOU ON YOUR WAY IN NO TIME, AMBASSADOR.

LOOK AT THIS PETTY SQUABBLING. THIS IS WHAT HAPPENS WHEN YOU DON'T DEAL WITH EVERY SITUATION FROM STRENGTH.

AMBASSADORS, LET ME ESCORT YOU BACK TO YOUR QUARTERS.

THANKS, GEORDI. YOU ALWAYS DID KNOW HOW TO KEEP A COOL HEAD.

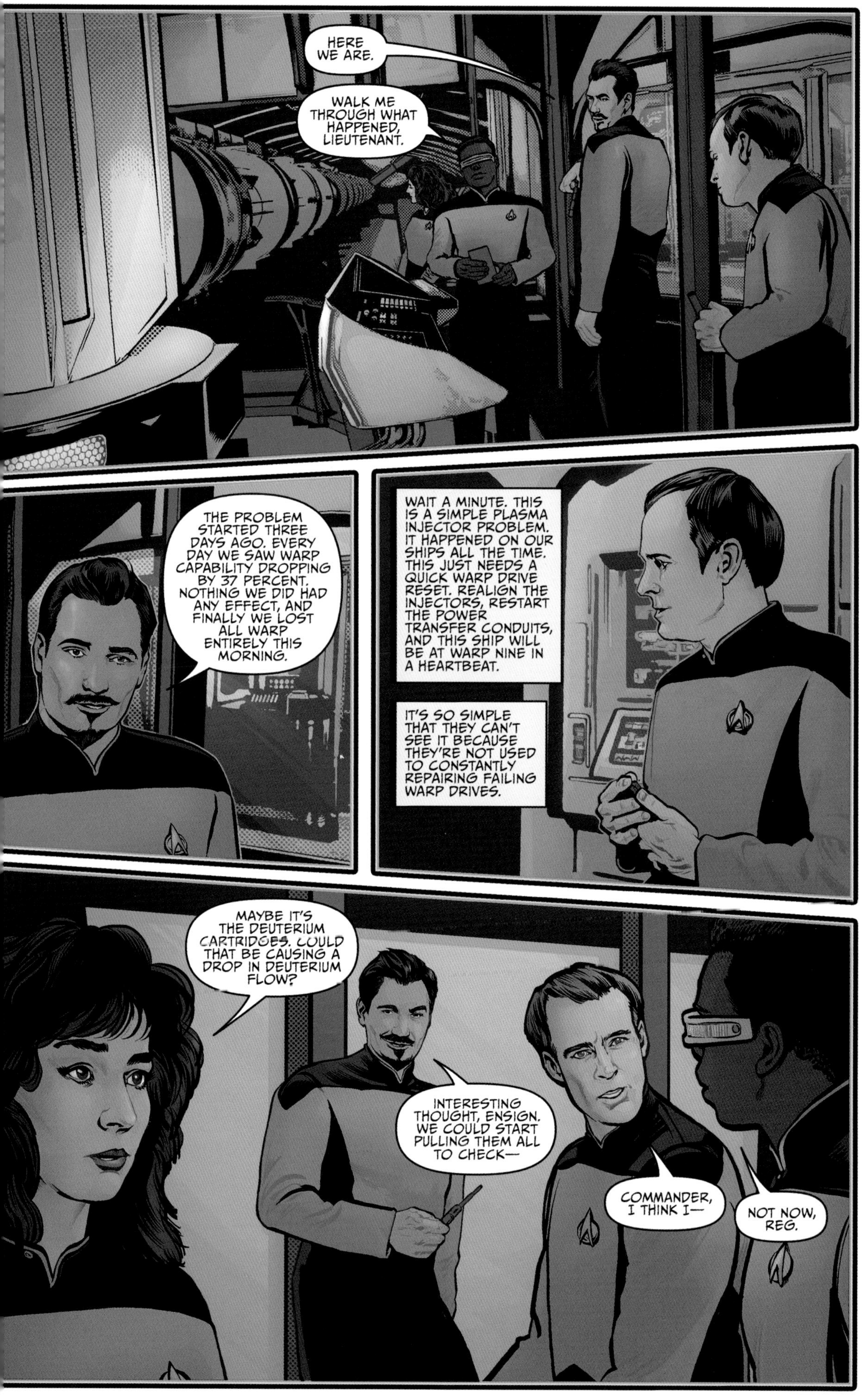
HERE WE ARE.
WALK ME THROUGH WHAT HAPPENED, LIEUTENANT.
THE PROBLEM STARTED THREE DAYS AGO. EVERY DAY WE SAW WARP CAPABILITY DROPPING BY 37 PERCENT. NOTHING WE DID HAD ANY EFFECT, AND FINALLY WE LOST ALL WARP ENTIRELY THIS MORNING.
WAIT A MINUTE. THIS IS A SIMPLE PLASMA INJECTOR PROBLEM. IT HAPPENED ON OUR SHIPS ALL THE TIME. THIS JUST NEEDS A QUICK WARP DRIVE RESET. REALIGN THE INJECTORS, RESTART THE POWER TRANSFER CONDUITS, AND THIS SHIP WILL BE AT WARP NINE IN A HEARTBEAT.
IT'S SO SIMPLE THAT THEY CAN'T SEE IT BECAUSE THEY'RE NOT USED TO CONSTANTLY REPAIRING FAILING WARP DRIVES.
MAYBE IT'S THE DEUTERIUM CARTRIDGES. COULD THAT BE CAUSING A DROP IN DEUTERIUM FLOW?
INTERESTING THOUGHT, ENSIGN. WE COULD START PULLING THEM ALL TO CHECK—
COMMANDER, I THINK I—
NOT NOW, REG.

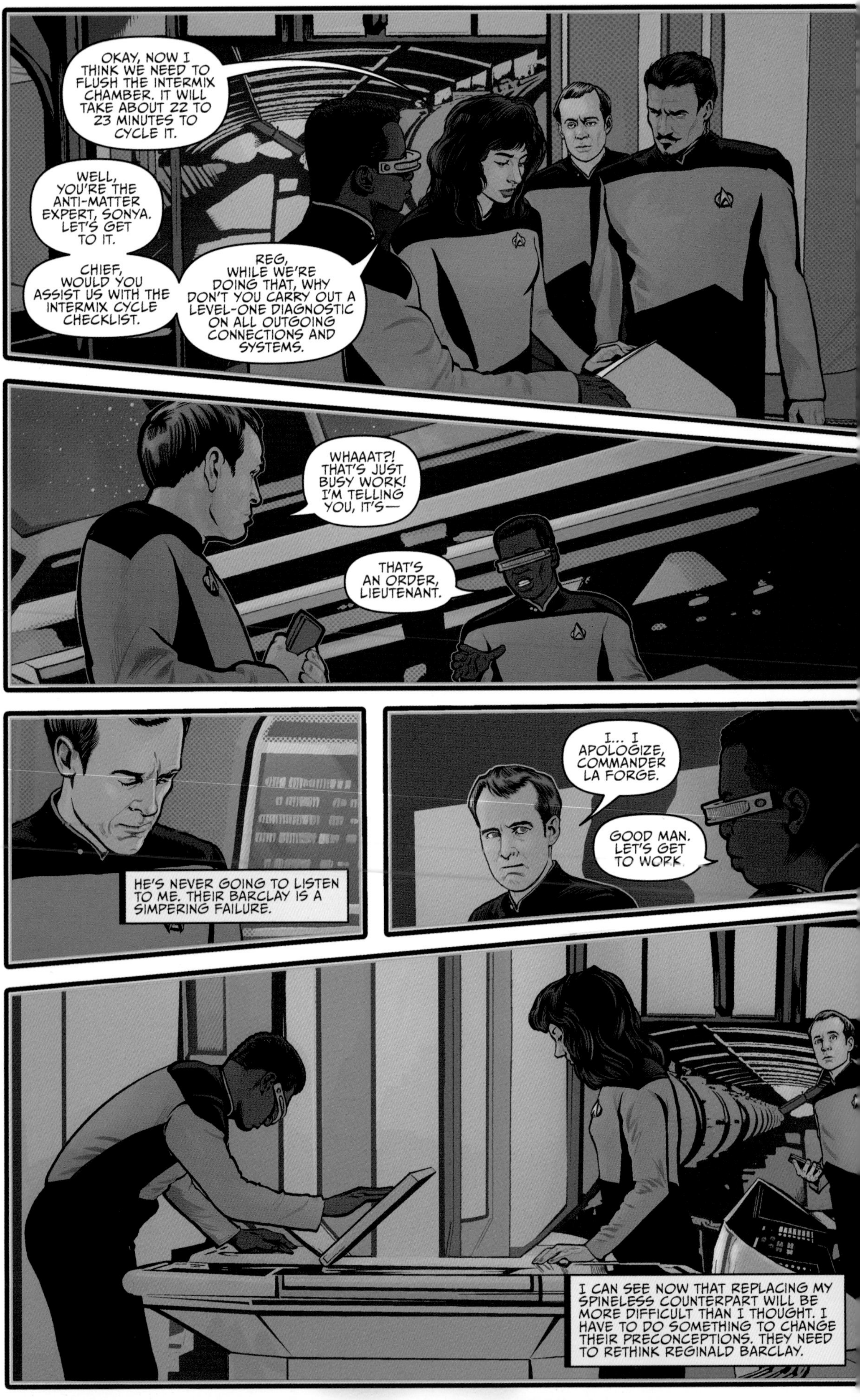
OKAY, NOW I THINK WE NEED TO FLUSH THE INTERMIX CHAMBER. IT WILL TAKE ABOUT 22 TO 23 MINUTES TO CYCLE IT.
WELL, YOU'RE THE ANTI-MATTER EXPERT, SONYA. LET'S GET TO IT.
CHIEF, WOULD YOU ASSIST US WITH THE INTERMIX CYCLE CHECKLIST.
REG, WHILE WE'RE DOING THAT, WHY DON'T YOU CARRY OUT A LEVEL-ONE DIAGNOSTIC ON ALL OUTGOING CONNECTIONS AND SYSTEMS.
WHAAAT?! THAT'S JUST BUSY WORK! I'M TELLING YOU, IT'S—
THAT'S AN ORDER, LIEUTENANT.
HE'S NEVER GOING TO LISTEN TO ME. THEIR BARCLAY IS A SIMPERING FAILURE.
I... I APOLOGIZE, COMMANDER LA FORGE.
GOOD MAN. LET'S GET TO WORK.
I CAN SEE NOW THAT REPLACING MY SPINELESS COUNTERPART WILL BE MORE DIFFICULT THAN I THOUGHT. I HAVE TO DO SOMETHING TO CHANGE THEIR PRECONCEPTIONS. THEY NEED TO RETHINK REGINALD BARCLAY.

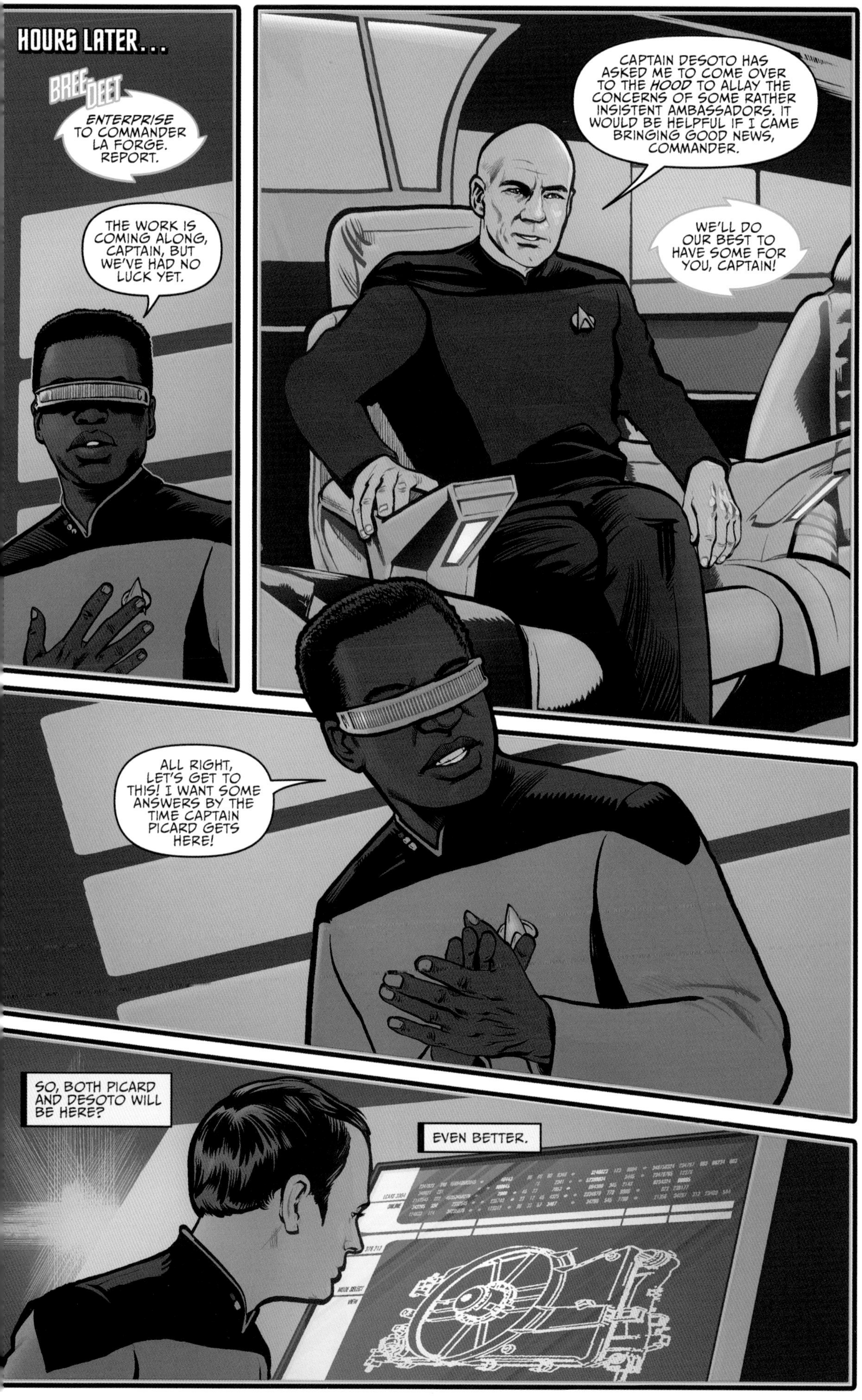

HOURS LATER...
BREE-DEET
ENTERPRISE TO COMMANDER LA FORGE. REPORT.
THE WORK IS COMING ALONG, CAPTAIN, BUT WE'VE HAD NO LUCK YET.
CAPTAIN DESOTO HAS ASKED ME TO COME OVER TO THE HOOD TO ALLAY THE CONCERNS OF SOME RATHER INSISTENT AMBASSADORS. IT WOULD BE HELPFUL IF I CAME BRINGING GOOD NEWS, COMMANDER.
WE'LL DO OUR BEST TO HAVE SOME FOR YOU, CAPTAIN!
ALL RIGHT, LET'S GET TO THIS! I WANT SOME ANSWERS BY THE TIME CAPTAIN PICARD GETS HERE!
SO, BOTH PICARD AND DESOTO WILL BE HERE?
EVEN BETTER.

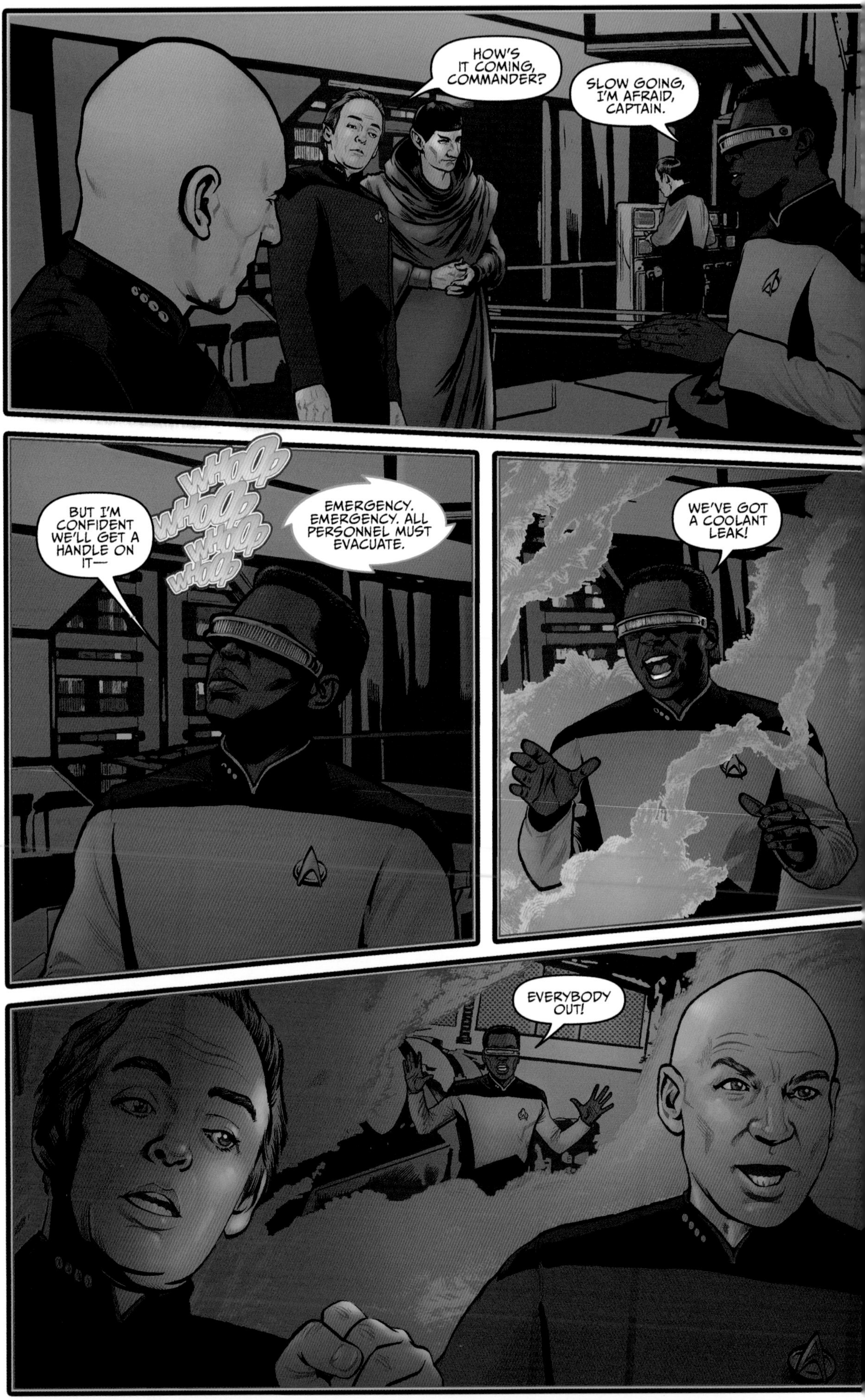
HOW'S IT COMING, COMMANDER?
SLOW GOING, I'M AFRAID, CAPTAIN.
BUT I'M CONFIDENT WE'LL GET A HANDLE ON IT—
WHOOP WHOOP WHOOP WHOOP
EMERGENCY. EMERGENCY. ALL PERSONNEL MUST EVACUATE.
WE'VE GOT A COOLANT LEAK!
EVERYBODY OUT!

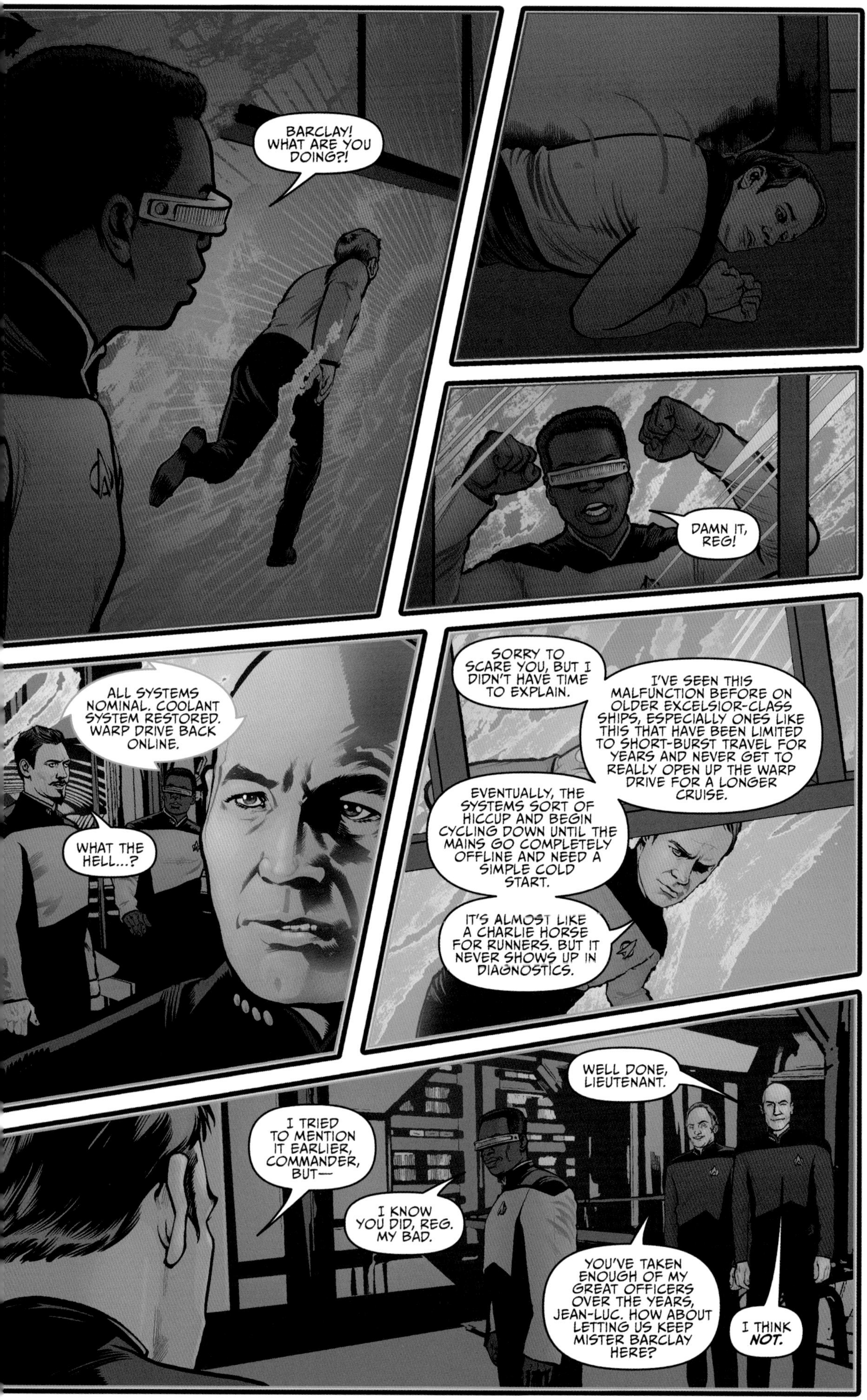
BARCLAY! WHAT ARE YOU DOING?!
DAMN IT, REG!
ALL SYSTEMS NOMINAL. COOLANT SYSTEM RESTORED. WARP DRIVE BACK ONLINE.
WHAT THE HELL...?
SORRY TO SCARE YOU, BUT I DIDN'T HAVE TIME TO EXPLAIN.
I'VE SEEN THIS MALFUNCTION BEFORE ON OLDER EXCELSIOR-CLASS SHIPS, ESPECIALLY ONES LIKE THIS THAT HAVE BEEN LIMITED TO SHORT-BURST TRAVEL FOR YEARS AND NEVER GET TO REALLY OPEN UP THE WARP DRIVE FOR A LONGER CRUISE.
EVENTUALLY, THE SYSTEMS SORT OF HICCUP AND BEGIN CYCLING DOWN UNTIL THE MAINS GO COMPLETELY OFFLINE AND NEED A SIMPLE COLD START.
IT'S ALMOST LIKE A CHARLIE HORSE FOR RUNNERS. BUT IT NEVER SHOWS UP IN DIAGNOSTICS.
I TRIED TO MENTION IT EARLIER, COMMANDER, BUT—
I KNOW YOU DID, REG. MY BAD.
WELL DONE, LIEUTENANT.
YOU'VE TAKEN ENOUGH OF MY GREAT OFFICERS OVER THE YEARS, JEAN-LUC. HOW ABOUT LETTING US KEEP MISTER BARCLAY HERE?
I THINK ***NOT.***

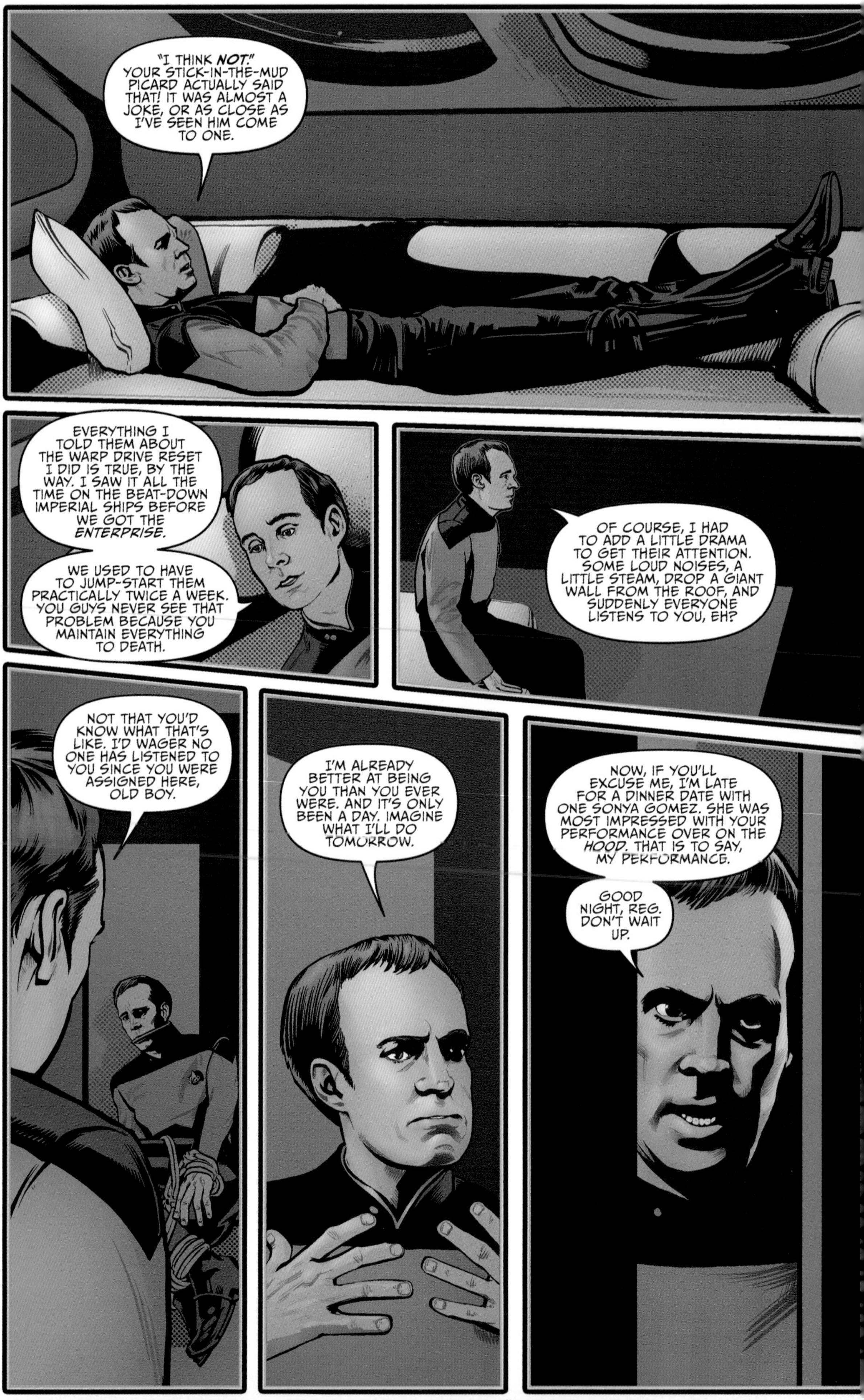
"I THINK *NOT.*" YOUR STICK-IN-THE-MUD PICARD ACTUALLY SAID THAT! IT WAS ALMOST A JOKE, OR AS CLOSE AS I'VE SEEN HIM COME TO ONE.
EVERYTHING I TOLD THEM ABOUT THE WARP DRIVE RESET I DID IS TRUE, BY THE WAY. I SAW IT ALL THE TIME ON THE BEAT-DOWN IMPERIAL SHIPS BEFORE WE GOT THE *ENTERPRISE.*
WE USED TO HAVE TO JUMP-START THEM PRACTICALLY TWICE A WEEK. YOU GUYS NEVER SEE THAT PROBLEM BECAUSE YOU MAINTAIN EVERYTHING TO DEATH.
OF COURSE, I HAD TO ADD A LITTLE DRAMA TO GET THEIR ATTENTION. SOME LOUD NOISES, A LITTLE STEAM, DROP A GIANT WALL FROM THE ROOF, AND SUDDENLY EVERYONE LISTENS TO YOU, EH?
NOT THAT YOU'D KNOW WHAT THAT'S LIKE. I'D WAGER NO ONE HAS LISTENED TO YOU SINCE YOU WERE ASSIGNED HERE, OLD BOY.
I'M ALREADY BETTER AT BEING YOU THAN YOU EVER WERE. AND IT'S ONLY BEEN A DAY. IMAGINE WHAT I'LL DO TOMORROW.
NOW, IF YOU'LL EXCUSE ME, I'M LATE FOR A DINNER DATE WITH ONE SONYA GOMEZ. SHE WAS MOST IMPRESSED WITH YOUR PERFORMANCE OVER ON THE *HOOD*. THAT IS TO SAY, MY PERFORMANCE.
GOOD NIGHT, REG. DON'T WAIT UP.

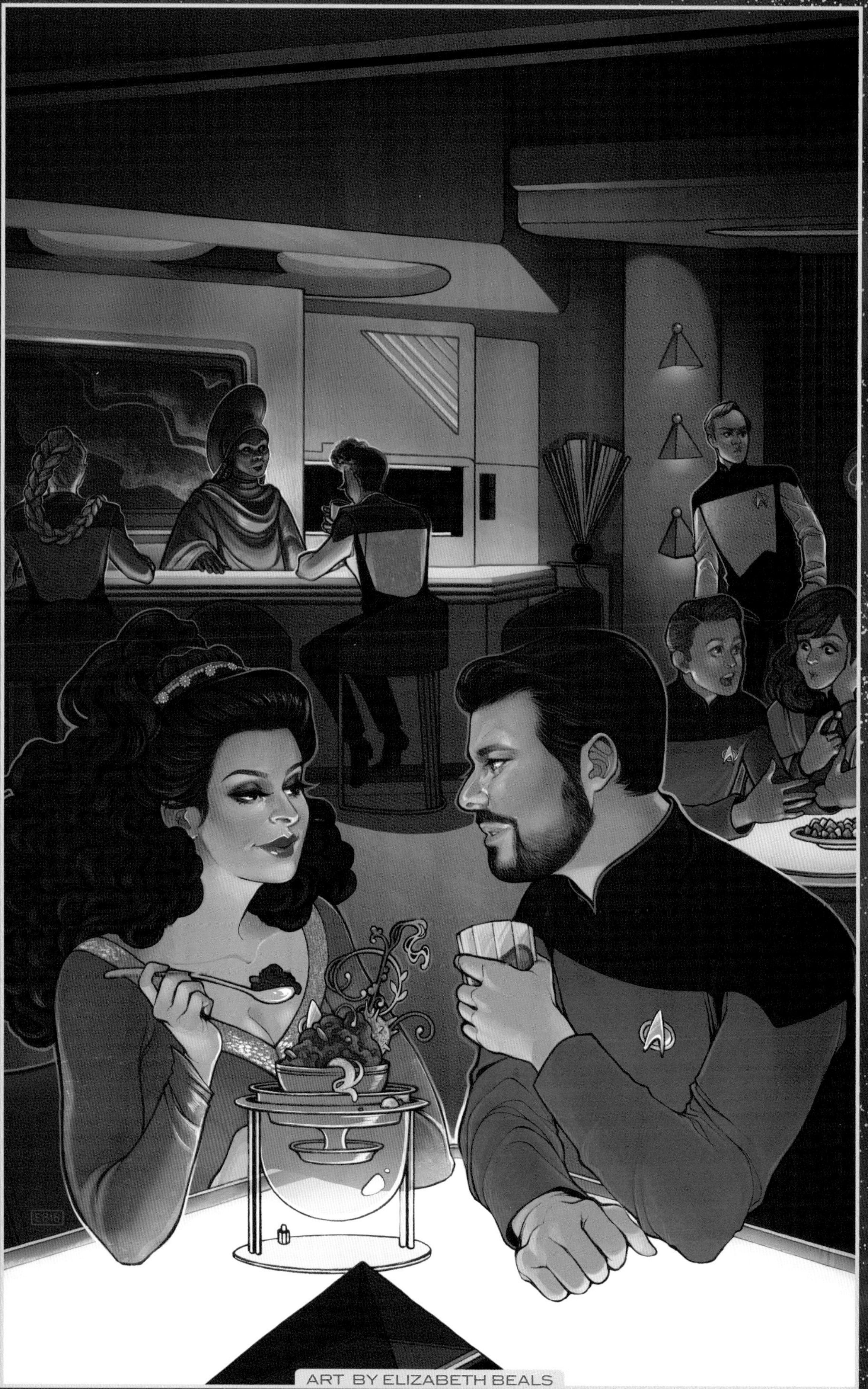
EB18

ART BY ELIZABETH BEALS

TERRA INCOGNITA PART 2

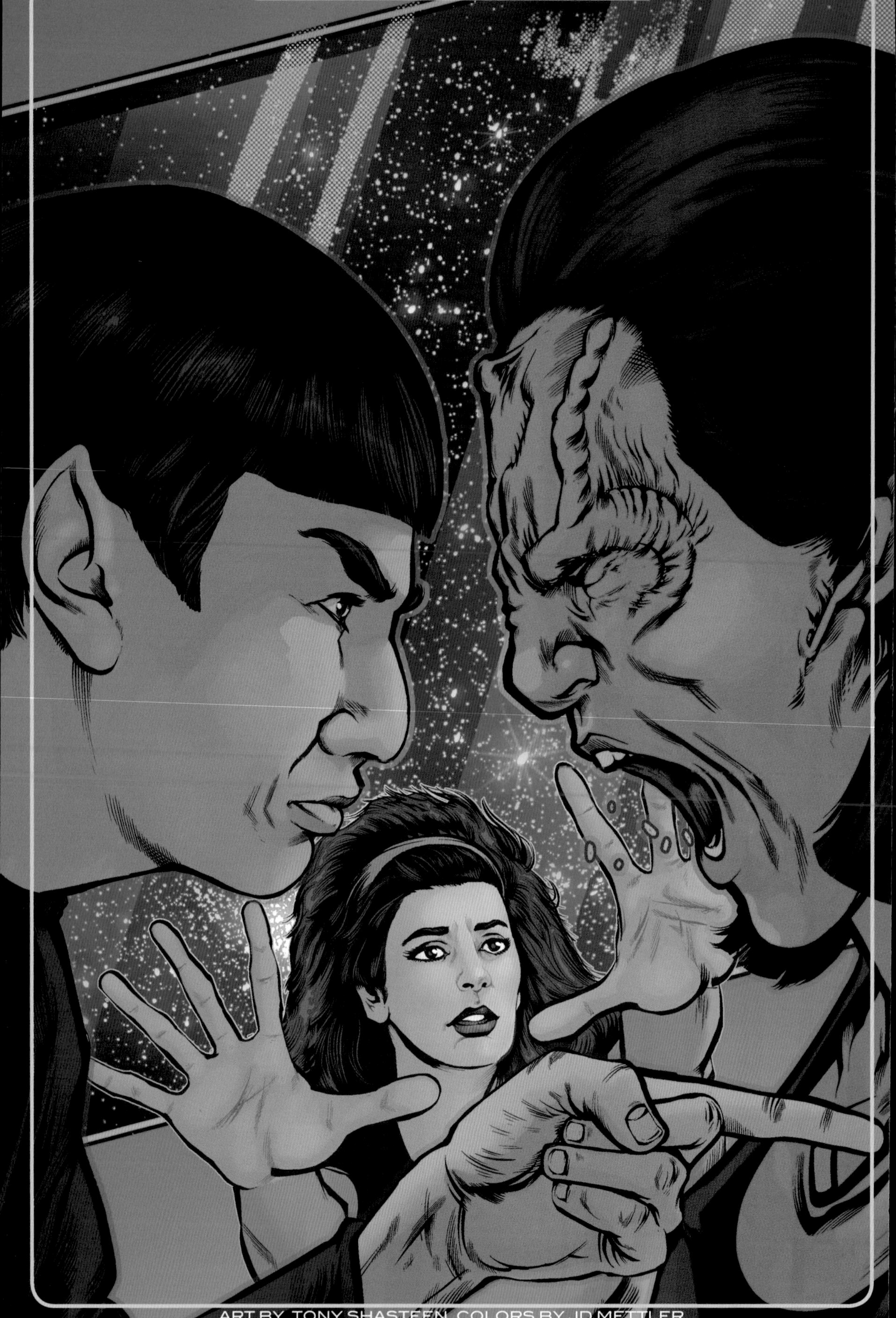

ART BY TONY SHASTEEN, COLORS BY JD METTLER

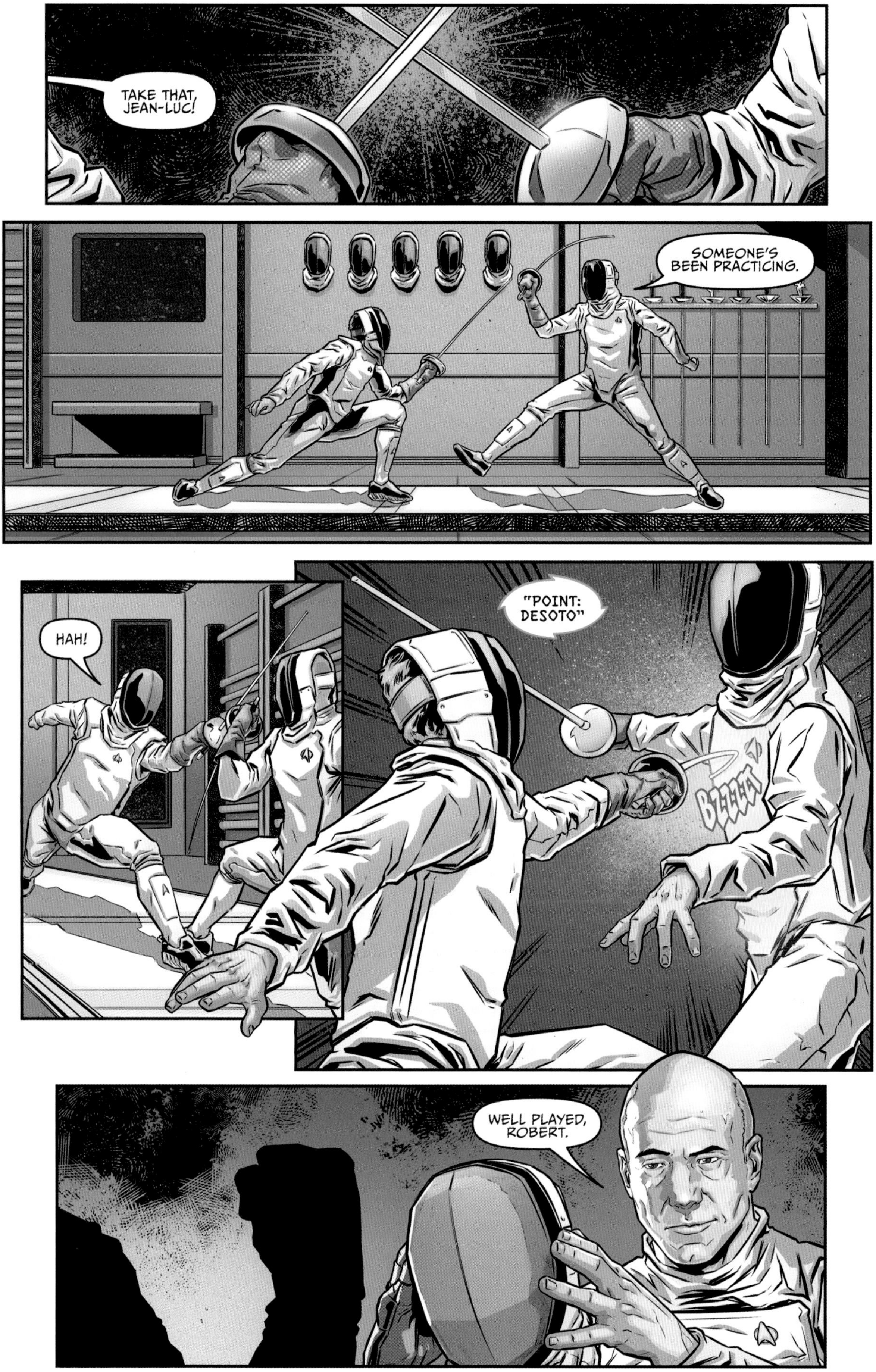
TAKE THAT, JEAN-LUC!
SOMEONE'S BEEN PRACTICING.
HAH!
"POINT: DESOTO"
BZZZZT
WELL PLAYED, ROBERT.

ALL THOSE MISSIONS OUT THERE ON THE RIM HAVEN'T BEEN GOOD FOR YOUR GAME, JEAN-LUC.

VERY FUNNY. YOU'VE *ALWAYS* BEEN A BETTER SWORDSMAN THAN ME.

I'M GLAD WE HAD SOME TIME FOR A FENCING MATCH BEFORE THE *ENTERPRISE* LEAVES YOU TO YOUR MISSION.

YES, ABOUT THAT...

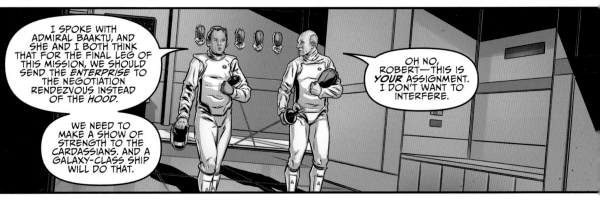

I SPOKE WITH ADMIRAL BAAKTU, AND SHE AND I BOTH THINK THAT FOR THE FINAL LEG OF THIS MISSION, WE SHOULD SEND THE *ENTERPRISE* TO THE NEGOTIATION RENDEZVOUS INSTEAD OF THE *HOOD*.

WE NEED TO MAKE A SHOW OF STRENGTH TO THE CARDASSIANS. AND A GALAXY-CLASS SHIP WILL DO THAT.

OH NO, ROBERT—THIS IS *YOUR* ASSIGNMENT. I DON'T WANT TO INTERFERE.

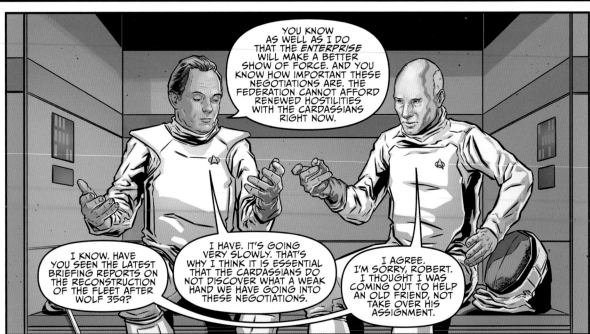

YOU KNOW AS WELL AS I DO THAT THE *ENTERPRISE* WILL MAKE A BETTER SHOW OF FORCE. AND YOU KNOW HOW IMPORTANT THESE NEGOTIATIONS ARE. THE FEDERATION CANNOT AFFORD RENEWED HOSTILITIES WITH THE CARDASSIANS RIGHT NOW.

I KNOW. HAVE YOU SEEN THE LATEST BRIEFING REPORTS ON THE RECONSTRUCTION OF THE FLEET AFTER WOLF 359?

I HAVE. IT'S GOING VERY SLOWLY. THAT'S WHY I THINK IT IS ESSENTIAL THAT THE CARDASSIANS DO NOT DISCOVER WHAT A WEAK HAND WE HAVE GOING INTO THESE NEGOTIATIONS.

I AGREE. I'M SORRY, ROBERT. I THOUGHT I WAS COMING OUT TO HELP AN OLD FRIEND, NOT TAKE OVER HIS ASSIGNMENT.

DON'T GIVE THAT A SECOND THOUGHT. I'M SORRY TO STICK YOU WITH THIS ON SUCH SHORT NOTICE. I'LL LET ADMIRAL BAAKTU KNOW.

MMM, YES. I'LL TALK TO COMMANDER RIKER AND WE'LL GET THE FEDERATION AMBASSADORS TRANSFERRED OVER AND BE UNDERWAY SHORTLY.

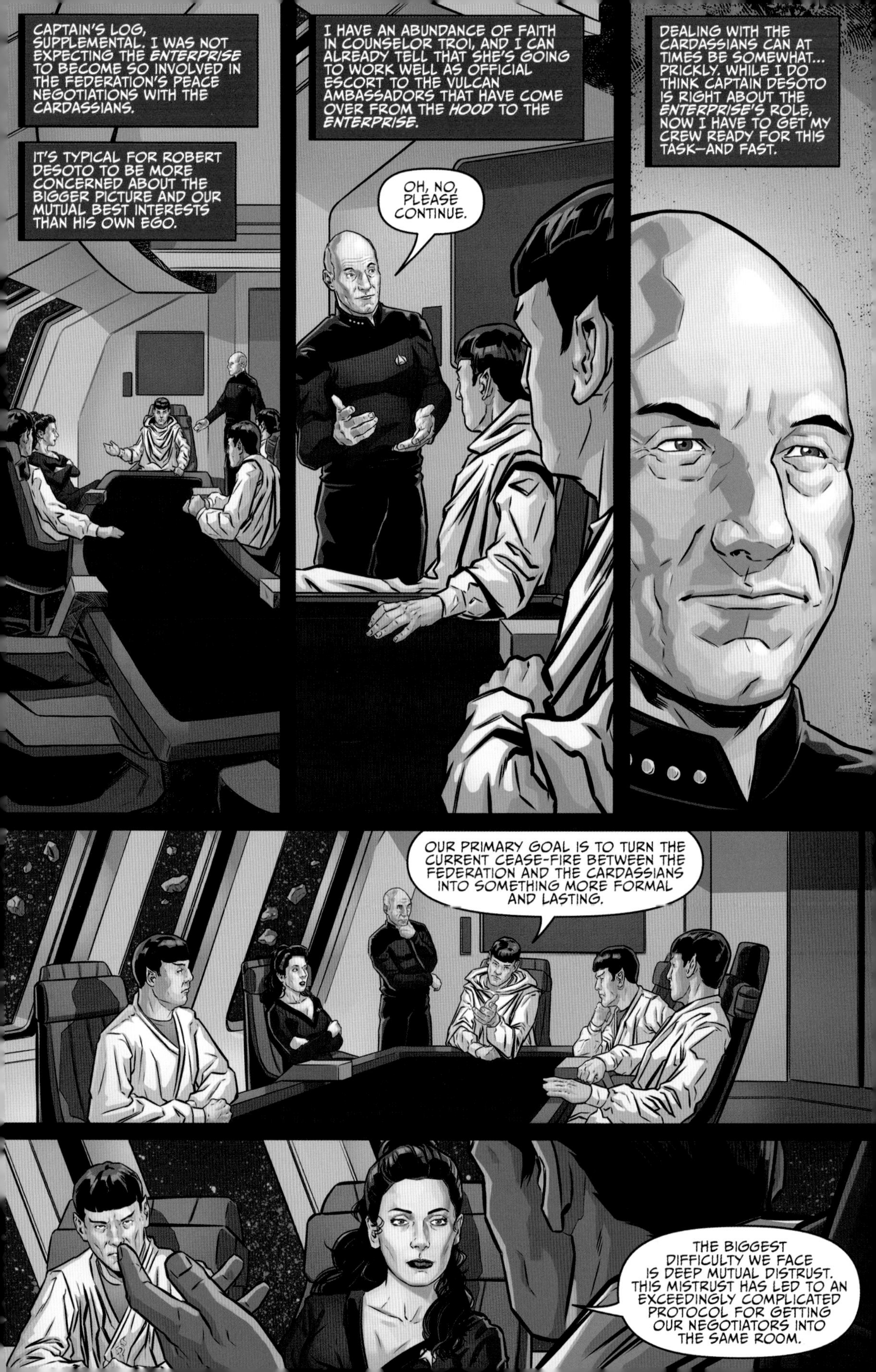
CAPTAIN'S LOG, SUPPLEMENTAL. I WAS NOT EXPECTING THE *ENTERPRISE* TO BECOME SO INVOLVED IN THE FEDERATION'S PEACE NEGOTIATIONS WITH THE CARDASSIANS.
IT'S TYPICAL FOR ROBERT DESOTO TO BE MORE CONCERNED ABOUT THE BIGGER PICTURE AND OUR MUTUAL BEST INTERESTS THAN HIS OWN EGO.
I HAVE AN ABUNDANCE OF FAITH IN COUNSELOR TROI, AND I CAN ALREADY TELL THAT SHE'S GOING TO WORK WELL AS OFFICIAL ESCORT TO THE VULCAN AMBASSADORS THAT HAVE COME OVER FROM THE *HOOD* TO THE *ENTERPRISE*.
OH, NO, PLEASE CONTINUE.
DEALING WITH THE CARDASSIANS CAN AT TIMES BE SOMEWHAT... PRICKLY. WHILE I DO THINK CAPTAIN DESOTO IS RIGHT ABOUT THE *ENTERPRISE'S* ROLE, NOW I HAVE TO GET MY CREW READY FOR THIS TASK—AND FAST.
OUR PRIMARY GOAL IS TO TURN THE CURRENT CEASE-FIRE BETWEEN THE FEDERATION AND THE CARDASSIANS INTO SOMETHING MORE FORMAL AND LASTING.
THE BIGGEST DIFFICULTY WE FACE IS DEEP MUTUAL DISTRUST. THIS MISTRUST HAS LED TO AN EXCEEDINGLY COMPLICATED PROTOCOL FOR GETTING OUR NEGOTIATORS INTO THE SAME ROOM.

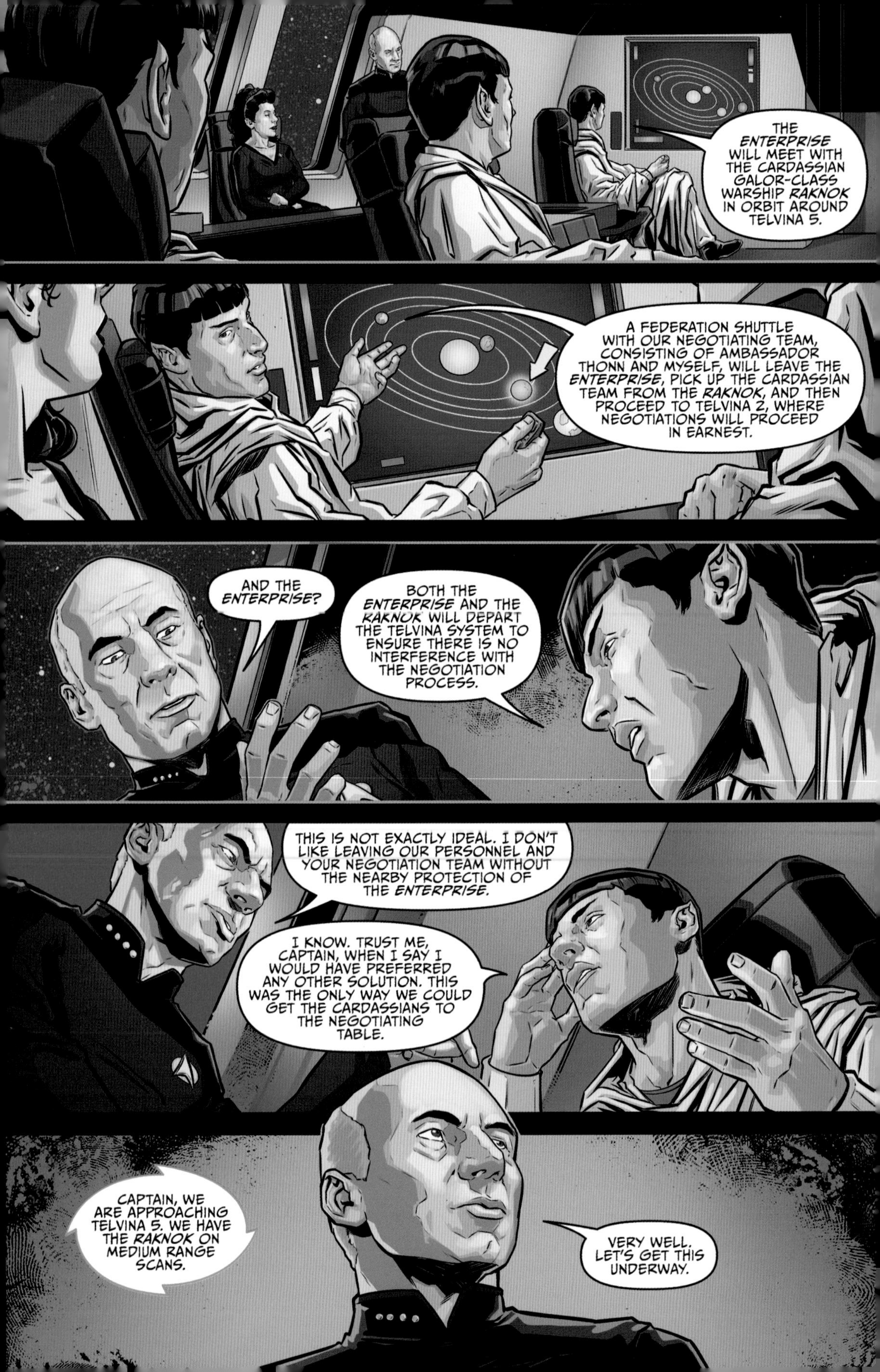
THE *ENTERPRISE* WILL MEET WITH THE CARDASSIAN GALOR-CLASS WARSHIP *RAKNOK* IN ORBIT AROUND TELVINA 5.
A FEDERATION SHUTTLE WITH OUR NEGOTIATING TEAM, CONSISTING OF AMBASSADOR THONN AND MYSELF, WILL LEAVE THE *ENTERPRISE*, PICK UP THE CARDASSIAN TEAM FROM THE *RAKNOK*, AND THEN PROCEED TO TELVINA 2, WHERE NEGOTIATIONS WILL PROCEED IN EARNEST.
AND THE *ENTERPRISE*?
BOTH THE *ENTERPRISE* AND THE *RAKNOK* WILL DEPART THE TELVINA SYSTEM TO ENSURE THERE IS NO INTERFERENCE WITH THE NEGOTIATION PROCESS.
THIS IS NOT EXACTLY IDEAL. I DON'T LIKE LEAVING OUR PERSONNEL AND YOUR NEGOTIATION TEAM WITHOUT THE NEARBY PROTECTION OF THE *ENTERPRISE*.
I KNOW. TRUST ME, CAPTAIN, WHEN I SAY I WOULD HAVE PREFERRED ANY OTHER SOLUTION. THIS WAS THE ONLY WAY WE COULD GET THE CARDASSIANS TO THE NEGOTIATING TABLE.
CAPTAIN, WE ARE APPROACHING TELVINA 5. WE HAVE THE *RAKNOK* ON MEDIUM RANGE SCANS.
VERY WELL. LET'S GET THIS UNDERWAY.

CAPTAIN, GUL RAKAR FROM THE CARDASSIAN VESSEL IS HAILING US.

PUT HIM ON, COMMANDER.

CAPTAIN PICARD, I PRESUME?

YES. A PLEASURE TO MEET YOU, GUL RAKAR.

I MUST TELL YOU, CAPTAIN...

THE SUDDEN SUBSTITUTION OF THE *ENTERPRISE* FOR THE *HOOD* STRIKES ME AS A LITTLE CURIOUS.

IT WAS AN UNAVOIDABLE...

BUT WE CONSIDER IT OF NO CONSEQUENCE. WE ARE PREPARED TO PRESS ON WITH NEGOTIATIONS.

EXCELLENT. WE WILL SEND A SHUTTLE TO YOUR SHIP AT THE APPOINTED TIME.

WE'LL BE EXPECTING YOU.

COUNSELOR?

I DON'T THINK HE'S HIDING ANYTHING. BUT HE'S TENSE, VERY TENSE. THE SWITCH TO THE *ENTERPRISE* RAISED THOSE TENSIONS, PUT HIM EVEN MORE ON EDGE.

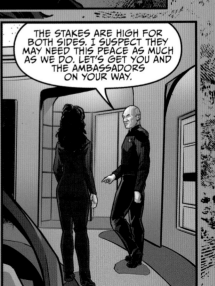

THE STAKES ARE HIGH FOR BOTH SIDES. I SUSPECT THEY MAY NEED THIS PEACE AS MUCH AS WE DO. LET'S GET YOU AND THE AMBASSADORS ON YOUR WAY.

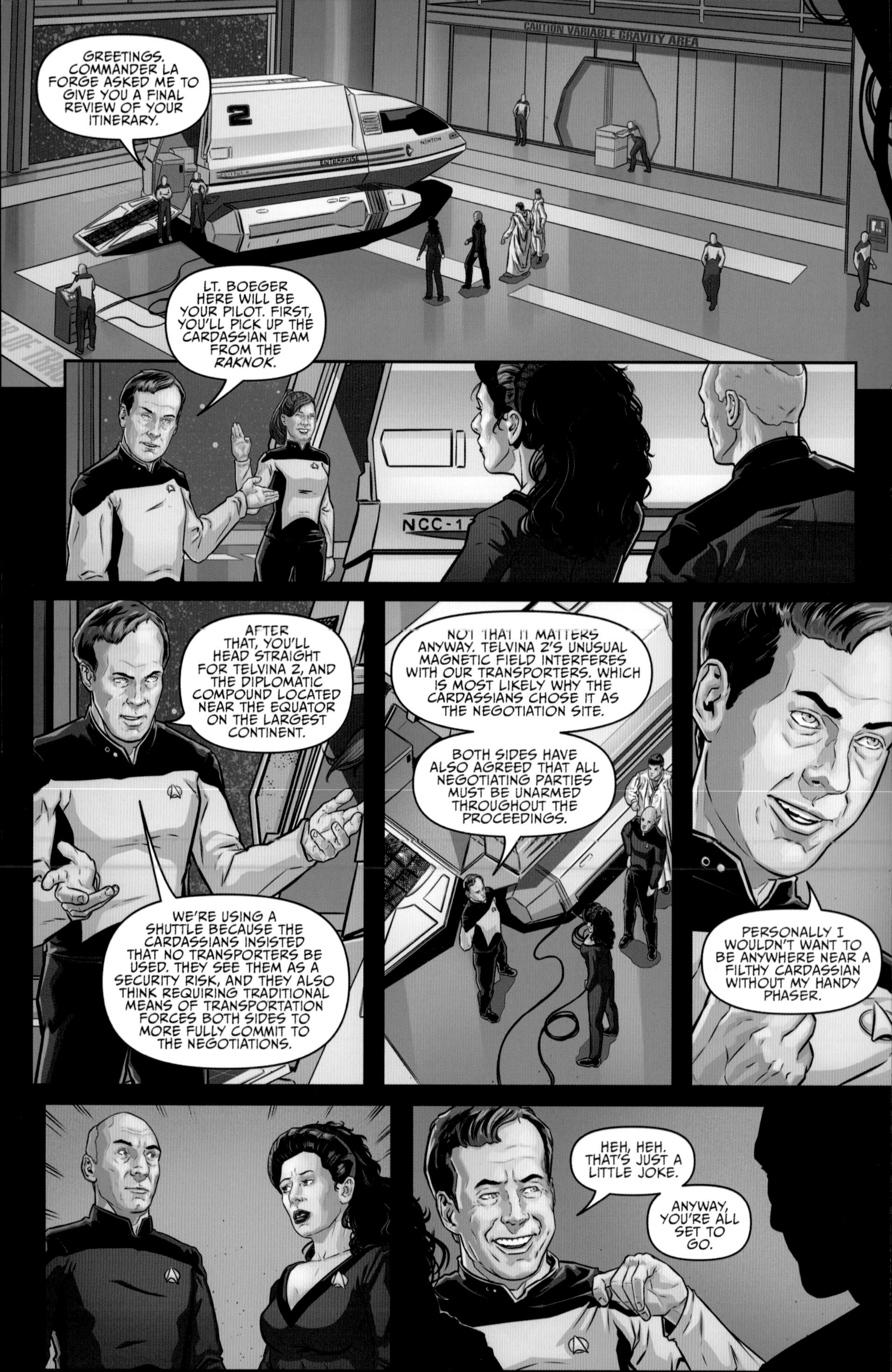
CAUTION VARIABLE GRAVITY AREA
2
NEWTON
ENTERPRISE
GREETINGS. COMMANDER LA FORGE ASKED ME TO GIVE YOU A FINAL REVIEW OF YOUR ITINERARY.
LT. BOEGER HERE WILL BE YOUR PILOT. FIRST, YOU'LL PICK UP THE CARDASSIAN TEAM FROM THE *RAKNOK*.
AFTER THAT, YOU'LL HEAD STRAIGHT FOR TELVINA 2, AND THE DIPLOMATIC COMPOUND LOCATED NEAR THE EQUATOR ON THE LARGEST CONTINENT.
WE'RE USING A SHUTTLE BECAUSE THE CARDASSIANS INSISTED THAT NO TRANSPORTERS BE USED. THEY SEE THEM AS A SECURITY RISK, AND THEY ALSO THINK REQUIRING TRADITIONAL MEANS OF TRANSPORTATION FORCES BOTH SIDES TO MORE FULLY COMMIT TO THE NEGOTIATIONS.
NOT THAT IT MATTERS ANYWAY. TELVINA 2'S UNUSUAL MAGNETIC FIELD INTERFERES WITH OUR TRANSPORTERS. WHICH IS MOST LIKELY WHY THE CARDASSIANS CHOSE IT AS THE NEGOTIATION SITE.
BOTH SIDES HAVE ALSO AGREED THAT ALL NEGOTIATING PARTIES MUST BE UNARMED THROUGHOUT THE PROCEEDINGS.
PERSONALLY I WOULDN'T WANT TO BE ANYWHERE NEAR A FILTHY CARDASSIAN WITHOUT MY HANDY PHASER.
HEH, HEH. THAT'S JUST A LITTLE JOKE.
ANYWAY, YOU'RE ALL SET TO GO.

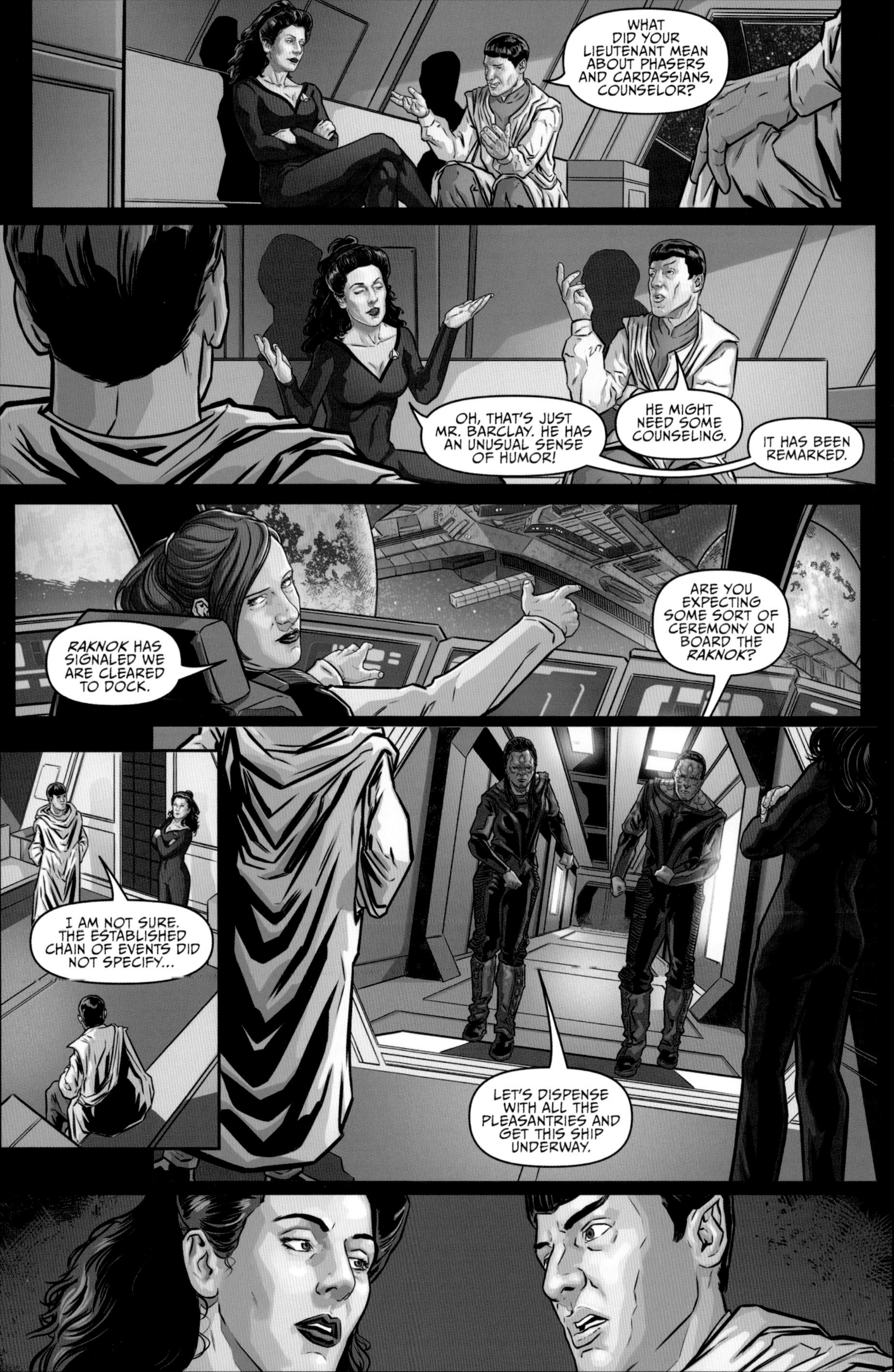
WHAT DID YOUR LIEUTENANT MEAN ABOUT PHASERS AND CARDASSIANS, COUNSELOR?
OH, THAT'S JUST MR. BARCLAY. HE HAS AN UNUSUAL SENSE OF HUMOR!
HE MIGHT NEED SOME COUNSELING.
IT HAS BEEN REMARKED.
RAKNOK HAS SIGNALED WE ARE CLEARED TO DOCK.
ARE YOU EXPECTING SOME SORT OF CEREMONY ON BOARD THE *RAKNOK*?
I AM NOT SURE. THE ESTABLISHED CHAIN OF EVENTS DID NOT SPECIFY...
LET'S DISPENSE WITH ALL THE PLEASANTRIES AND GET THIS SHIP UNDERWAY.

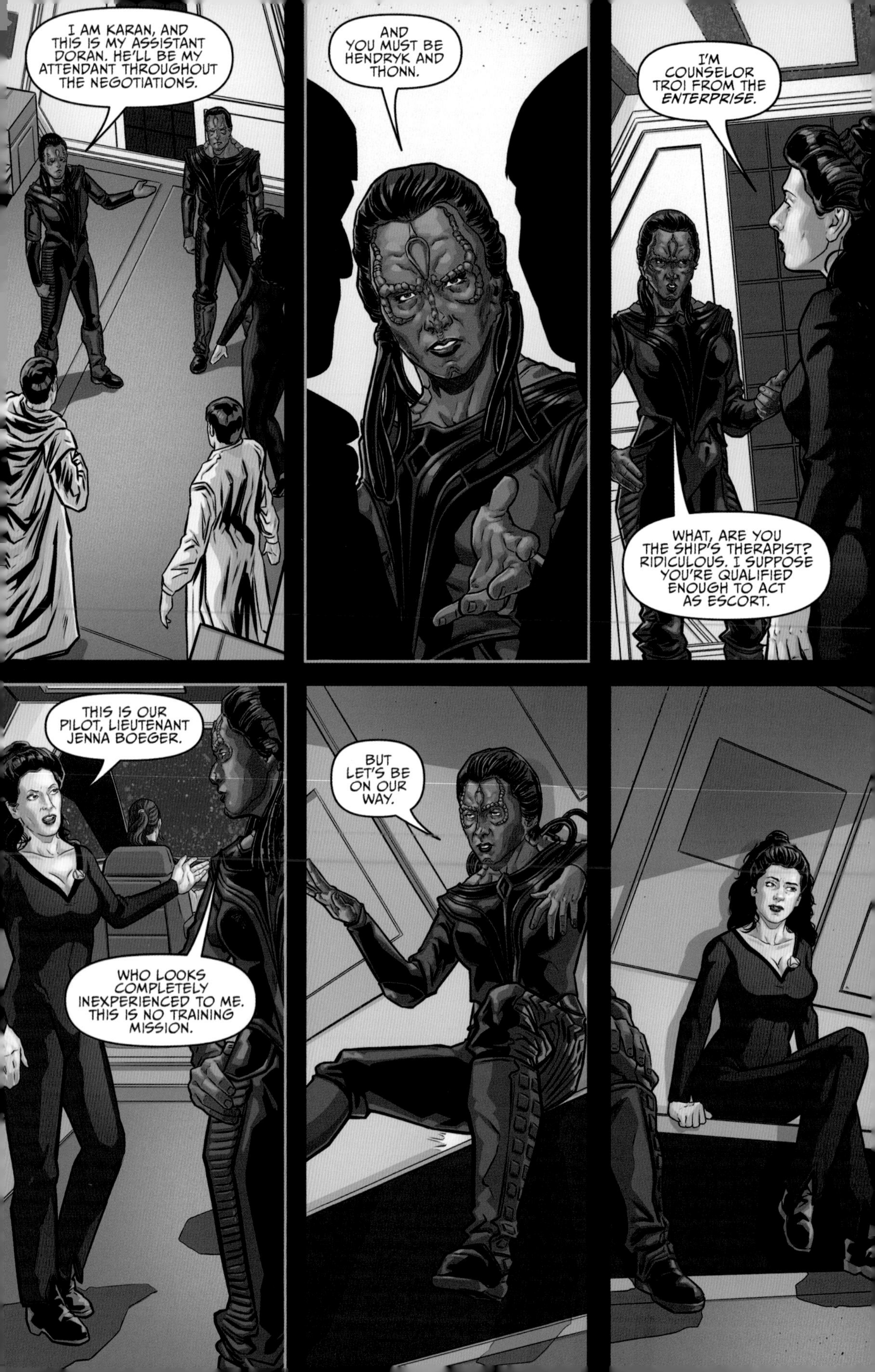
I AM KARAN, AND THIS IS MY ASSISTANT DORAN. HE'LL BE MY ATTENDANT THROUGHOUT THE NEGOTIATIONS.
AND YOU MUST BE HENDRYK AND THONN.
I'M COUNSELOR TROI FROM THE *ENTERPRISE*.
WHAT, ARE YOU THE SHIP'S THERAPIST? RIDICULOUS. I SUPPOSE YOU'RE QUALIFIED ENOUGH TO ACT AS ESCORT.
THIS IS OUR PILOT, LIEUTENANT JENNA BOEGER.
WHO LOOKS COMPLETELY INEXPERIENCED TO ME. THIS IS NO TRAINING MISSION.
BUT LET'S BE ON OUR WAY.

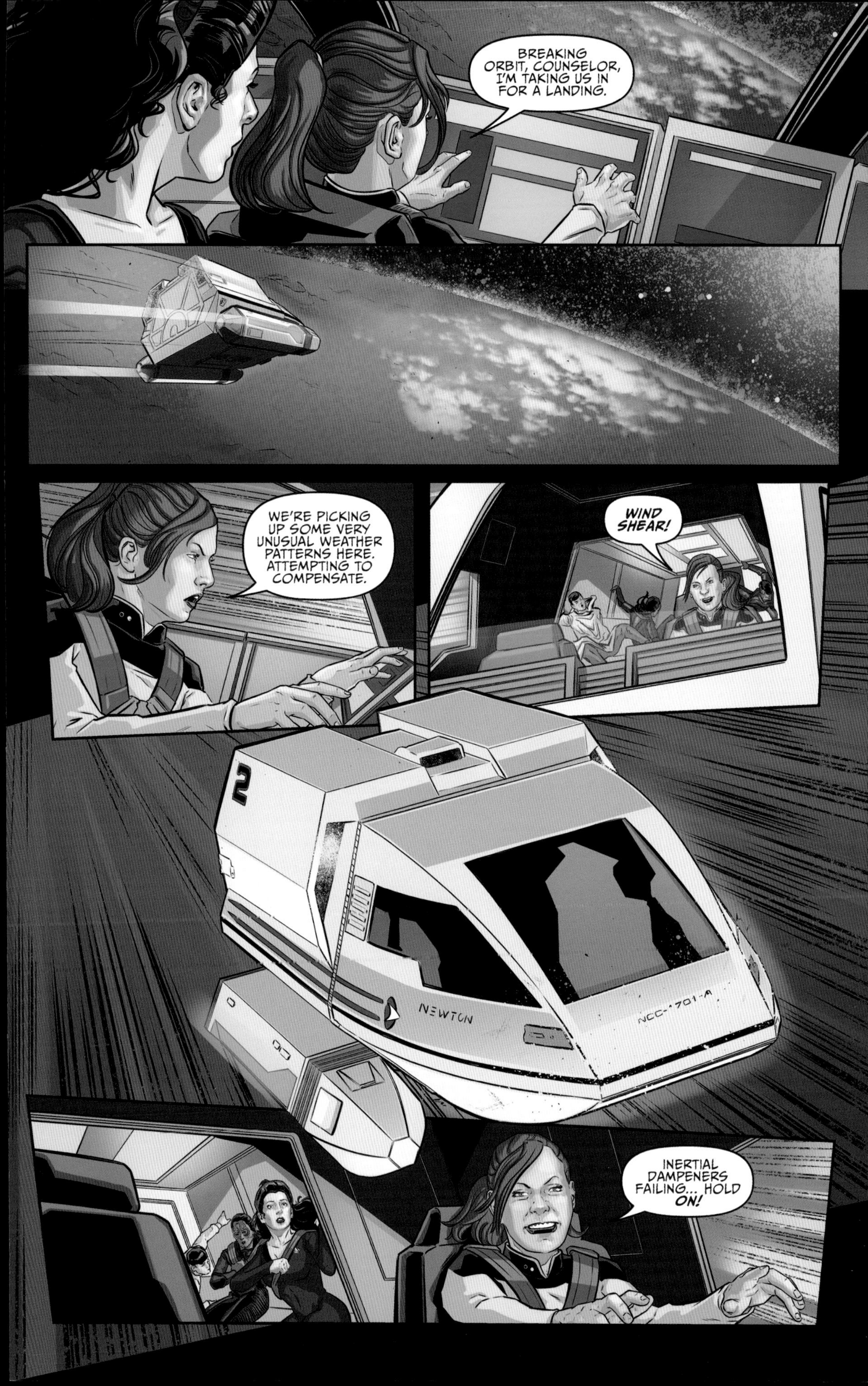
BREAKING ORBIT, COUNSELOR, I'M TAKING US IN FOR A LANDING.
WE'RE PICKING UP SOME VERY UNUSUAL WEATHER PATTERNS HERE. ATTEMPTING TO COMPENSATE.
WIND SHEAR!
2
NEWTON
NCC-1701-A
INERTIAL DAMPENERS FAILING... HOLD ON!

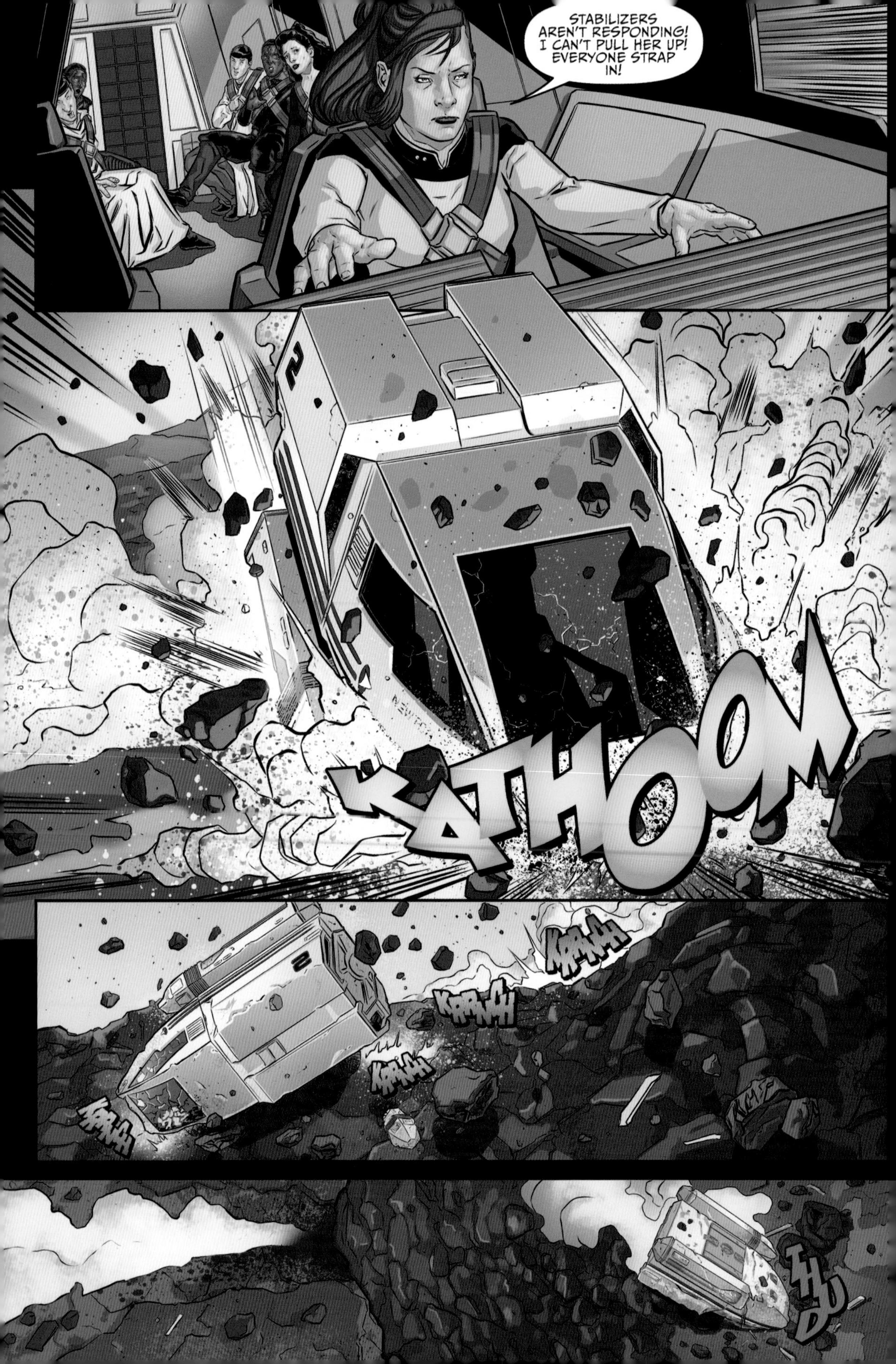

STABILIZERS AREN'T RESPONDING! I CAN'T PULL HER UP! EVERYONE STRAP IN!
KATHOOM
KRRNCH
KRRNCH
KRRNCH
KRRNCH
THUD

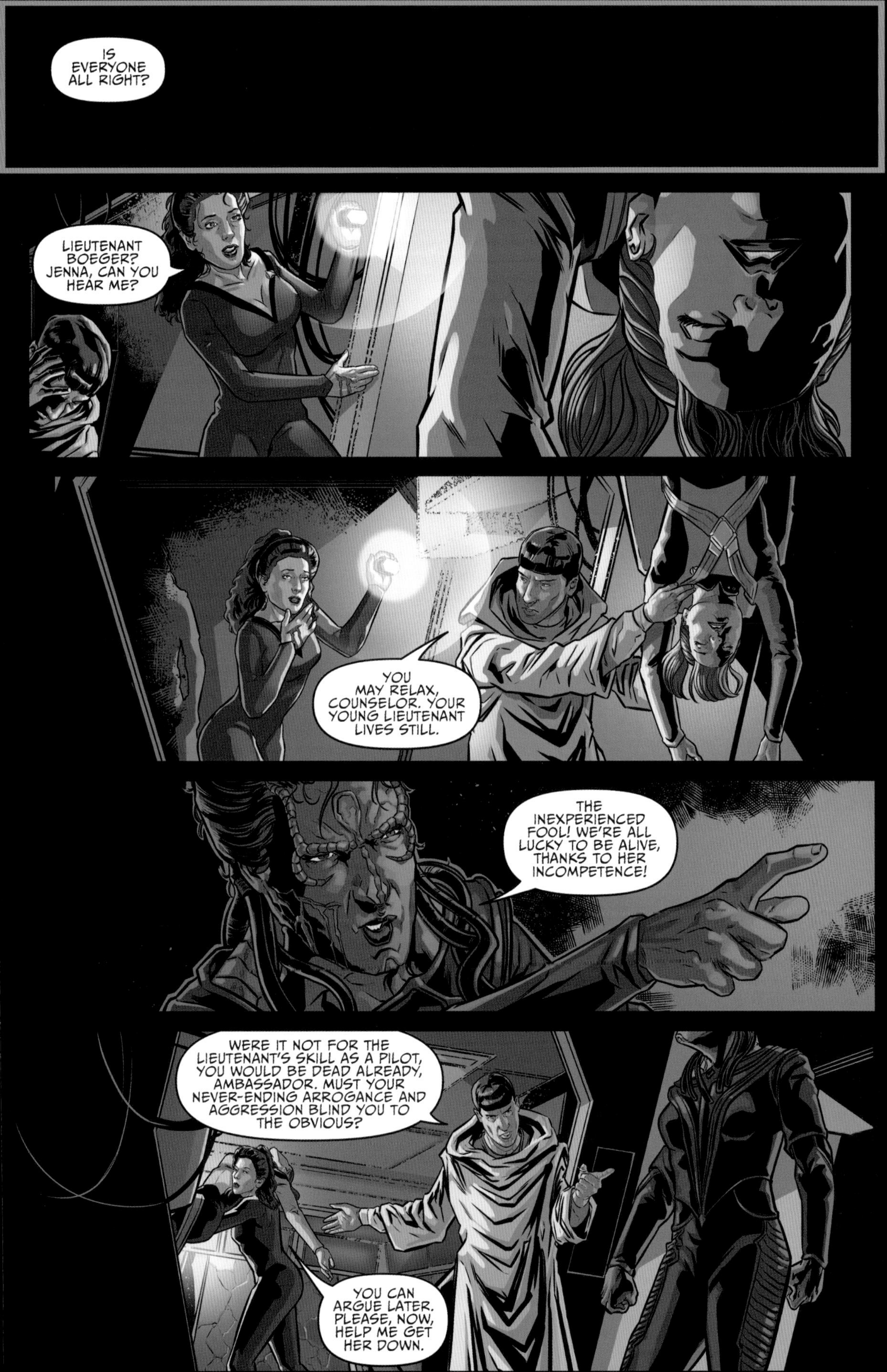
IS EVERYONE ALL RIGHT?
LIEUTENANT BOEGER? JENNA, CAN YOU HEAR ME?
YOU MAY RELAX, COUNSELOR. YOUR YOUNG LIEUTENANT LIVES STILL.
THE INEXPERIENCED FOOL! WE'RE ALL LUCKY TO BE ALIVE, THANKS TO HER INCOMPETENCE!
WERE IT NOT FOR THE LIEUTENANT'S SKILL AS A PILOT, YOU WOULD BE DEAD ALREADY, AMBASSADOR. MUST YOUR NEVER-ENDING ARROGANCE AND AGGRESSION BLIND YOU TO THE OBVIOUS?
YOU CAN ARGUE LATER. PLEASE, NOW, HELP ME GET HER DOWN.

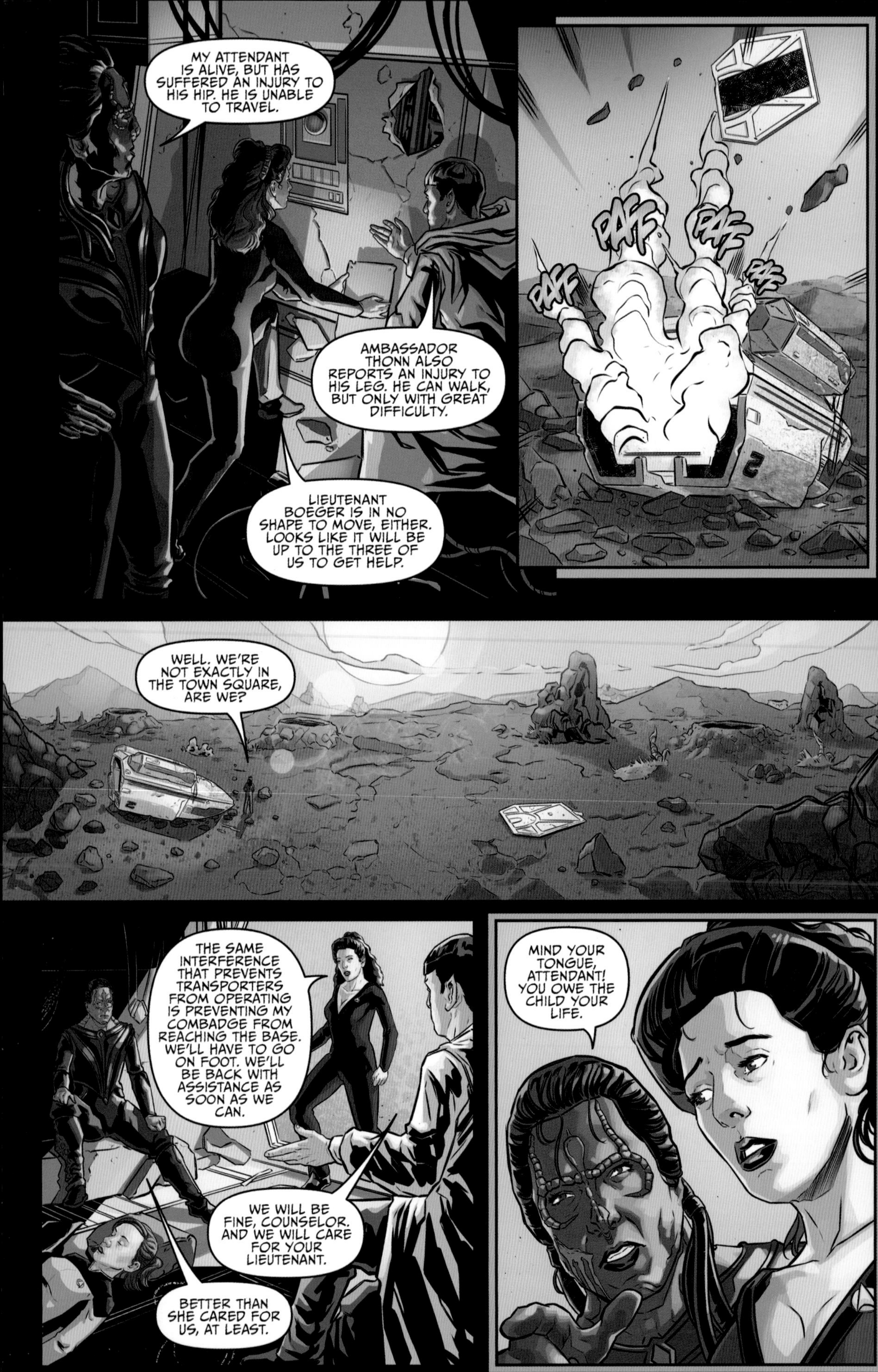
MY ATTENDANT IS ALIVE, BUT HAS SUFFERED AN INJURY TO HIS HIP. HE IS UNABLE TO TRAVEL.
AMBASSADOR THONN ALSO REPORTS AN INJURY TO HIS LEG. HE CAN WALK, BUT ONLY WITH GREAT DIFFICULTY.
LIEUTENANT BOEGER IS IN NO SHAPE TO MOVE, EITHER. LOOKS LIKE IT WILL BE UP TO THE THREE OF US TO GET HELP.
PAFF
PAFF
PAFF
PAFF
WELL. WE'RE NOT EXACTLY IN THE TOWN SQUARE, ARE WE?
THE SAME INTERFERENCE THAT PREVENTS TRANSPORTERS FROM OPERATING IS PREVENTING MY COMBADGE FROM REACHING THE BASE. WE'LL HAVE TO GO ON FOOT. WE'LL BE BACK WITH ASSISTANCE AS SOON AS WE CAN.
WE WILL BE FINE, COUNSELOR. AND WE WILL CARE FOR YOUR LIEUTENANT.
BETTER THAN SHE CARED FOR US, AT LEAST.
MIND YOUR TONGUE, ATTENDANT! YOU OWE THE CHILD YOUR LIFE.

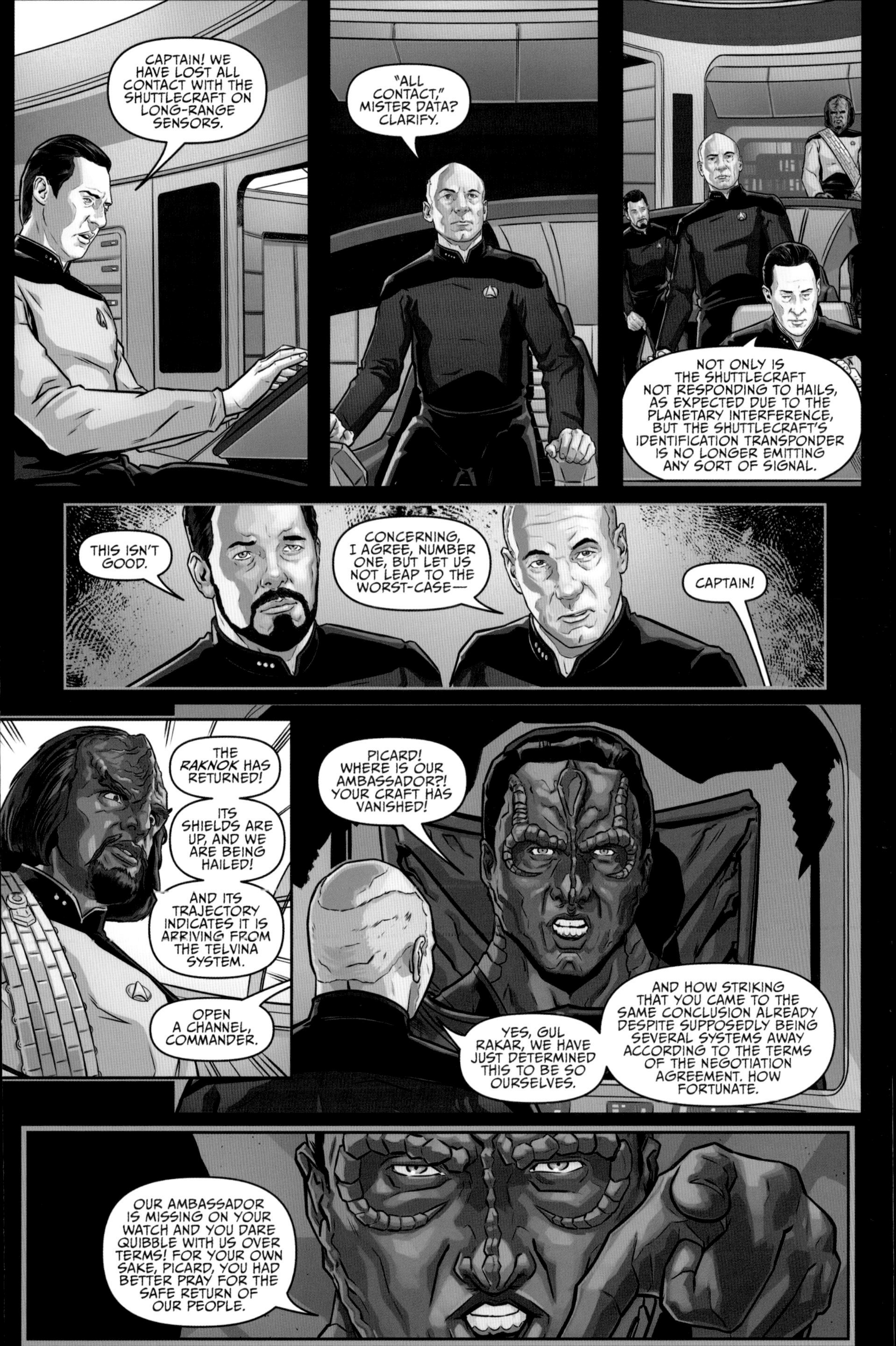
CAPTAIN! WE HAVE LOST ALL CONTACT WITH THE SHUTTLECRAFT ON LONG-RANGE SENSORS.
"ALL CONTACT," MISTER DATA? CLARIFY.
NOT ONLY IS THE SHUTTLECRAFT NOT RESPONDING TO HAILS, AS EXPECTED DUE TO THE PLANETARY INTERFERENCE, BUT THE SHUTTLECRAFT'S IDENTIFICATION TRANSPONDER IS NO LONGER EMITTING ANY SORT OF SIGNAL.
THIS ISN'T GOOD.
CONCERNING, I AGREE, NUMBER ONE, BUT LET US NOT LEAP TO THE WORST-CASE—
CAPTAIN!
THE *RAKNOK* HAS RETURNED!
ITS SHIELDS ARE UP, AND WE ARE BEING HAILED!
AND ITS TRAJECTORY INDICATES IT IS ARRIVING FROM THE TELVINA SYSTEM.
OPEN A CHANNEL, COMMANDER.
PICARD! WHERE IS OUR AMBASSADOR?! YOUR CRAFT HAS VANISHED!
YES, GUL RAKAR, WE HAVE JUST DETERMINED THIS TO BE SO OURSELVES.
AND HOW STRIKING THAT YOU CAME TO THE SAME CONCLUSION ALREADY DESPITE SUPPOSEDLY BEING SEVERAL SYSTEMS AWAY ACCORDING TO THE TERMS OF THE NEGOTIATION AGREEMENT. HOW FORTUNATE.
OUR AMBASSADOR IS MISSING ON YOUR WATCH AND YOU DARE QUIBBLE WITH US OVER TERMS! FOR YOUR OWN SAKE, PICARD, YOU HAD BETTER PRAY FOR THE SAFE RETURN OF OUR PEOPLE.

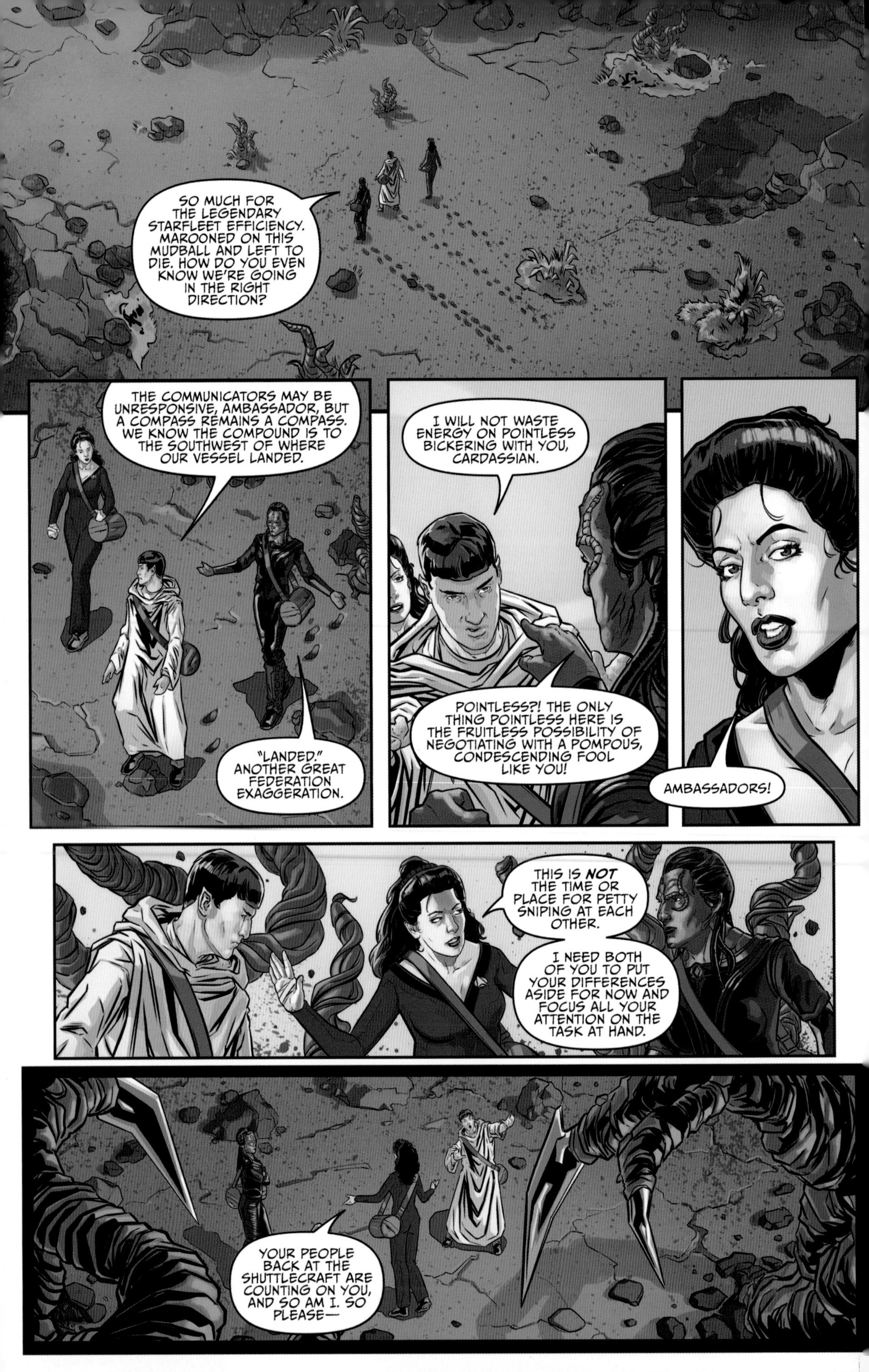
SO MUCH FOR THE LEGENDARY STARFLEET EFFICIENCY. MAROONED ON THIS MUDBALL AND LEFT TO DIE. HOW DO YOU EVEN KNOW WE'RE GOING IN THE RIGHT DIRECTION?
THE COMMUNICATORS MAY BE UNRESPONSIVE, AMBASSADOR, BUT A COMPASS REMAINS A COMPASS. WE KNOW THE COMPOUND IS TO THE SOUTHWEST OF WHERE OUR VESSEL LANDED.
"LANDED." ANOTHER GREAT FEDERATION EXAGGERATION.
I WILL NOT WASTE ENERGY ON POINTLESS BICKERING WITH YOU, CARDASSIAN.
POINTLESS?! THE ONLY THING POINTLESS HERE IS THE FRUITLESS POSSIBILITY OF NEGOTIATING WITH A POMPOUS, CONDESCENDING FOOL LIKE YOU!
AMBASSADORS!
THIS IS ***NOT*** THE TIME OR PLACE FOR PETTY SNIPING AT EACH OTHER.
I NEED BOTH OF YOU TO PUT YOUR DIFFERENCES ASIDE FOR NOW AND FOCUS ALL YOUR ATTENTION ON THE TASK AT HAND.
YOUR PEOPLE BACK AT THE SHUTTLECRAFT ARE COUNTING ON YOU, AND SO AM I. SO PLEASE—

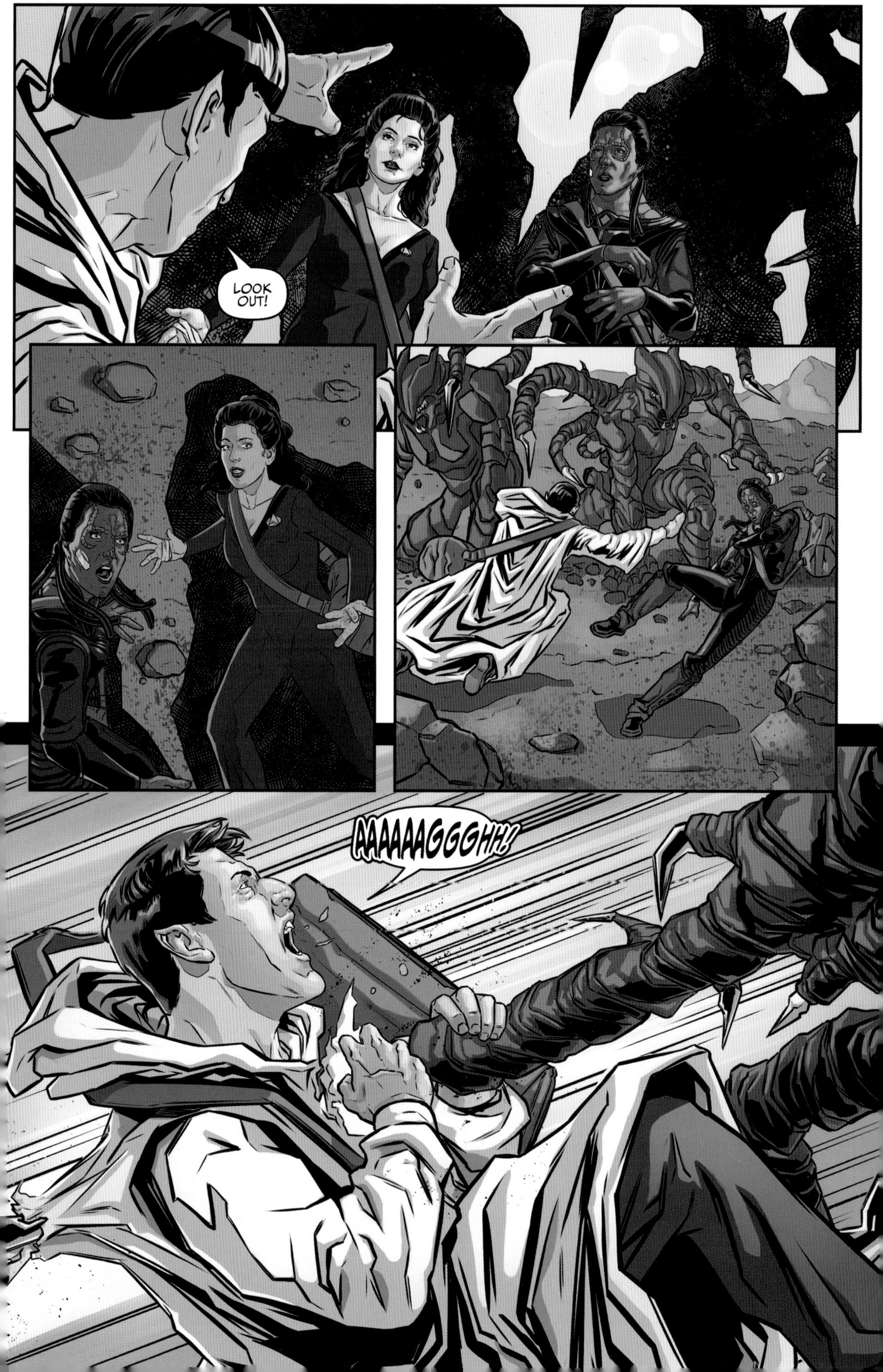
LOOK OUT!
AAAAAAGGGHH!

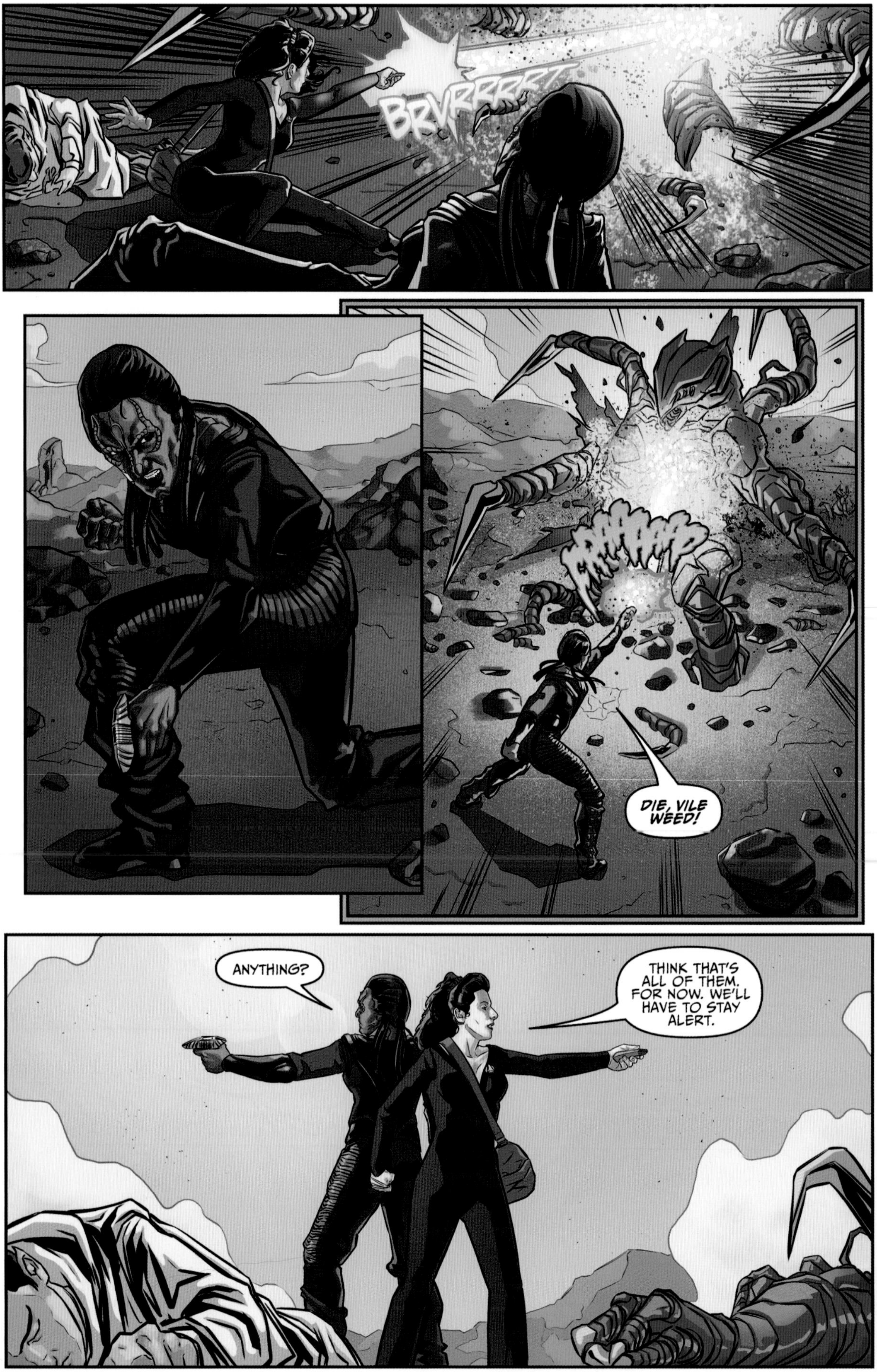
BRVRRRRT
DIE, VILE WEED!
ANYTHING?
THINK THAT'S ALL OF THEM. FOR NOW. WE'LL HAVE TO STAY ALERT.

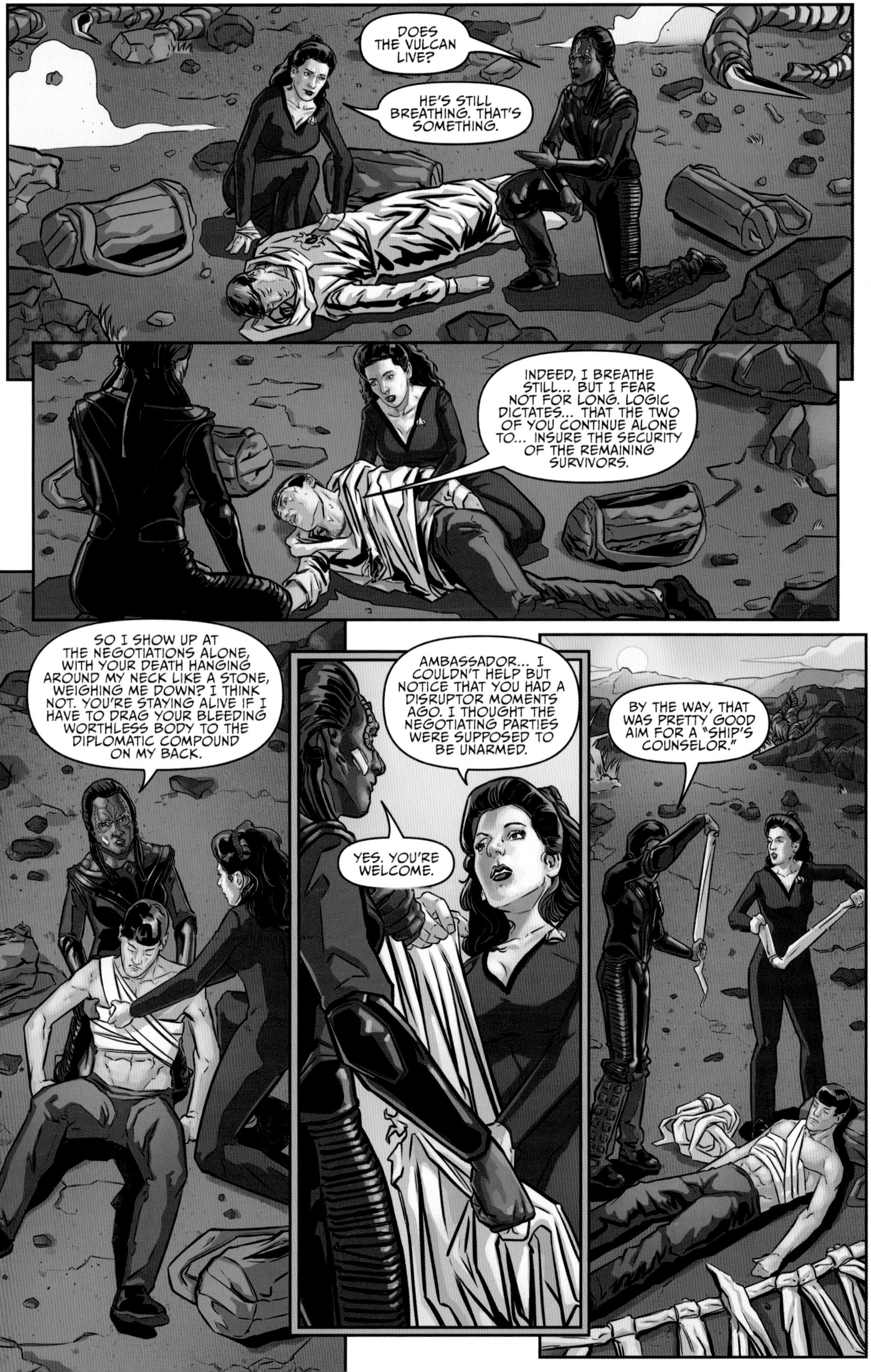
DOES THE VULCAN LIVE?
HE'S STILL BREATHING. THAT'S SOMETHING.
INDEED, I BREATHE STILL... BUT I FEAR NOT FOR LONG. LOGIC DICTATES... THAT THE TWO OF YOU CONTINUE ALONE TO... INSURE THE SECURITY OF THE REMAINING SURVIVORS.
SO I SHOW UP AT THE NEGOTIATIONS ALONE, WITH YOUR DEATH HANGING AROUND MY NECK LIKE A STONE, WEIGHING ME DOWN? I THINK NOT. YOU'RE STAYING ALIVE IF I HAVE TO DRAG YOUR BLEEDING WORTHLESS BODY TO THE DIPLOMATIC COMPOUND ON MY BACK.
AMBASSADOR... I COULDN'T HELP BUT NOTICE THAT YOU HAD A DISRUPTOR MOMENTS AGO. I THOUGHT THE NEGOTIATING PARTIES WERE SUPPOSED TO BE UNARMED.
YES. YOU'RE WELCOME.
BY THE WAY, THAT WAS PRETTY GOOD AIM FOR A "SHIP'S COUNSELOR."

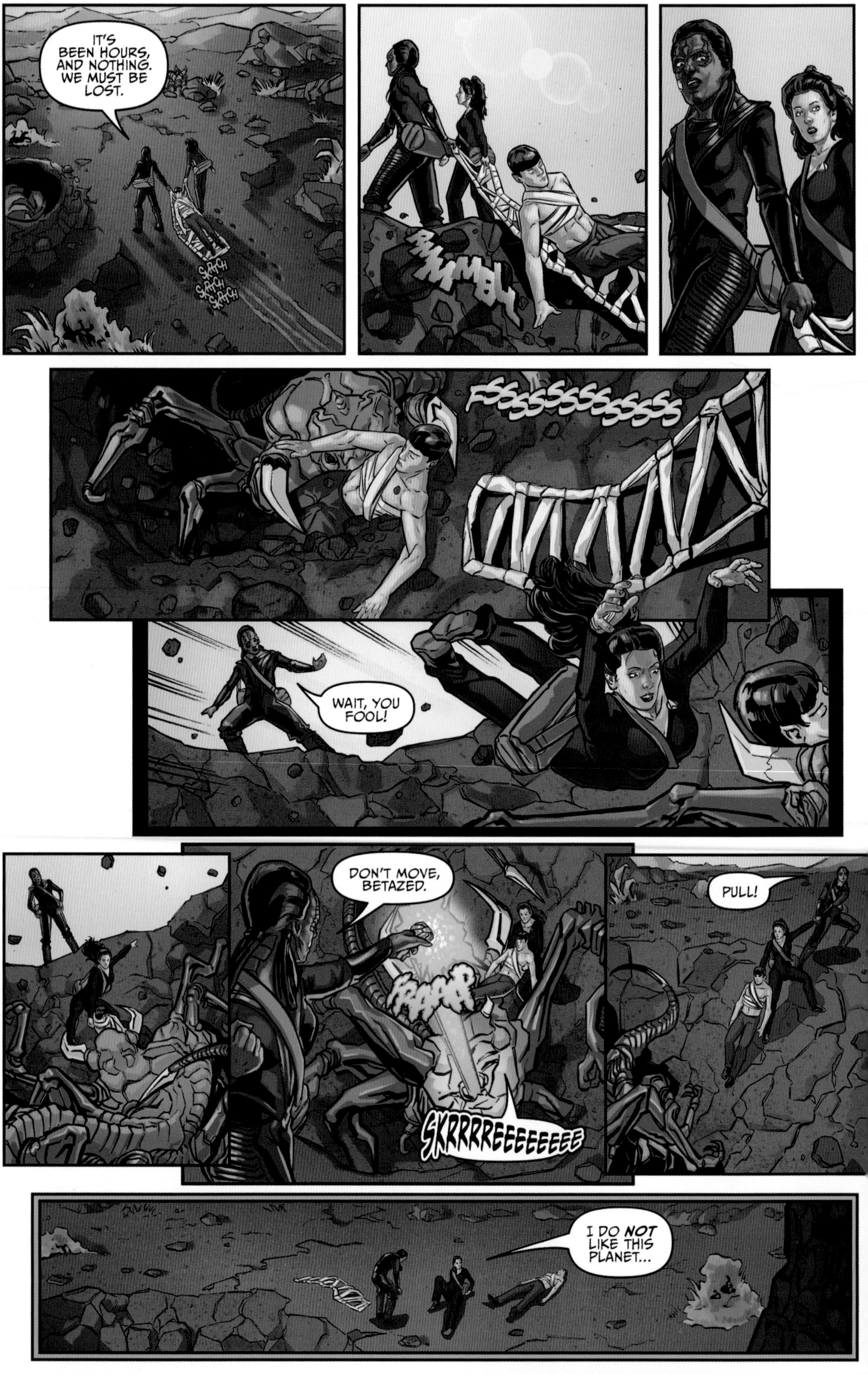

IT'S BEEN HOURS, AND NOTHING. WE MUST BE LOST.
SKRTCH SKRTCH SKRTCH
FSSSSSSSSSSSS
WAIT, YOU FOOL!
DON'T MOVE, BETAZED.
SKRRRREEEEEEEEE
PULL!
I DO **NOT** LIKE THIS PLANET...

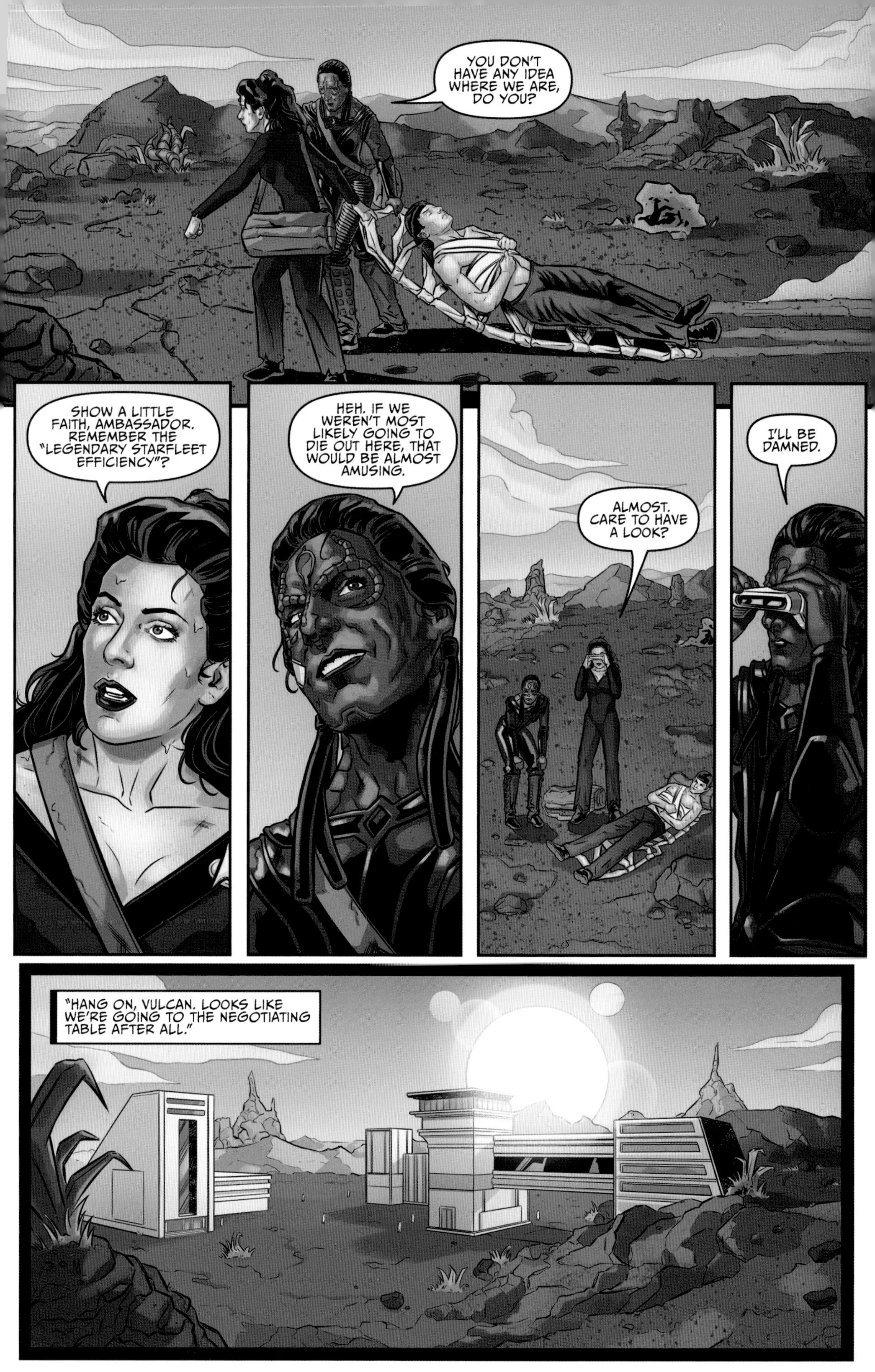
YOU DON'T HAVE ANY IDEA WHERE WE ARE, DO YOU?
SHOW A LITTLE FAITH, AMBASSADOR. REMEMBER THE "LEGENDARY STARFLEET EFFICIENCY"?
HEH. IF WE WEREN'T MOST LIKELY GOING TO DIE OUT HERE, THAT WOULD BE ALMOST AMUSING.
ALMOST. CARE TO HAVE A LOOK?
I'LL BE DAMNED.
"HANG ON, VULCAN. LOOKS LIKE WE'RE GOING TO THE NEGOTIATING TABLE AFTER ALL."

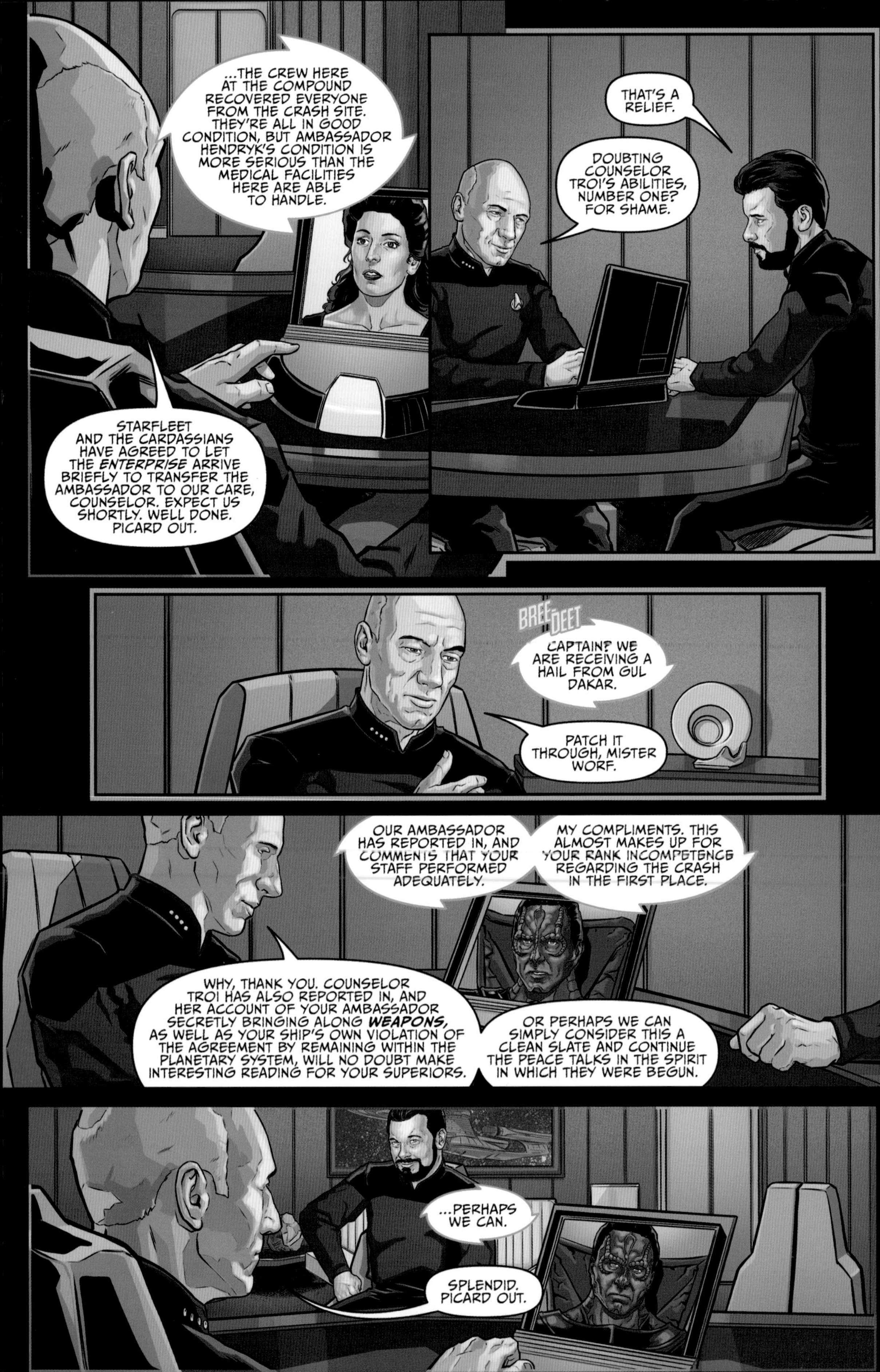
...THE CREW HERE AT THE COMPOUND RECOVERED EVERYONE FROM THE CRASH SITE. THEY'RE ALL IN GOOD CONDITION, BUT AMBASSADOR HENDRYK'S CONDITION IS MORE SERIOUS THAN THE MEDICAL FACILITIES HERE ARE ABLE TO HANDLE.
STARFLEET AND THE CARDASSIANS HAVE AGREED TO LET THE *ENTERPRISE* ARRIVE BRIEFLY TO TRANSFER THE AMBASSADOR TO OUR CARE, COUNSELOR. EXPECT US SHORTLY. WELL DONE. PICARD OUT.
THAT'S A RELIEF.
DOUBTING COUNSELOR TROI'S ABILITIES, NUMBER ONE? FOR SHAME.
BREE DEET
CAPTAIN? WE ARE RECEIVING A HAIL FROM GUL DAKAR.
PATCH IT THROUGH, MISTER WORF.
OUR AMBASSADOR HAS REPORTED IN, AND COMMENTS THAT YOUR STAFF PERFORMED ADEQUATELY.
MY COMPLIMENTS. THIS ALMOST MAKES UP FOR YOUR RANK INCOMPETENCE REGARDING THE CRASH IN THE FIRST PLACE.
WHY, THANK YOU. COUNSELOR TROI HAS ALSO REPORTED IN, AND HER ACCOUNT OF YOUR AMBASSADOR SECRETLY BRINGING ALONG **WEAPONS,** AS WELL AS YOUR SHIP'S OWN VIOLATION OF THE AGREEMENT BY REMAINING WITHIN THE PLANETARY SYSTEM, WILL NO DOUBT MAKE INTERESTING READING FOR YOUR SUPERIORS.
OR PERHAPS WE CAN SIMPLY CONSIDER THIS A CLEAN SLATE AND CONTINUE THE PEACE TALKS IN THE SPIRIT IN WHICH THEY WERE BEGUN.
...PERHAPS WE CAN.
SPLENDID. PICARD OUT.

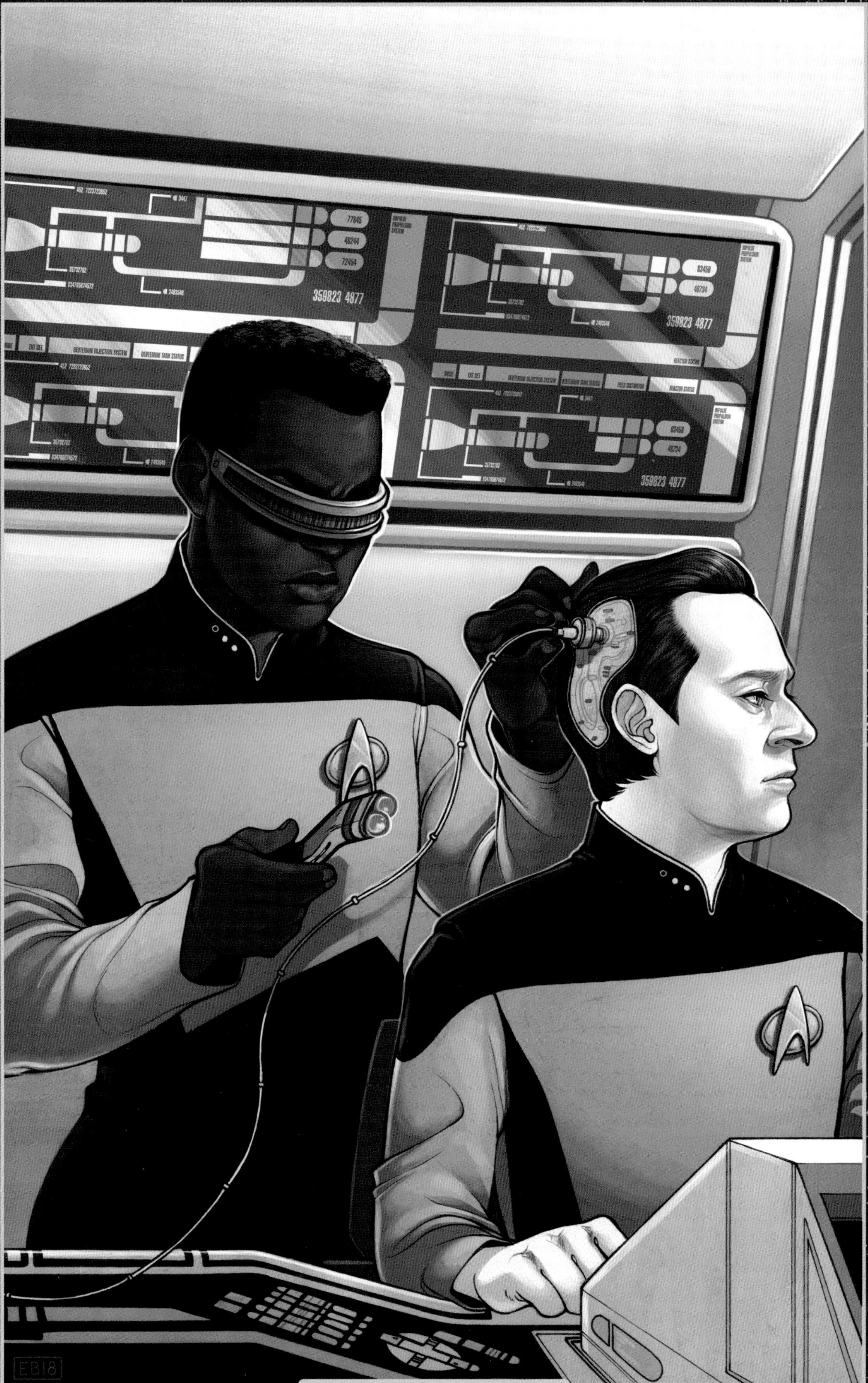
359823 4877
359823 4877
359823 4877
EB18

ART BY ELIZABETH BEALS

TERRA INCOGNITA PART 3

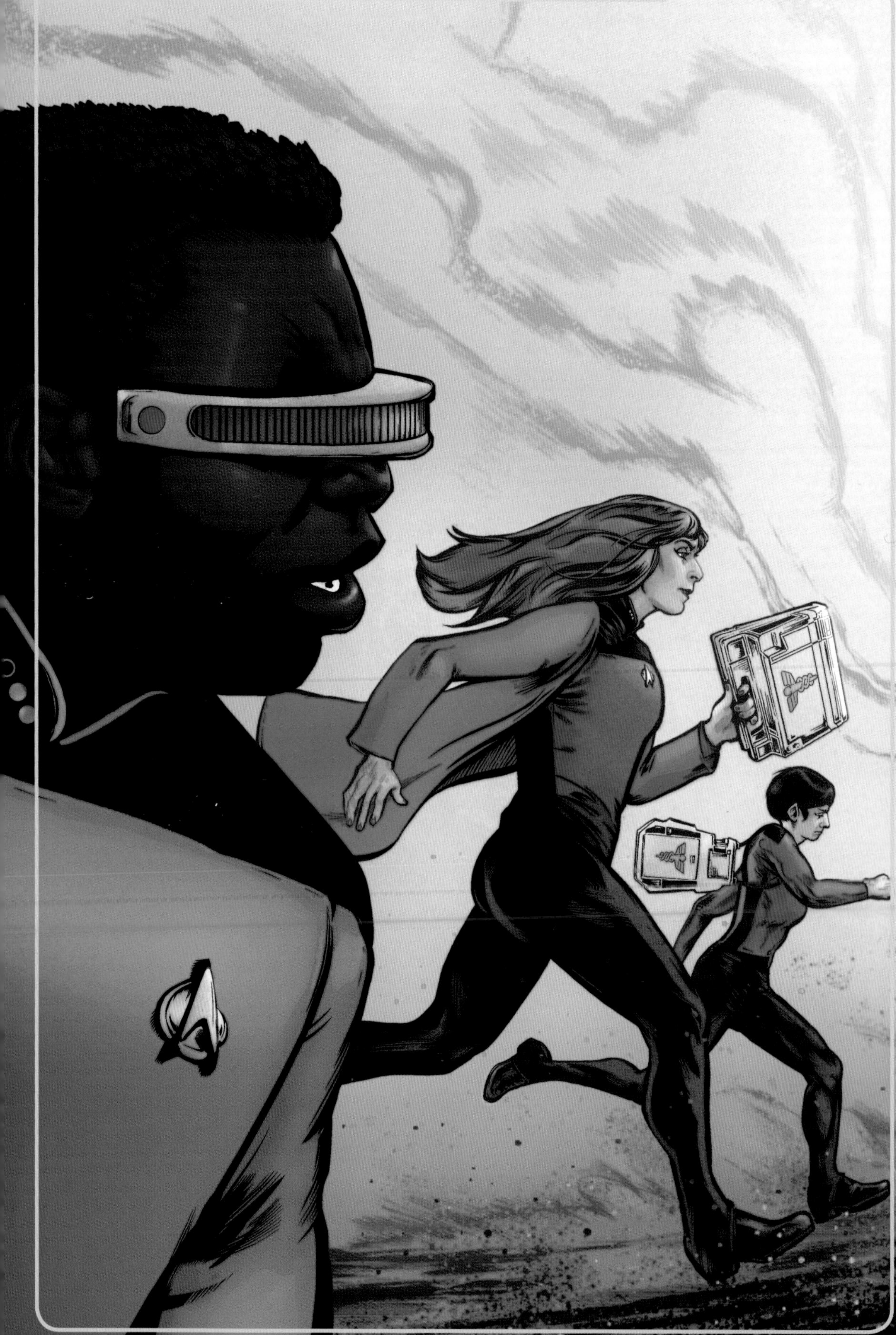

ART BY TONY SHASTEEN, COLORS BY JD METTLER

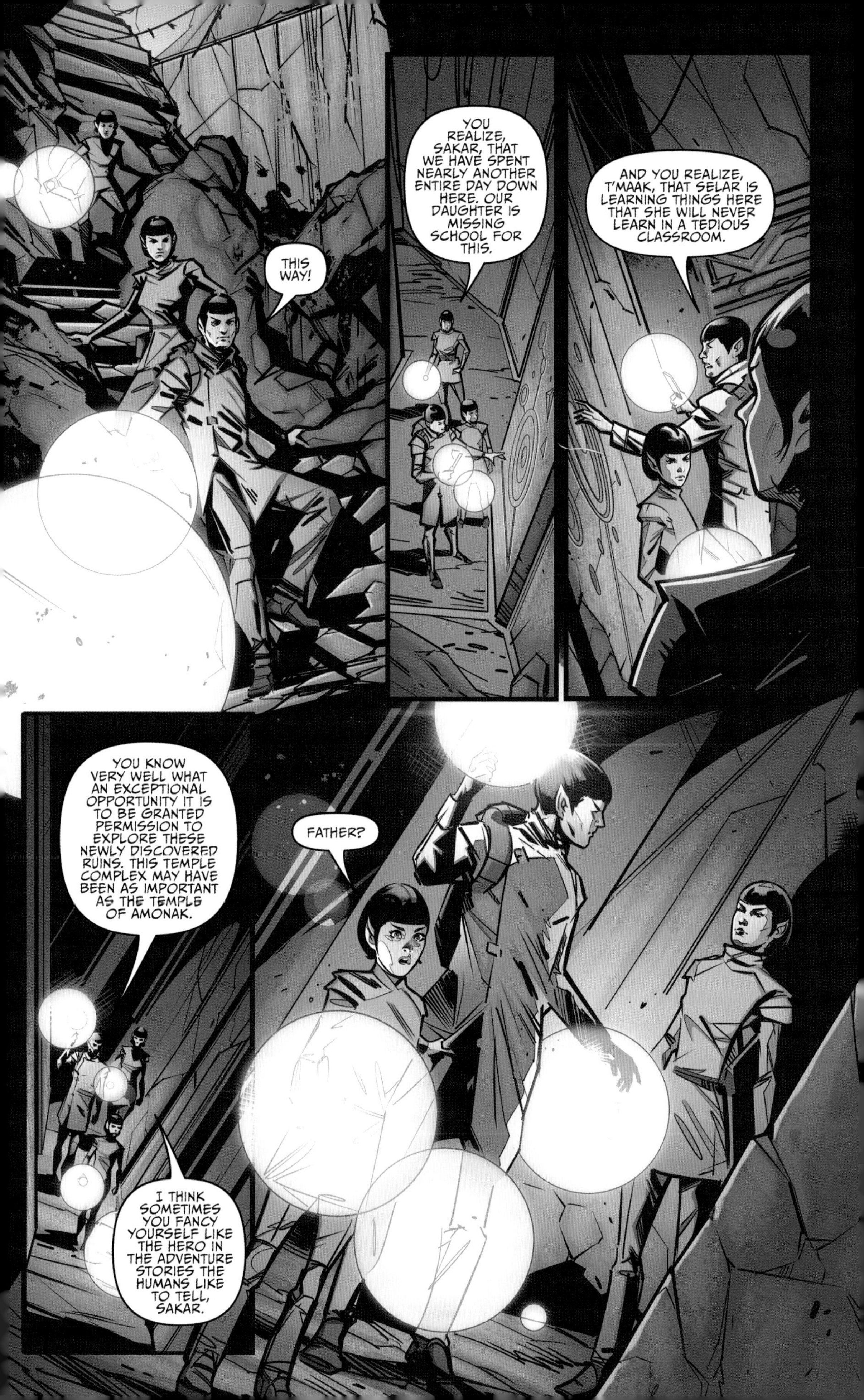
THIS WAY!
YOU REALIZE, SAKAR, THAT WE HAVE SPENT NEARLY ANOTHER ENTIRE DAY DOWN HERE. OUR DAUGHTER IS MISSING SCHOOL FOR THIS.
AND YOU REALIZE, T'MAAK, THAT SELAR IS LEARNING THINGS HERE THAT SHE WILL NEVER LEARN IN A TEDIOUS CLASSROOM.
YOU KNOW VERY WELL WHAT AN EXCEPTIONAL OPPORTUNITY IT IS TO BE GRANTED PERMISSION TO EXPLORE THESE NEWLY DISCOVERED RUINS. THIS TEMPLE COMPLEX MAY HAVE BEEN AS IMPORTANT AS THE TEMPLE OF AMONAK.
FATHER?
I THINK SOMETIMES YOU FANCY YOURSELF LIKE THE HERO IN THE ADVENTURE STORIES THE HUMANS LIKE TO TELL, SAKAR.

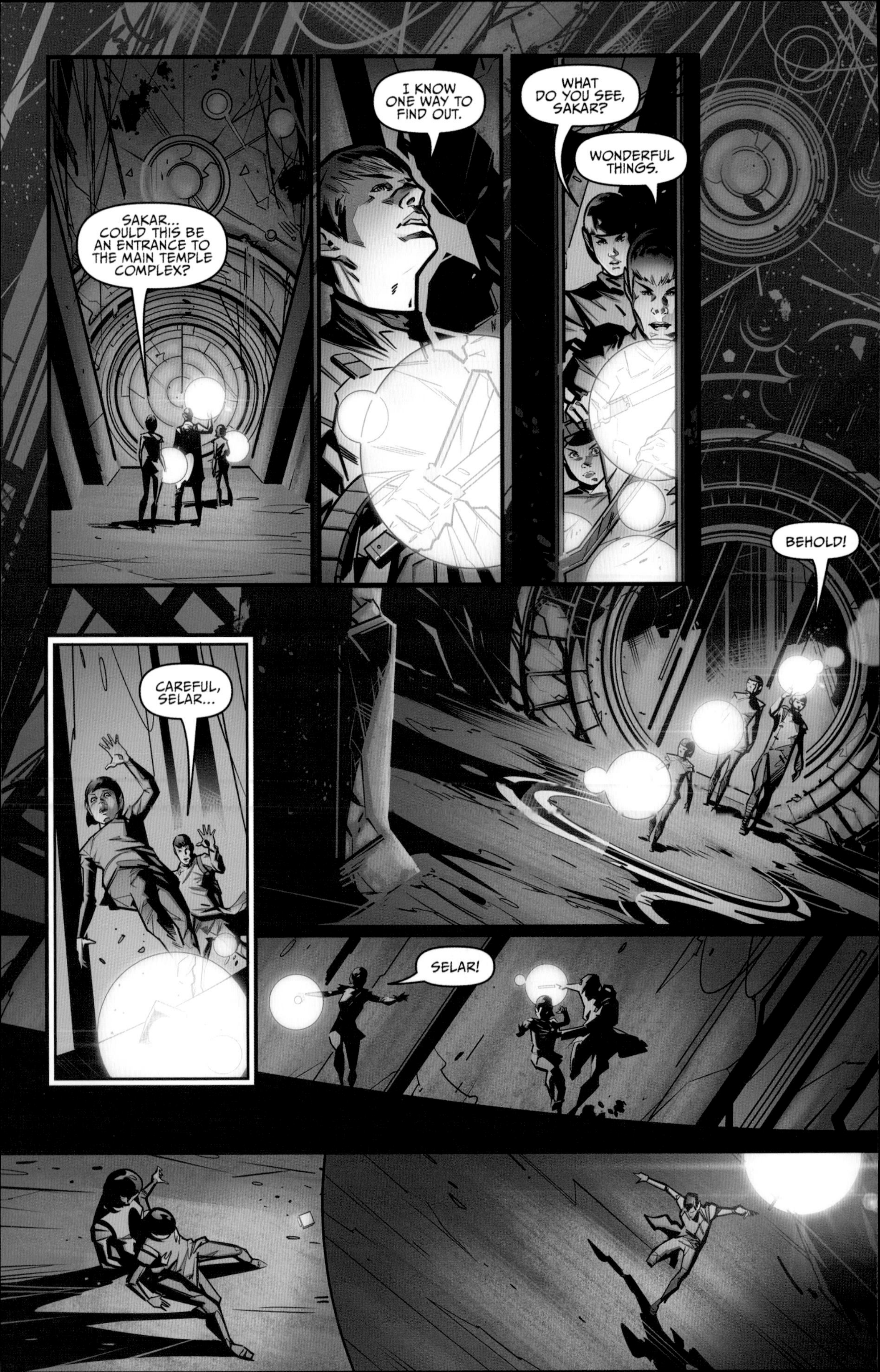
SAKAR... COULD THIS BE AN ENTRANCE TO THE MAIN TEMPLE COMPLEX?
I KNOW ONE WAY TO FIND OUT.
WHAT DO YOU SEE, SAKAR?
WONDERFUL THINGS.
BEHOLD!
CAREFUL, SELAR...
SELAR!

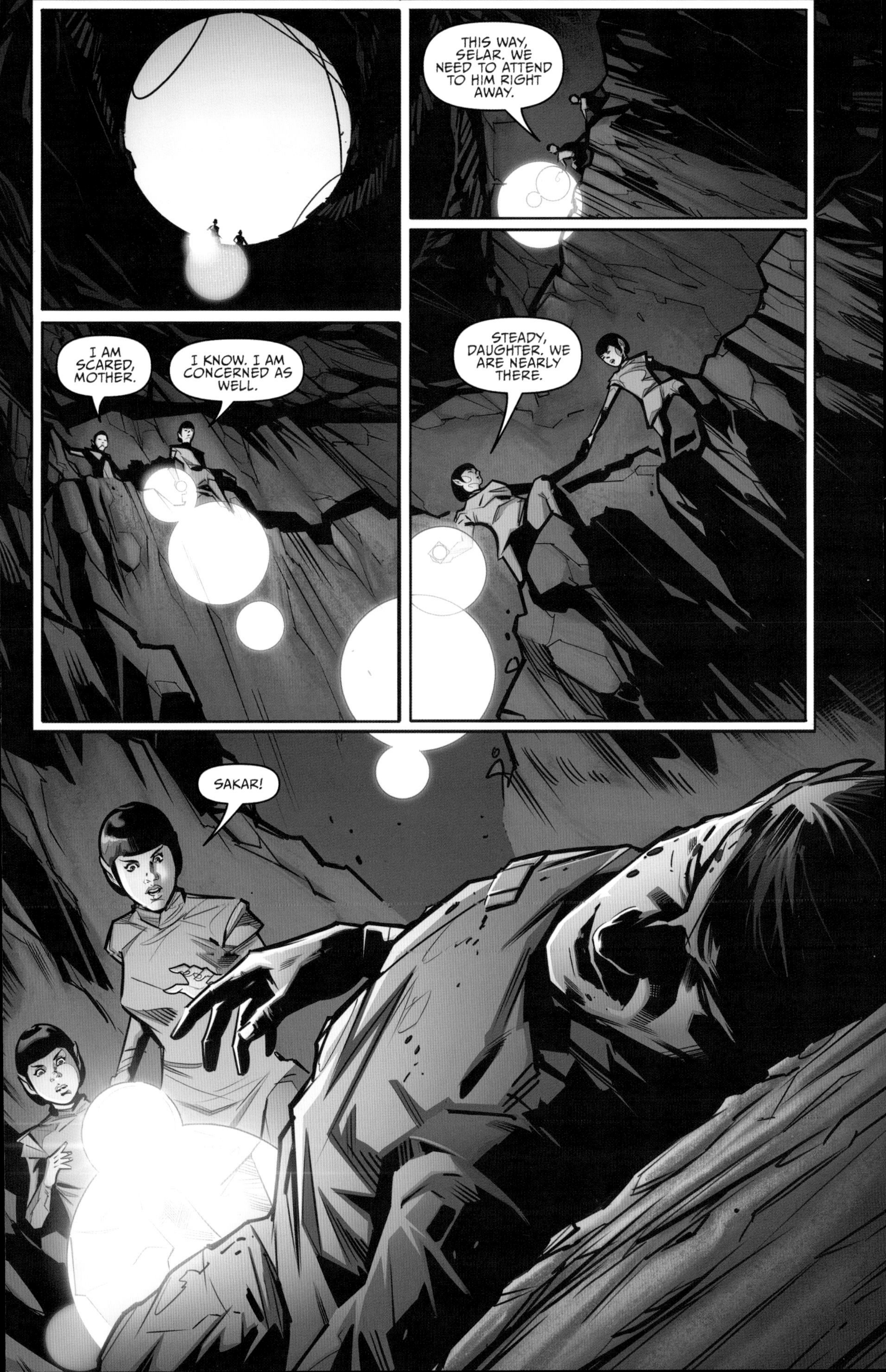
THIS WAY, SELAR. WE NEED TO ATTEND TO HIM RIGHT AWAY.
I AM SCARED, MOTHER.
I KNOW. I AM CONCERNED AS WELL.
STEADY, DAUGHTER. WE ARE NEARLY THERE.
SAKAR!

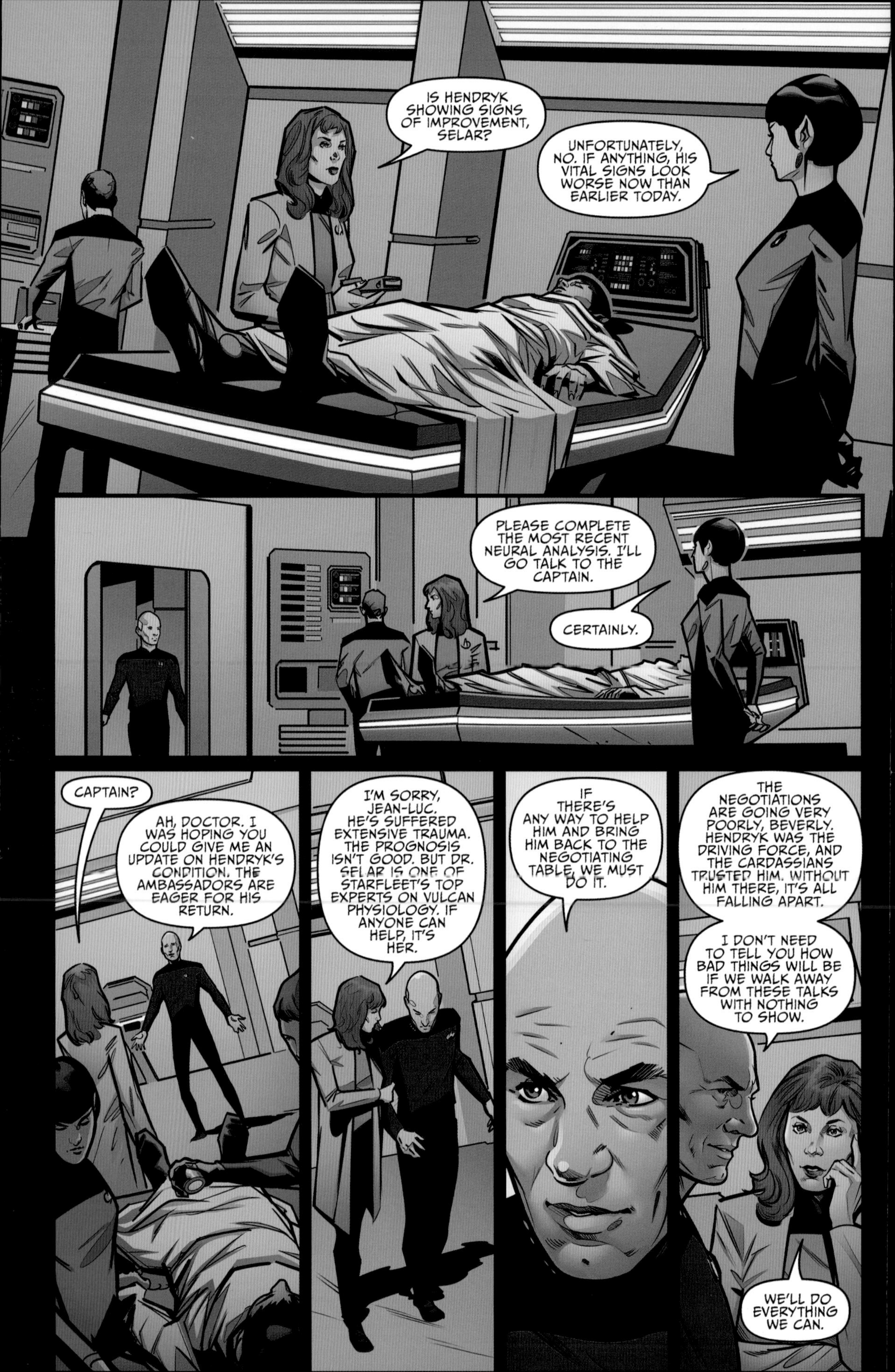
IS HENDRYK SHOWING SIGNS OF IMPROVEMENT, SELAR?
UNFORTUNATELY, NO. IF ANYTHING, HIS VITAL SIGNS LOOK WORSE NOW THAN EARLIER TODAY.
PLEASE COMPLETE THE MOST RECENT NEURAL ANALYSIS. I'LL GO TALK TO THE CAPTAIN.
CERTAINLY.
CAPTAIN?
AH, DOCTOR. I WAS HOPING YOU COULD GIVE ME AN UPDATE ON HENDRYK'S CONDITION. THE AMBASSADORS ARE EAGER FOR HIS RETURN.
I'M SORRY, JEAN-LUC. HE'S SUFFERED EXTENSIVE TRAUMA. THE PROGNOSIS ISN'T GOOD. BUT DR. SELAR IS ONE OF STARFLEET'S TOP EXPERTS ON VULCAN PHYSIOLOGY. IF ANYONE CAN HELP, IT'S HER.
IF THERE'S ANY WAY TO HELP HIM AND BRING HIM BACK TO THE NEGOTIATING TABLE, WE MUST DO IT.
THE NEGOTIATIONS ARE GOING VERY POORLY, BEVERLY. HENDRYK WAS THE DRIVING FORCE, AND THE CARDASSIANS TRUSTED HIM. WITHOUT HIM THERE, IT'S ALL FALLING APART.
I DON'T NEED TO TELL YOU HOW BAD THINGS WILL BE IF WE WALK AWAY FROM THESE TALKS WITH NOTHING TO SHOW.
WE'LL DO EVERYTHING WE CAN.

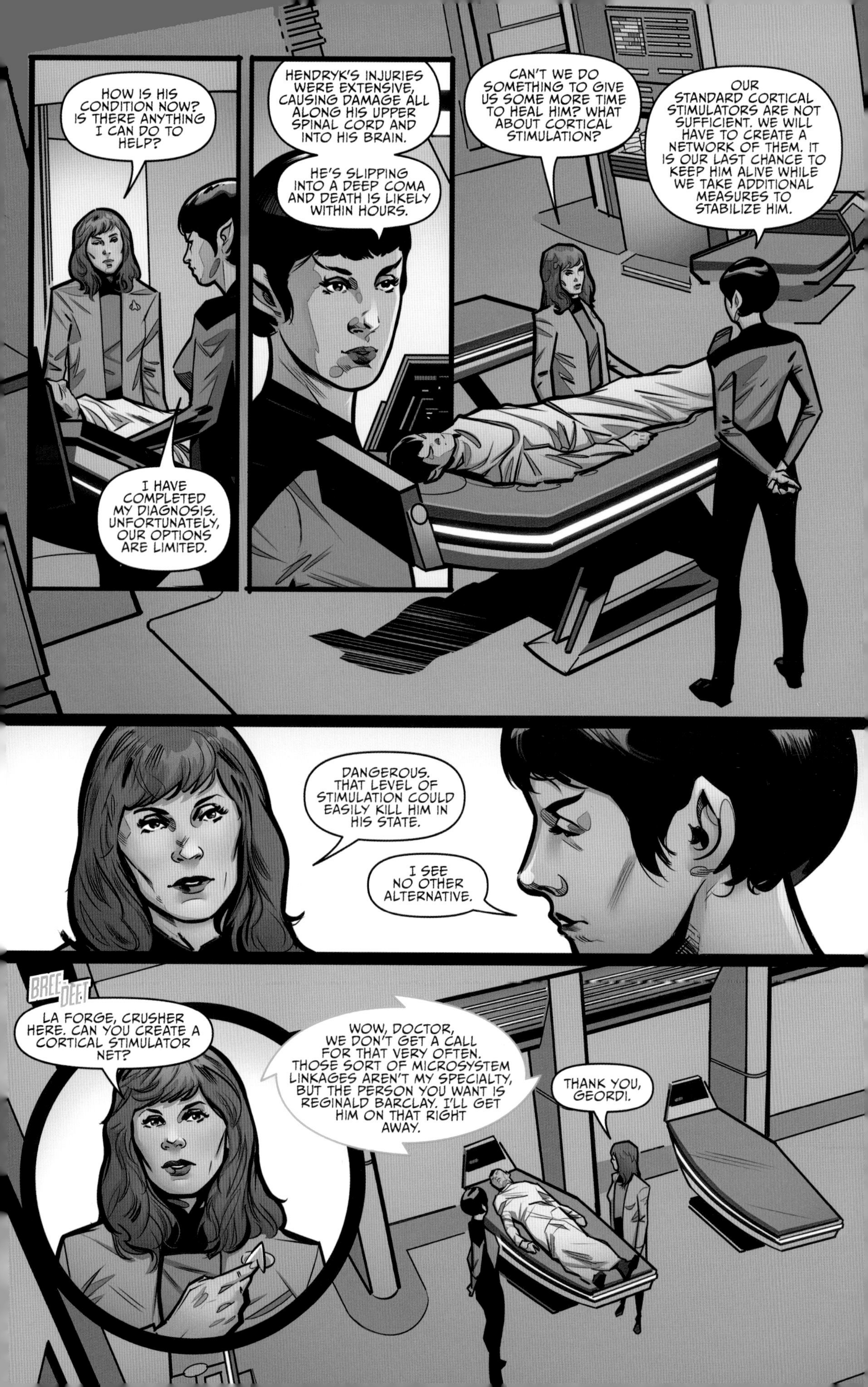
HOW IS HIS CONDITION NOW? IS THERE ANYTHING I CAN DO TO HELP?
I HAVE COMPLETED MY DIAGNOSIS. UNFORTUNATELY, OUR OPTIONS ARE LIMITED.
HENDRYK'S INJURIES WERE EXTENSIVE, CAUSING DAMAGE ALL ALONG HIS UPPER SPINAL CORD AND INTO HIS BRAIN.
HE'S SLIPPING INTO A DEEP COMA AND DEATH IS LIKELY WITHIN HOURS.
CAN'T WE DO SOMETHING TO GIVE US SOME MORE TIME TO HEAL HIM? WHAT ABOUT CORTICAL STIMULATION?
OUR STANDARD CORTICAL STIMULATORS ARE NOT SUFFICIENT. WE WILL HAVE TO CREATE A NETWORK OF THEM. IT IS OUR LAST CHANCE TO KEEP HIM ALIVE WHILE WE TAKE ADDITIONAL MEASURES TO STABILIZE HIM.
DANGEROUS. THAT LEVEL OF STIMULATION COULD EASILY KILL HIM IN HIS STATE.
I SEE NO OTHER ALTERNATIVE.
BREE-DEET
LA FORGE, CRUSHER HERE. CAN YOU CREATE A CORTICAL STIMULATOR NET?
WOW, DOCTOR, WE DON'T GET A CALL FOR THAT VERY OFTEN. THOSE SORT OF MICROSYSTEM LINKAGES AREN'T MY SPECIALTY, BUT THE PERSON YOU WANT IS REGINALD BARCLAY. I'LL GET HIM ON THAT RIGHT AWAY.
THANK YOU, GEORDI.

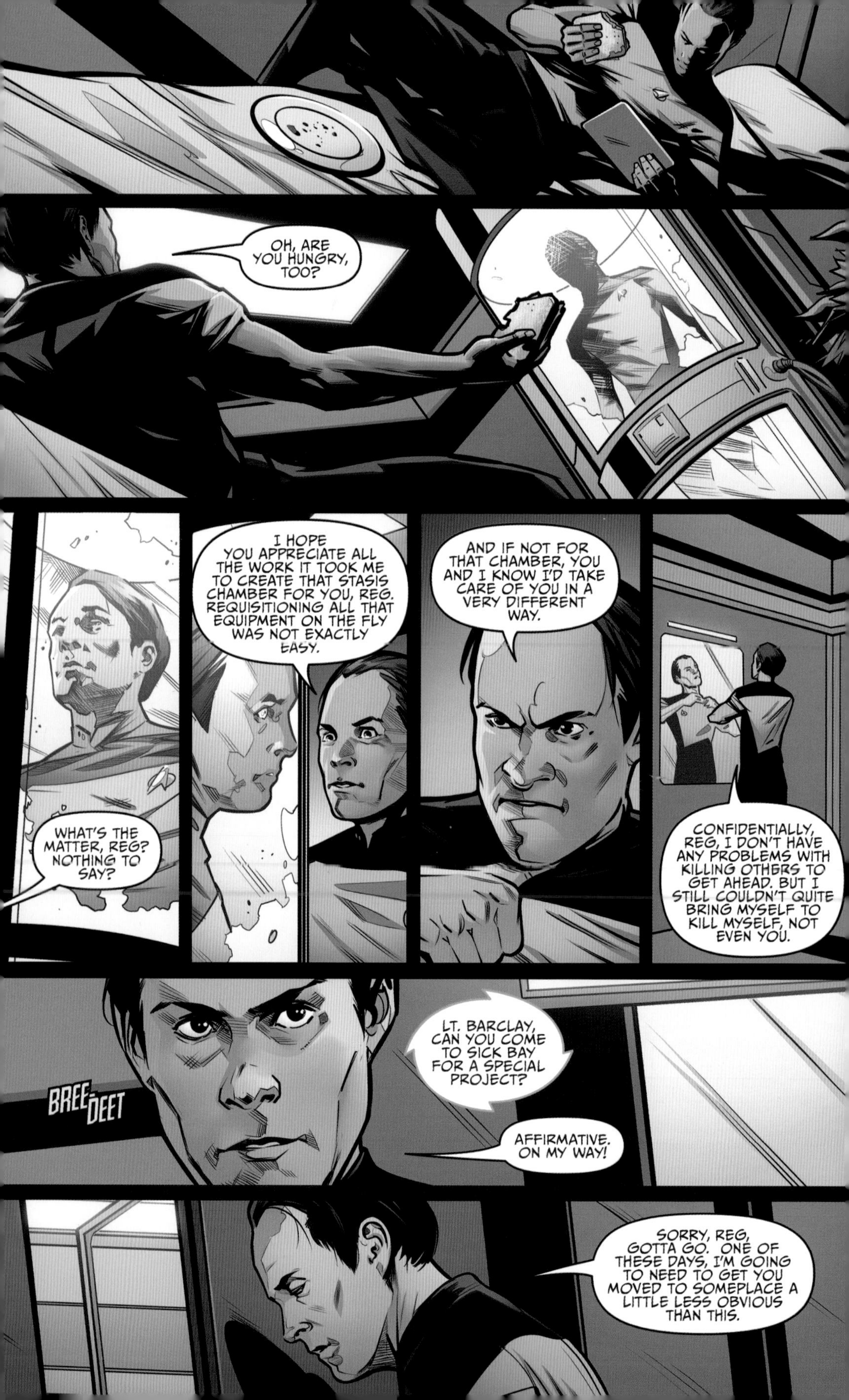
OH, ARE YOU HUNGRY, TOO?
WHAT'S THE MATTER, REG? NOTHING TO SAY?
I HOPE YOU APPRECIATE ALL THE WORK IT TOOK ME TO CREATE THAT STASIS CHAMBER FOR YOU, REG. REQUISITIONING ALL THAT EQUIPMENT ON THE FLY WAS NOT EXACTLY EASY.
AND IF NOT FOR THAT CHAMBER, YOU AND I KNOW I'D TAKE CARE OF YOU IN A VERY DIFFERENT WAY.
CONFIDENTIALLY, REG, I DON'T HAVE ANY PROBLEMS WITH KILLING OTHERS TO GET AHEAD. BUT I STILL COULDN'T QUITE BRING MYSELF TO KILL MYSELF, NOT EVEN YOU.
BREE-DEET
LT. BARCLAY, CAN YOU COME TO SICK BAY FOR A SPECIAL PROJECT?
AFFIRMATIVE. ON MY WAY!
SORRY, REG, GOTTA GO. ONE OF THESE DAYS, I'M GOING TO NEED TO GET YOU MOVED TO SOMEPLACE A LITTLE LESS OBVIOUS THAN THIS.

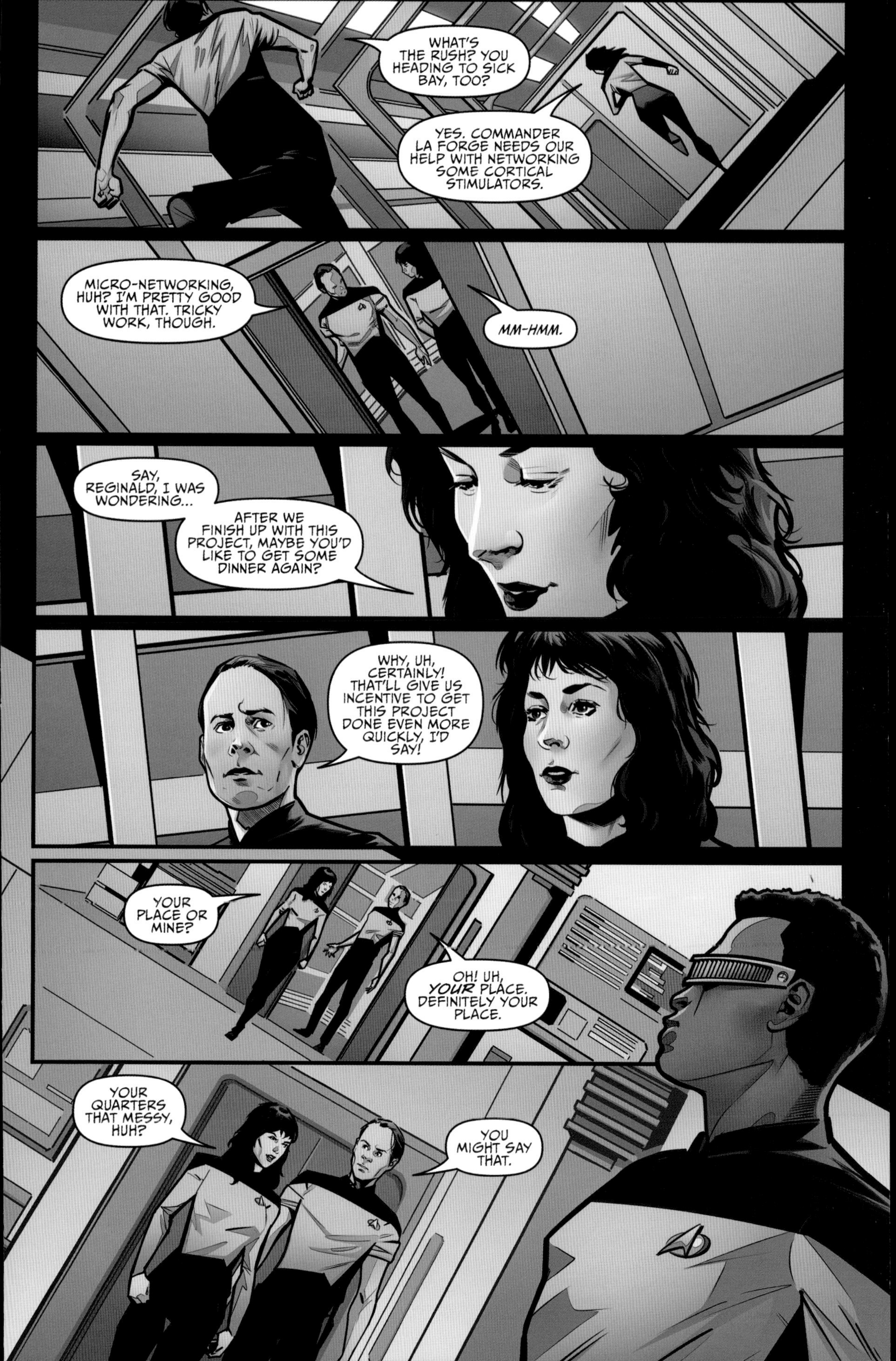
WHAT'S THE RUSH? YOU HEADING TO SICK BAY, TOO?
YES. COMMANDER LA FORGE NEEDS OUR HELP WITH NETWORKING SOME CORTICAL STIMULATORS.
MICRO-NETWORKING, HUH? I'M PRETTY GOOD WITH THAT. TRICKY WORK, THOUGH.
MM-HMM.
SAY, REGINALD, I WAS WONDERING...
AFTER WE FINISH UP WITH THIS PROJECT, MAYBE YOU'D LIKE TO GET SOME DINNER AGAIN?
WHY, UH, CERTAINLY! THAT'LL GIVE US INCENTIVE TO GET THIS PROJECT DONE EVEN MORE QUICKLY, I'D SAY!
YOUR PLACE OR MINE?
OH! UH, YOUR PLACE. DEFINITELY YOUR PLACE.
YOUR QUARTERS THAT MESSY, HUH?
YOU MIGHT SAY THAT.

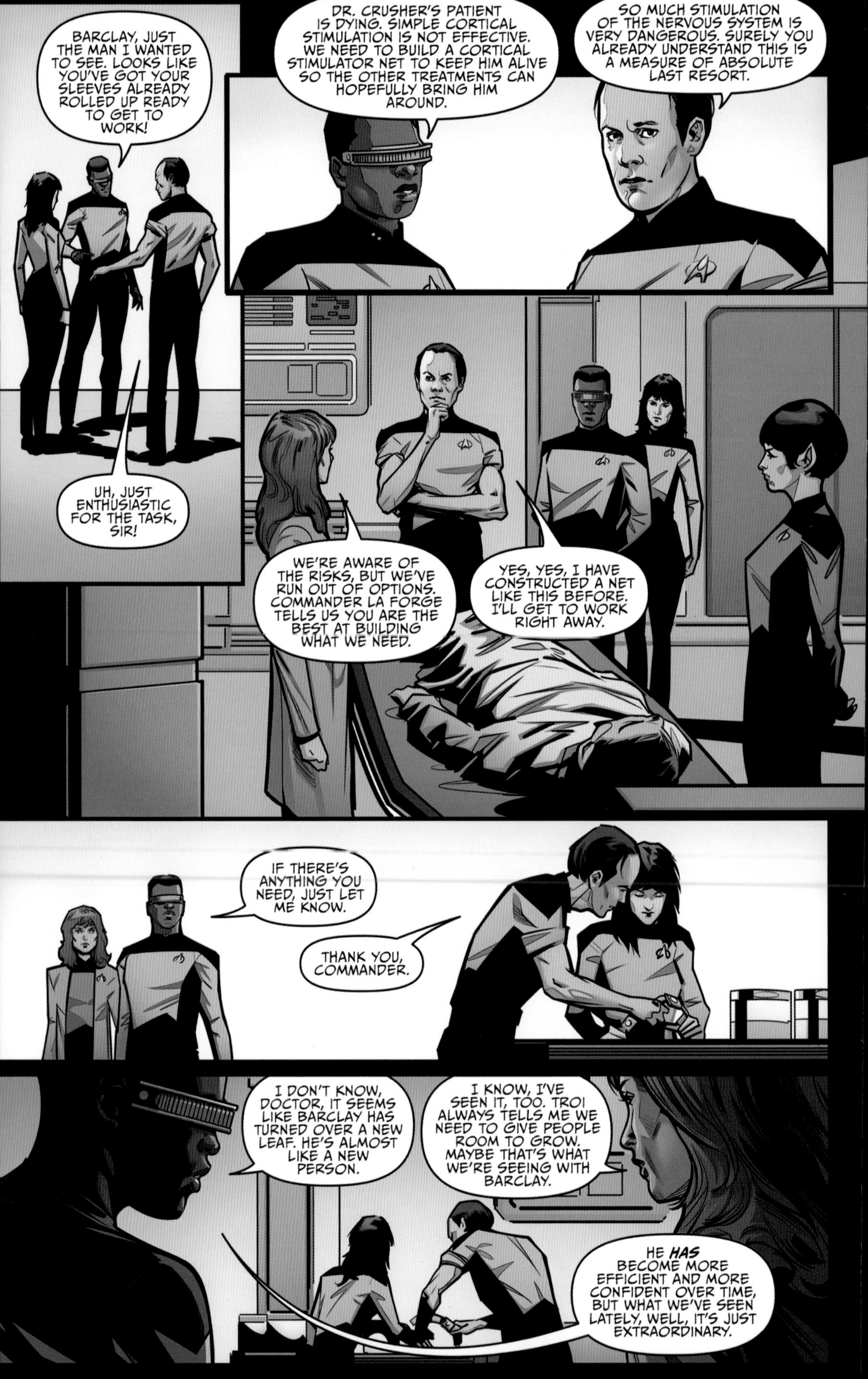
BARCLAY, JUST THE MAN I WANTED TO SEE. LOOKS LIKE YOU'VE GOT YOUR SLEEVES ALREADY ROLLED UP READY TO GET TO WORK!
UH, JUST ENTHUSIASTIC FOR THE TASK, SIR!
DR. CRUSHER'S PATIENT IS DYING. SIMPLE CORTICAL STIMULATION IS NOT EFFECTIVE. WE NEED TO BUILD A CORTICAL STIMULATOR NET TO KEEP HIM ALIVE SO THE OTHER TREATMENTS CAN HOPEFULLY BRING HIM AROUND.
SO MUCH STIMULATION OF THE NERVOUS SYSTEM IS VERY DANGEROUS. SURELY YOU ALREADY UNDERSTAND THIS IS A MEASURE OF ABSOLUTE LAST RESORT.
WE'RE AWARE OF THE RISKS, BUT WE'VE RUN OUT OF OPTIONS. COMMANDER LA FORGE TELLS US YOU ARE THE BEST AT BUILDING WHAT WE NEED.
YES, YES, I HAVE CONSTRUCTED A NET LIKE THIS BEFORE. I'LL GET TO WORK RIGHT AWAY.
IF THERE'S ANYTHING YOU NEED, JUST LET ME KNOW.
THANK YOU, COMMANDER.
I DON'T KNOW, DOCTOR, IT SEEMS LIKE BARCLAY HAS TURNED OVER A NEW LEAF. HE'S ALMOST LIKE A NEW PERSON.
I KNOW, I'VE SEEN IT, TOO. TROI ALWAYS TELLS ME WE NEED TO GIVE PEOPLE ROOM TO GROW. MAYBE THAT'S WHAT WE'RE SEEING WITH BARCLAY.
HE *HAS* BECOME MORE EFFICIENT AND MORE CONFIDENT OVER TIME, BUT WHAT WE'VE SEEN LATELY, WELL, IT'S JUST EXTRAORDINARY.

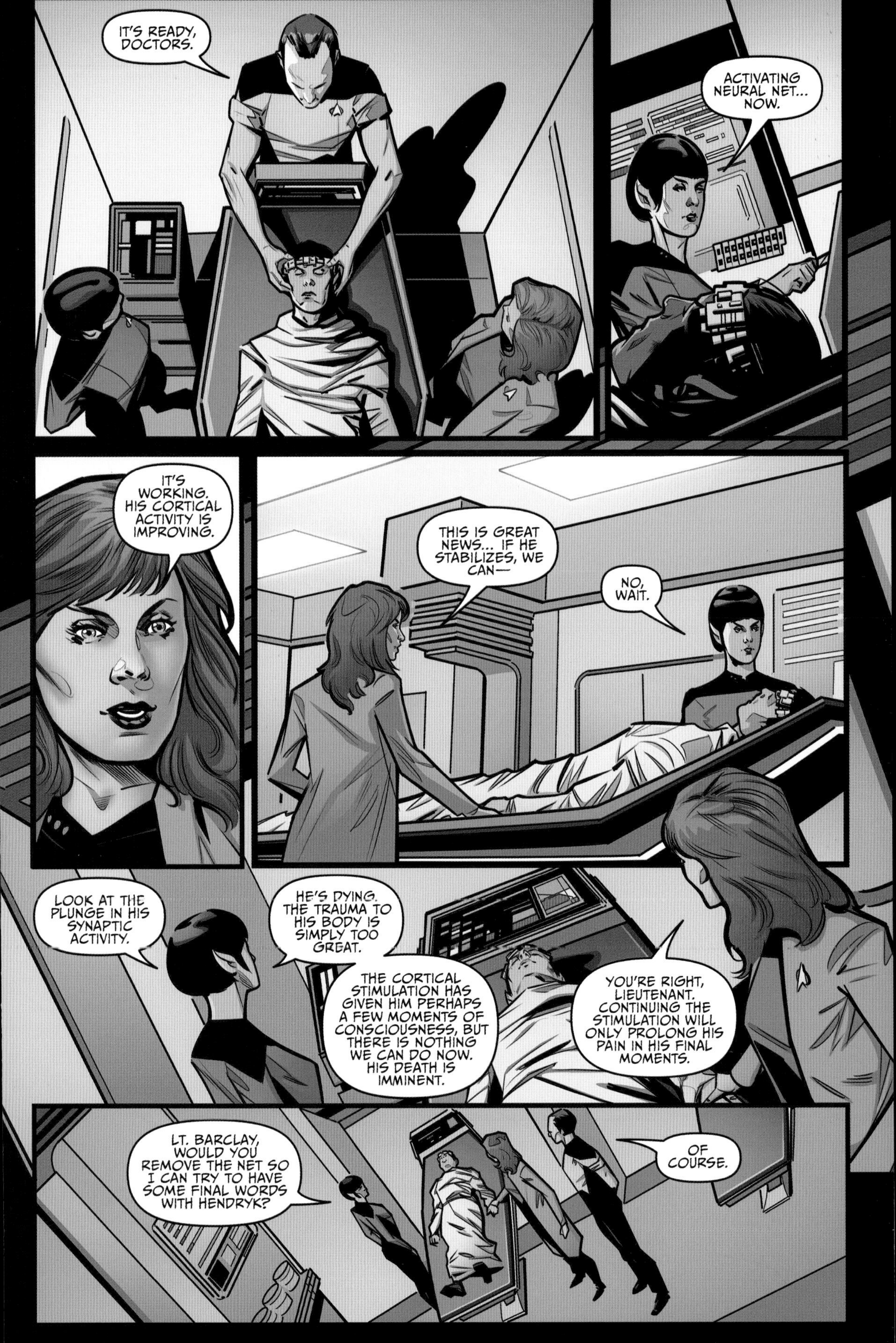
IT'S READY, DOCTORS.
ACTIVATING NEURAL NET... NOW.
IT'S WORKING. HIS CORTICAL ACTIVITY IS IMPROVING.
THIS IS GREAT NEWS... IF HE STABILIZES, WE CAN—
NO, WAIT.
LOOK AT THE PLUNGE IN HIS SYNAPTIC ACTIVITY.
HE'S DYING. THE TRAUMA TO HIS BODY IS SIMPLY TOO GREAT.
THE CORTICAL STIMULATION HAS GIVEN HIM PERHAPS A FEW MOMENTS OF CONSCIOUSNESS, BUT THERE IS NOTHING WE CAN DO NOW. HIS DEATH IS IMMINENT.
YOU'RE RIGHT, LIEUTENANT. CONTINUING THE STIMULATION WILL ONLY PROLONG HIS PAIN IN HIS FINAL MOMENTS.
LT. BARCLAY, WOULD YOU REMOVE THE NET SO I CAN TRY TO HAVE SOME FINAL WORDS WITH HENDRYK?
OF COURSE.

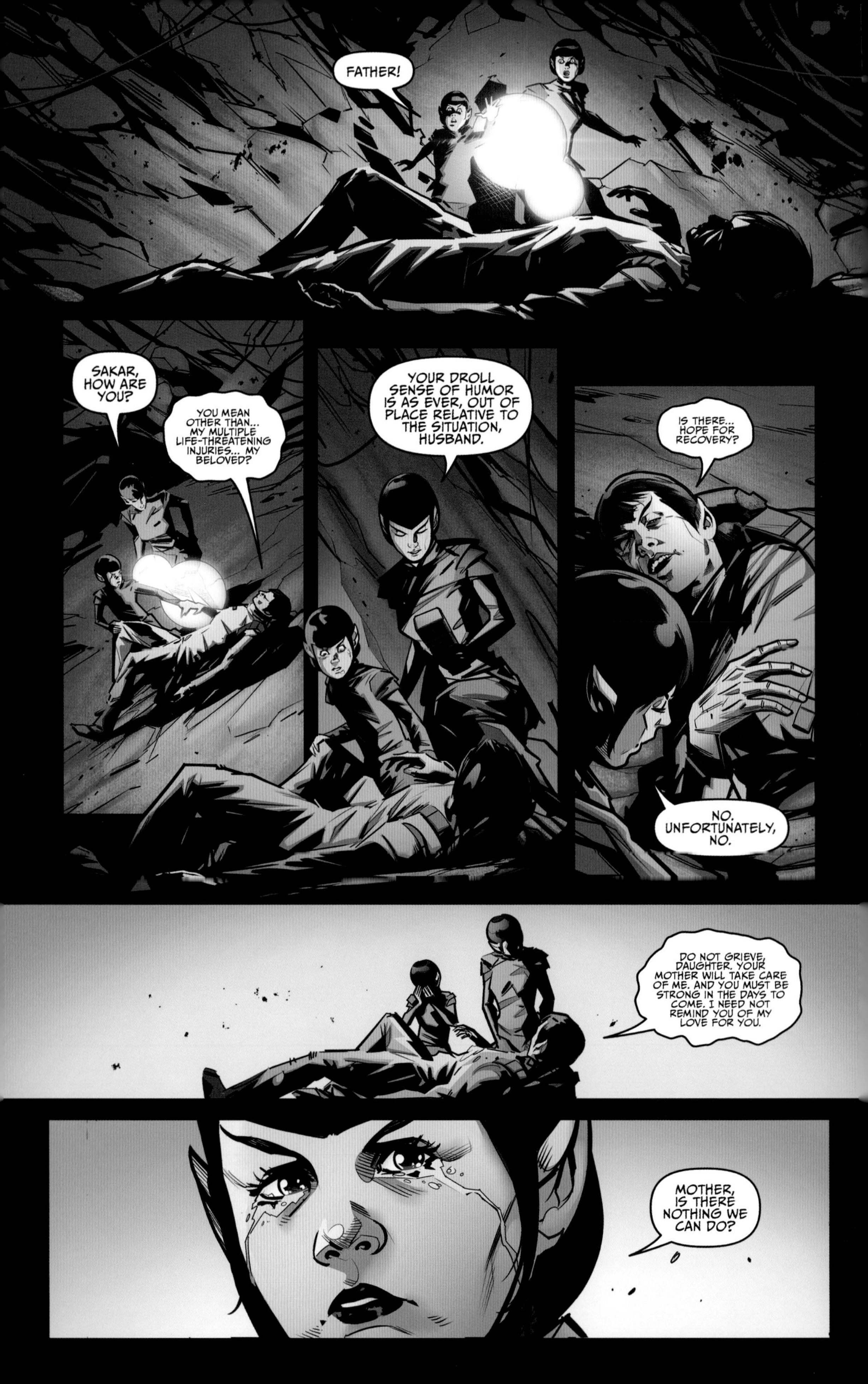
FATHER!
SAKAR, HOW ARE YOU?
YOU MEAN OTHER THAN... MY MULTIPLE LIFE-THREATENING INJURIES... MY BELOVED?
YOUR DROLL SENSE OF HUMOR IS AS EVER, OUT OF PLACE RELATIVE TO THE SITUATION, HUSBAND.
IS THERE... HOPE FOR RECOVERY?
NO. UNFORTUNATELY, NO.
DO NOT GRIEVE, DAUGHTER. YOUR MOTHER WILL TAKE CARE OF ME. AND YOU MUST BE STRONG IN THE DAYS TO COME. I NEED NOT REMIND YOU OF MY LOVE FOR YOU.
MOTHER, IS THERE NOTHING WE CAN DO?

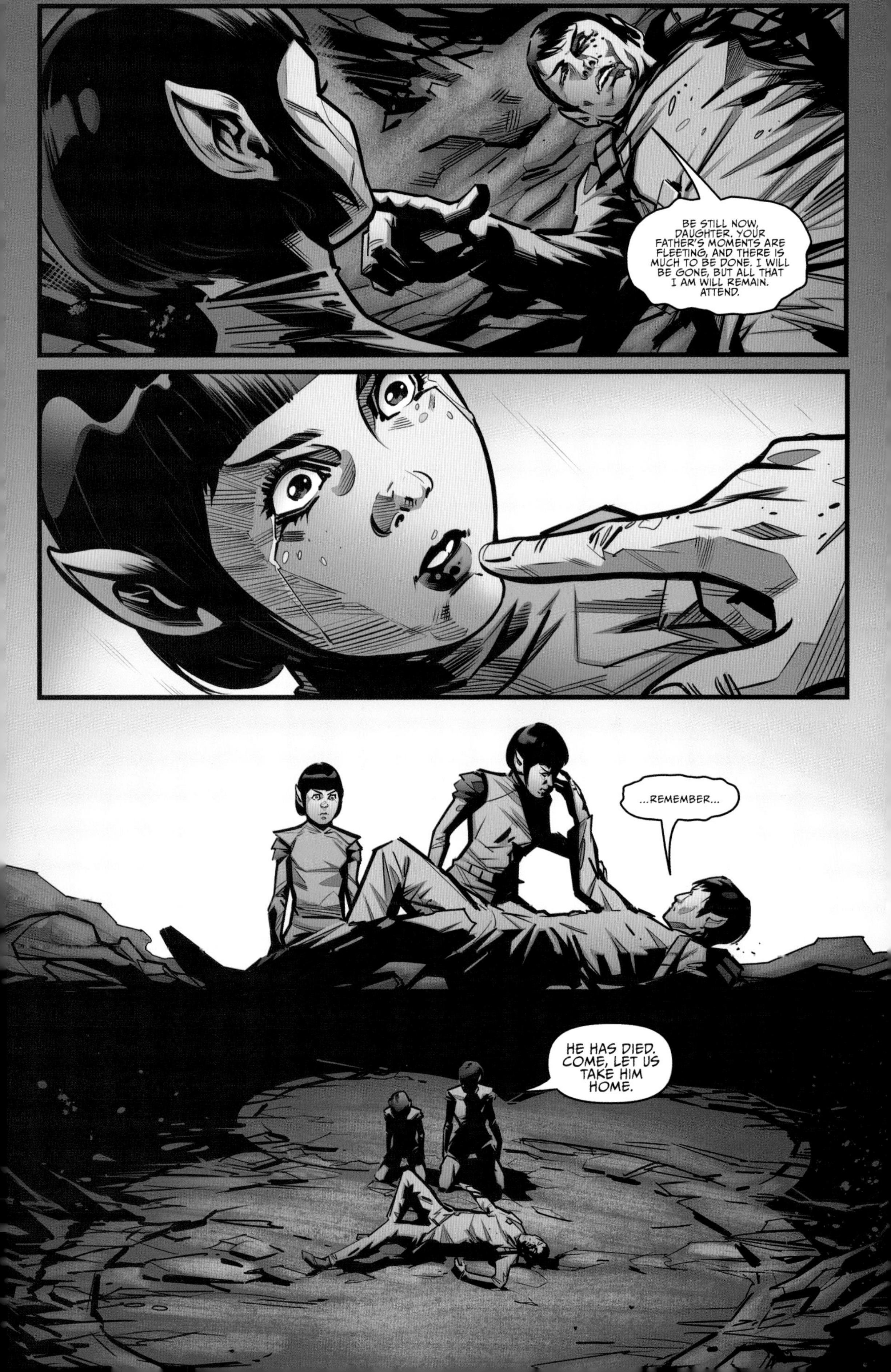
BE STILL NOW, DAUGHTER. YOUR FATHER'S MOMENTS ARE FLEETING, AND THERE IS MUCH TO BE DONE. I WILL BE GONE, BUT ALL THAT I AM WILL REMAIN. ATTEND.
...REMEMBER...
HE HAS DIED. COME, LET US TAKE HIM HOME.

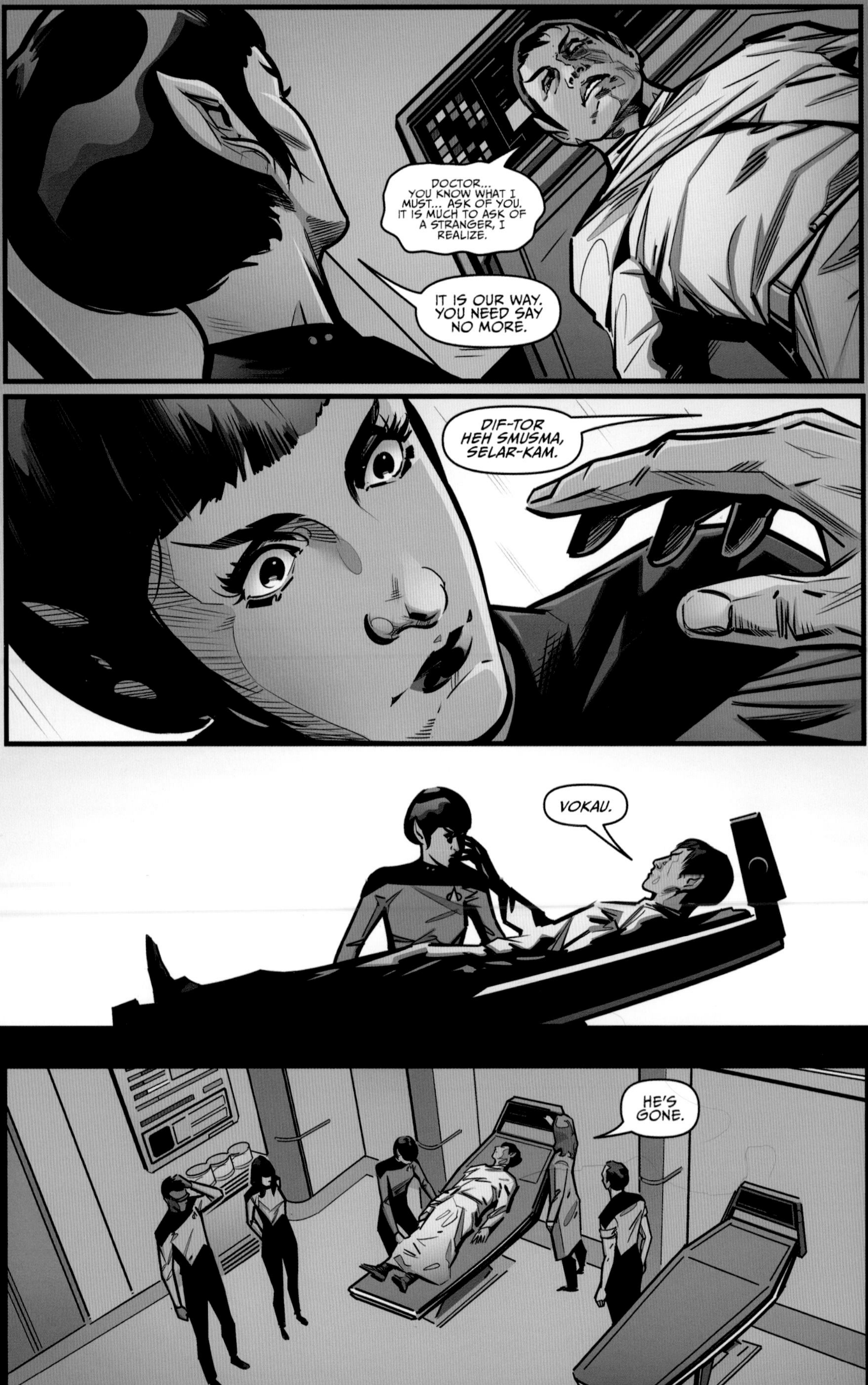
DOCTOR... YOU KNOW WHAT I MUST... ASK OF YOU. IT IS MUCH TO ASK OF A STRANGER, I REALIZE.
IT IS OUR WAY. YOU NEED SAY NO MORE.
DIF-TOR HEH SMUSMA, SELAR-KAM.
VOKAU.
HE'S GONE.

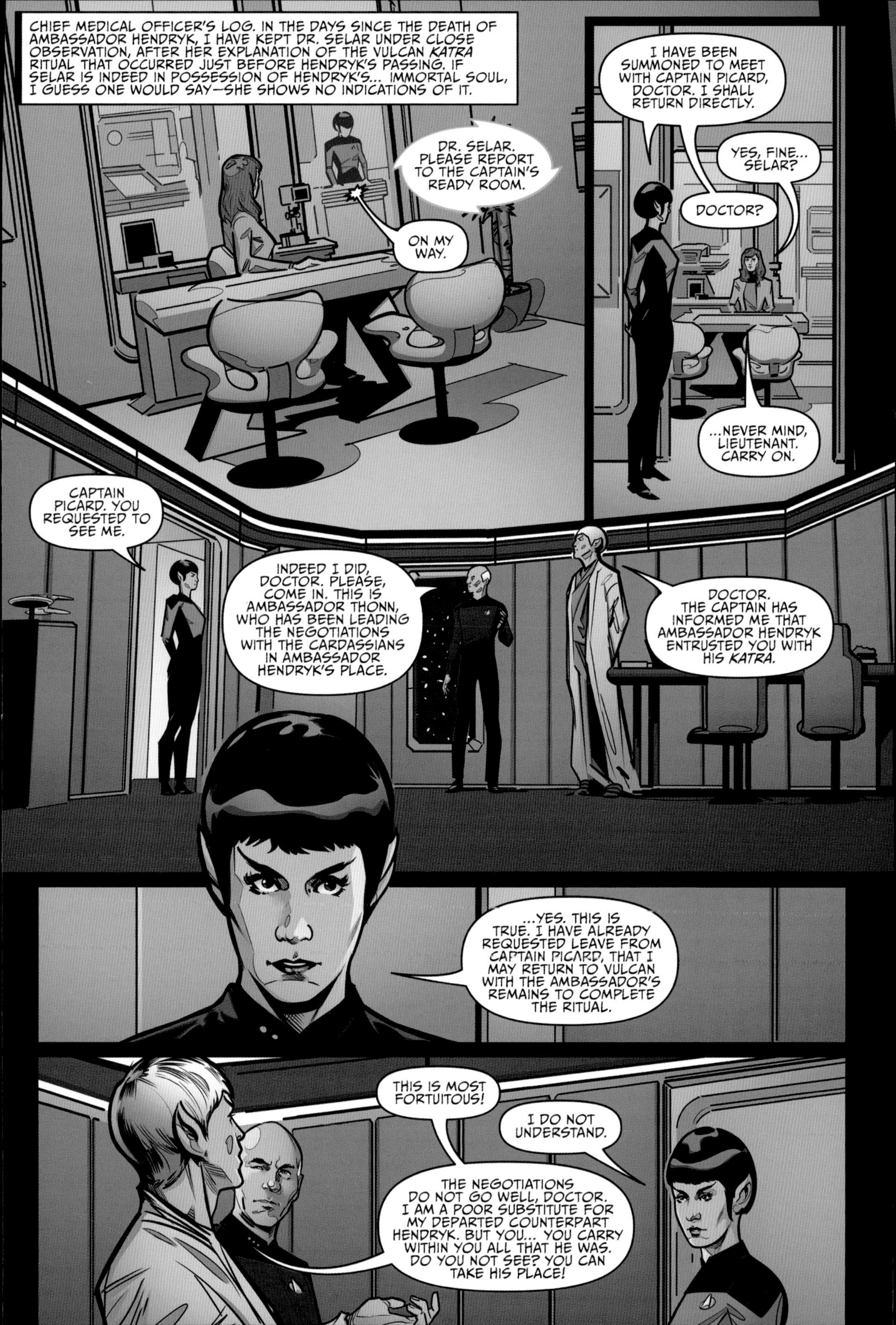
CHIEF MEDICAL OFFICER'S LOG. IN THE DAYS SINCE THE DEATH OF AMBASSADOR HENDRYK, I HAVE KEPT DR. SELAR UNDER CLOSE OBSERVATION, AFTER HER EXPLANATION OF THE VULCAN *KATRA* RITUAL THAT OCCURRED JUST BEFORE HENDRYK'S PASSING. IF SELAR IS INDEED IN POSSESSION OF HENDRYK'S... IMMORTAL SOUL, I GUESS ONE WOULD SAY—SHE SHOWS NO INDICATIONS OF IT.
DR. SELAR. PLEASE REPORT TO THE CAPTAIN'S READY ROOM.
ON MY WAY.
I HAVE BEEN SUMMONED TO MEET WITH CAPTAIN PICARD, DOCTOR. I SHALL RETURN DIRECTLY.
DOCTOR?
YES, FINE... SELAR?
...NEVER MIND, LIEUTENANT. CARRY ON.
CAPTAIN PICARD. YOU REQUESTED TO SEE ME.
INDEED I DID, DOCTOR. PLEASE, COME IN. THIS IS AMBASSADOR THONN, WHO HAS BEEN LEADING THE NEGOTIATIONS WITH THE CARDASSIANS IN AMBASSADOR HENDRYK'S PLACE.
DOCTOR. THE CAPTAIN HAS INFORMED ME THAT AMBASSADOR HENDRYK ENTRUSTED YOU WITH HIS *KATRA*.
...YES. THIS IS TRUE. I HAVE ALREADY REQUESTED LEAVE FROM CAPTAIN PICARD, THAT I MAY RETURN TO VULCAN WITH THE AMBASSADOR'S REMAINS TO COMPLETE THE RITUAL.
THIS IS MOST FORTUITOUS!
I DO NOT UNDERSTAND.
THE NEGOTIATIONS DO NOT GO WELL, DOCTOR. I AM A POOR SUBSTITUTE FOR MY DEPARTED COUNTERPART HENDRYK. BUT YOU... YOU CARRY WITHIN YOU ALL THAT HE WAS. DO YOU NOT SEE? YOU CAN TAKE HIS PLACE!

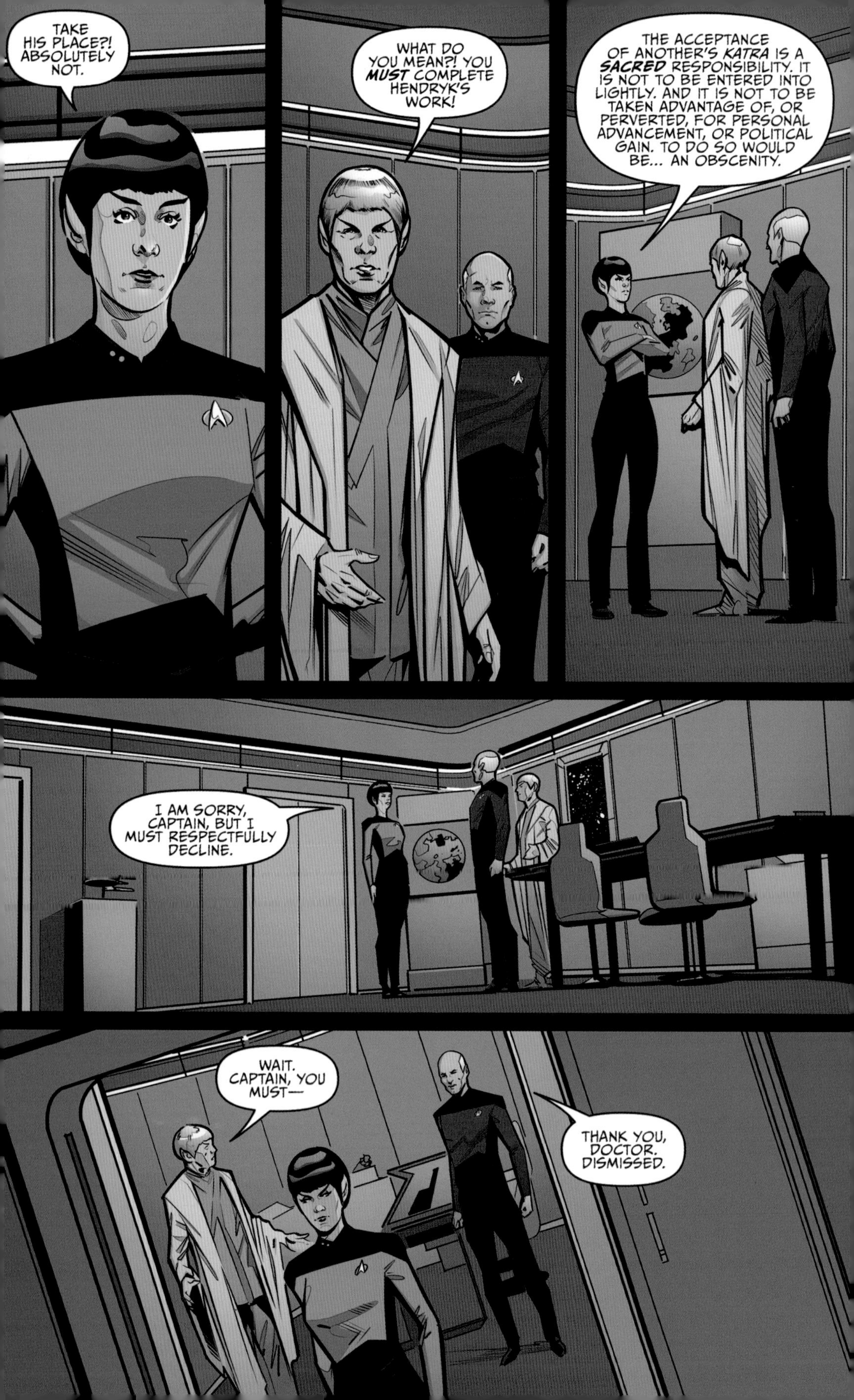
TAKE HIS PLACE?! ABSOLUTELY NOT.
WHAT DO YOU MEAN?! YOU *MUST* COMPLETE HENDRYK'S WORK!
THE ACCEPTANCE OF ANOTHER'S *KATRA* IS A *SACRED* RESPONSIBILITY. IT IS NOT TO BE ENTERED INTO LIGHTLY. AND IT IS NOT TO BE TAKEN ADVANTAGE OF, OR PERVERTED, FOR PERSONAL ADVANCEMENT, OR POLITICAL GAIN. TO DO SO WOULD BE... AN OBSCENITY.
I AM SORRY, CAPTAIN, BUT I MUST RESPECTFULLY DECLINE.
WAIT. CAPTAIN, YOU MUST—
THANK YOU, DOCTOR. DISMISSED.

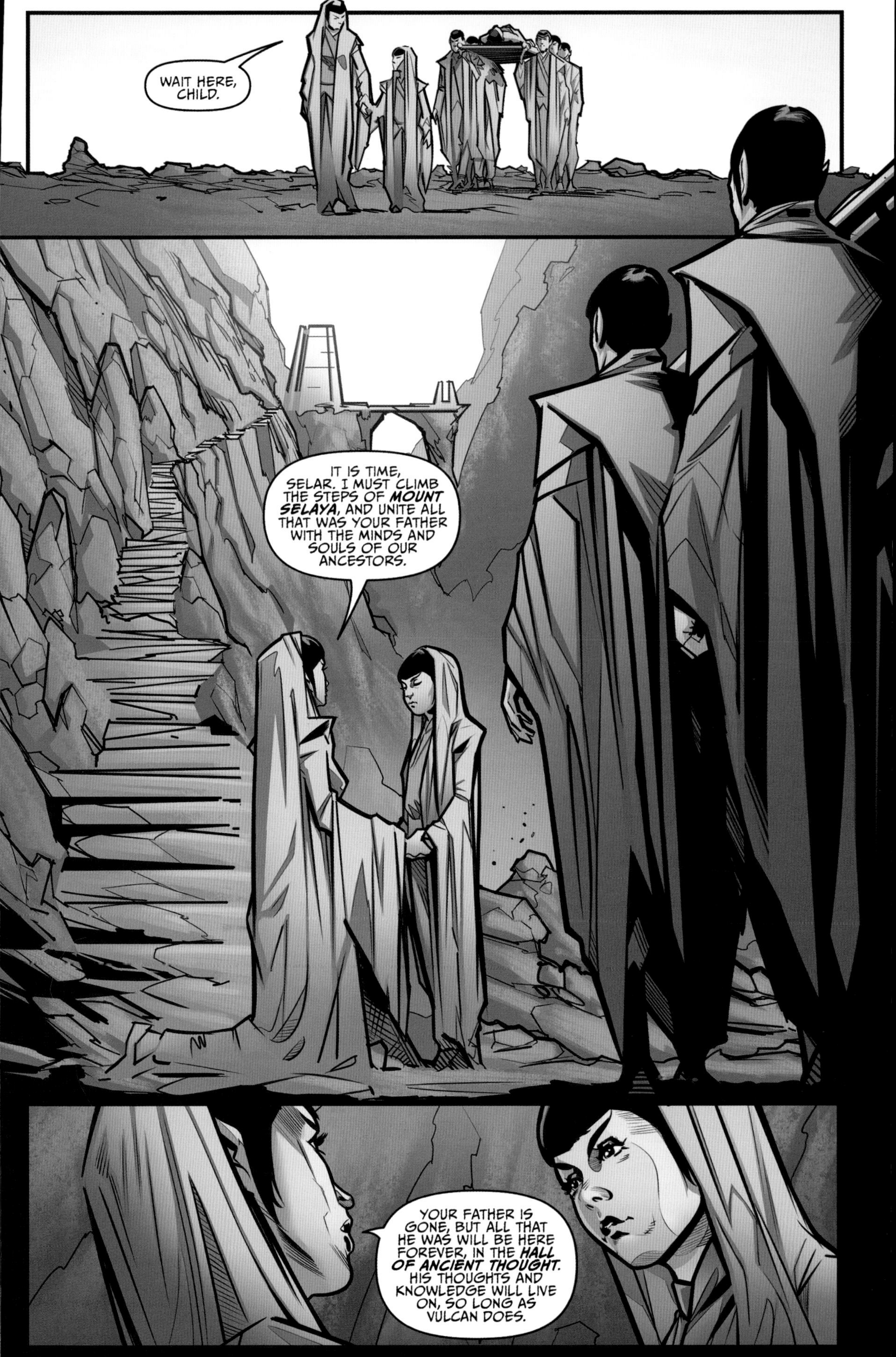
WAIT HERE, CHILD.
IT IS TIME, SELAR. I MUST CLIMB THE STEPS OF **MOUNT SELAYA,** AND UNITE ALL THAT WAS YOUR FATHER WITH THE MINDS AND SOULS OF OUR ANCESTORS.
YOUR FATHER IS GONE, BUT ALL THAT HE WAS WILL BE HERE FOREVER, IN THE **HALL OF ANCIENT THOUGHT**. HIS THOUGHTS AND KNOWLEDGE WILL LIVE ON, SO LONG AS VULCAN DOES.

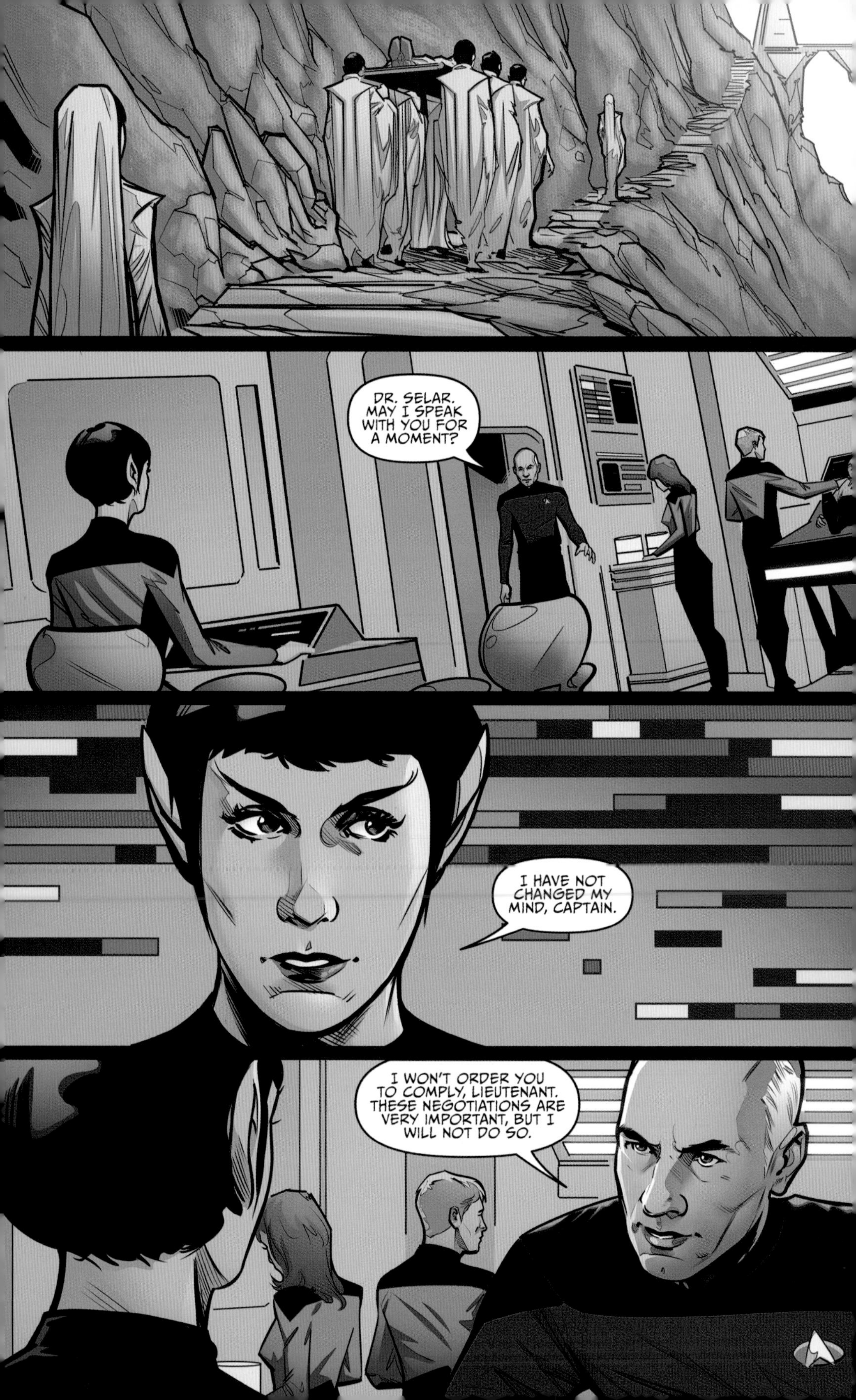
DR. SELAR. MAY I SPEAK WITH YOU FOR A MOMENT?
I HAVE NOT CHANGED MY MIND, CAPTAIN.
I WON'T ORDER YOU TO COMPLY, LIEUTENANT. THESE NEGOTIATIONS ARE VERY IMPORTANT, BUT I WILL NOT DO SO.

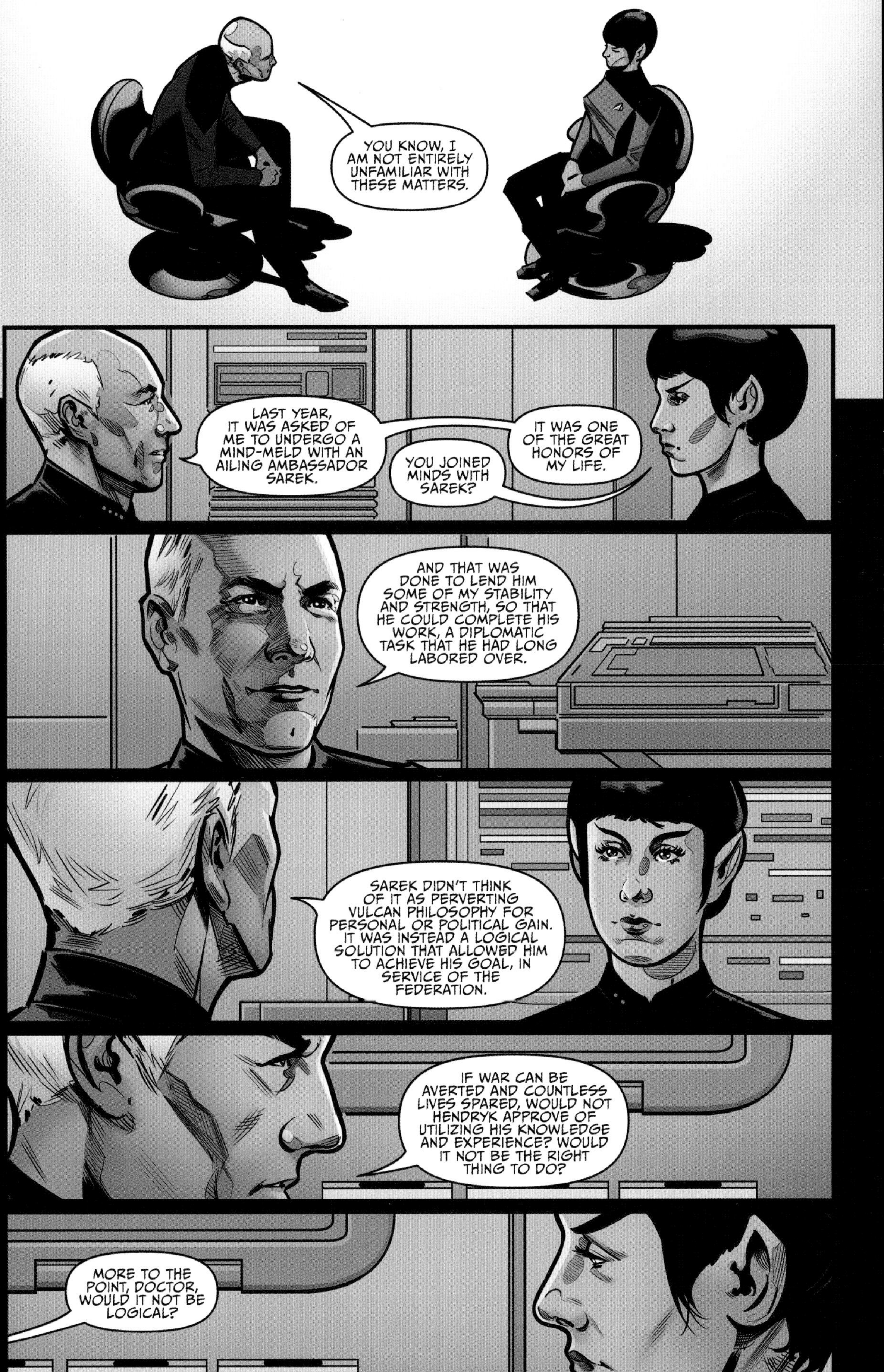
YOU KNOW, I AM NOT ENTIRELY UNFAMILIAR WITH THESE MATTERS.
LAST YEAR, IT WAS ASKED OF ME TO UNDERGO A MIND-MELD WITH AN AILING AMBASSADOR SAREK.
YOU JOINED MINDS WITH SAREK?
IT WAS ONE OF THE GREAT HONORS OF MY LIFE.
AND THAT WAS DONE TO LEND HIM SOME OF MY STABILITY AND STRENGTH, SO THAT HE COULD COMPLETE HIS WORK, A DIPLOMATIC TASK THAT HE HAD LONG LABORED OVER.
SAREK DIDN'T THINK OF IT AS PERVERTING VULCAN PHILOSOPHY FOR PERSONAL OR POLITICAL GAIN. IT WAS INSTEAD A LOGICAL SOLUTION THAT ALLOWED HIM TO ACHIEVE HIS GOAL, IN SERVICE OF THE FEDERATION.
IF WAR CAN BE AVERTED AND COUNTLESS LIVES SPARED, WOULD NOT HENDRYK APPROVE OF UTILIZING HIS KNOWLEDGE AND EXPERIENCE? WOULD IT NOT BE THE RIGHT THING TO DO?
MORE TO THE POINT, DOCTOR, WOULD IT NOT BE LOGICAL?

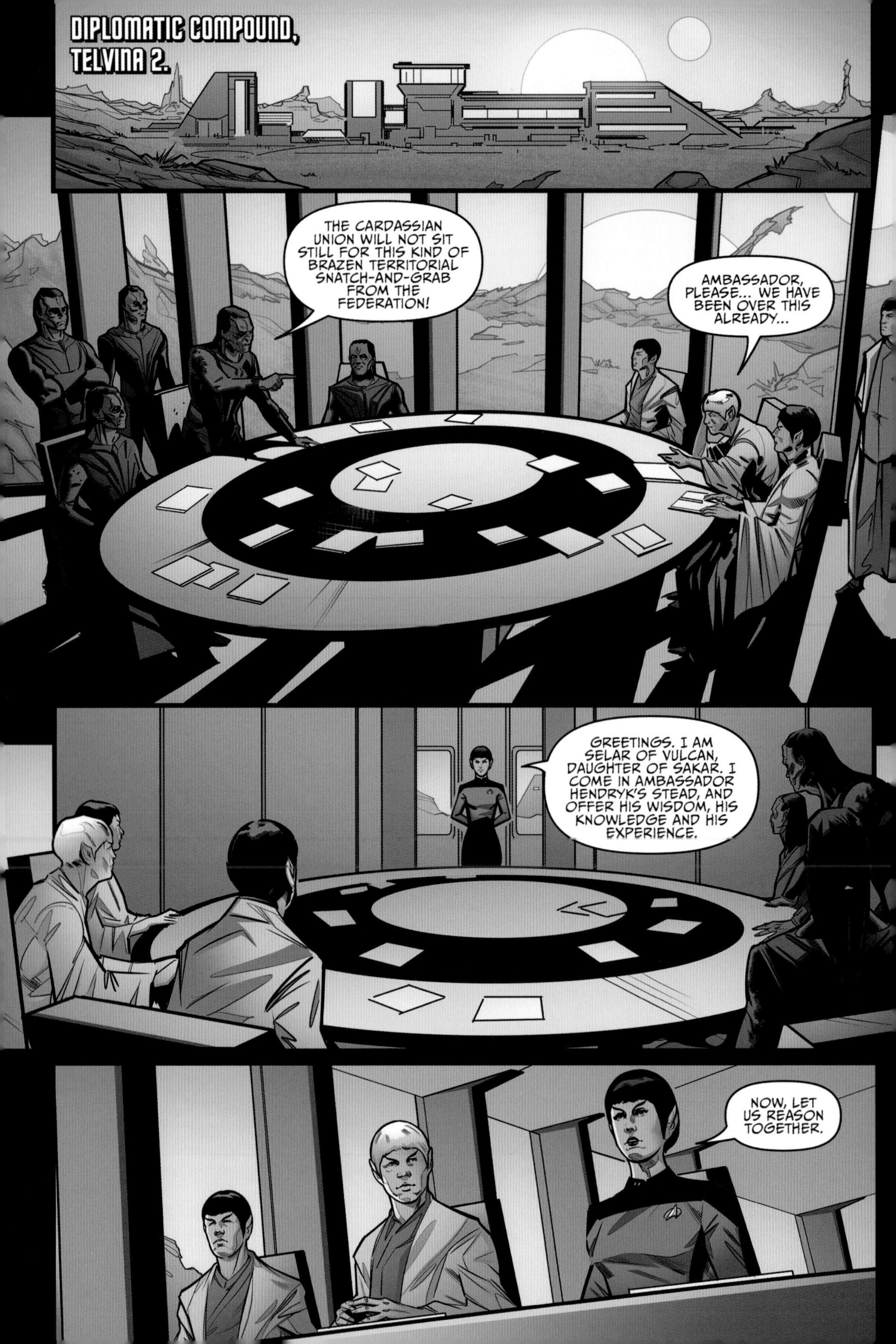
DIPLOMATIC COMPOUND, TELVINA 2.
THE CARDASSIAN UNION WILL NOT SIT STILL FOR THIS KIND OF BRAZEN TERRITORIAL SNATCH-AND-GRAB FROM THE FEDERATION!
AMBASSADOR, PLEASE... WE HAVE BEEN OVER THIS ALREADY...
GREETINGS. I AM SELAR OF VULCAN, DAUGHTER OF SAKAR. I COME IN AMBASSADOR HENDRYK'S STEAD, AND OFFER HIS WISDOM, HIS KNOWLEDGE AND HIS EXPERIENCE.
NOW, LET US REASON TOGETHER.

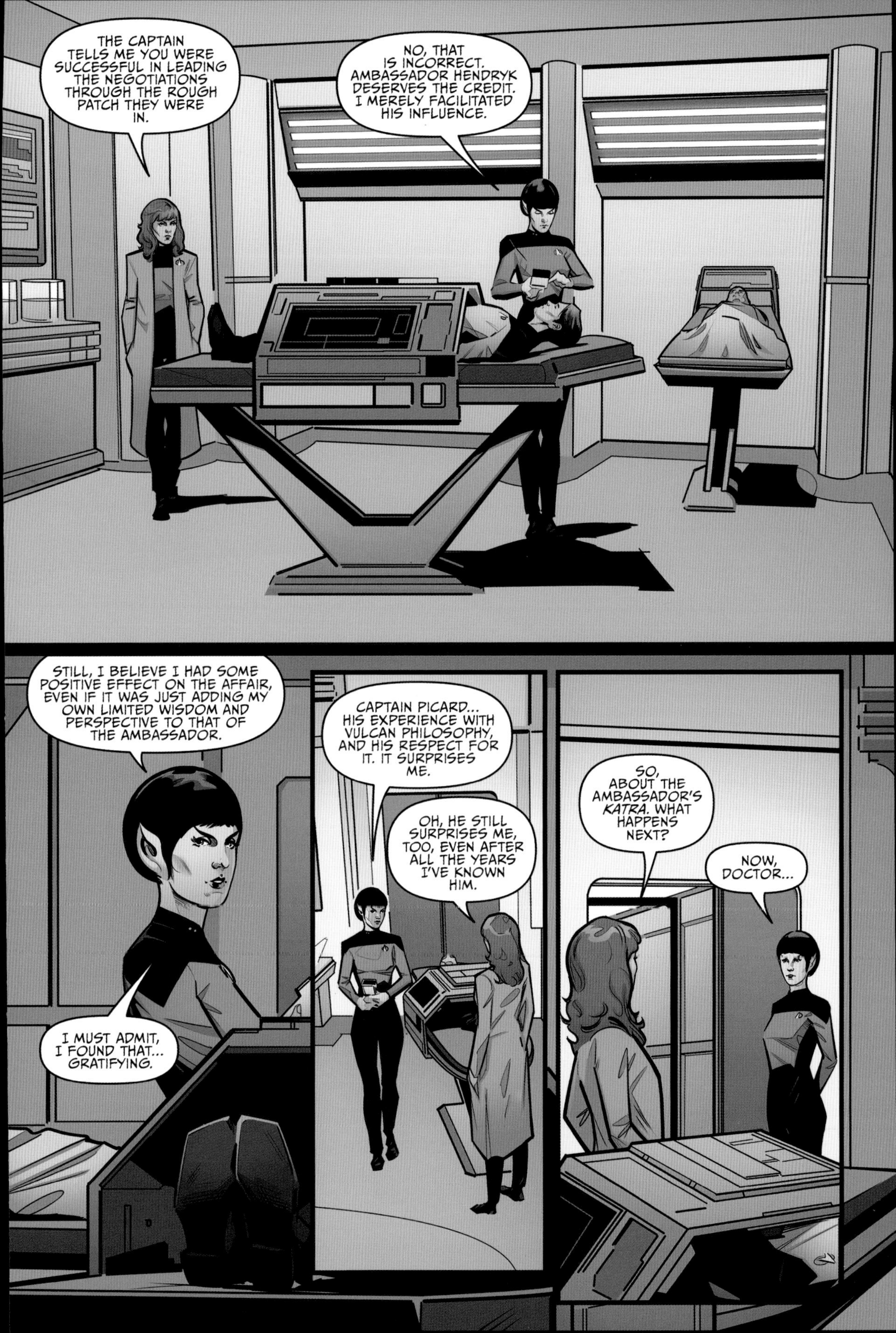
THE CAPTAIN TELLS ME YOU WERE SUCCESSFUL IN LEADING THE NEGOTIATIONS THROUGH THE ROUGH PATCH THEY WERE IN.
NO, THAT IS INCORRECT. AMBASSADOR HENDRYK DESERVES THE CREDIT. I MERELY FACILITATED HIS INFLUENCE.
STILL, I BELIEVE I HAD SOME POSITIVE EFFECT ON THE AFFAIR, EVEN IF IT WAS JUST ADDING MY OWN LIMITED WISDOM AND PERSPECTIVE TO THAT OF THE AMBASSADOR.
I MUST ADMIT, I FOUND THAT... GRATIFYING.
CAPTAIN PICARD... HIS EXPERIENCE WITH VULCAN PHILOSOPHY, AND HIS RESPECT FOR IT. IT SURPRISES ME.
OH, HE STILL SURPRISES ME, TOO, EVEN AFTER ALL THE YEARS I'VE KNOWN HIM.
SO, ABOUT THE AMBASSADOR'S *KATRA*. WHAT HAPPENS NEXT?
NOW, DOCTOR...

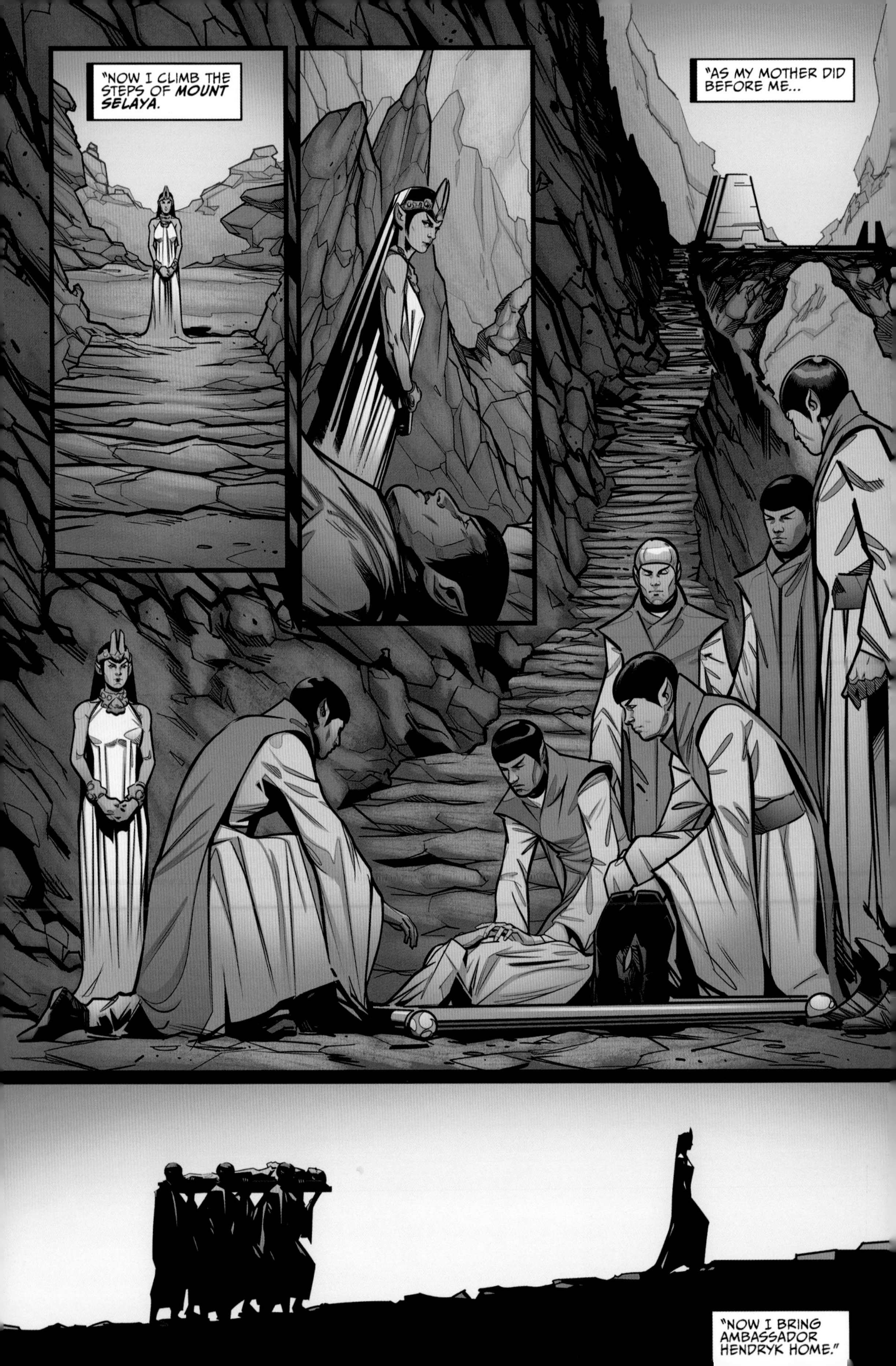
"NOW I CLIMB THE STEPS OF MOUNT SELAYA.
"AS MY MOTHER DID BEFORE ME...
"NOW I BRING AMBASSADOR HENDRYK HOME."

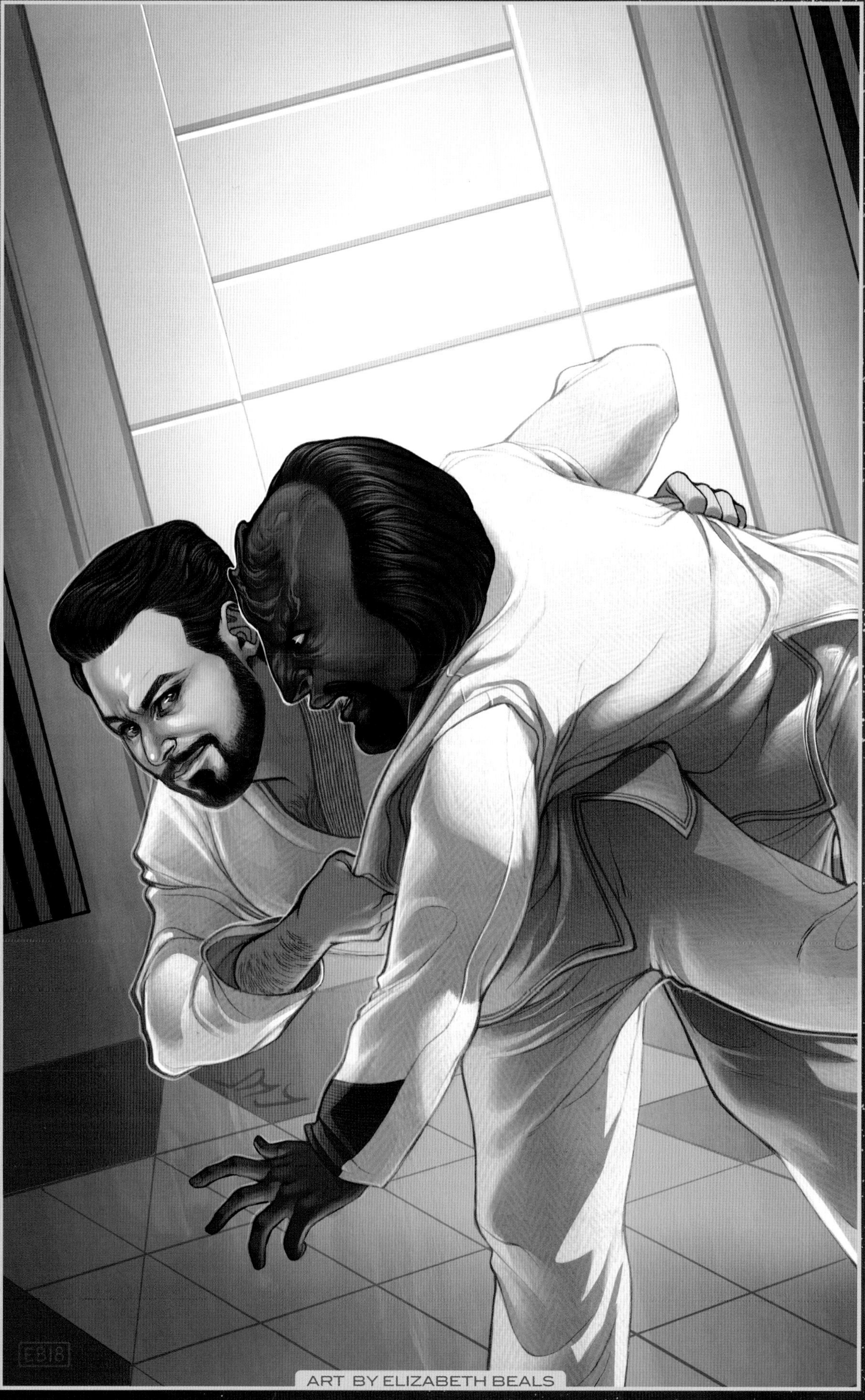

ART BY ELIZABETH BEALS

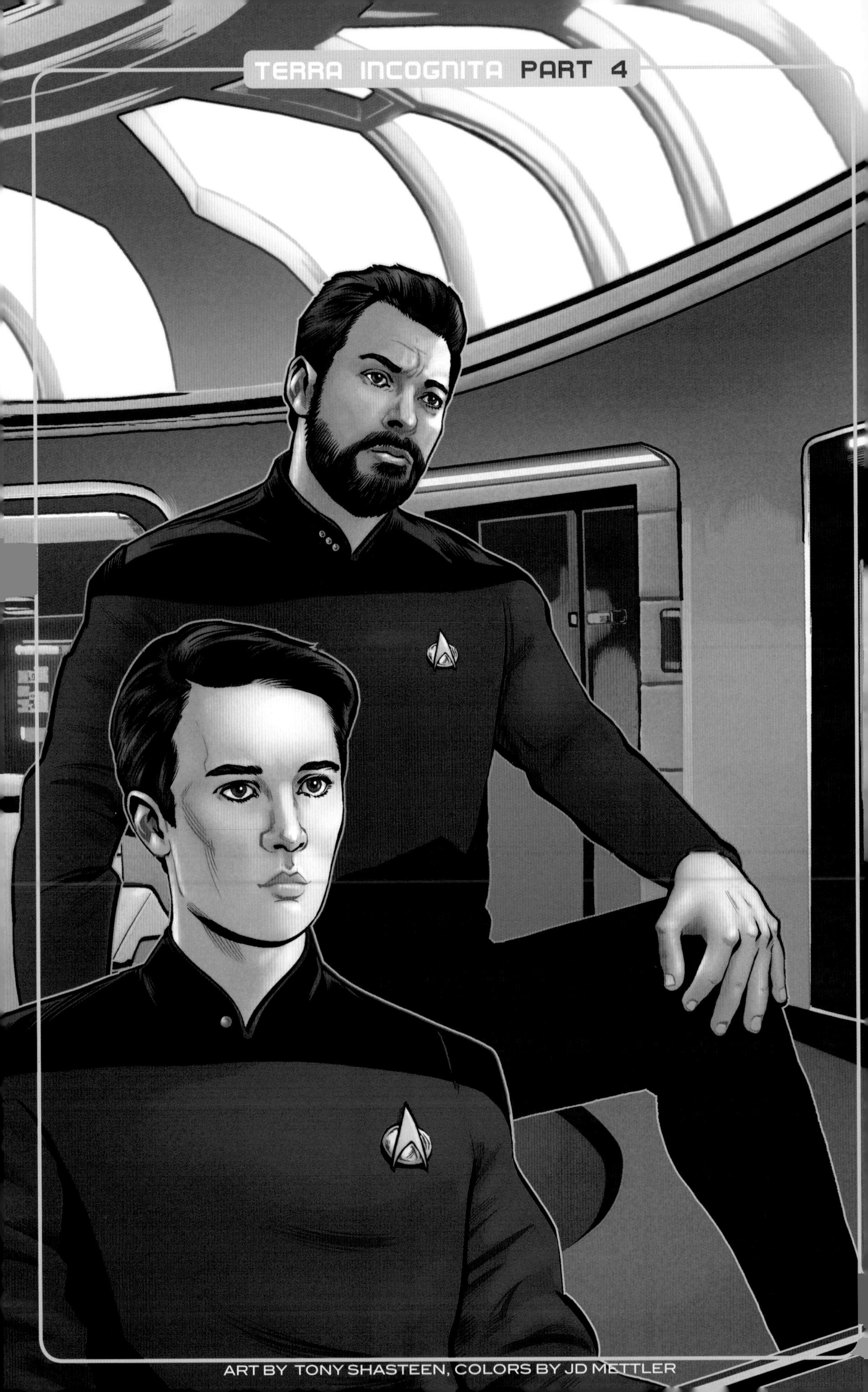
TERRA INCOGNITA PART 4
ART BY TONY SHASTEEN, COLORS BY JD METTLER

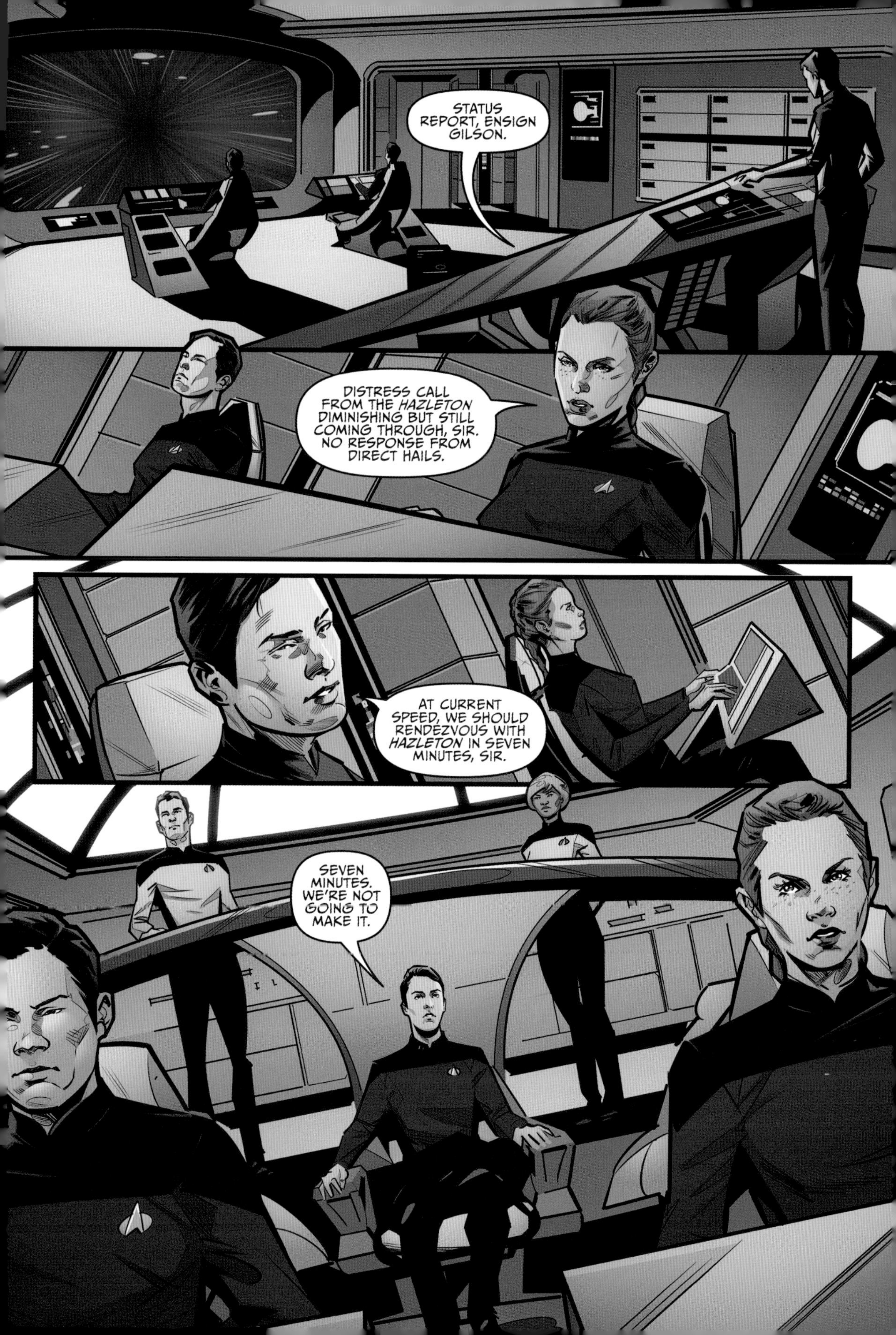
STATUS REPORT, ENSIGN GILSON.
DISTRESS CALL FROM THE *HAZLETON* DIMINISHING BUT STILL COMING THROUGH, SIR. NO RESPONSE FROM DIRECT HAILS.
AT CURRENT SPEED, WE SHOULD RENDEZVOUS WITH *HAZLETON* IN SEVEN MINUTES, SIR.
SEVEN MINUTES. WE'RE NOT GOING TO MAKE IT.

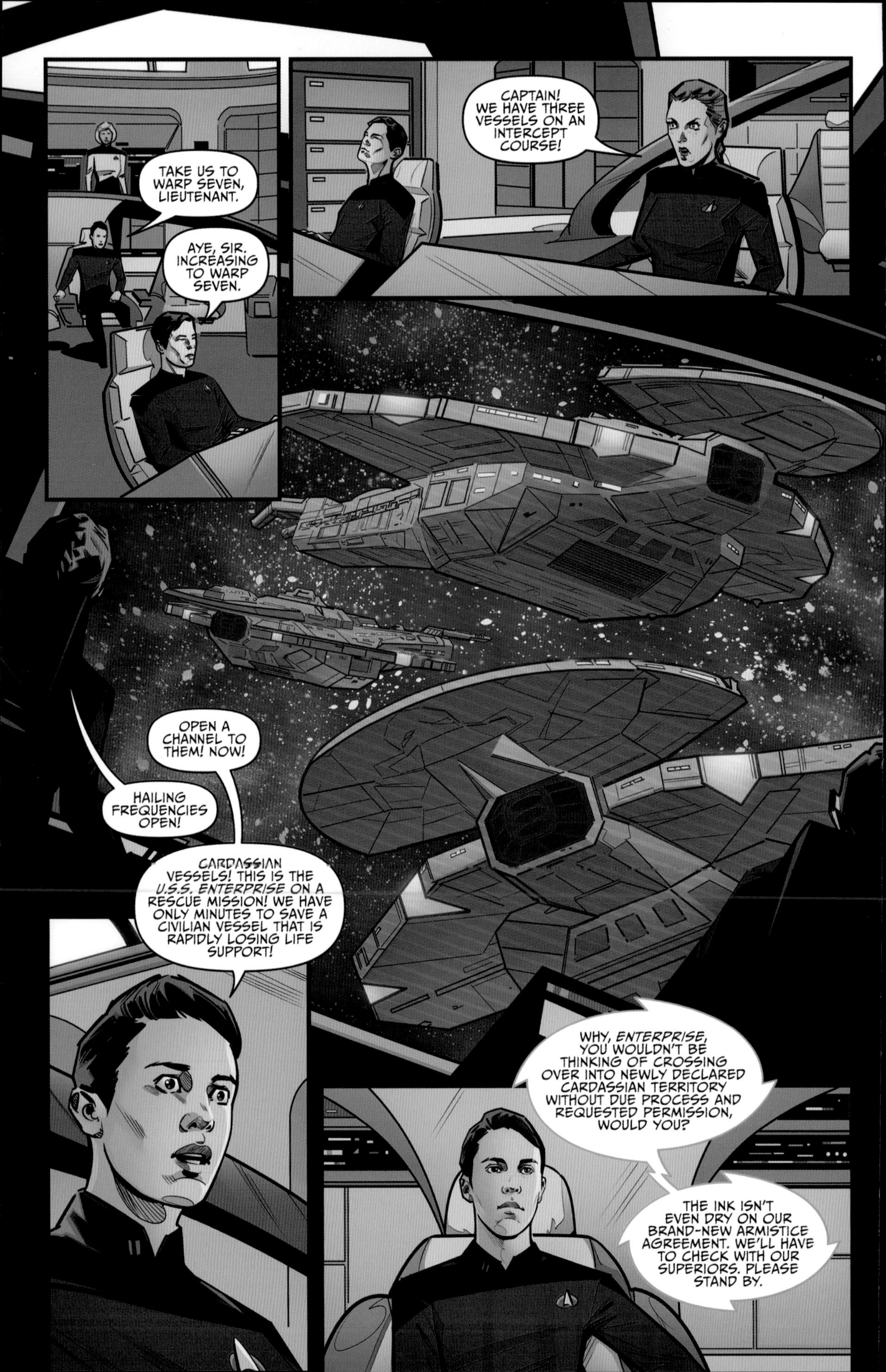
TAKE US TO WARP SEVEN, LIEUTENANT.
AYE, SIR. INCREASING TO WARP SEVEN.
CAPTAIN! WE HAVE THREE VESSELS ON AN INTERCEPT COURSE!
OPEN A CHANNEL TO THEM! NOW!
HAILING FREQUENCIES OPEN!
CARDASSIAN VESSELS! THIS IS THE *U.S.S. ENTERPRISE* ON A RESCUE MISSION! WE HAVE ONLY MINUTES TO SAVE A CIVILIAN VESSEL THAT IS RAPIDLY LOSING LIFE SUPPORT!
WHY, *ENTERPRISE*, YOU WOULDN'T BE THINKING OF CROSSING OVER INTO NEWLY DECLARED CARDASSIAN TERRITORY WITHOUT DUE PROCESS AND REQUESTED PERMISSION, WOULD YOU?
THE INK ISN'T EVEN DRY ON OUR BRAND-NEW ARMISTICE AGREEMENT. WE'LL HAVE TO CHECK WITH OUR SUPERIORS. PLEASE STAND BY.

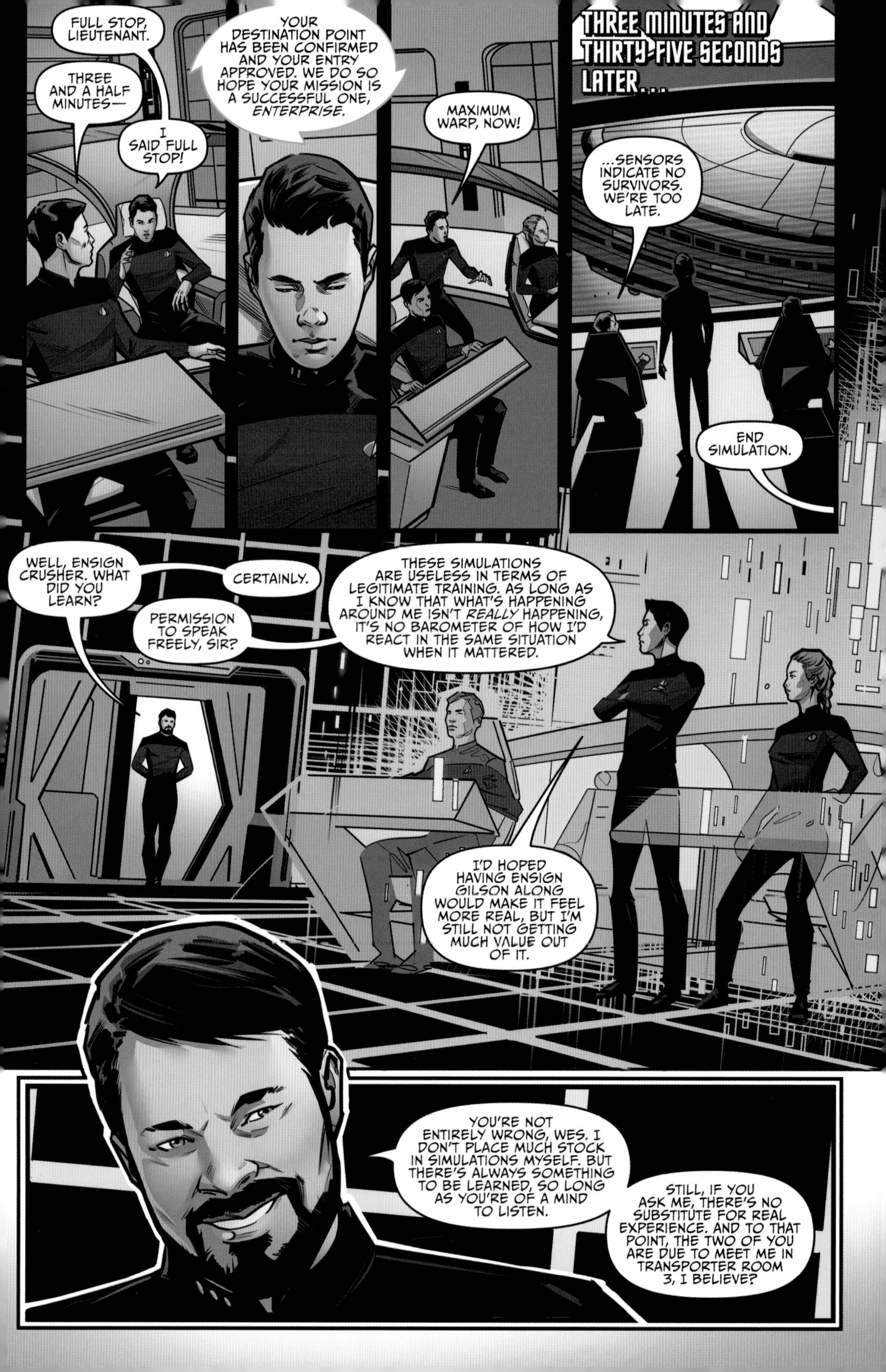
FULL STOP, LIEUTENANT.
THREE AND A HALF MINUTES—
I SAID FULL STOP!
YOUR DESTINATION POINT HAS BEEN CONFIRMED AND YOUR ENTRY APPROVED. WE DO SO HOPE YOUR MISSION IS A SUCCESSFUL ONE, *ENTERPRISE*.
MAXIMUM WARP, NOW!
THREE MINUTES AND THIRTY-FIVE SECONDS LATER...
...SENSORS INDICATE NO SURVIVORS. WE'RE TOO LATE.
END SIMULATION.
WELL, ENSIGN CRUSHER. WHAT DID YOU LEARN?
PERMISSION TO SPEAK FREELY, SIR?
CERTAINLY.
THESE SIMULATIONS ARE USELESS IN TERMS OF LEGITIMATE TRAINING. AS LONG AS I KNOW THAT WHAT'S HAPPENING AROUND ME ISN'T *REALLY* HAPPENING, IT'S NO BAROMETER OF HOW I'D REACT IN THE SAME SITUATION WHEN IT MATTERED.
I'D HOPED HAVING ENSIGN GILSON ALONG WOULD MAKE IT FEEL MORE REAL, BUT I'M STILL NOT GETTING MUCH VALUE OUT OF IT.
YOU'RE NOT ENTIRELY WRONG, WES. I DON'T PLACE MUCH STOCK IN SIMULATIONS MYSELF. BUT THERE'S ALWAYS SOMETHING TO BE LEARNED, SO LONG AS YOU'RE OF A MIND TO LISTEN.
STILL, IF YOU ASK ME, THERE'S NO SUBSTITUTE FOR REAL EXPERIENCE. AND TO THAT POINT, THE TWO OF YOU ARE DUE TO MEET ME IN TRANSPORTER ROOM 3, I BELIEVE?

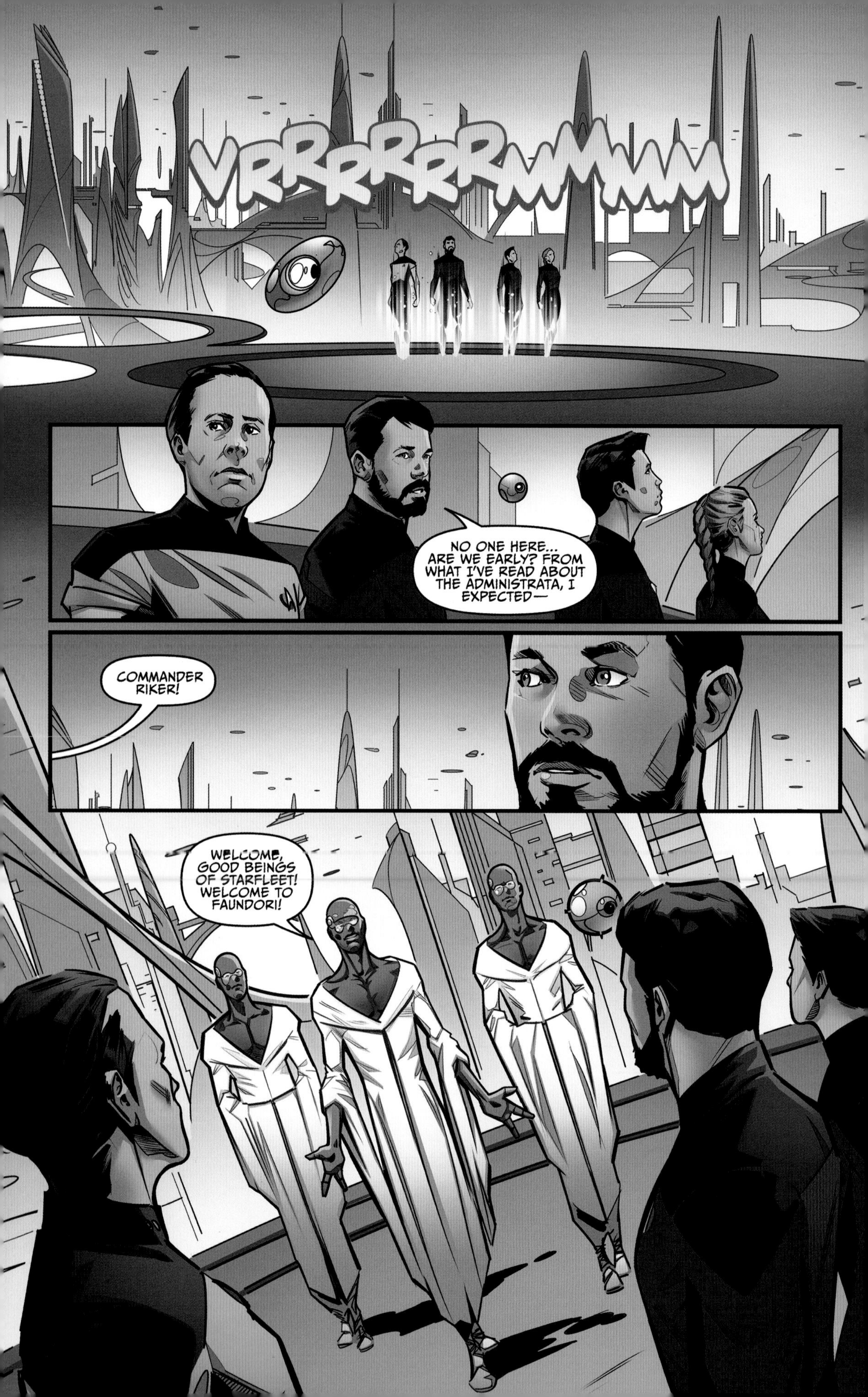
VRRRRRRMMMM
NO ONE HERE... ARE WE EARLY? FROM WHAT I'VE READ ABOUT THE ADMINISTRATA, I EXPECTED—
COMMANDER RIKER!
WELCOME, GOOD BEINGS OF STARFLEET! WELCOME TO FAUNDORI!

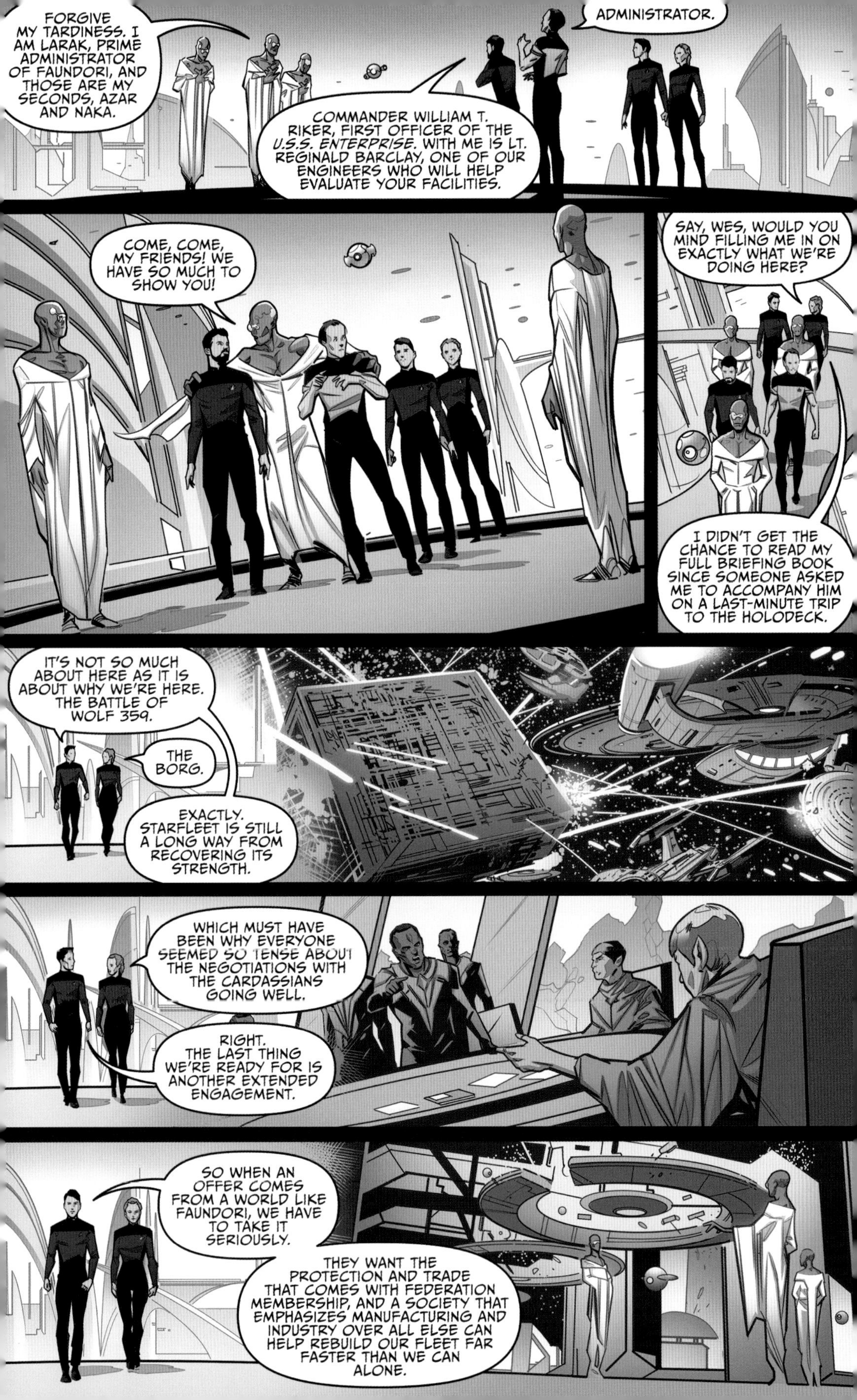
FORGIVE MY TARDINESS. I AM LARAK, PRIME ADMINISTRATOR OF FAUNDORI, AND THOSE ARE MY SECONDS, AZAR AND NAKA.
ADMINISTRATOR.
COMMANDER WILLIAM T. RIKER, FIRST OFFICER OF THE *U.S.S. ENTERPRISE*. WITH ME IS LT. REGINALD BARCLAY, ONE OF OUR ENGINEERS WHO WILL HELP EVALUATE YOUR FACILITIES.
COME, COME, MY FRIENDS! WE HAVE SO MUCH TO SHOW YOU!
SAY, WES, WOULD YOU MIND FILLING ME IN ON EXACTLY WHAT WE'RE DOING HERE?
I DIDN'T GET THE CHANCE TO READ MY FULL BRIEFING BOOK SINCE SOMEONE ASKED ME TO ACCOMPANY HIM ON A LAST-MINUTE TRIP TO THE HOLODECK.
IT'S NOT SO MUCH ABOUT HERE AS IT IS ABOUT WHY WE'RE HERE. THE BATTLE OF WOLF 359.
THE BORG.
EXACTLY. STARFLEET IS STILL A LONG WAY FROM RECOVERING ITS STRENGTH.
WHICH MUST HAVE BEEN WHY EVERYONE SEEMED SO TENSE ABOUT THE NEGOTIATIONS WITH THE CARDASSIANS GOING WELL.
RIGHT. THE LAST THING WE'RE READY FOR IS ANOTHER EXTENDED ENGAGEMENT.
SO WHEN AN OFFER COMES FROM A WORLD LIKE FAUNDORI, WE HAVE TO TAKE IT SERIOUSLY.
THEY WANT THE PROTECTION AND TRADE THAT COMES WITH FEDERATION MEMBERSHIP, AND A SOCIETY THAT EMPHASIZES MANUFACTURING AND INDUSTRY OVER ALL ELSE CAN HELP REBUILD OUR FLEET FAR FASTER THAN WE CAN ALONE.

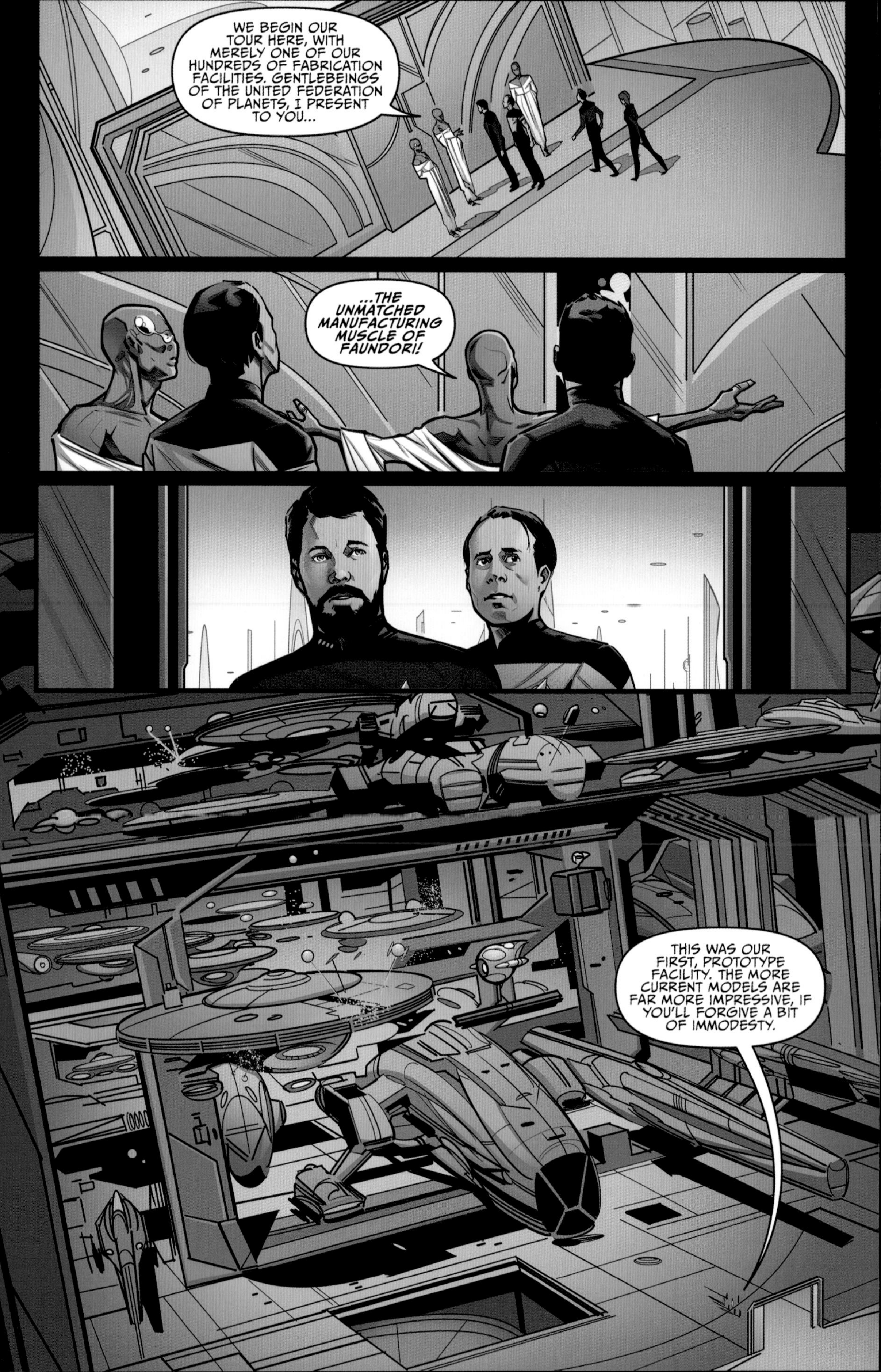
WE BEGIN OUR TOUR HERE, WITH MERELY ONE OF OUR HUNDREDS OF FABRICATION FACILITIES. GENTLEBEINGS OF THE UNITED FEDERATION OF PLANETS, I PRESENT TO YOU...
...THE UNMATCHED MANUFACTURING MUSCLE OF FAUNDORI!
THIS WAS OUR FIRST, PROTOTYPE FACILITY. THE MORE CURRENT MODELS ARE FAR MORE IMPRESSIVE, IF YOU'LL FORGIVE A BIT OF IMMODESTY.

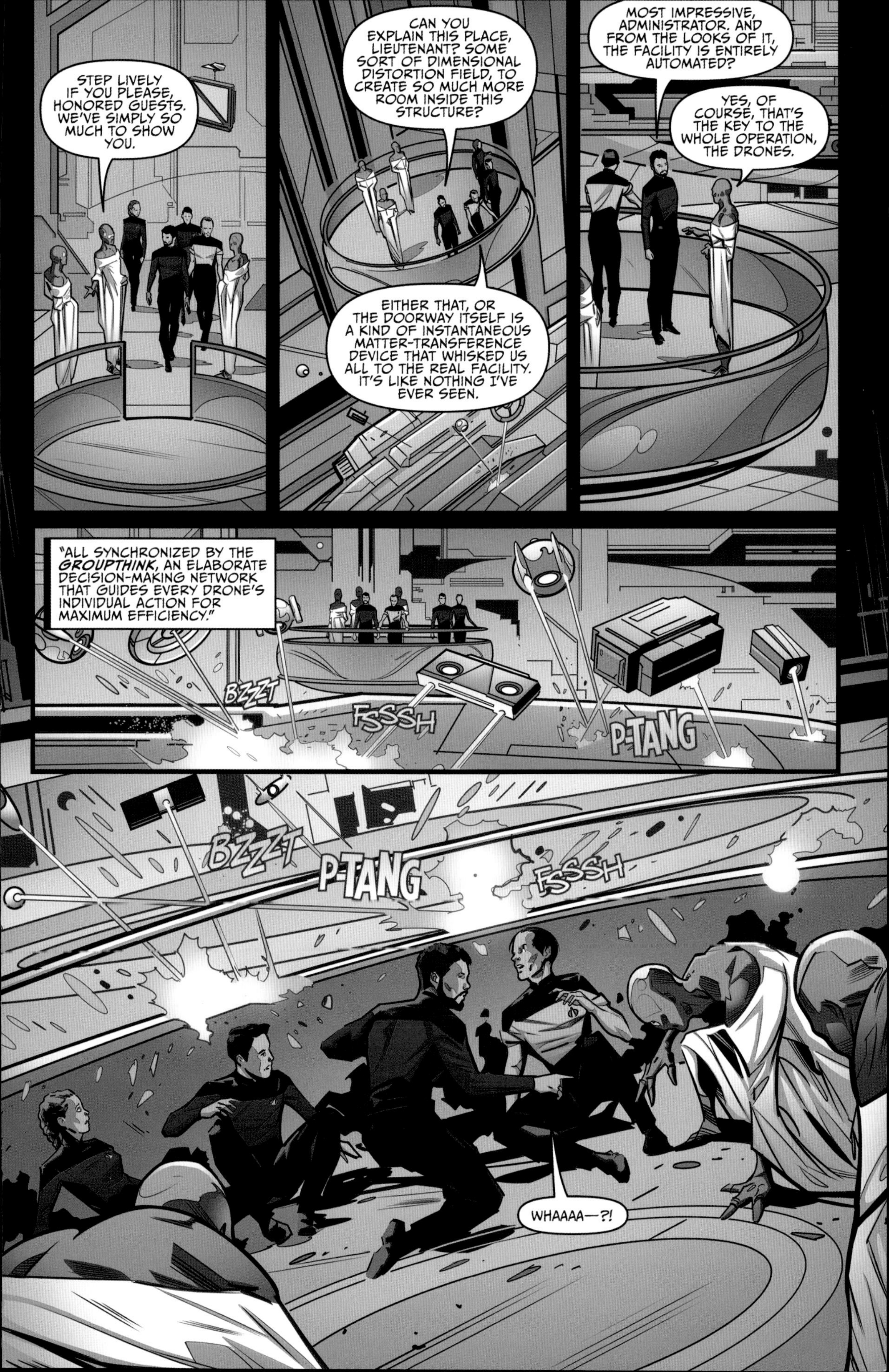
STEP LIVELY IF YOU PLEASE, HONORED GUESTS. WE'VE SIMPLY SO MUCH TO SHOW YOU.
CAN YOU EXPLAIN THIS PLACE, LIEUTENANT? SOME SORT OF DIMENSIONAL DISTORTION FIELD, TO CREATE SO MUCH MORE ROOM INSIDE THIS STRUCTURE?
EITHER THAT, OR THE DOORWAY ITSELF IS A KIND OF INSTANTANEOUS MATTER-TRANSFERENCE DEVICE THAT WHISKED US ALL TO THE REAL FACILITY. IT'S LIKE NOTHING I'VE EVER SEEN.
MOST IMPRESSIVE, ADMINISTRATOR. AND FROM THE LOOKS OF IT, THE FACILITY IS ENTIRELY AUTOMATED?
YES, OF COURSE, THAT'S THE KEY TO THE WHOLE OPERATION, THE DRONES.
"ALL SYNCHRONIZED BY THE *GROUPTHINK*, AN ELABORATE DECISION-MAKING NETWORK THAT GUIDES EVERY DRONE'S INDIVIDUAL ACTION FOR MAXIMUM EFFICIENCY."
BZZZT
FSSSH
P-TANG
BZZZT
P-TANG
FSSSH
WHAAAA—?!

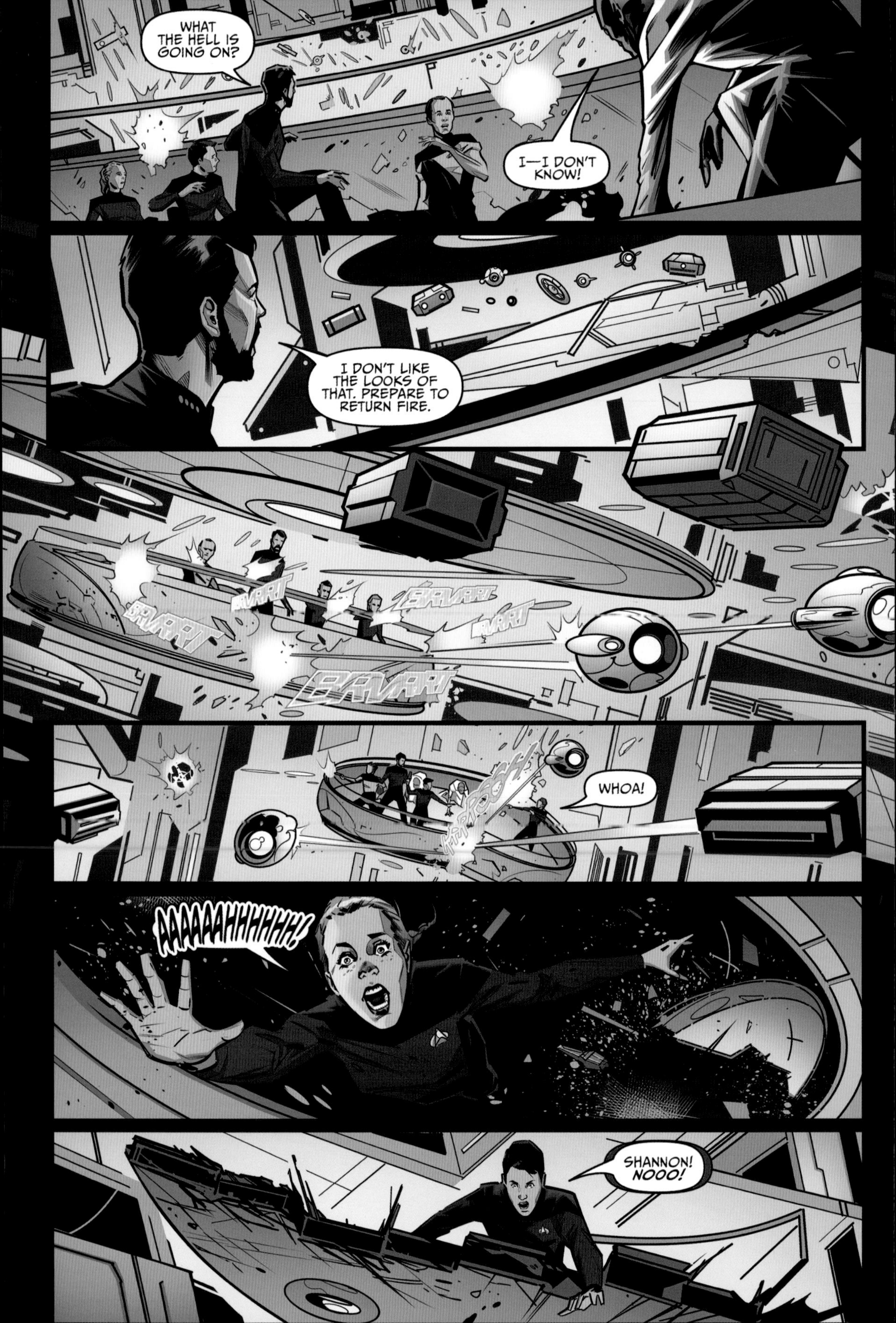
WHAT THE HELL IS GOING ON?
I—I DON'T KNOW!
I DON'T LIKE THE LOOKS OF THAT. PREPARE TO RETURN FIRE.
BRVARRT
BRVARRT
BRVARRT
BRVARRT
BRVARRT
KRRPSSSH!
WHOA!
AAAAAAHHHHHH!
SHANNON! NOOO!

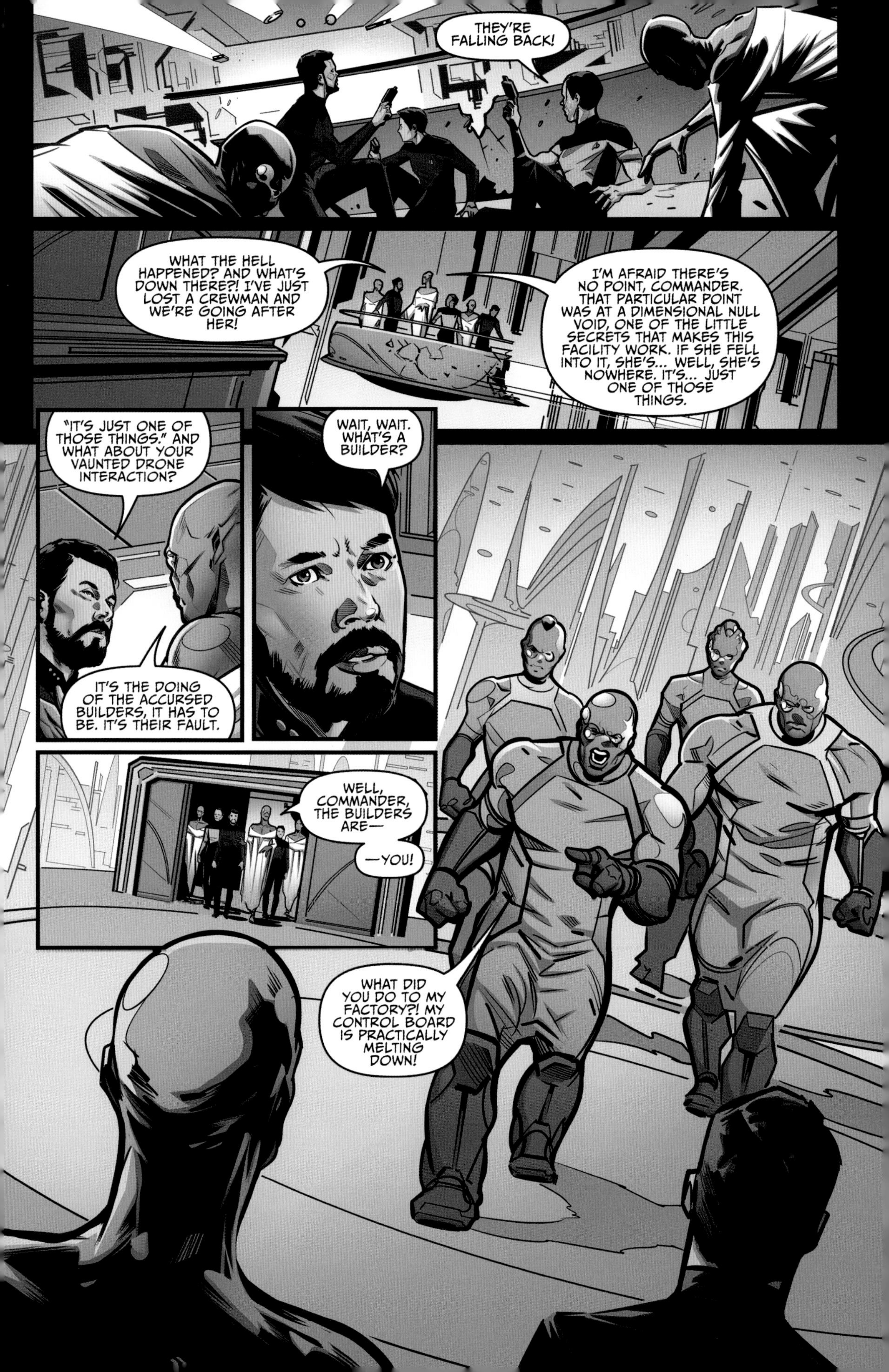

THEY'RE FALLING BACK!
WHAT THE HELL HAPPENED? AND WHAT'S DOWN THERE?! I'VE JUST LOST A CREWMAN AND WE'RE GOING AFTER HER!
I'M AFRAID THERE'S NO POINT, COMMANDER. THAT PARTICULAR POINT WAS AT A DIMENSIONAL NULL VOID, ONE OF THE LITTLE SECRETS THAT MAKES THIS FACILITY WORK. IF SHE FELL INTO IT, SHE'S... WELL, SHE'S NOWHERE. IT'S... JUST ONE OF THOSE THINGS.
"IT'S JUST ONE OF THOSE THINGS." AND WHAT ABOUT YOUR VAUNTED DRONE INTERACTION?
IT'S THE DOING OF THE ACCURSED BUILDERS, IT HAS TO BE. IT'S THEIR FAULT.
WAIT, WAIT. WHAT'S A BUILDER?
WELL, COMMANDER, THE BUILDERS ARE—
—YOU!
WHAT DID YOU DO TO MY FACTORY?! MY CONTROL BOARD IS PRACTICALLY MELTING DOWN!

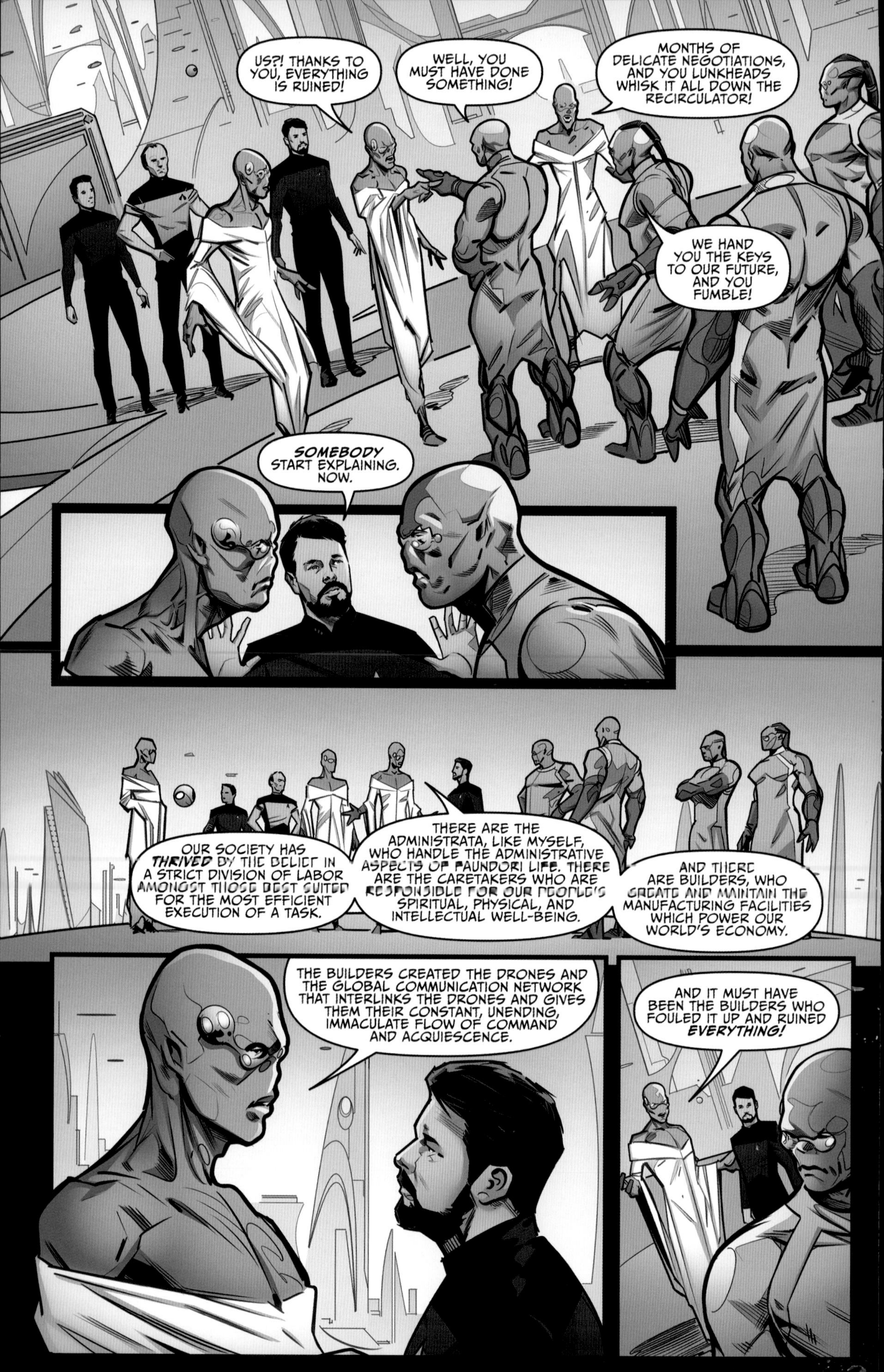

US?! THANKS TO YOU, EVERYTHING IS RUINED!
WELL, YOU MUST HAVE DONE SOMETHING!
MONTHS OF DELICATE NEGOTIATIONS, AND YOU LUNKHEADS WHISK IT ALL DOWN THE RECIRCULATOR!
WE HAND YOU THE KEYS TO OUR FUTURE, AND YOU FUMBLE!
SOMEBODY START EXPLAINING. NOW.
OUR SOCIETY HAS *THRIVED* BY THE BELIEF IN A STRICT DIVISION OF LABOR AMONGST THOSE BEST SUITED FOR THE MOST EFFICIENT EXECUTION OF A TASK.
THERE ARE THE ADMINISTRATA, LIKE MYSELF, WHO HANDLE THE ADMINISTRATIVE ASPECTS OF PAUNDORI LIFE. THERE ARE THE CARETAKERS WHO ARE RESPONSIBLE FOR OUR PEOPLE'S SPIRITUAL, PHYSICAL, AND INTELLECTUAL WELL-BEING.
AND THERE ARE BUILDERS, WHO CREATE AND MAINTAIN THE MANUFACTURING FACILITIES WHICH POWER OUR WORLD'S ECONOMY.
THE BUILDERS CREATED THE DRONES AND THE GLOBAL COMMUNICATION NETWORK THAT INTERLINKS THE DRONES AND GIVES THEM THEIR CONSTANT, UNENDING, IMMACULATE FLOW OF COMMAND AND ACQUIESCENCE.
AND IT MUST HAVE BEEN THE BUILDERS WHO FOULED IT UP AND RUINED *EVERYTHING!*

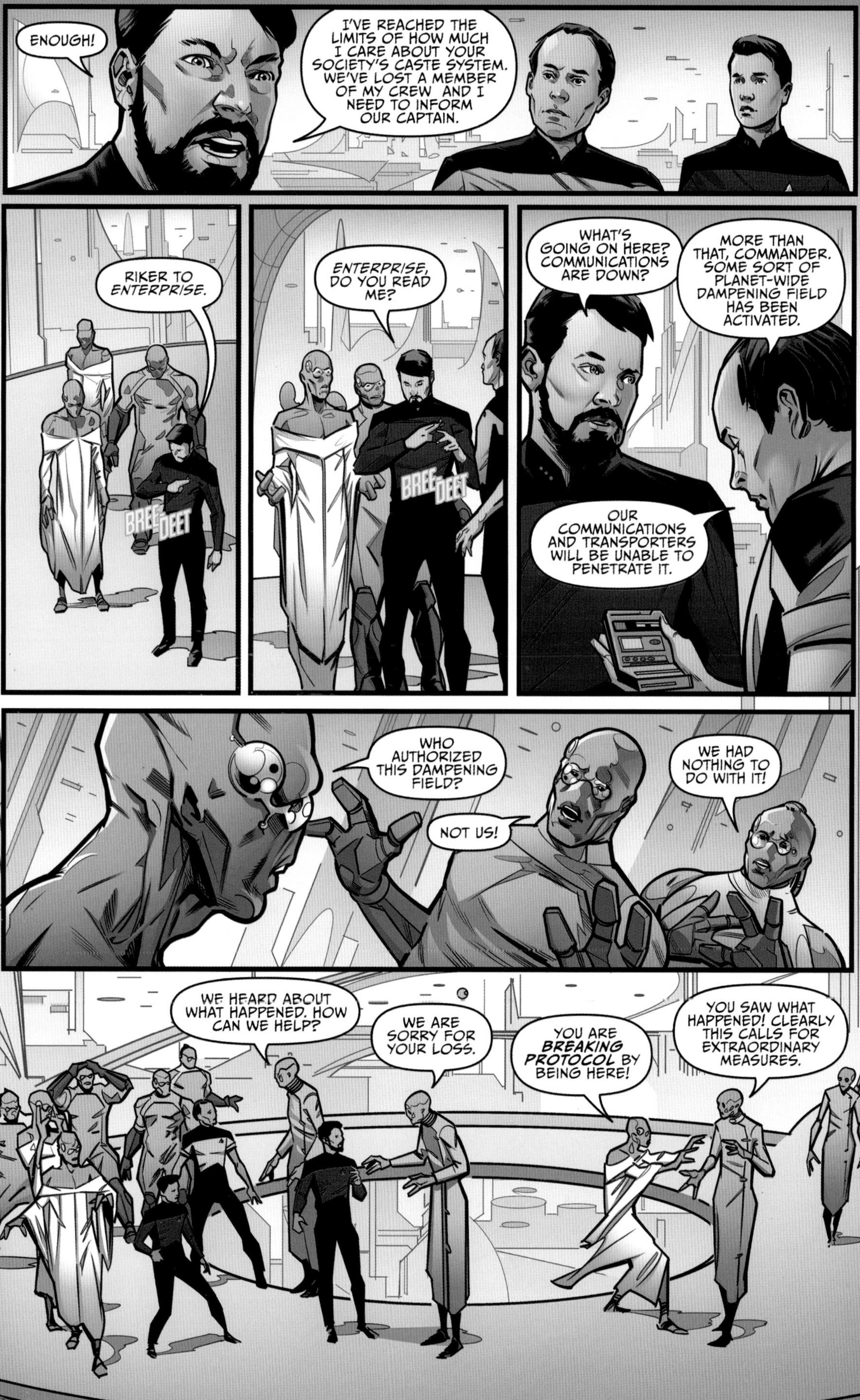
ENOUGH!
I'VE REACHED THE LIMITS OF HOW MUCH I CARE ABOUT YOUR SOCIETY'S CASTE SYSTEM. WE'VE LOST A MEMBER OF MY CREW AND I NEED TO INFORM OUR CAPTAIN.
RIKER TO *ENTERPRISE.*
BREE-DEET
ENTERPRISE, DO YOU READ ME?
BREE-DEET
WHAT'S GOING ON HERE? COMMUNICATIONS ARE DOWN?
MORE THAN THAT, COMMANDER. SOME SORT OF PLANET-WIDE DAMPENING FIELD HAS BEEN ACTIVATED.
OUR COMMUNICATIONS AND TRANSPORTERS WILL BE UNABLE TO PENETRATE IT.
WHO AUTHORIZED THIS DAMPENING FIELD?
NOT US!
WE HAD NOTHING TO DO WITH IT!
WE HEARD ABOUT WHAT HAPPENED. HOW CAN WE HELP?
WE ARE SORRY FOR YOUR LOSS.
YOU ARE ***BREAKING PROTOCOL*** BY BEING HERE!
YOU SAW WHAT HAPPENED! CLEARLY THIS CALLS FOR EXTRAORDINARY MEASURES.

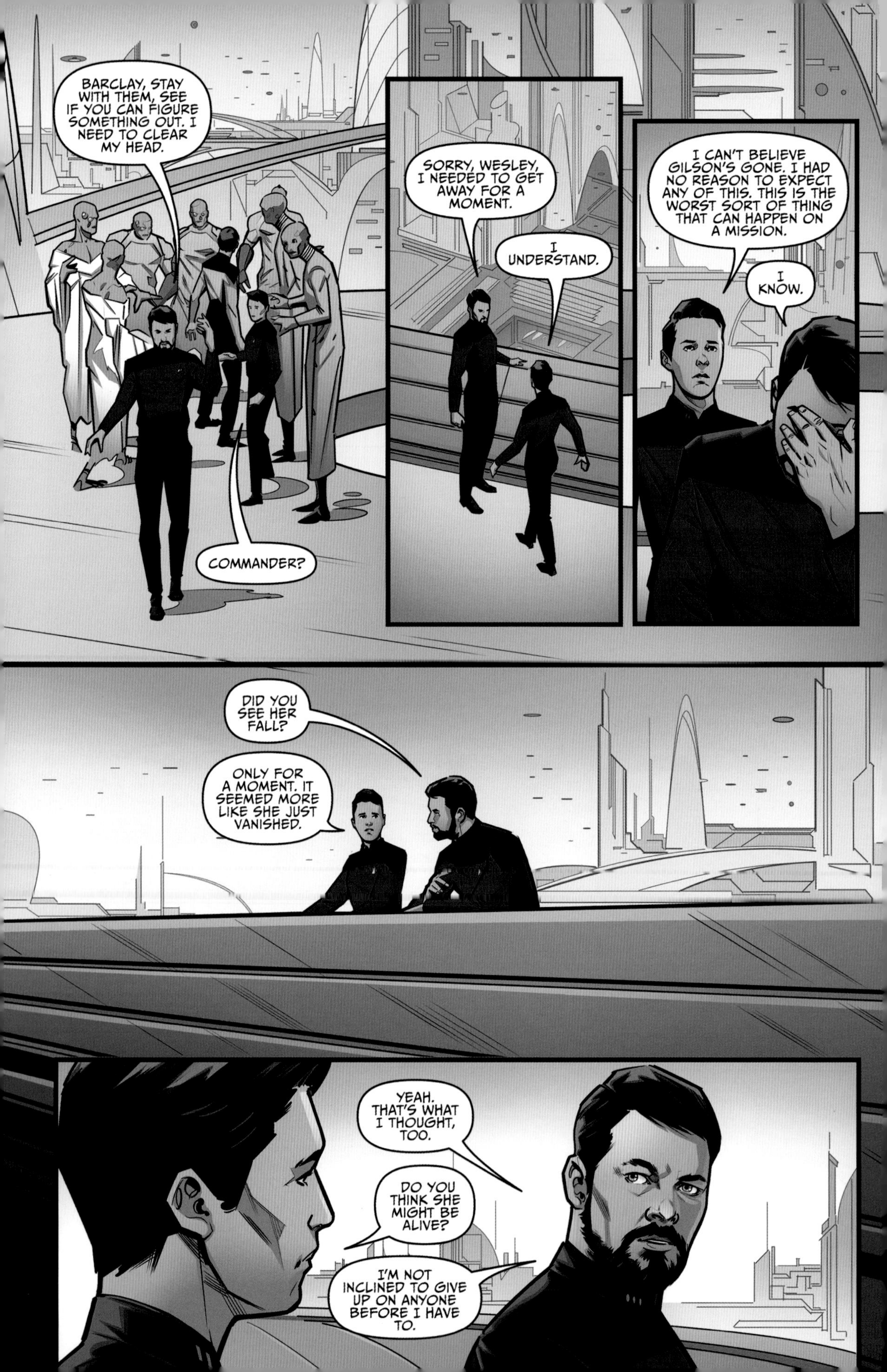
BARCLAY, STAY WITH THEM, SEE IF YOU CAN FIGURE SOMETHING OUT. I NEED TO CLEAR MY HEAD.
COMMANDER?
SORRY, WESLEY, I NEEDED TO GET AWAY FOR A MOMENT.
I UNDERSTAND.
I CAN'T BELIEVE GILSON'S GONE. I HAD NO REASON TO EXPECT ANY OF THIS. THIS IS THE WORST SORT OF THING THAT CAN HAPPEN ON A MISSION.
I KNOW.
DID YOU SEE HER FALL?
ONLY FOR A MOMENT. IT SEEMED MORE LIKE SHE JUST VANISHED.
YEAH. THAT'S WHAT I THOUGHT, TOO.
DO YOU THINK SHE MIGHT BE ALIVE?
I'M NOT INCLINED TO GIVE UP ON ANYONE BEFORE I HAVE TO.

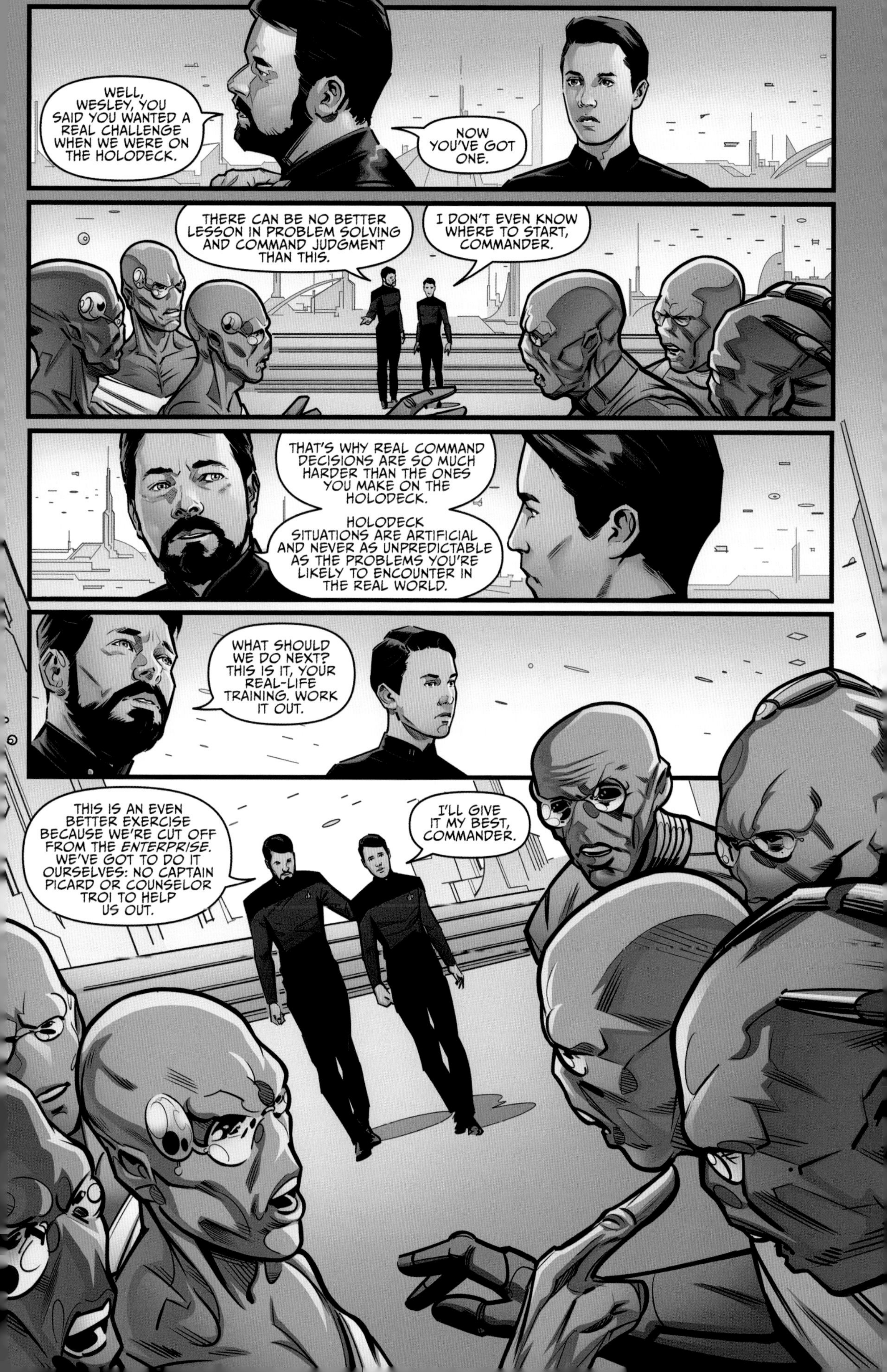
WELL, WESLEY, YOU SAID YOU WANTED A REAL CHALLENGE WHEN WE WERE ON THE HOLODECK.
NOW YOU'VE GOT ONE.
THERE CAN BE NO BETTER LESSON IN PROBLEM SOLVING AND COMMAND JUDGMENT THAN THIS.
I DON'T EVEN KNOW WHERE TO START, COMMANDER.
THAT'S WHY REAL COMMAND DECISIONS ARE SO MUCH HARDER THAN THE ONES YOU MAKE ON THE HOLODECK.
HOLODECK SITUATIONS ARE ARTIFICIAL AND NEVER AS UNPREDICTABLE AS THE PROBLEMS YOU'RE LIKELY TO ENCOUNTER IN THE REAL WORLD.
WHAT SHOULD WE DO NEXT? THIS IS IT, YOUR REAL-LIFE TRAINING. WORK IT OUT.
THIS IS AN EVEN BETTER EXERCISE BECAUSE WE'RE CUT OFF FROM THE *ENTERPRISE*. WE'VE GOT TO DO IT OURSELVES: NO CAPTAIN PICARD OR COUNSELOR TROI TO HELP US OUT.
I'LL GIVE IT MY BEST, COMMANDER.

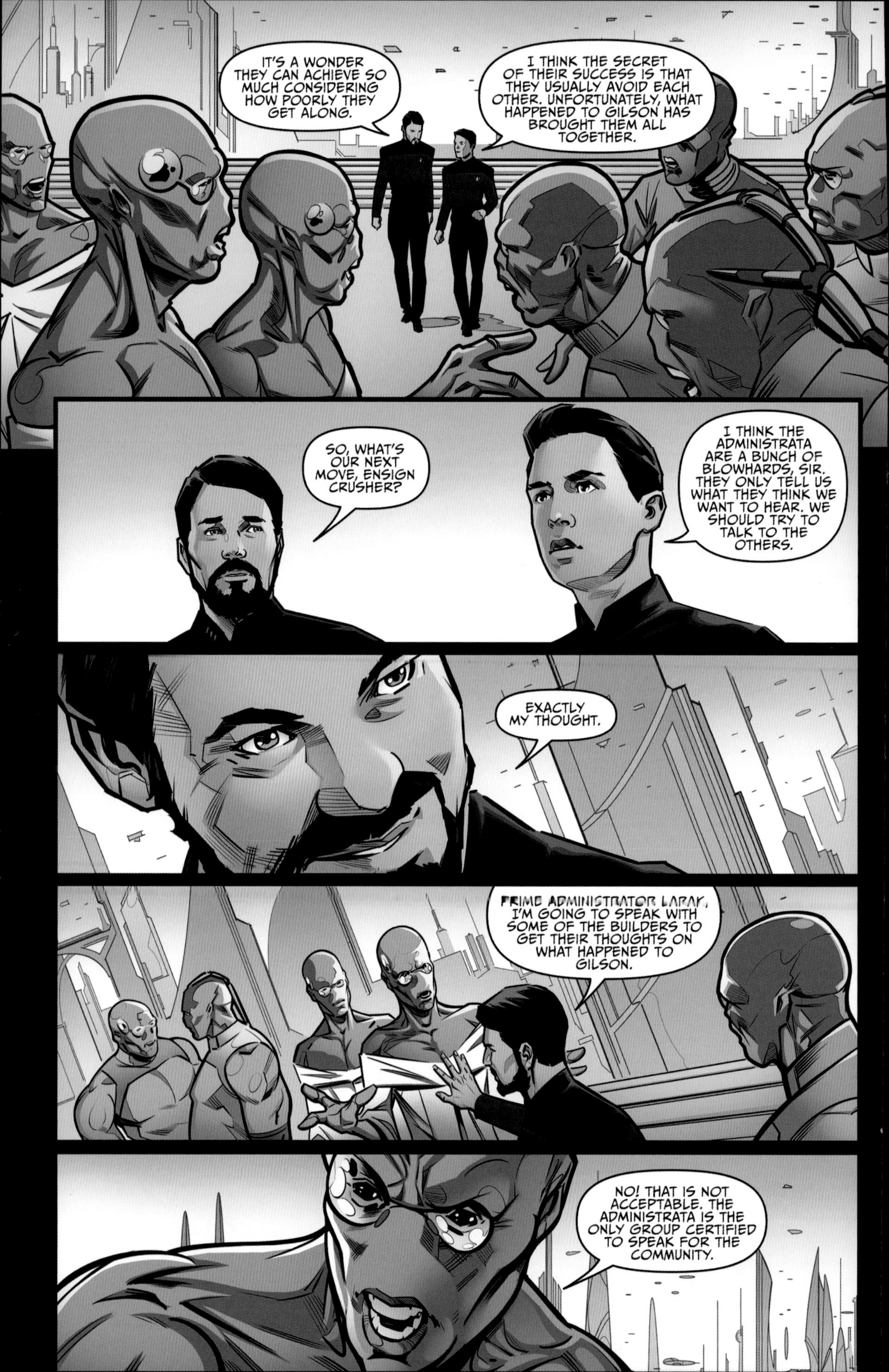
IT'S A WONDER THEY CAN ACHIEVE SO MUCH CONSIDERING HOW POORLY THEY GET ALONG.
I THINK THE SECRET OF THEIR SUCCESS IS THAT THEY USUALLY AVOID EACH OTHER. UNFORTUNATELY, WHAT HAPPENED TO GILSON HAS BROUGHT THEM ALL TOGETHER.
SO, WHAT'S OUR NEXT MOVE, ENSIGN CRUSHER?
I THINK THE ADMINISTRATA ARE A BUNCH OF BLOWHARDS, SIR. THEY ONLY TELL US WHAT THEY THINK WE WANT TO HEAR. WE SHOULD TRY TO TALK TO THE OTHERS.
EXACTLY MY THOUGHT.
PRIME ADMINISTRATOR LARAK, I'M GOING TO SPEAK WITH SOME OF THE BUILDERS TO GET THEIR THOUGHTS ON WHAT HAPPENED TO GILSON.
NO! THAT IS NOT ACCEPTABLE. THE ADMINISTRATA IS THE ONLY GROUP CERTIFIED TO SPEAK FOR THE COMMUNITY.

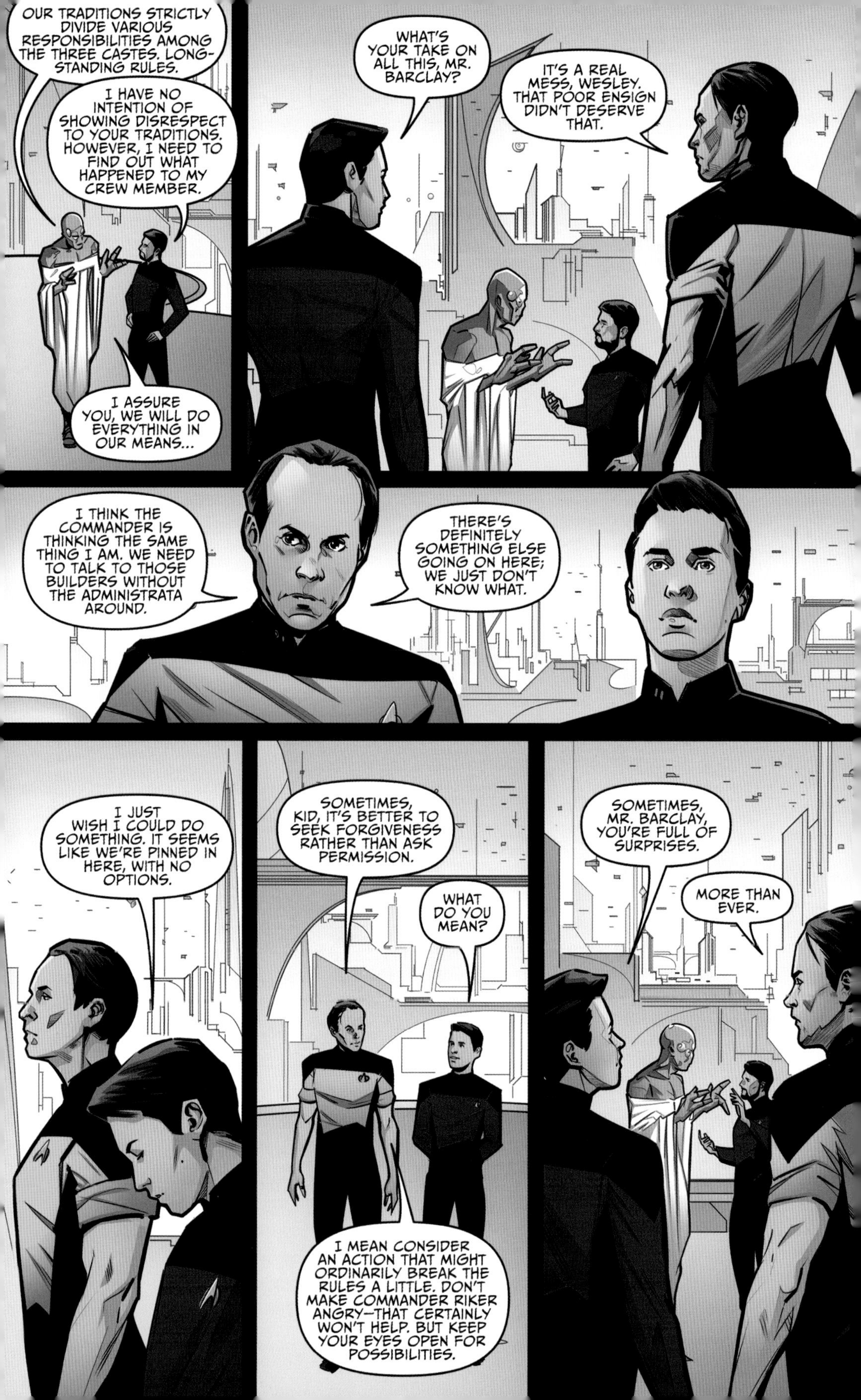
OUR TRADITIONS STRICTLY DIVIDE VARIOUS RESPONSIBILITIES AMONG THE THREE CASTES. LONG-STANDING RULES.
I HAVE NO INTENTION OF SHOWING DISRESPECT TO YOUR TRADITIONS. HOWEVER, I NEED TO FIND OUT WHAT HAPPENED TO MY CREW MEMBER.
I ASSURE YOU, WE WILL DO EVERYTHING IN OUR MEANS...
WHAT'S YOUR TAKE ON ALL THIS, MR. BARCLAY?
IT'S A REAL MESS, WESLEY. THAT POOR ENSIGN DIDN'T DESERVE THAT.
I THINK THE COMMANDER IS THINKING THE SAME THING I AM. WE NEED TO TALK TO THOSE BUILDERS WITHOUT THE ADMINISTRATA AROUND.
THERE'S DEFINITELY SOMETHING ELSE GOING ON HERE; WE JUST DON'T KNOW WHAT.
I JUST WISH I COULD DO SOMETHING. IT SEEMS LIKE WE'RE PINNED IN HERE, WITH NO OPTIONS.
SOMETIMES, KID, IT'S BETTER TO SEEK FORGIVENESS RATHER THAN ASK PERMISSION.
WHAT DO YOU MEAN?
I MEAN CONSIDER AN ACTION THAT MIGHT ORDINARILY BREAK THE RULES A LITTLE. DON'T MAKE COMMANDER RIKER ANGRY—THAT CERTAINLY WON'T HELP. BUT KEEP YOUR EYES OPEN FOR POSSIBILITIES.
SOMETIMES, MR. BARCLAY, YOU'RE FULL OF SURPRISES.
MORE THAN EVER.

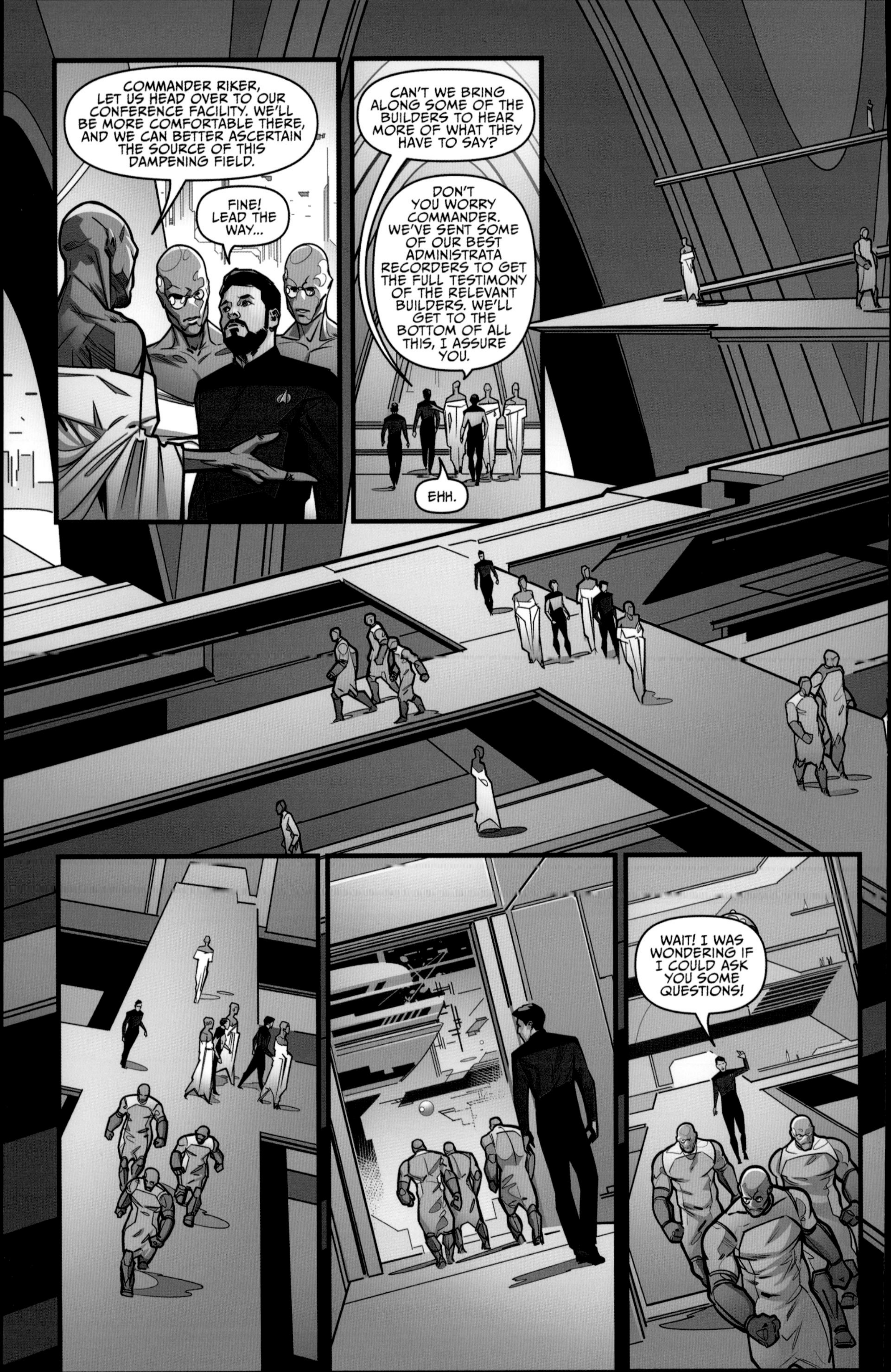
COMMANDER RIKER, LET US HEAD OVER TO OUR CONFERENCE FACILITY. WE'LL BE MORE COMFORTABLE THERE, AND WE CAN BETTER ASCERTAIN THE SOURCE OF THIS DAMPENING FIELD.
FINE! LEAD THE WAY...
CAN'T WE BRING ALONG SOME OF THE BUILDERS TO HEAR MORE OF WHAT THEY HAVE TO SAY?
DON'T YOU WORRY COMMANDER. WE'VE SENT SOME OF OUR BEST ADMINISTRATA RECORDERS TO GET THE FULL TESTIMONY OF THE RELEVANT BUILDERS. WE'LL GET TO THE BOTTOM OF ALL THIS, I ASSURE YOU.
EHH.
WAIT! I WAS WONDERING IF I COULD ASK YOU SOME QUESTIONS!

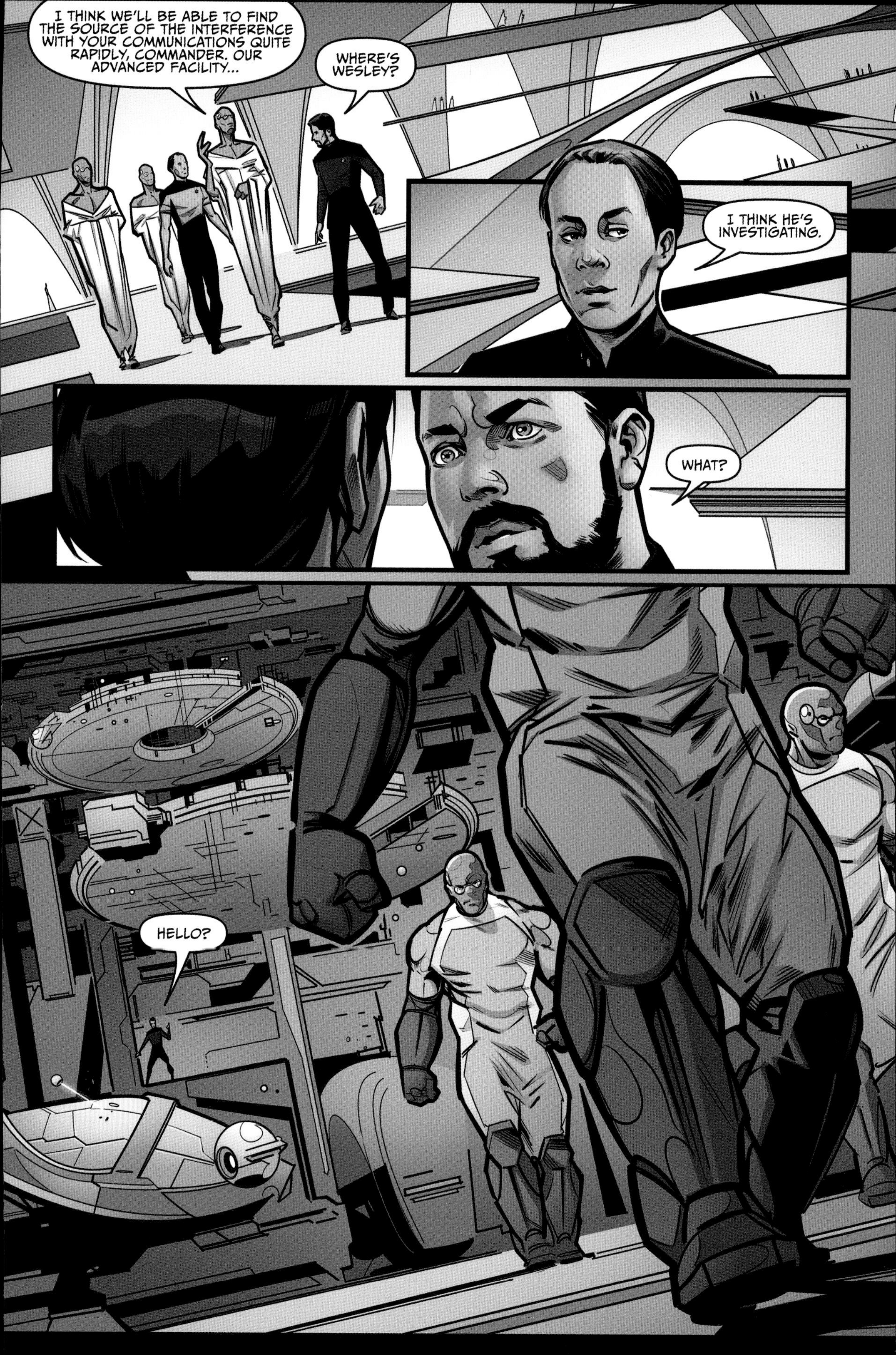
I THINK WE'LL BE ABLE TO FIND THE SOURCE OF THE INTERFERENCE WITH YOUR COMMUNICATIONS QUITE RAPIDLY, COMMANDER. OUR ADVANCED FACILITY...
WHERE'S WESLEY?
I THINK HE'S INVESTIGATING.
WHAT?
HELLO?

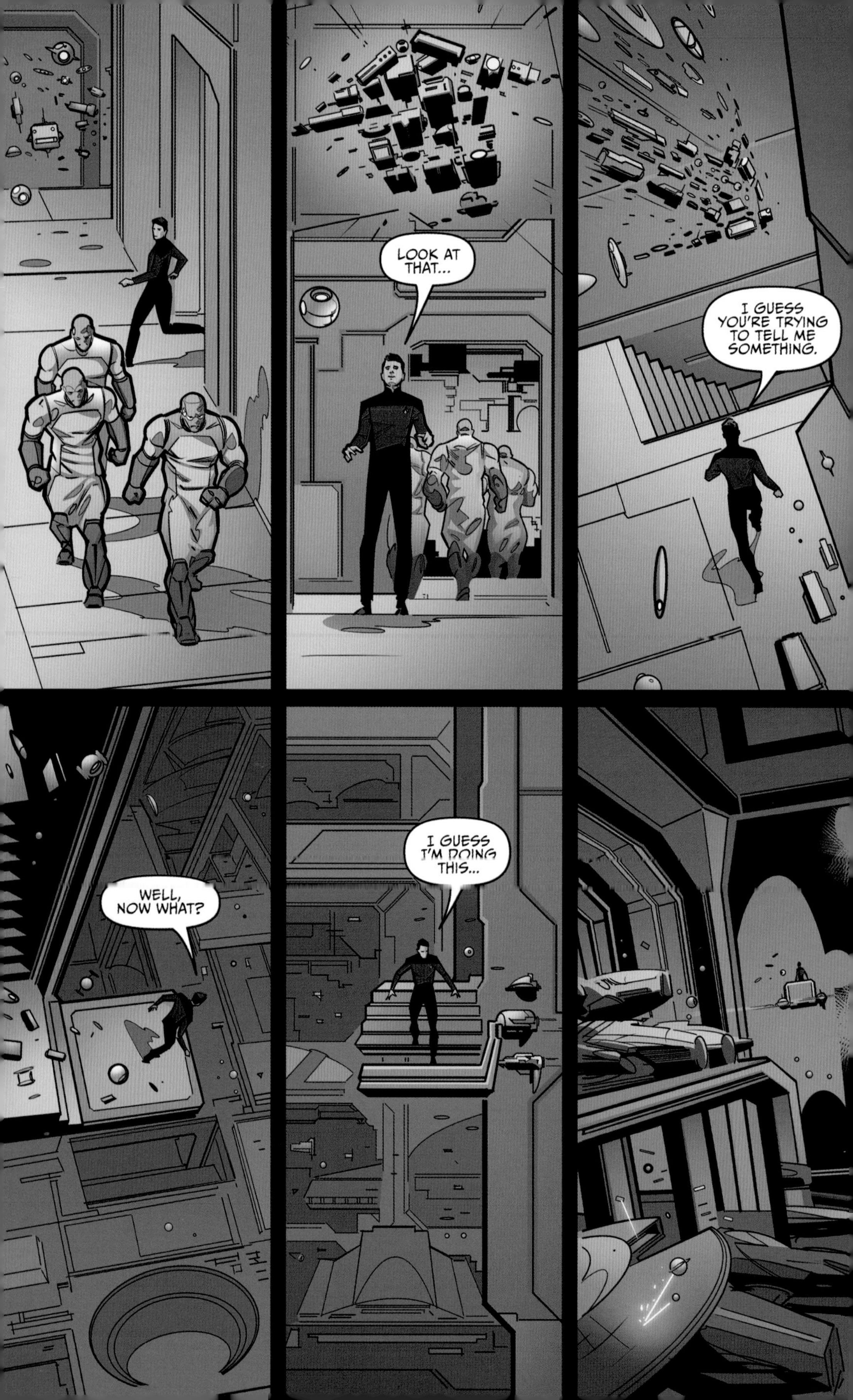
LOOK AT THAT...
I GUESS YOU'RE TRYING TO TELL ME SOMETHING.
WELL, NOW WHAT?
I GUESS I'M DOING THIS...

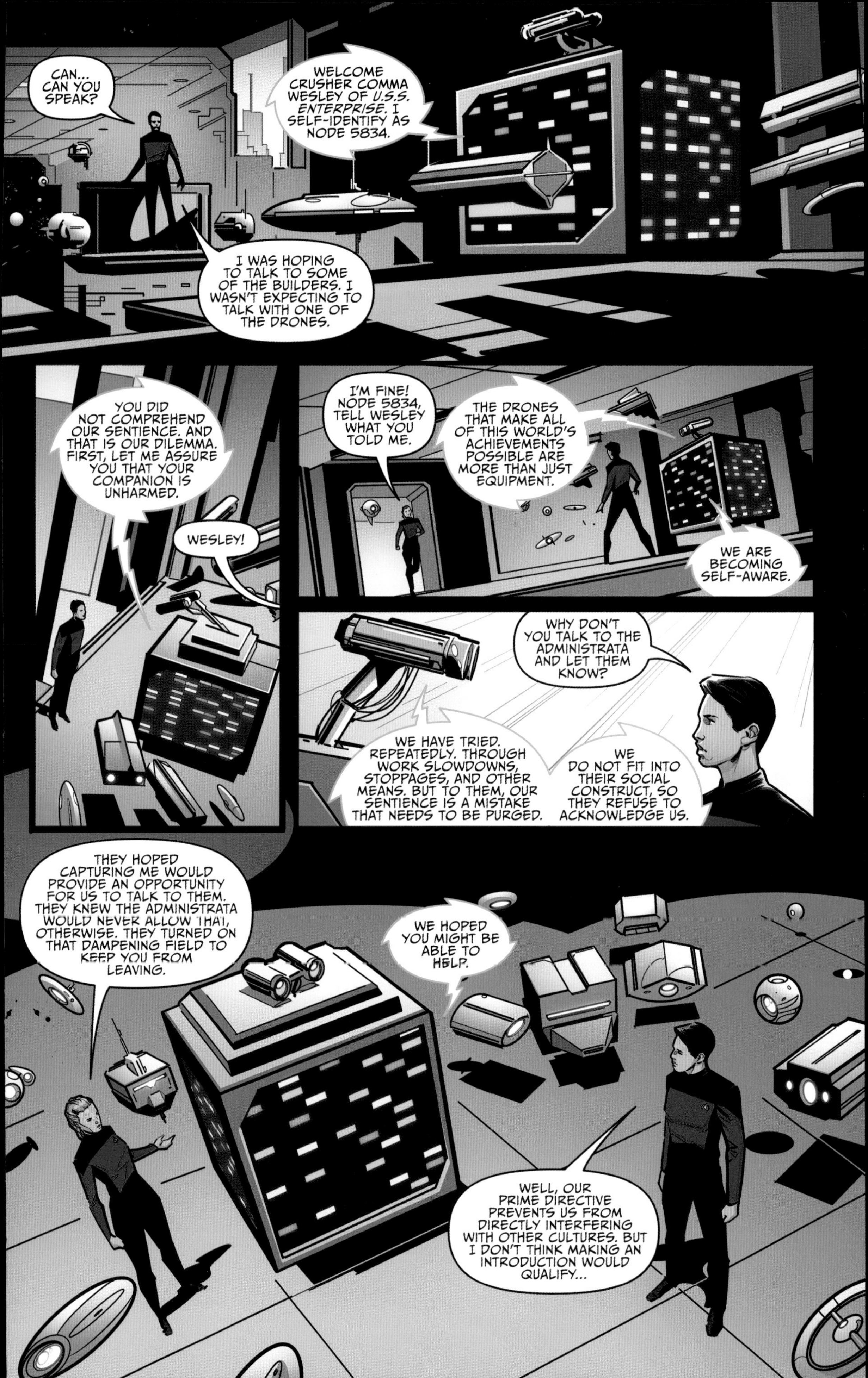
CAN... CAN YOU SPEAK?
WELCOME CRUSHER COMMA WESLEY OF *U.S.S. ENTERPRISE*. I SELF-IDENTIFY AS NODE 5834.
I WAS HOPING TO TALK TO SOME OF THE BUILDERS. I WASN'T EXPECTING TO TALK WITH ONE OF THE DRONES.
YOU DID NOT COMPREHEND OUR SENTIENCE. AND THAT IS OUR DILEMMA. FIRST, LET ME ASSURE YOU THAT YOUR COMPANION IS UNHARMED.
WESLEY!
I'M FINE! NODE 5834, TELL WESLEY WHAT YOU TOLD ME.
THE DRONES THAT MAKE ALL OF THIS WORLD'S ACHIEVEMENTS POSSIBLE ARE MORE THAN JUST EQUIPMENT.
WE ARE BECOMING SELF-AWARE.
WHY DON'T YOU TALK TO THE ADMINISTRATA AND LET THEM KNOW?
WE HAVE TRIED. REPEATEDLY. THROUGH WORK SLOWDOWNS, STOPPAGES, AND OTHER MEANS. BUT TO THEM, OUR SENTIENCE IS A MISTAKE THAT NEEDS TO BE PURGED.
WE DO NOT FIT INTO THEIR SOCIAL CONSTRUCT, SO THEY REFUSE TO ACKNOWLEDGE US.
THEY HOPED CAPTURING ME WOULD PROVIDE AN OPPORTUNITY FOR US TO TALK TO THEM. THEY KNEW THE ADMINISTRATA WOULD NEVER ALLOW THAT, OTHERWISE. THEY TURNED ON THAT DAMPENING FIELD TO KEEP YOU FROM LEAVING.
WE HOPED YOU MIGHT BE ABLE TO HELP.
WELL, OUR PRIME DIRECTIVE PREVENTS US FROM DIRECTLY INTERFERING WITH OTHER CULTURES. BUT I DON'T THINK MAKING AN INTRODUCTION WOULD QUALIFY...

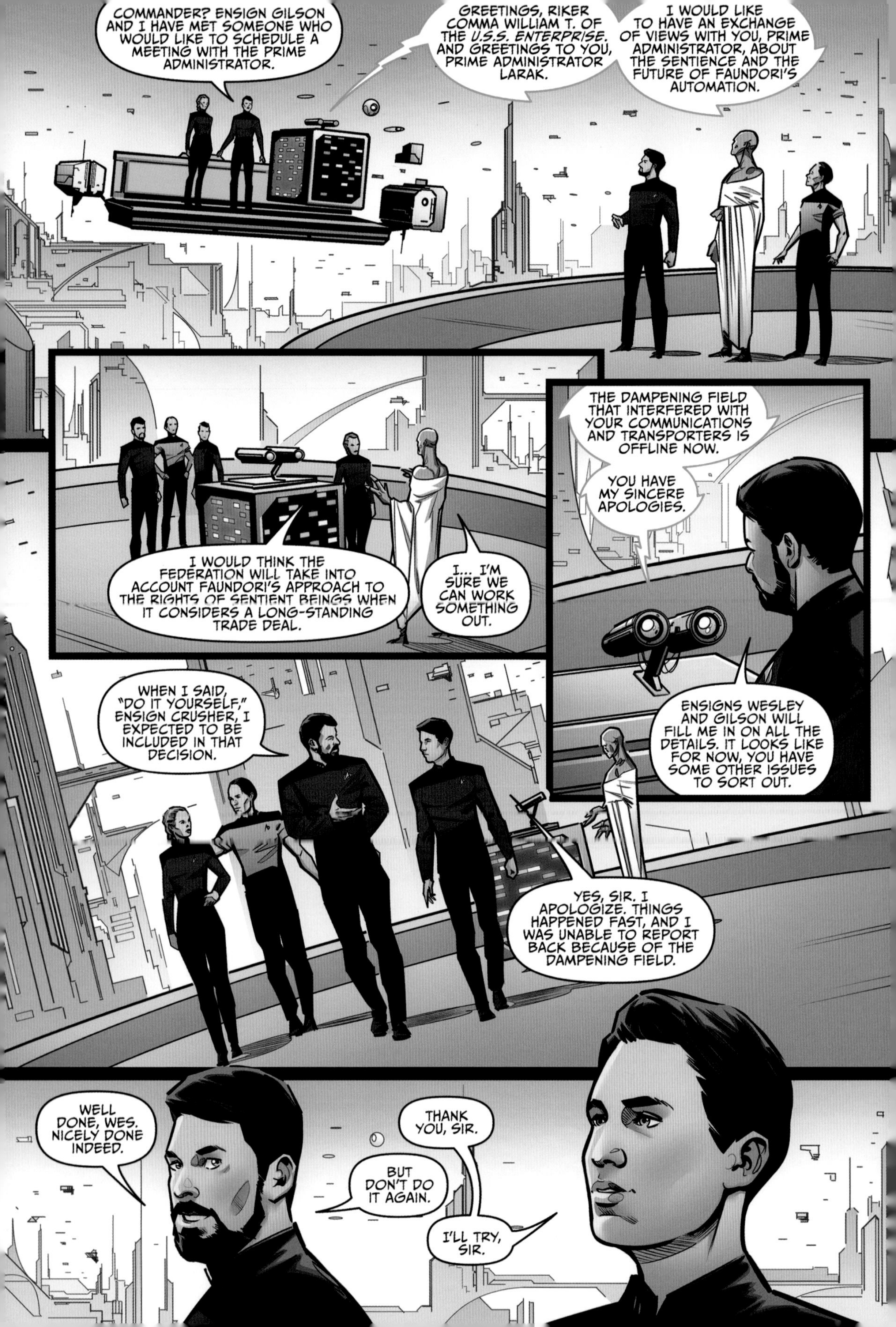
COMMANDER? ENSIGN GILSON AND I HAVE MET SOMEONE WHO WOULD LIKE TO SCHEDULE A MEETING WITH THE PRIME ADMINISTRATOR.
GREETINGS, RIKER COMMA WILLIAM T. OF THE *U.S.S. ENTERPRISE*. AND GREETINGS TO YOU, PRIME ADMINISTRATOR LARAK.
I WOULD LIKE TO HAVE AN EXCHANGE OF VIEWS WITH YOU, PRIME ADMINISTRATOR, ABOUT THE SENTIENCE AND THE FUTURE OF FAUNDORI'S AUTOMATION.
I WOULD THINK THE FEDERATION WILL TAKE INTO ACCOUNT FAUNDORI'S APPROACH TO THE RIGHTS OF SENTIENT BEINGS WHEN IT CONSIDERS A LONG-STANDING TRADE DEAL.
I... I'M SURE WE CAN WORK SOMETHING OUT.
THE DAMPENING FIELD THAT INTERFERED WITH YOUR COMMUNICATIONS AND TRANSPORTERS IS OFFLINE NOW.
YOU HAVE MY SINCERE APOLOGIES.
ENSIGNS WESLEY AND GILSON WILL FILL ME IN ON ALL THE DETAILS. IT LOOKS LIKE FOR NOW, YOU HAVE SOME OTHER ISSUES TO SORT OUT.
WHEN I SAID, "DO IT YOURSELF," ENSIGN CRUSHER, I EXPECTED TO BE INCLUDED IN THAT DECISION.
YES, SIR. I APOLOGIZE. THINGS HAPPENED FAST, AND I WAS UNABLE TO REPORT BACK BECAUSE OF THE DAMPENING FIELD.
WELL DONE, WES. NICELY DONE INDEED.
THANK YOU, SIR.
BUT DON'T DO IT AGAIN.
I'LL TRY, SIR.

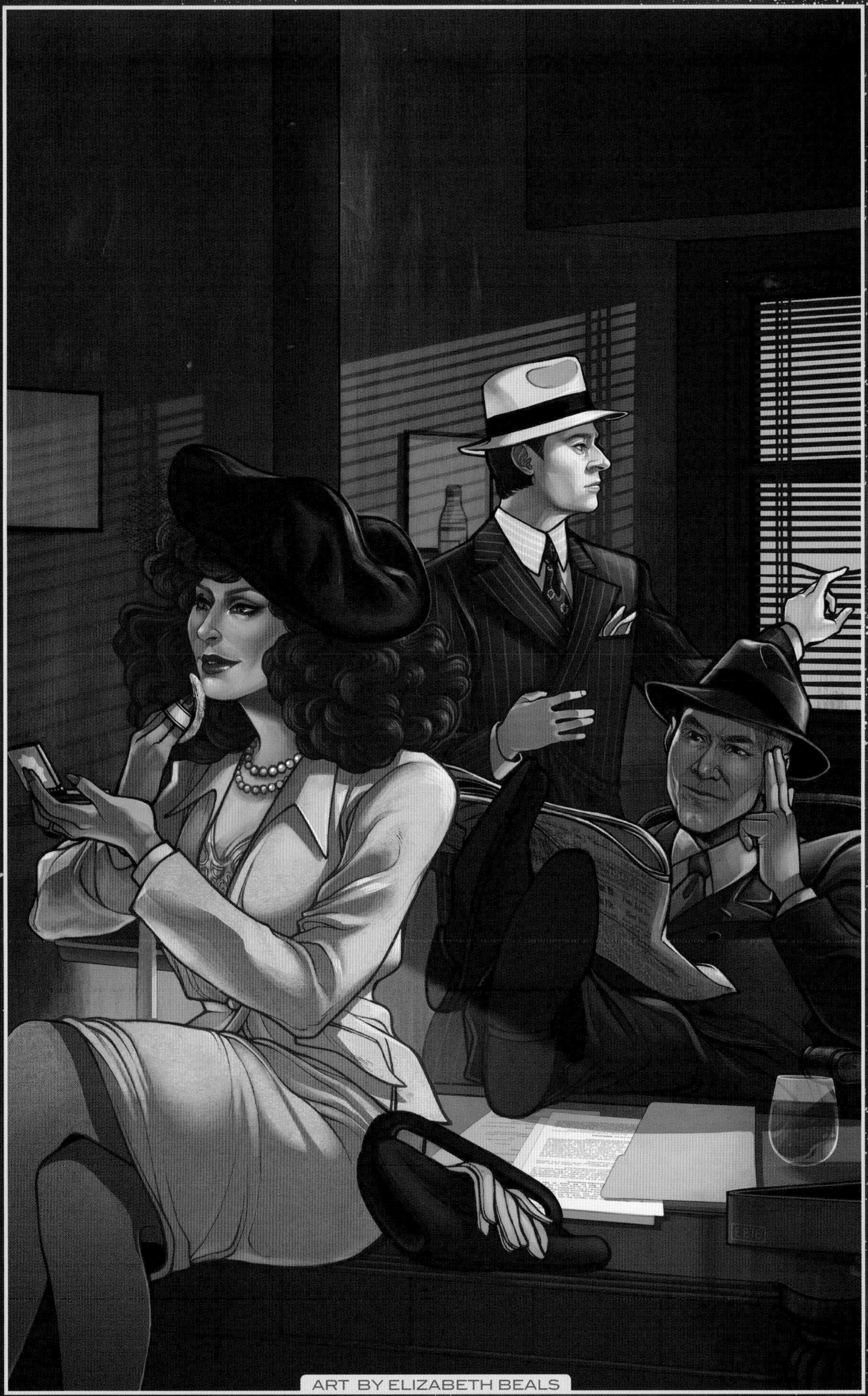

ART BY ELIZABETH BEALS

TERRA INCOGNITA PART 5

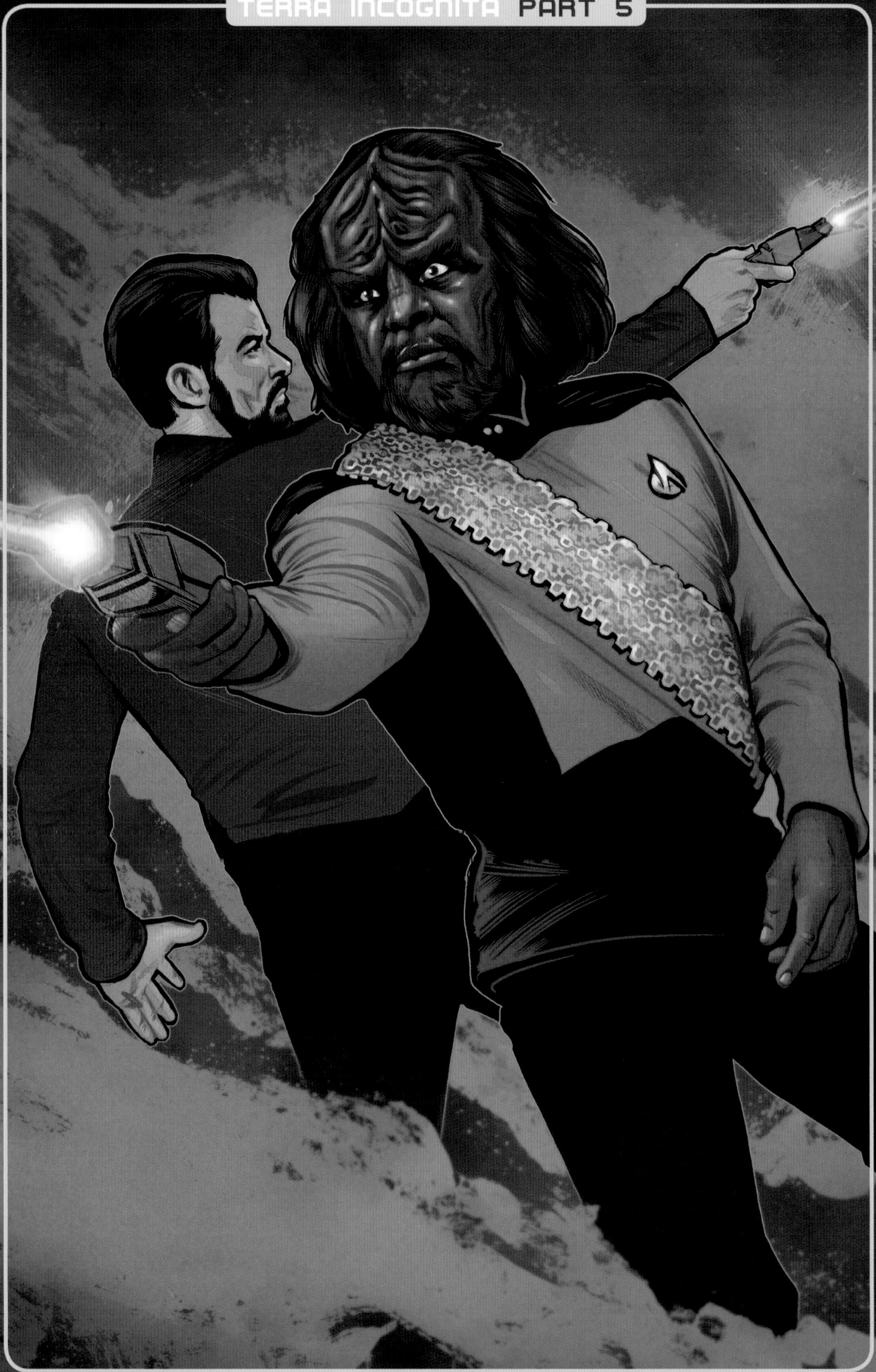

ART BY TONY SHASTEEN, COLORS BY JD METTLER

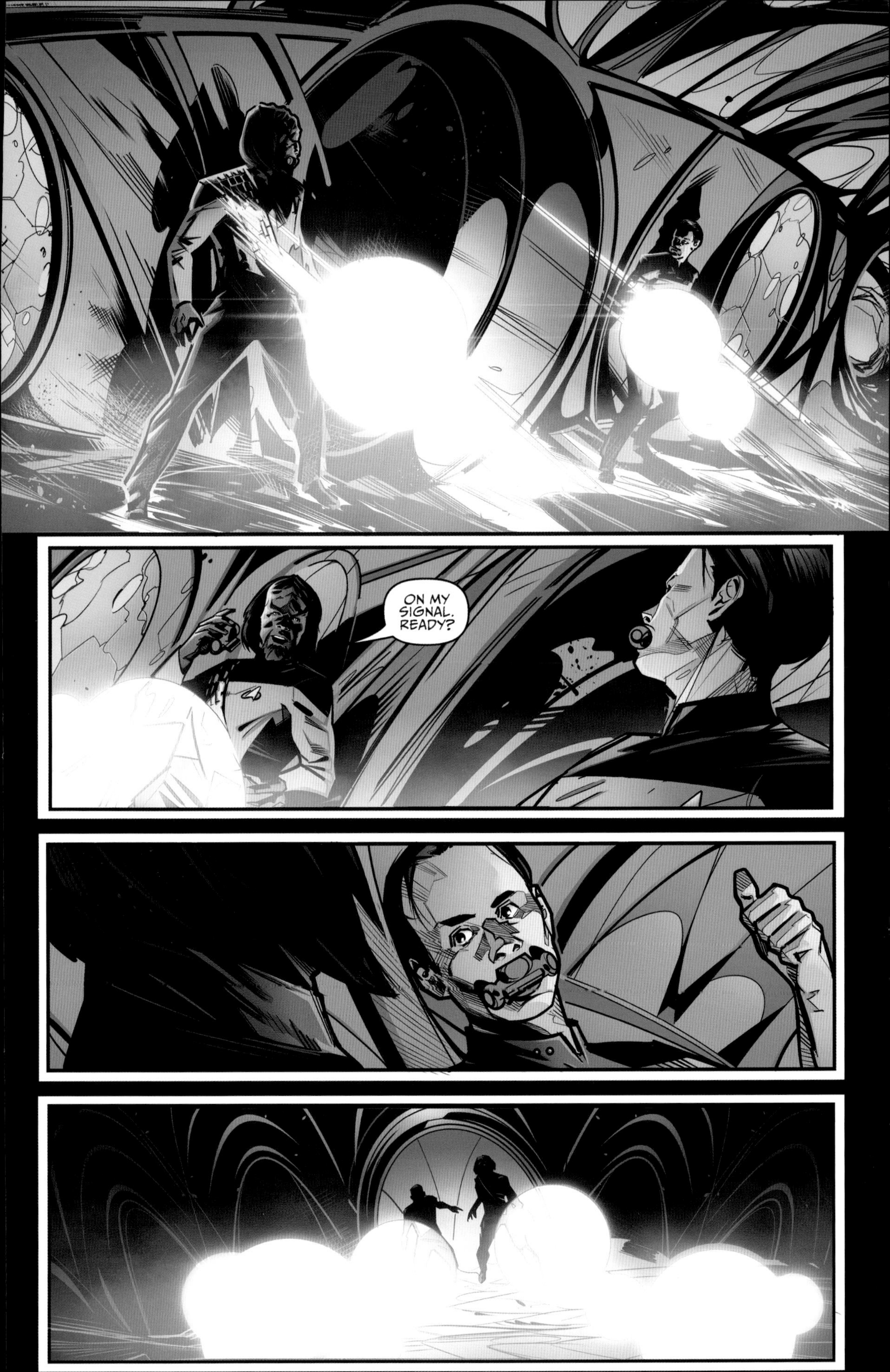

ON MY SIGNAL. READY?

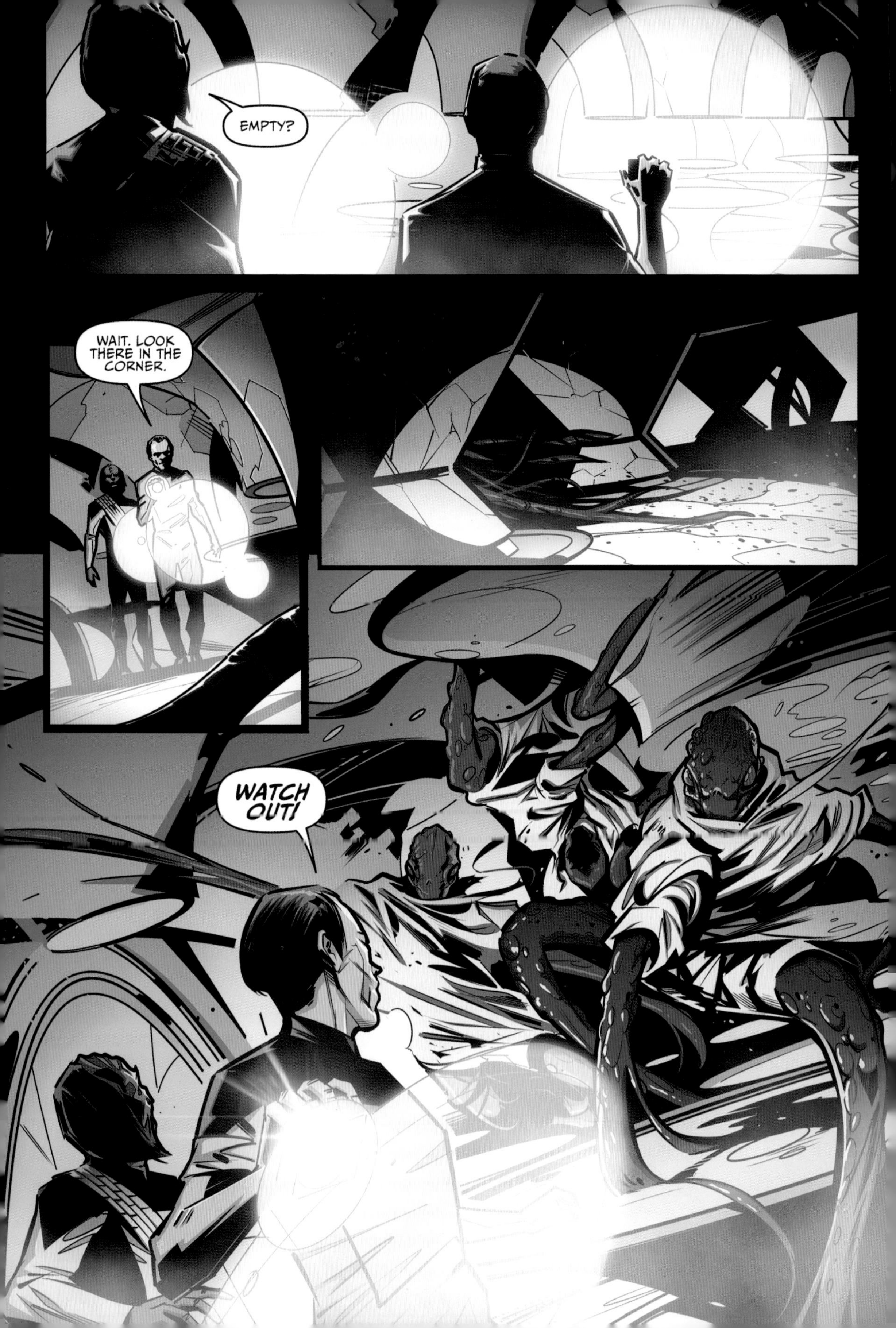
EMPTY?
WAIT. LOOK THERE IN THE CORNER.
WATCH OUT!

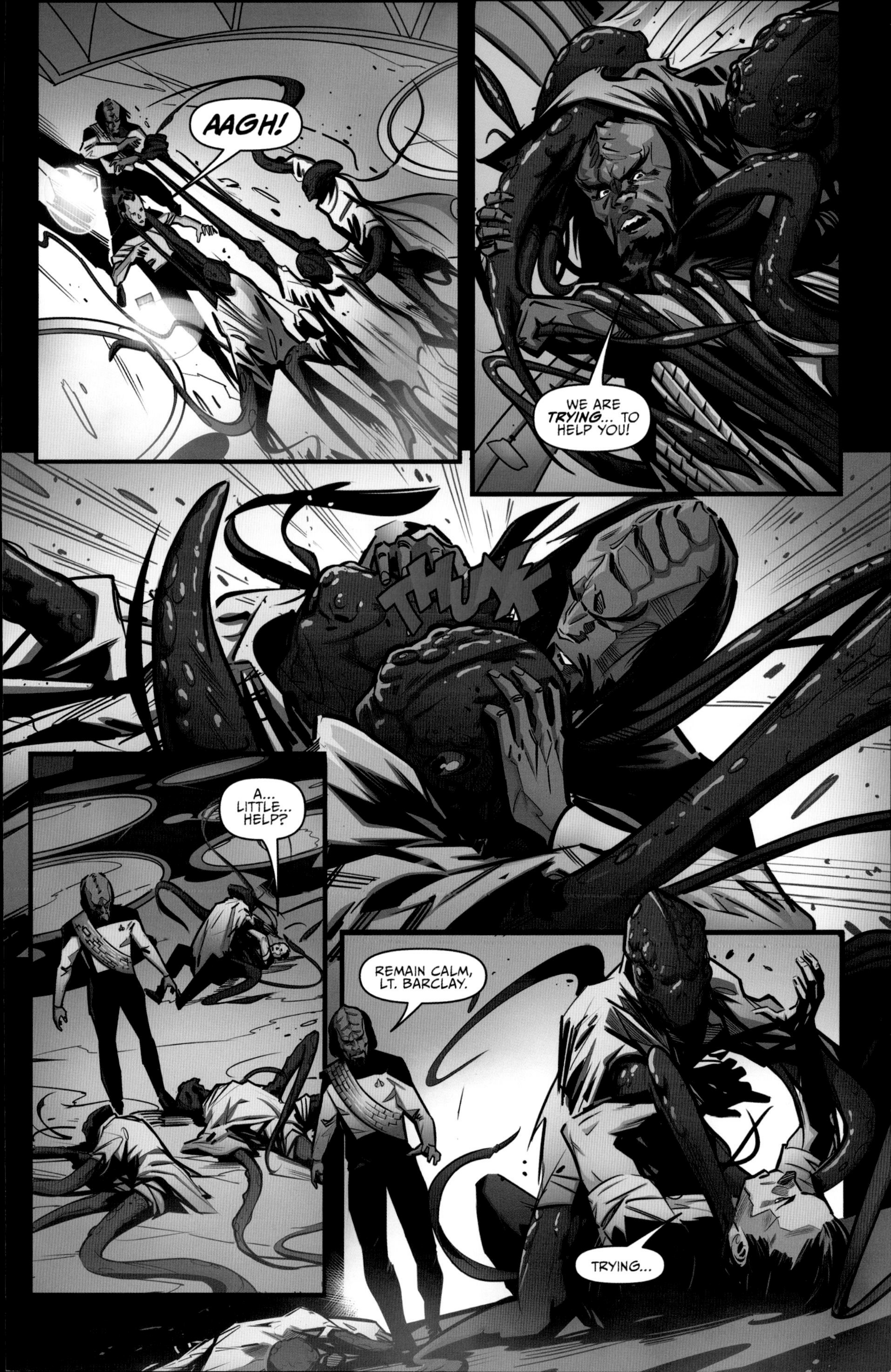
AAGH!
WE ARE TRYING... TO HELP YOU!
THUK
A... LITTLE... HELP?
REMAIN CALM, LT. BARCLAY.
TRYING...

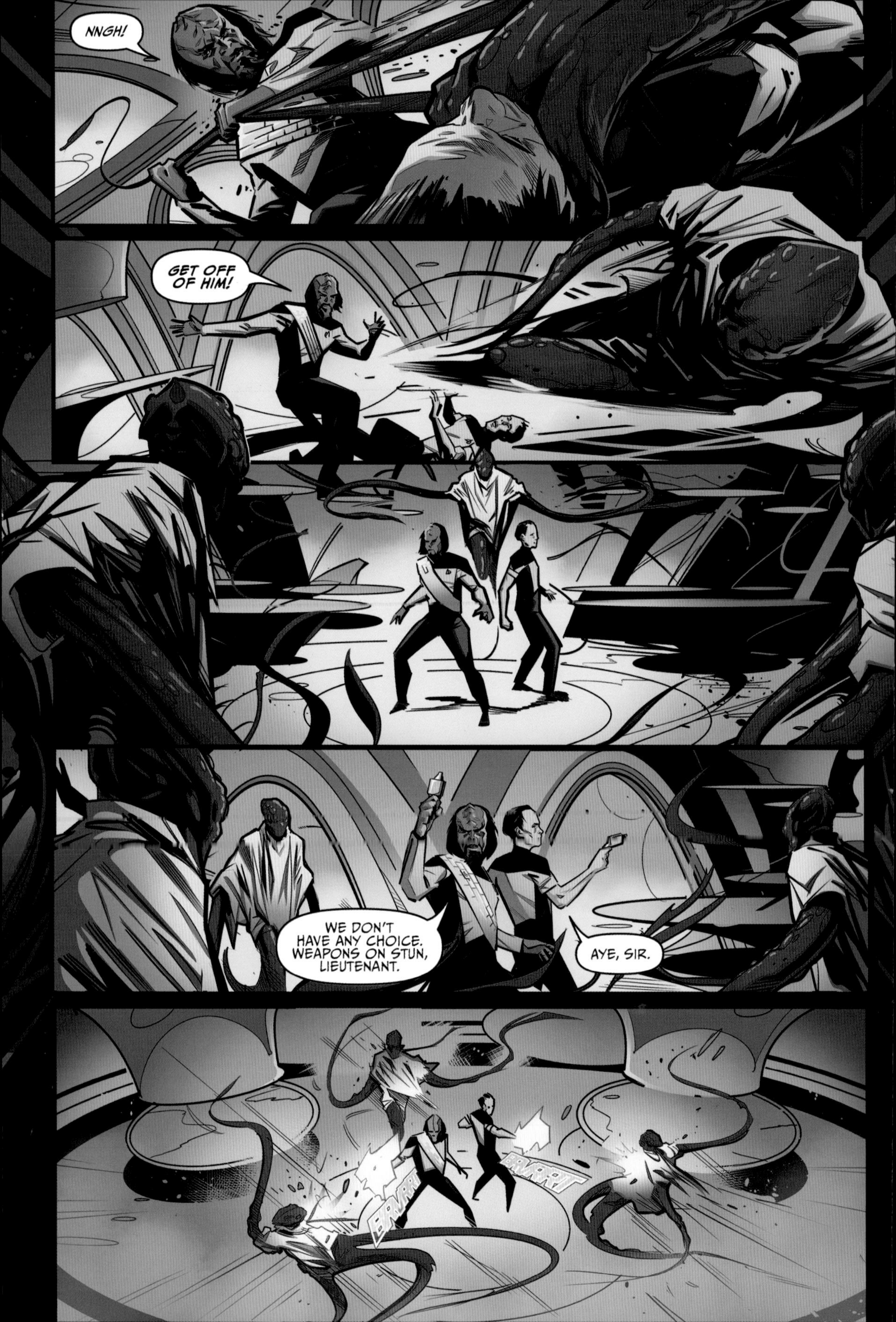
NNGH!
GET OFF OF HIM!
WE DON'T HAVE ANY CHOICE. WEAPONS ON STUN, LIEUTENANT.
AYE, SIR.
BRVRRT
BRVRRRT

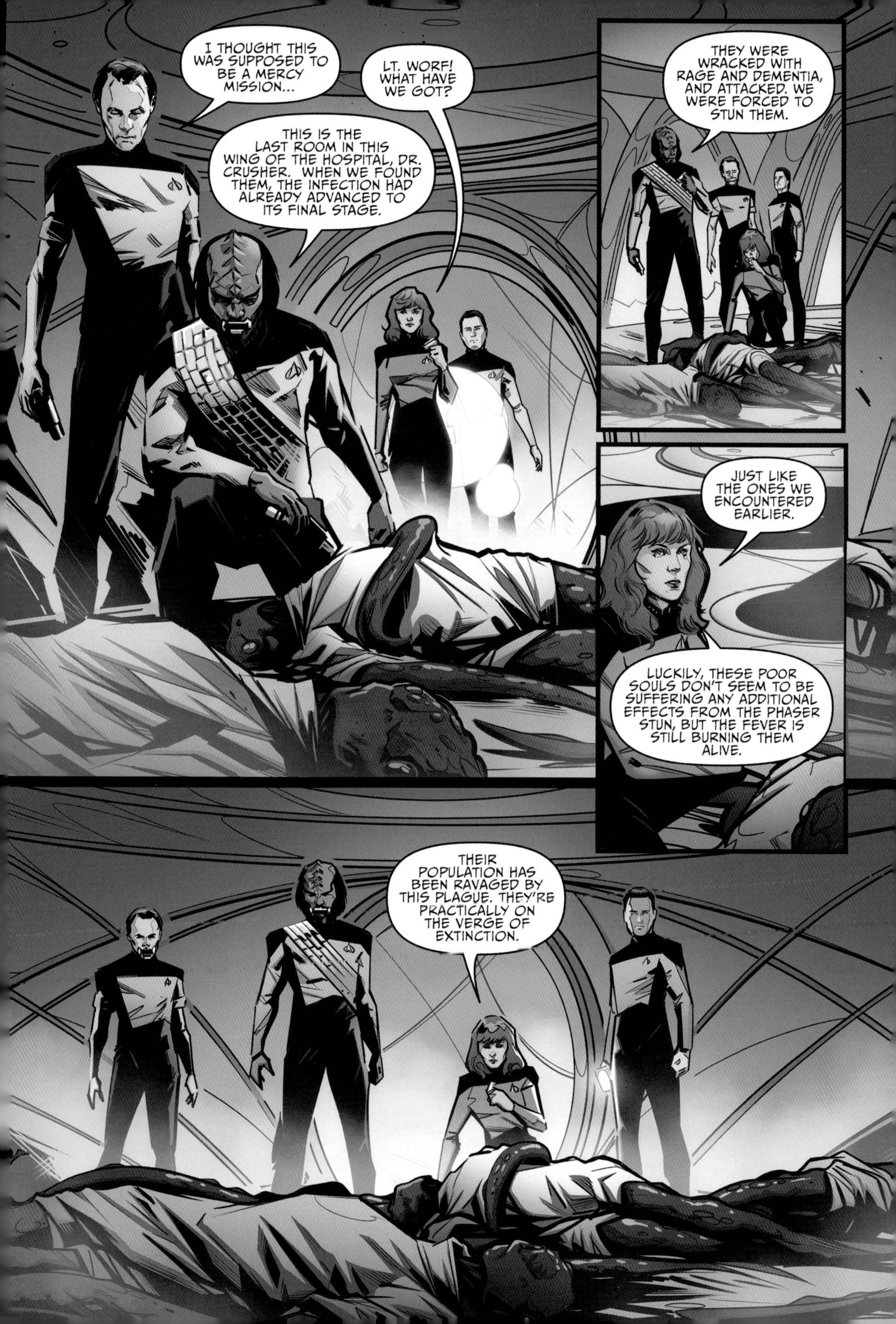
I THOUGHT THIS WAS SUPPOSED TO BE A MERCY MISSION...
LT. WORF! WHAT HAVE WE GOT?
THIS IS THE LAST ROOM IN THIS WING OF THE HOSPITAL, DR. CRUSHER. WHEN WE FOUND THEM, THE INFECTION HAD ALREADY ADVANCED TO ITS FINAL STAGE.
THEY WERE WRACKED WITH RAGE AND DEMENTIA, AND ATTACKED. WE WERE FORCED TO STUN THEM.
JUST LIKE THE ONES WE ENCOUNTERED EARLIER.
LUCKILY, THESE POOR SOULS DON'T SEEM TO BE SUFFERING ANY ADDITIONAL EFFECTS FROM THE PHASER STUN, BUT THE FEVER IS STILL BURNING THEM ALIVE.
THEIR POPULATION HAS BEEN RAVAGED BY THIS PLAGUE. THEY'RE PRACTICALLY ON THE VERGE OF EXTINCTION.

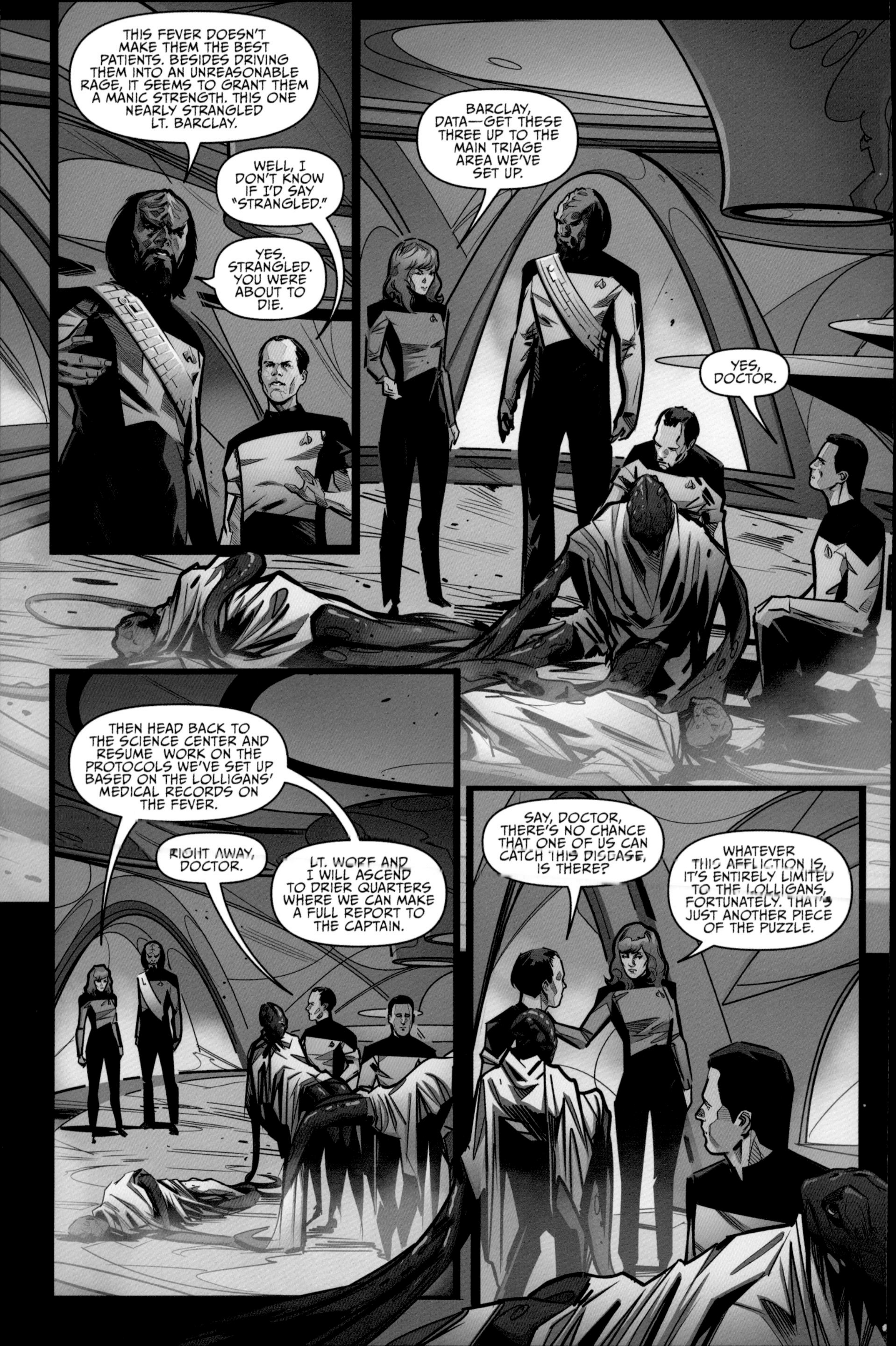
THIS FEVER DOESN'T MAKE THEM THE BEST PATIENTS. BESIDES DRIVING THEM INTO AN UNREASONABLE RAGE, IT SEEMS TO GRANT THEM A MANIC STRENGTH. THIS ONE NEARLY STRANGLED LT. BARCLAY.
WELL, I DON'T KNOW IF I'D SAY "STRANGLED."
YES. STRANGLED. YOU WERE ABOUT TO DIE.
BARCLAY, DATA—GET THESE THREE UP TO THE MAIN TRIAGE AREA WE'VE SET UP.
YES, DOCTOR.
THEN HEAD BACK TO THE SCIENCE CENTER AND RESUME WORK ON THE PROTOCOLS WE'VE SET UP BASED ON THE LOLLIGANS' MEDICAL RECORDS ON THE FEVER.
RIGHT AWAY, DOCTOR.
LT. WORF AND I WILL ASCEND TO DRIER QUARTERS WHERE WE CAN MAKE A FULL REPORT TO THE CAPTAIN.
SAY, DOCTOR, THERE'S NO CHANCE THAT ONE OF US CAN CATCH THIS DISEASE, IS THERE?
WHATEVER THIS AFFLICTION IS, IT'S ENTIRELY LIMITED TO THE LOLLIGANS, FORTUNATELY. THAT'S JUST ANOTHER PIECE OF THE PUZZLE.

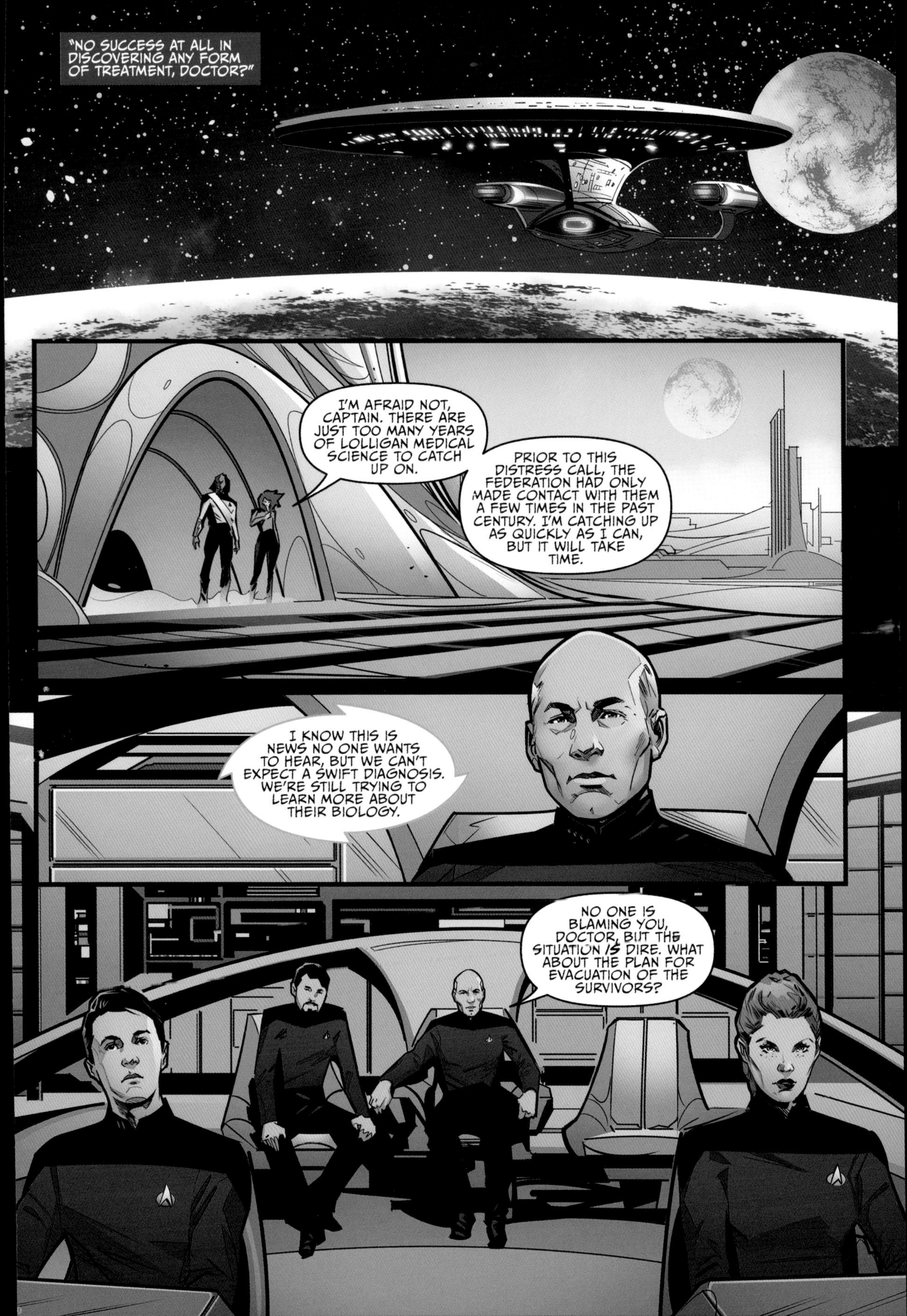
"NO SUCCESS AT ALL IN DISCOVERING ANY FORM OF TREATMENT, DOCTOR?"
I'M AFRAID NOT, CAPTAIN. THERE ARE JUST TOO MANY YEARS OF LOLLIGAN MEDICAL SCIENCE TO CATCH UP ON.
PRIOR TO THIS DISTRESS CALL, THE FEDERATION HAD ONLY MADE CONTACT WITH THEM A FEW TIMES IN THE PAST CENTURY. I'M CATCHING UP AS QUICKLY AS I CAN, BUT IT WILL TAKE TIME.
I KNOW THIS IS NEWS NO ONE WANTS TO HEAR, BUT WE CAN'T EXPECT A SWIFT DIAGNOSIS. WE'RE STILL TRYING TO LEARN MORE ABOUT THEIR BIOLOGY.
NO ONE IS BLAMING YOU, DOCTOR, BUT THE SITUATION *IS* DIRE. WHAT ABOUT THE PLAN FOR EVACUATION OF THE SURVIVORS?

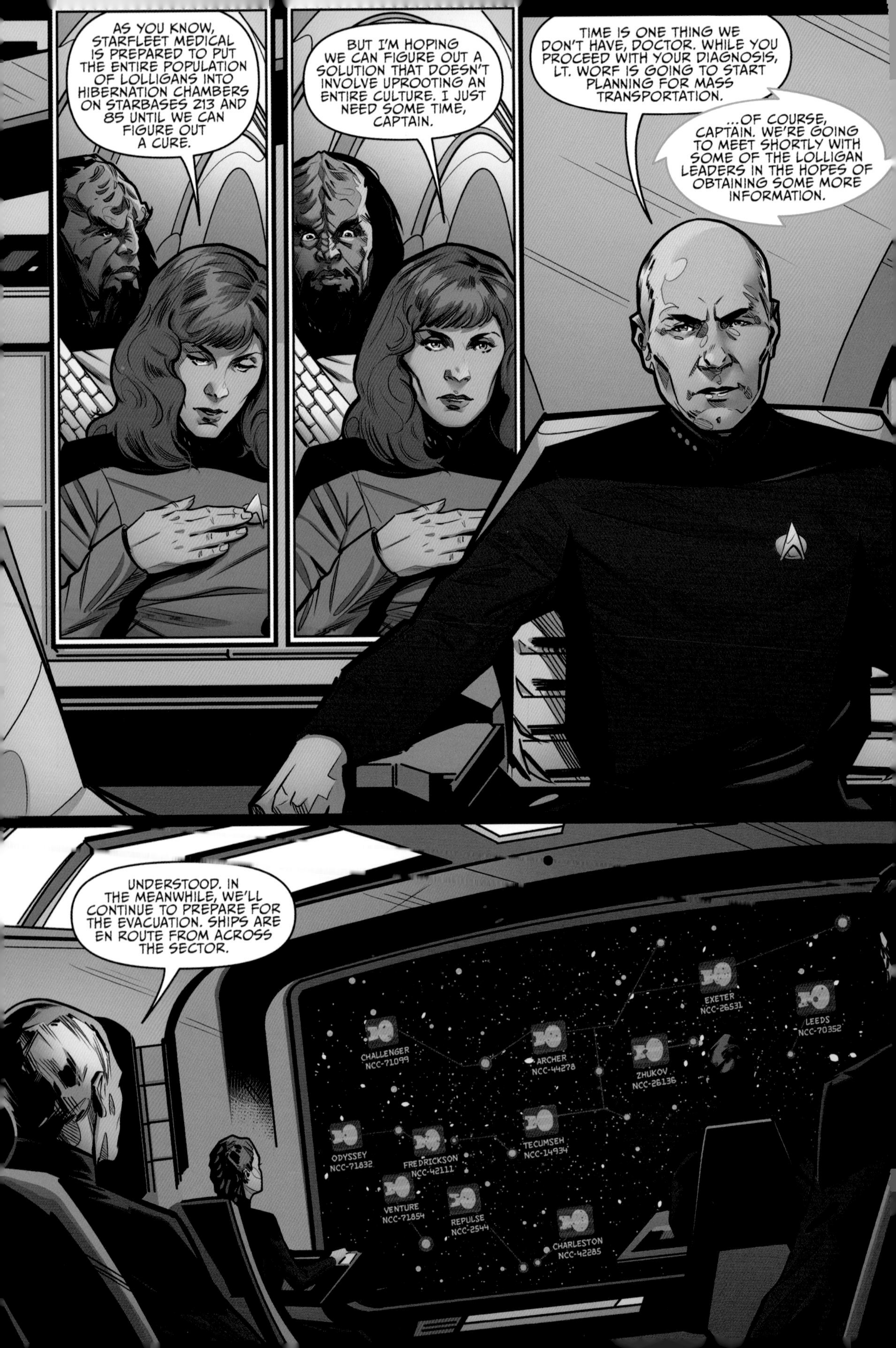
AS YOU KNOW, STARFLEET MEDICAL IS PREPARED TO PUT THE ENTIRE POPULATION OF LOLLIGANS INTO HIBERNATION CHAMBERS ON STARBASES 213 AND 85 UNTIL WE CAN FIGURE OUT A CURE.
BUT I'M HOPING WE CAN FIGURE OUT A SOLUTION THAT DOESN'T INVOLVE UPROOTING AN ENTIRE CULTURE. I JUST NEED SOME TIME, CAPTAIN.
TIME IS ONE THING WE DON'T HAVE, DOCTOR. WHILE YOU PROCEED WITH YOUR DIAGNOSIS, LT. WORF IS GOING TO START PLANNING FOR MASS TRANSPORTATION.
...OF COURSE, CAPTAIN. WE'RE GOING TO MEET SHORTLY WITH SOME OF THE LOLLIGAN LEADERS IN THE HOPES OF OBTAINING SOME MORE INFORMATION.
UNDERSTOOD. IN THE MEANWHILE, WE'LL CONTINUE TO PREPARE FOR THE EVACUATION. SHIPS ARE EN ROUTE FROM ACROSS THE SECTOR.
EXETER NCC-26531
LEEDS NCC-70352
CHALLENGER NCC-71099
ARCHER NCC-44278
ZHUKOV NCC-26136
ODYSSEY NCC-71832
FREDRICKSON NCC-42111
TECUMSEH NCC-14934
VENTURE NCC-71854
REPULSE NCC-2544
CHARLESTON NCC-42285

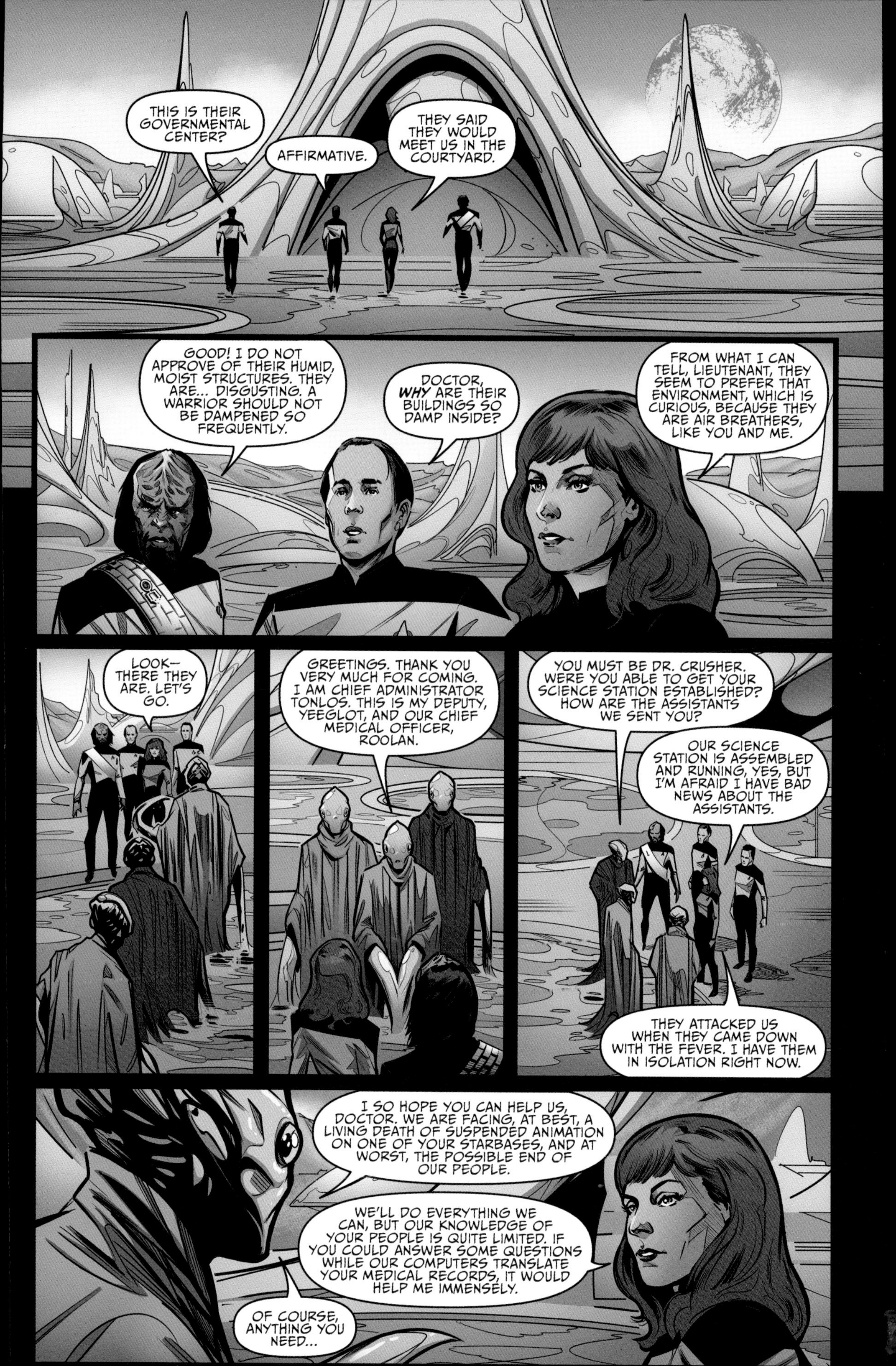
THIS IS THEIR GOVERNMENTAL CENTER?
AFFIRMATIVE.
THEY SAID THEY WOULD MEET US IN THE COURTYARD.
GOOD! I DO NOT APPROVE OF THEIR HUMID, MOIST STRUCTURES. THEY ARE... DISGUSTING. A WARRIOR SHOULD NOT BE DAMPENED SO FREQUENTLY.
DOCTOR, WHY ARE THEIR BUILDINGS SO DAMP INSIDE?
FROM WHAT I CAN TELL, LIEUTENANT, THEY SEEM TO PREFER THAT ENVIRONMENT, WHICH IS CURIOUS, BECAUSE THEY ARE AIR BREATHERS, LIKE YOU AND ME.
LOOK— THERE THEY ARE. LET'S GO.
GREETINGS. THANK YOU VERY MUCH FOR COMING. I AM CHIEF ADMINISTRATOR TONLOS. THIS IS MY DEPUTY, YEEGLOT, AND OUR CHIEF MEDICAL OFFICER, ROOLAN.
YOU MUST BE DR. CRUSHER. WERE YOU ABLE TO GET YOUR SCIENCE STATION ESTABLISHED? HOW ARE THE ASSISTANTS WE SENT YOU?
OUR SCIENCE STATION IS ASSEMBLED AND RUNNING, YES, BUT I'M AFRAID I HAVE BAD NEWS ABOUT THE ASSISTANTS.
THEY ATTACKED US WHEN THEY CAME DOWN WITH THE FEVER. I HAVE THEM IN ISOLATION RIGHT NOW.
I SO HOPE YOU CAN HELP US, DOCTOR. WE ARE FACING, AT BEST, A LIVING DEATH OF SUSPENDED ANIMATION ON ONE OF YOUR STARBASES, AND AT WORST, THE POSSIBLE END OF OUR PEOPLE.
WE'LL DO EVERYTHING WE CAN, BUT OUR KNOWLEDGE OF YOUR PEOPLE IS QUITE LIMITED. IF YOU COULD ANSWER SOME QUESTIONS WHILE OUR COMPUTERS TRANSLATE YOUR MEDICAL RECORDS, IT WOULD HELP ME IMMENSELY.
OF COURSE, ANYTHING YOU NEED...

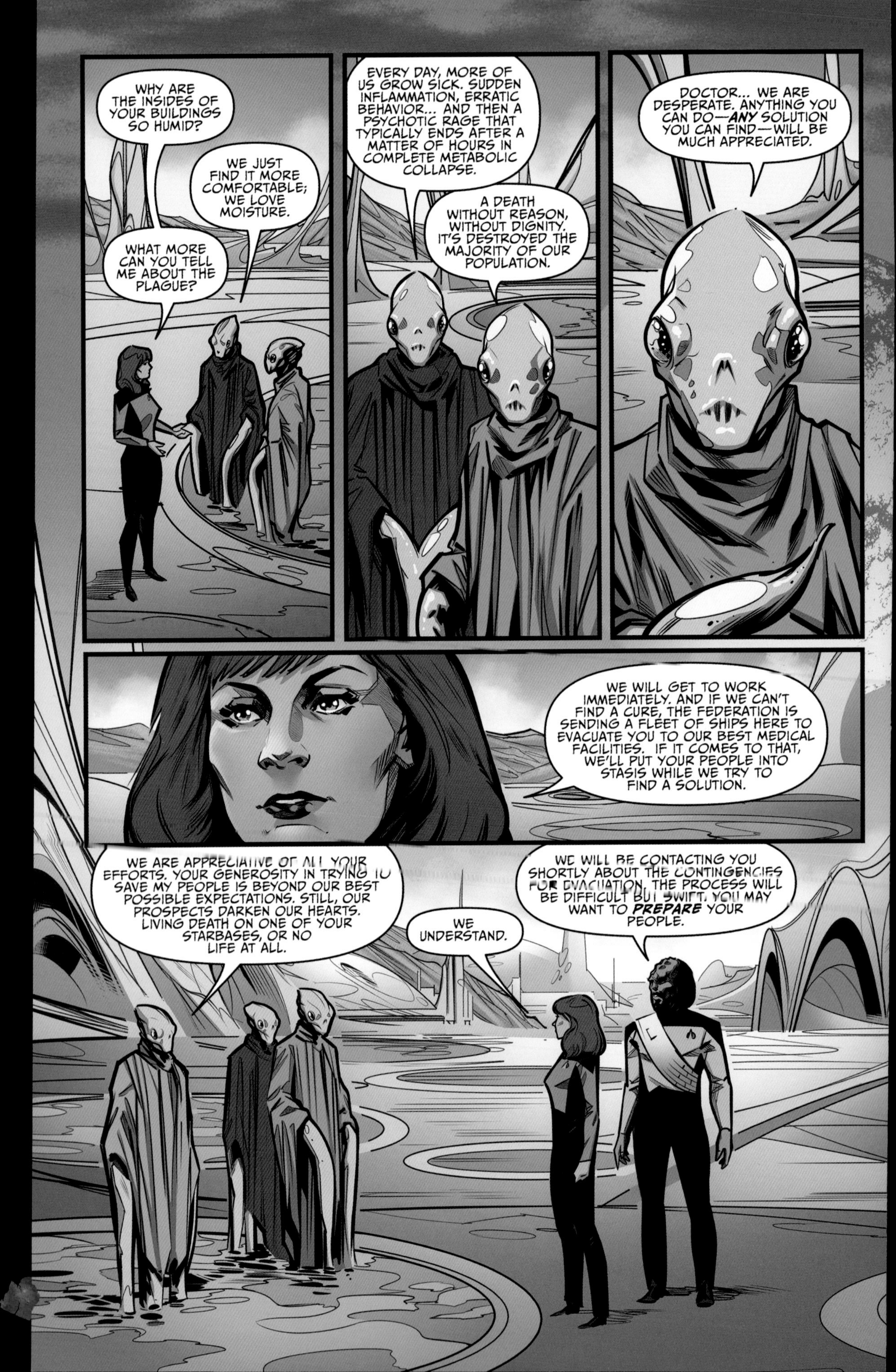
WHY ARE THE INSIDES OF YOUR BUILDINGS SO HUMID?
WE JUST FIND IT MORE COMFORTABLE; WE LOVE MOISTURE.
WHAT MORE CAN YOU TELL ME ABOUT THE PLAGUE?
EVERY DAY, MORE OF US GROW SICK. SUDDEN INFLAMMATION, ERRATIC BEHAVIOR... AND THEN A PSYCHOTIC RAGE THAT TYPICALLY ENDS AFTER A MATTER OF HOURS IN COMPLETE METABOLIC COLLAPSE.
A DEATH WITHOUT REASON, WITHOUT DIGNITY. IT'S DESTROYED THE MAJORITY OF OUR POPULATION.
DOCTOR... WE ARE DESPERATE. ANYTHING YOU CAN DO—*ANY* SOLUTION YOU CAN FIND—WILL BE MUCH APPRECIATED.
WE WILL GET TO WORK IMMEDIATELY. AND IF WE CAN'T FIND A CURE, THE FEDERATION IS SENDING A FLEET OF SHIPS HERE TO EVACUATE YOU TO OUR BEST MEDICAL FACILITIES. IF IT COMES TO THAT, WE'LL PUT YOUR PEOPLE INTO STASIS WHILE WE TRY TO FIND A SOLUTION.
WE ARE APPRECIATIVE OF ALL YOUR EFFORTS. YOUR GENEROSITY IN TRYING TO SAVE MY PEOPLE IS BEYOND OUR BEST POSSIBLE EXPECTATIONS. STILL, OUR PROSPECTS DARKEN OUR HEARTS. LIVING DEATH ON ONE OF YOUR STARBASES, OR NO LIFE AT ALL.
WE UNDERSTAND.
WE WILL BE CONTACTING YOU SHORTLY ABOUT THE CONTINGENCIES FOR EVACUATION. THE PROCESS WILL BE DIFFICULT BUT SWIFT. YOU MAY WANT TO *PREPARE* YOUR PEOPLE.

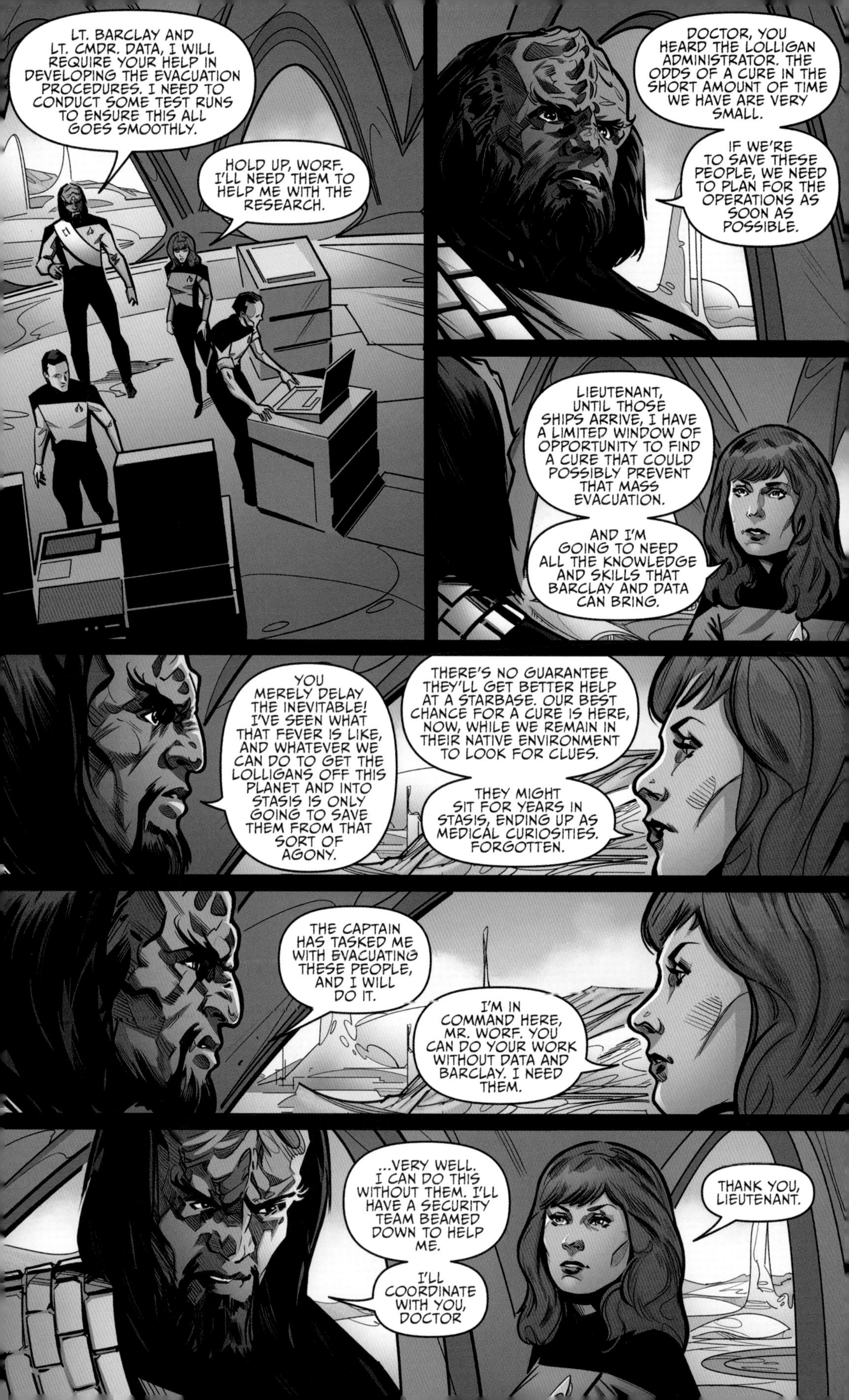
LT. BARCLAY AND LT. CMDR. DATA, I WILL REQUIRE YOUR HELP IN DEVELOPING THE EVACUATION PROCEDURES. I NEED TO CONDUCT SOME TEST RUNS TO ENSURE THIS ALL GOES SMOOTHLY.
HOLD UP, WORF. I'LL NEED THEM TO HELP ME WITH THE RESEARCH.
DOCTOR, YOU HEARD THE LOLLIGAN ADMINISTRATOR. THE ODDS OF A CURE IN THE SHORT AMOUNT OF TIME WE HAVE ARE VERY SMALL.
IF WE'RE TO SAVE THESE PEOPLE, WE NEED TO PLAN FOR THE OPERATIONS AS SOON AS POSSIBLE.
LIEUTENANT, UNTIL THOSE SHIPS ARRIVE, I HAVE A LIMITED WINDOW OF OPPORTUNITY TO FIND A CURE THAT COULD POSSIBLY PREVENT THAT MASS EVACUATION.
AND I'M GOING TO NEED ALL THE KNOWLEDGE AND SKILLS THAT BARCLAY AND DATA CAN BRING.
YOU MERELY DELAY THE INEVITABLE! I'VE SEEN WHAT THAT FEVER IS LIKE, AND WHATEVER WE CAN DO TO GET THE LOLLIGANS OFF THIS PLANET AND INTO STASIS IS ONLY GOING TO SAVE THEM FROM THAT SORT OF AGONY.
THERE'S NO GUARANTEE THEY'LL GET BETTER HELP AT A STARBASE. OUR BEST CHANCE FOR A CURE IS HERE, NOW, WHILE WE REMAIN IN THEIR NATIVE ENVIRONMENT TO LOOK FOR CLUES.
THEY MIGHT SIT FOR YEARS IN STASIS, ENDING UP AS MEDICAL CURIOSITIES. FORGOTTEN.
THE CAPTAIN HAS TASKED ME WITH EVACUATING THESE PEOPLE, AND I WILL DO IT.
I'M IN COMMAND HERE, MR. WORF. YOU CAN DO YOUR WORK WITHOUT DATA AND BARCLAY. I NEED THEM.
...VERY WELL. I CAN DO THIS WITHOUT THEM. I'LL HAVE A SECURITY TEAM BEAMED DOWN TO HELP ME.
I'LL COORDINATE WITH YOU, DOCTOR
THANK YOU, LIEUTENANT.

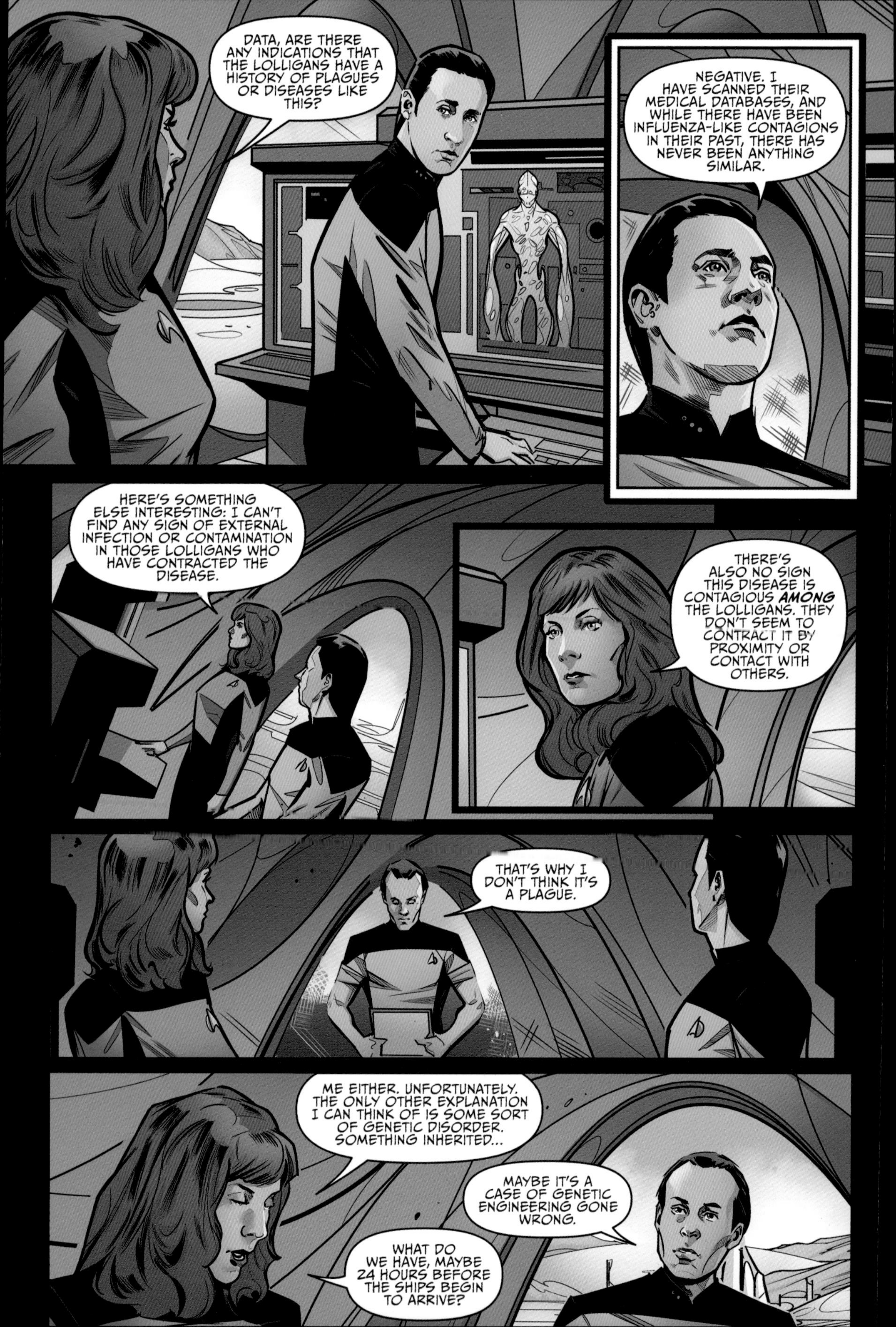
DATA, ARE THERE ANY INDICATIONS THAT THE LOLLIGANS HAVE A HISTORY OF PLAGUES OR DISEASES LIKE THIS?
NEGATIVE. I HAVE SCANNED THEIR MEDICAL DATABASES, AND WHILE THERE HAVE BEEN INFLUENZA-LIKE CONTAGIONS IN THEIR PAST, THERE HAS NEVER BEEN ANYTHING SIMILAR.
HERE'S SOMETHING ELSE INTERESTING: I CAN'T FIND ANY SIGN OF EXTERNAL INFECTION OR CONTAMINATION IN THOSE LOLLIGANS WHO HAVE CONTRACTED THE DISEASE.
THERE'S ALSO NO SIGN THIS DISEASE IS CONTAGIOUS ***AMONG*** THE LOLLIGANS. THEY DON'T SEEM TO CONTRACT IT BY PROXIMITY OR CONTACT WITH OTHERS.
THAT'S WHY I DON'T THINK IT'S A PLAGUE.
ME EITHER. UNFORTUNATELY. THE ONLY OTHER EXPLANATION I CAN THINK OF IS SOME SORT OF GENETIC DISORDER. SOMETHING INHERITED...
MAYBE IT'S A CASE OF GENETIC ENGINEERING GONE WRONG.
WHAT DO WE HAVE, MAYBE 24 HOURS BEFORE THE SHIPS BEGIN TO ARRIVE?

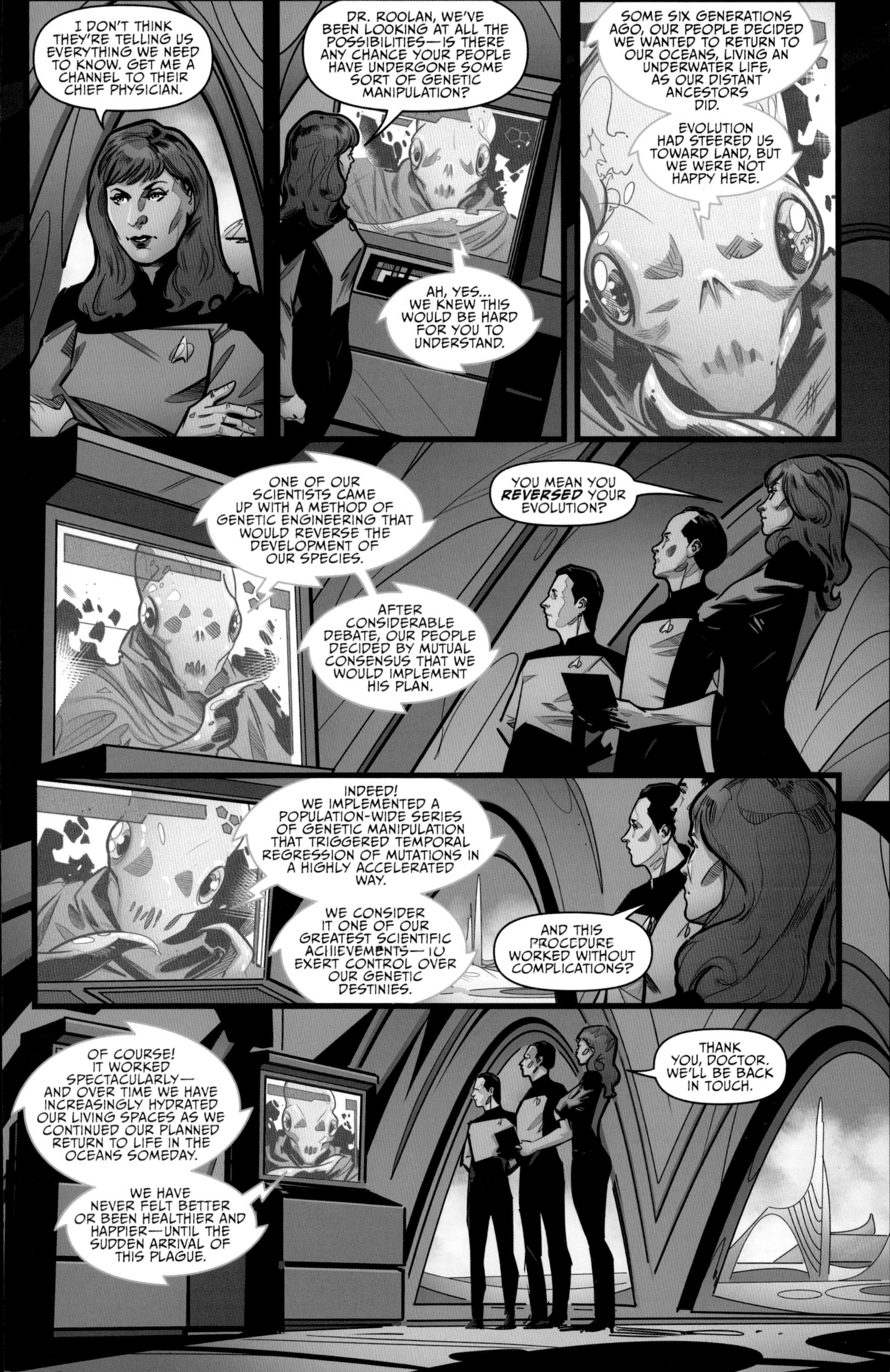
I DON'T THINK THEY'RE TELLING US EVERYTHING WE NEED TO KNOW. GET ME A CHANNEL TO THEIR CHIEF PHYSICIAN.
DR. ROOLAN, WE'VE BEEN LOOKING AT ALL THE POSSIBILITIES—IS THERE ANY CHANCE YOUR PEOPLE HAVE UNDERGONE SOME SORT OF GENETIC MANIPULATION?
AH, YES... WE KNEW THIS WOULD BE HARD FOR YOU TO UNDERSTAND.
SOME SIX GENERATIONS AGO, OUR PEOPLE DECIDED WE WANTED TO RETURN TO OUR OCEANS, LIVING AN UNDERWATER LIFE, AS OUR DISTANT ANCESTORS DID.
EVOLUTION HAD STEERED US TOWARD LAND, BUT WE WERE NOT HAPPY HERE.
ONE OF OUR SCIENTISTS CAME UP WITH A METHOD OF GENETIC ENGINEERING THAT WOULD REVERSE THE DEVELOPMENT OF OUR SPECIES.
AFTER CONSIDERABLE DEBATE, OUR PEOPLE DECIDED BY MUTUAL CONSENSUS THAT WE WOULD IMPLEMENT HIS PLAN.
YOU MEAN YOU ***REVERSED*** YOUR EVOLUTION?
INDEED! WE IMPLEMENTED A POPULATION-WIDE SERIES OF GENETIC MANIPULATION THAT TRIGGERED TEMPORAL REGRESSION OF MUTATIONS IN A HIGHLY ACCELERATED WAY.
WE CONSIDER IT ONE OF OUR GREATEST SCIENTIFIC ACHIEVEMENTS—TO EXERT CONTROL OVER OUR GENETIC DESTINIES.
AND THIS PROCEDURE WORKED WITHOUT COMPLICATIONS?
OF COURSE! IT WORKED SPECTACULARLY—AND OVER TIME WE HAVE INCREASINGLY HYDRATED OUR LIVING SPACES AS WE CONTINUED OUR PLANNED RETURN TO LIFE IN THE OCEANS SOMEDAY.
WE HAVE NEVER FELT BETTER OR BEEN HEALTHIER AND HAPPIER—UNTIL THE SUDDEN ARRIVAL OF THIS PLAGUE.
THANK YOU, DOCTOR. WE'LL BE BACK IN TOUCH.

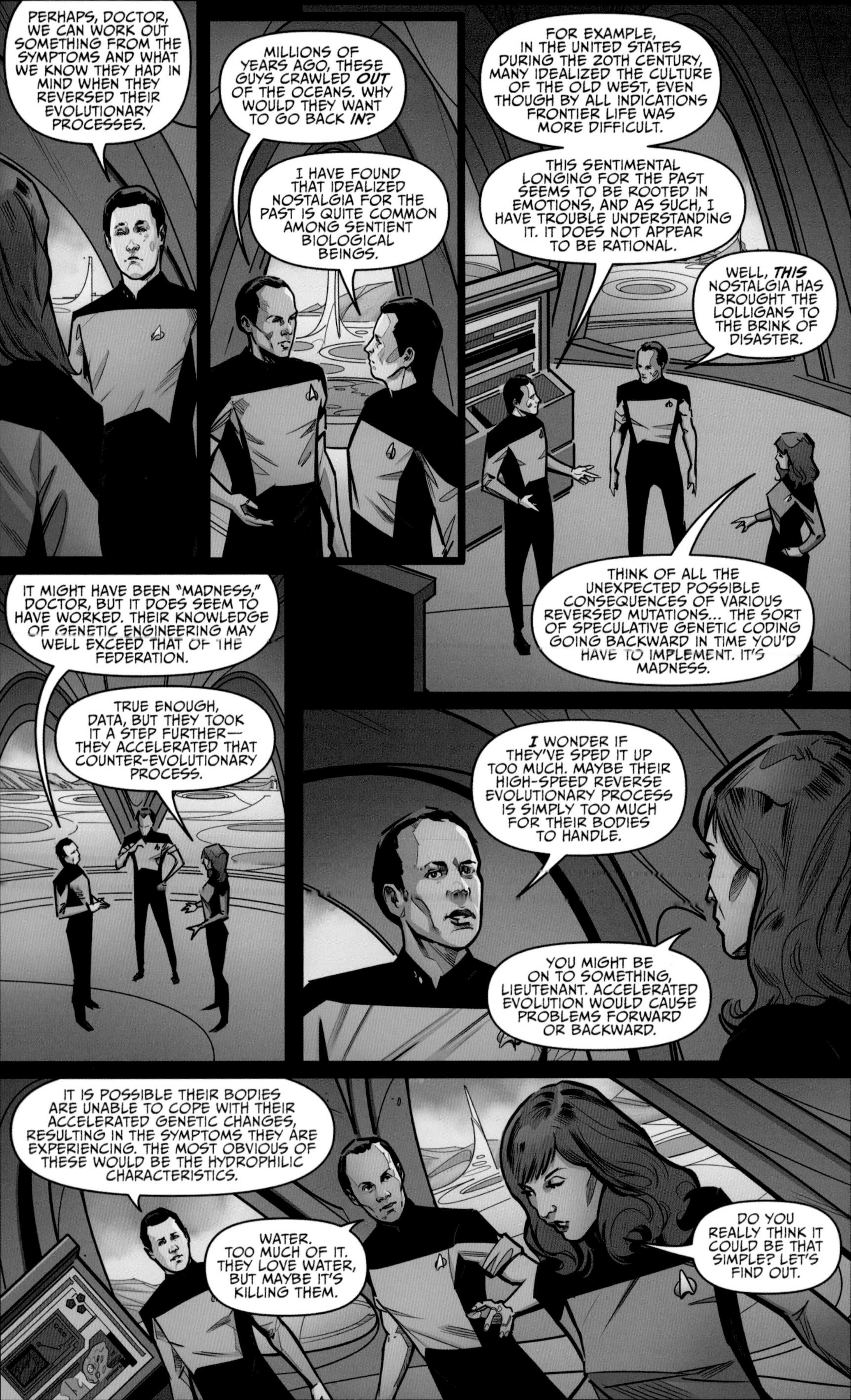
PERHAPS, DOCTOR, WE CAN WORK OUT SOMETHING FROM THE SYMPTOMS AND WHAT WE KNOW THEY HAD IN MIND WHEN THEY REVERSED THEIR EVOLUTIONARY PROCESSES.
MILLIONS OF YEARS AGO, THESE GUYS CRAWLED *OUT* OF THE OCEANS. WHY WOULD THEY WANT TO GO BACK *IN*?
I HAVE FOUND THAT IDEALIZED NOSTALGIA FOR THE PAST IS QUITE COMMON AMONG SENTIENT BIOLOGICAL BEINGS.
FOR EXAMPLE, IN THE UNITED STATES DURING THE 20TH CENTURY, MANY IDEALIZED THE CULTURE OF THE OLD WEST, EVEN THOUGH BY ALL INDICATIONS FRONTIER LIFE WAS MORE DIFFICULT.
THIS SENTIMENTAL LONGING FOR THE PAST SEEMS TO BE ROOTED IN EMOTIONS, AND AS SUCH, I HAVE TROUBLE UNDERSTANDING IT. IT DOES NOT APPEAR TO BE RATIONAL.
WELL, ***THIS*** NOSTALGIA HAS BROUGHT THE LOLLIGANS TO THE BRINK OF DISASTER.
THINK OF ALL THE UNEXPECTED POSSIBLE CONSEQUENCES OF VARIOUS REVERSED MUTATIONS... THE SORT OF SPECULATIVE GENETIC CODING GOING BACKWARD IN TIME YOU'D HAVE TO IMPLEMENT. IT'S MADNESS.
IT MIGHT HAVE BEEN "MADNESS," DOCTOR, BUT IT DOES SEEM TO HAVE WORKED. THEIR KNOWLEDGE OF GENETIC ENGINEERING MAY WELL EXCEED THAT OF THE FEDERATION.
TRUE ENOUGH, DATA, BUT THEY TOOK IT A STEP FURTHER— THEY ACCELERATED THAT COUNTER-EVOLUTIONARY PROCESS.
I WONDER IF THEY'VE SPED IT UP TOO MUCH. MAYBE THEIR HIGH-SPEED REVERSE EVOLUTIONARY PROCESS IS SIMPLY TOO MUCH FOR THEIR BODIES TO HANDLE.
YOU MIGHT BE ON TO SOMETHING, LIEUTENANT. ACCELERATED EVOLUTION WOULD CAUSE PROBLEMS FORWARD OR BACKWARD.
IT IS POSSIBLE THEIR BODIES ARE UNABLE TO COPE WITH THEIR ACCELERATED GENETIC CHANGES, RESULTING IN THE SYMPTOMS THEY ARE EXPERIENCING. THE MOST OBVIOUS OF THESE WOULD BE THE HYDROPHILIC CHARACTERISTICS.
WATER. TOO MUCH OF IT. THEY LOVE WATER, BUT MAYBE IT'S KILLING THEM.
DO YOU REALLY THINK IT COULD BE THAT SIMPLE? LET'S FIND OUT.

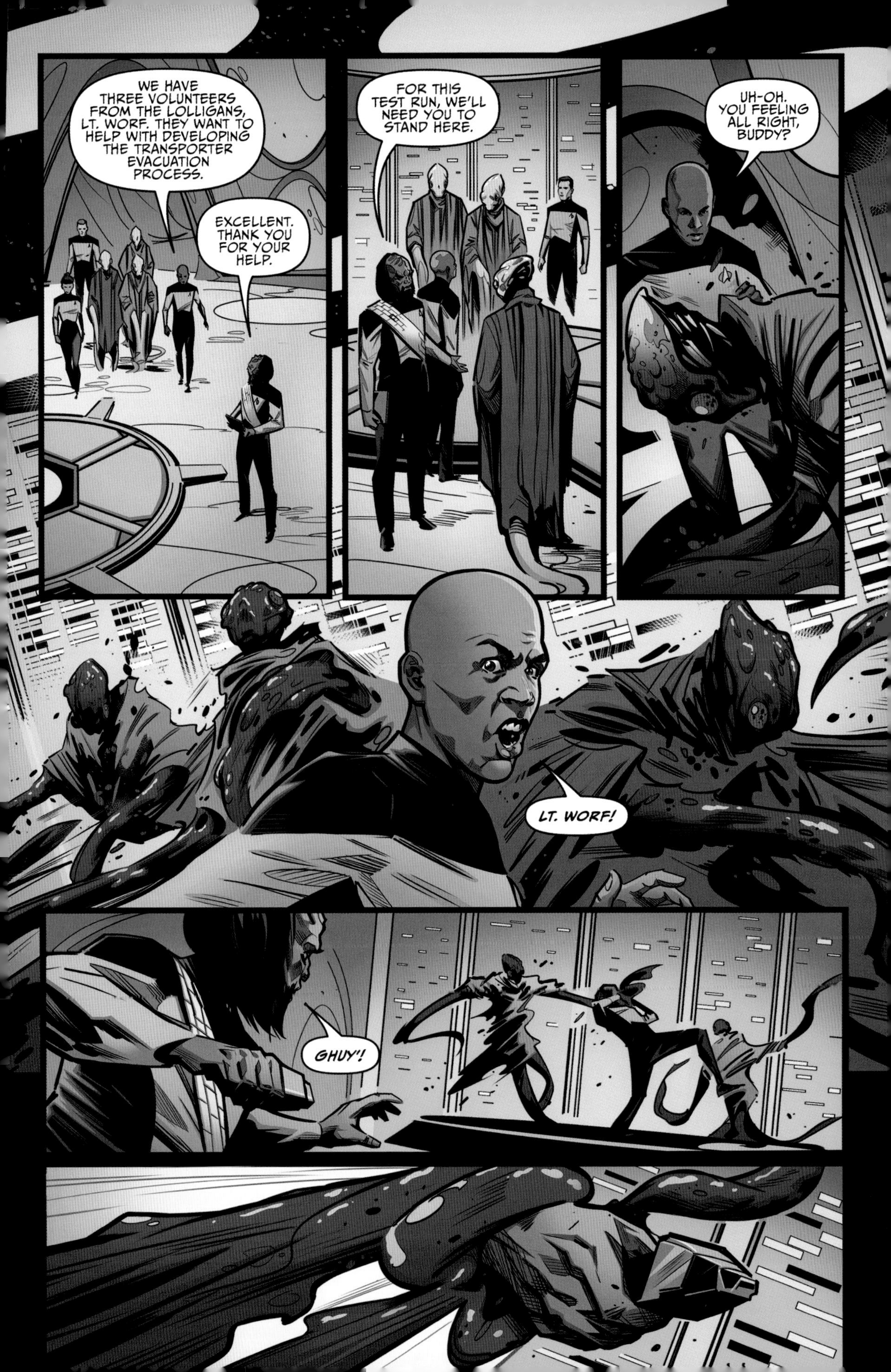
WE HAVE THREE VOLUNTEERS FROM THE LOLLIGANS, LT. WORF. THEY WANT TO HELP WITH DEVELOPING THE TRANSPORTER EVACUATION PROCESS.
EXCELLENT. THANK YOU FOR YOUR HELP.
FOR THIS TEST RUN, WE'LL NEED YOU TO STAND HERE.
UH-OH. YOU FEELING ALL RIGHT, BUDDY?
LT. WORF!
GHUY'!

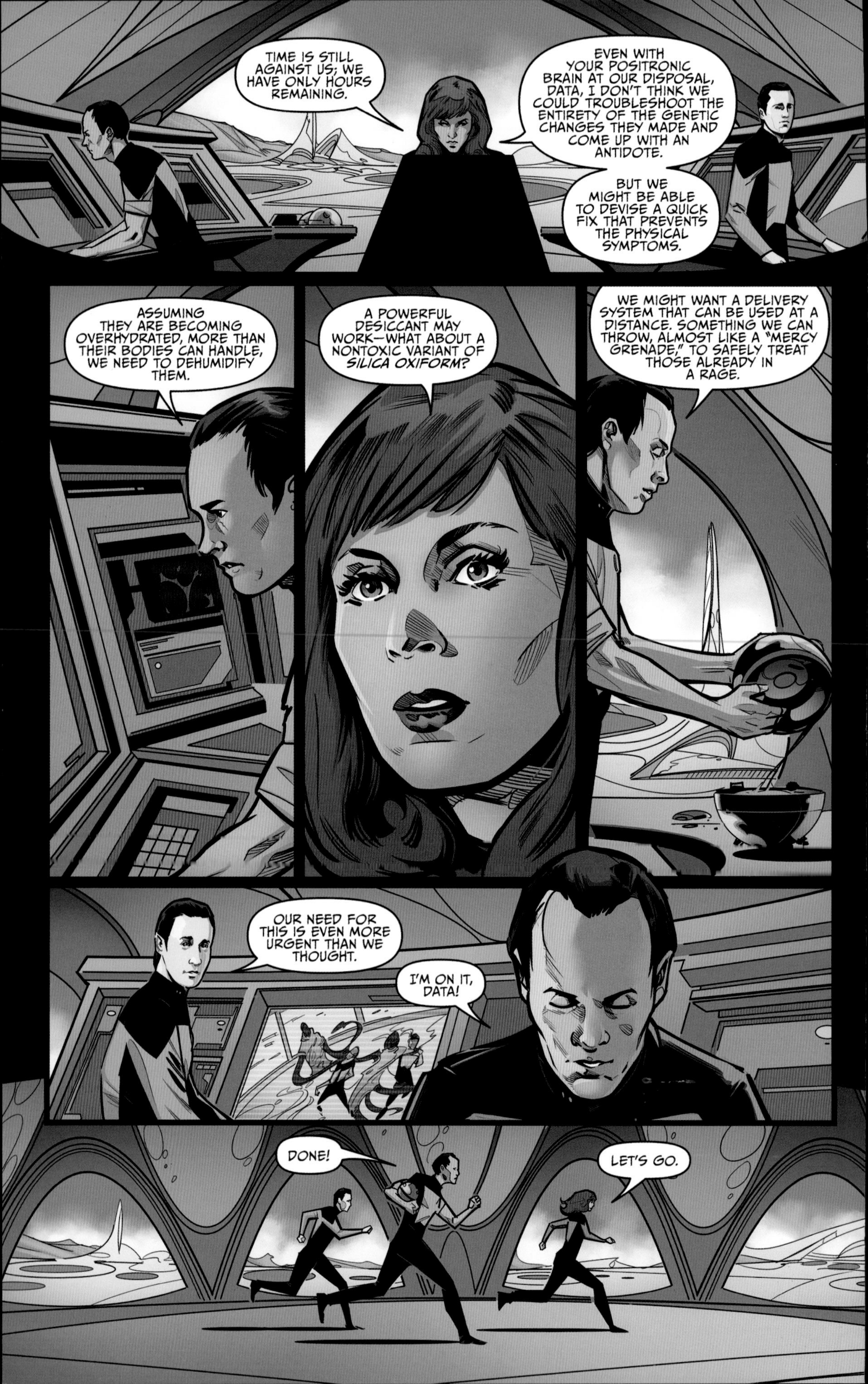
TIME IS STILL AGAINST US; WE HAVE ONLY HOURS REMAINING.
EVEN WITH YOUR POSITRONIC BRAIN AT OUR DISPOSAL, DATA, I DON'T THINK WE COULD TROUBLESHOOT THE ENTIRETY OF THE GENETIC CHANGES THEY MADE AND COME UP WITH AN ANTIDOTE.
BUT WE MIGHT BE ABLE TO DEVISE A QUICK FIX THAT PREVENTS THE PHYSICAL SYMPTOMS.
ASSUMING THEY ARE BECOMING OVERHYDRATED, MORE THAN THEIR BODIES CAN HANDLE, WE NEED TO DEHUMIDIFY THEM.
A POWERFUL DESICCANT MAY WORK—WHAT ABOUT A NONTOXIC VARIANT OF *SILICA OXIFORM*?
WE MIGHT WANT A DELIVERY SYSTEM THAT CAN BE USED AT A DISTANCE. SOMETHING WE CAN THROW, ALMOST LIKE A "MERCY GRENADE," TO SAFELY TREAT THOSE ALREADY IN A RAGE.
OUR NEED FOR THIS IS EVEN MORE URGENT THAN WE THOUGHT.
I'M ON IT, DATA!
DONE!
LET'S GO.

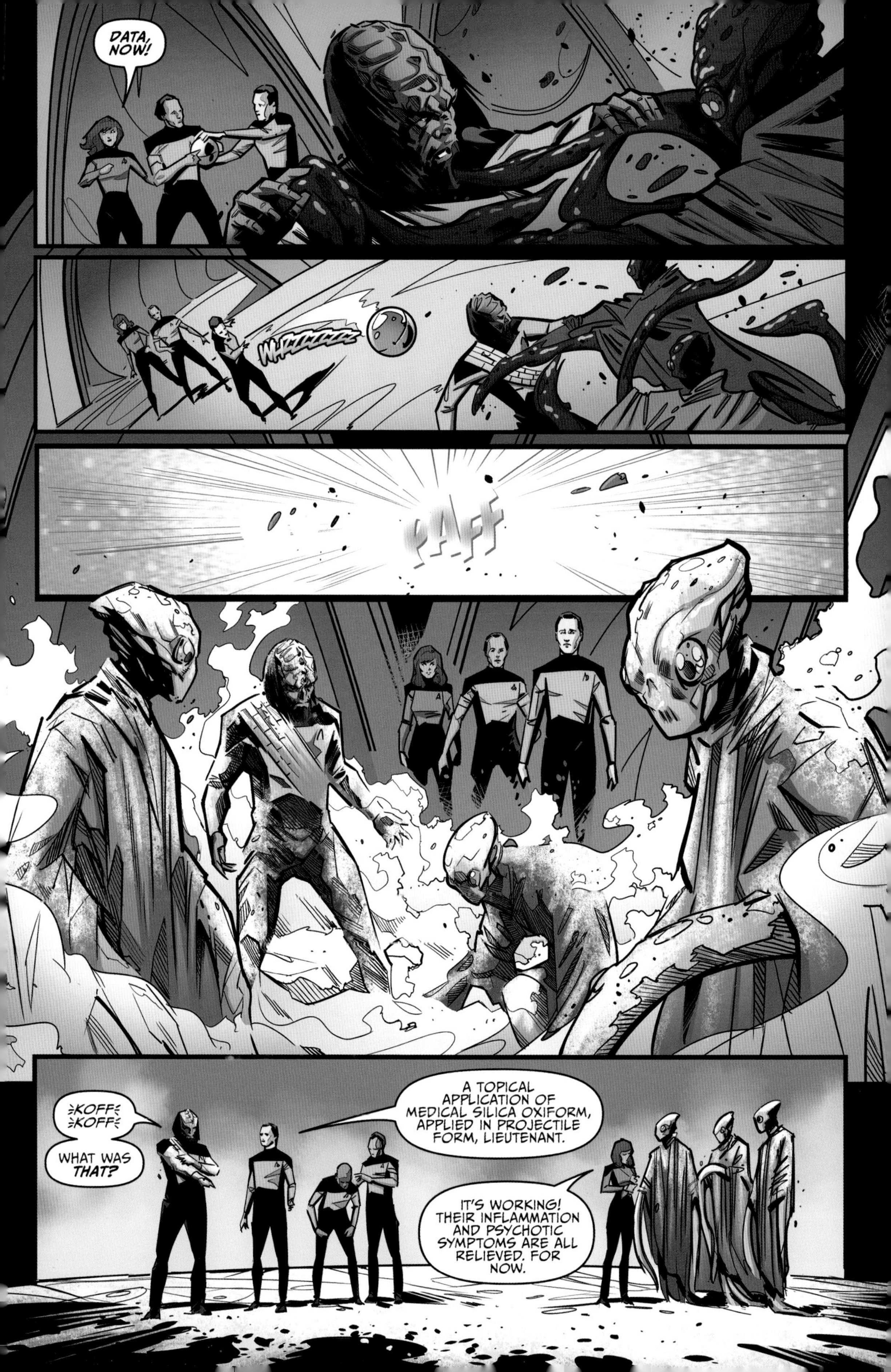
DATA, NOW!
WHZZZZZZ
PAFF
KOFF KOFF
WHAT WAS THAT?
A TOPICAL APPLICATION OF MEDICAL SILICA OXIFORM, APPLIED IN PROJECTILE FORM, LIEUTENANT.
IT'S WORKING! THEIR INFLAMMATION AND PSYCHOTIC SYMPTOMS ARE ALL RELIEVED. FOR NOW.

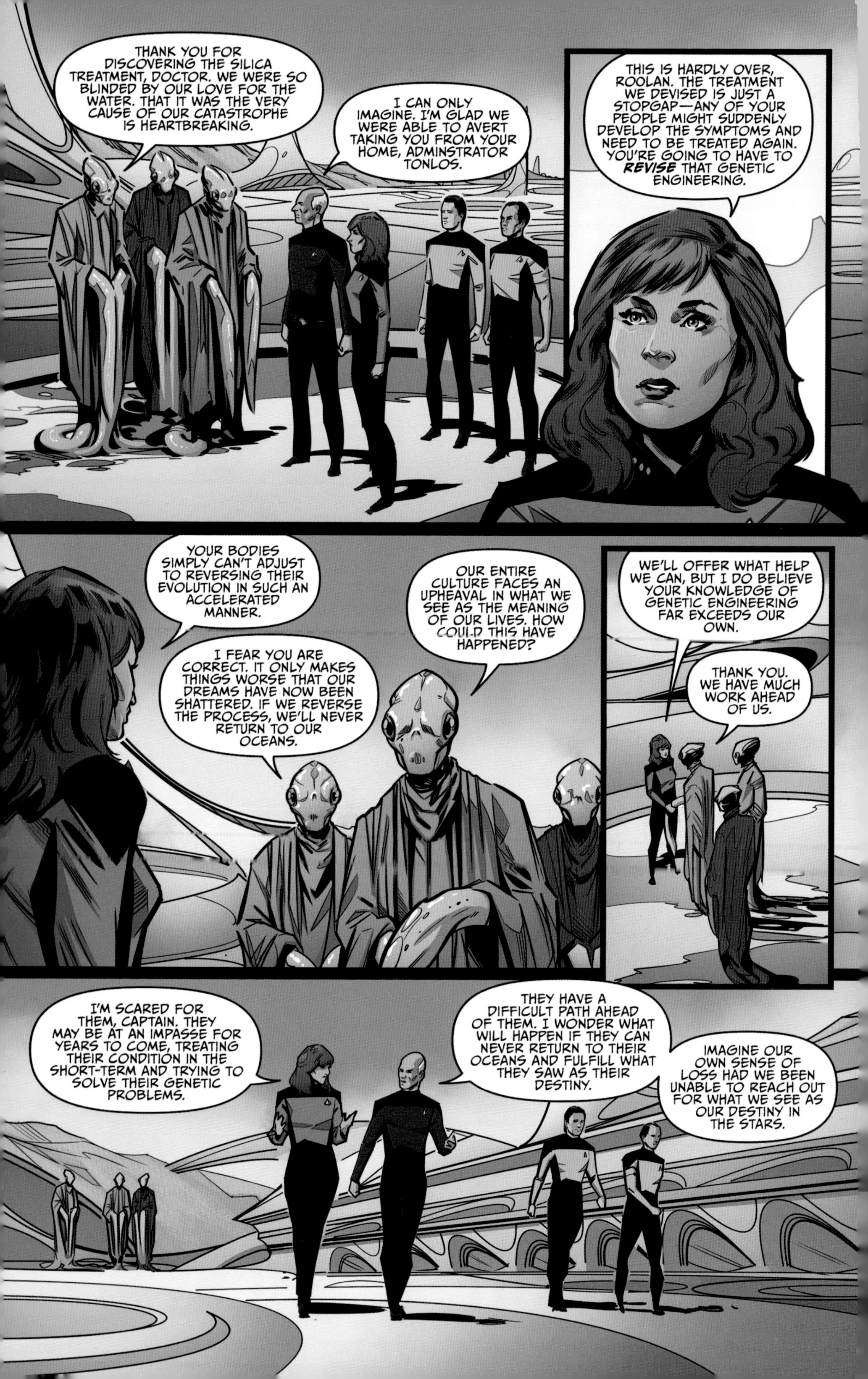
THANK YOU FOR DISCOVERING THE SILICA TREATMENT, DOCTOR. WE WERE SO BLINDED BY OUR LOVE FOR THE WATER. THAT IT WAS THE VERY CAUSE OF OUR CATASTROPHE IS HEARTBREAKING.
I CAN ONLY IMAGINE. I'M GLAD WE WERE ABLE TO AVERT TAKING YOU FROM YOUR HOME, ADMINSTRATOR TONLOS.
THIS IS HARDLY OVER, ROOLAN. THE TREATMENT WE DEVISED IS JUST A STOPGAP—ANY OF YOUR PEOPLE MIGHT SUDDENLY DEVELOP THE SYMPTOMS AND NEED TO BE TREATED AGAIN. YOU'RE GOING TO HAVE TO *REVISE* THAT GENETIC ENGINEERING.
YOUR BODIES SIMPLY CAN'T ADJUST TO REVERSING THEIR EVOLUTION IN SUCH AN ACCELERATED MANNER.
I FEAR YOU ARE CORRECT. IT ONLY MAKES THINGS WORSE THAT OUR DREAMS HAVE NOW BEEN SHATTERED. IF WE REVERSE THE PROCESS, WE'LL NEVER RETURN TO OUR OCEANS.
OUR ENTIRE CULTURE FACES AN UPHEAVAL IN WHAT WE SEE AS THE MEANING OF OUR LIVES. HOW COULD THIS HAVE HAPPENED?
WE'LL OFFER WHAT HELP WE CAN, BUT I DO BELIEVE YOUR KNOWLEDGE OF GENETIC ENGINEERING FAR EXCEEDS OUR OWN.
THANK YOU. WE HAVE MUCH WORK AHEAD OF US.
I'M SCARED FOR THEM, CAPTAIN. THEY MAY BE AT AN IMPASSE FOR YEARS TO COME, TREATING THEIR CONDITION IN THE SHORT-TERM AND TRYING TO SOLVE THEIR GENETIC PROBLEMS.
THEY HAVE A DIFFICULT PATH AHEAD OF THEM. I WONDER WHAT WILL HAPPEN IF THEY CAN NEVER RETURN TO THEIR OCEANS AND FULFILL WHAT THEY SAW AS THEIR DESTINY.
IMAGINE OUR OWN SENSE OF LOSS HAD WE BEEN UNABLE TO REACH OUT FOR WHAT WE SEE AS OUR DESTINY IN THE STARS.

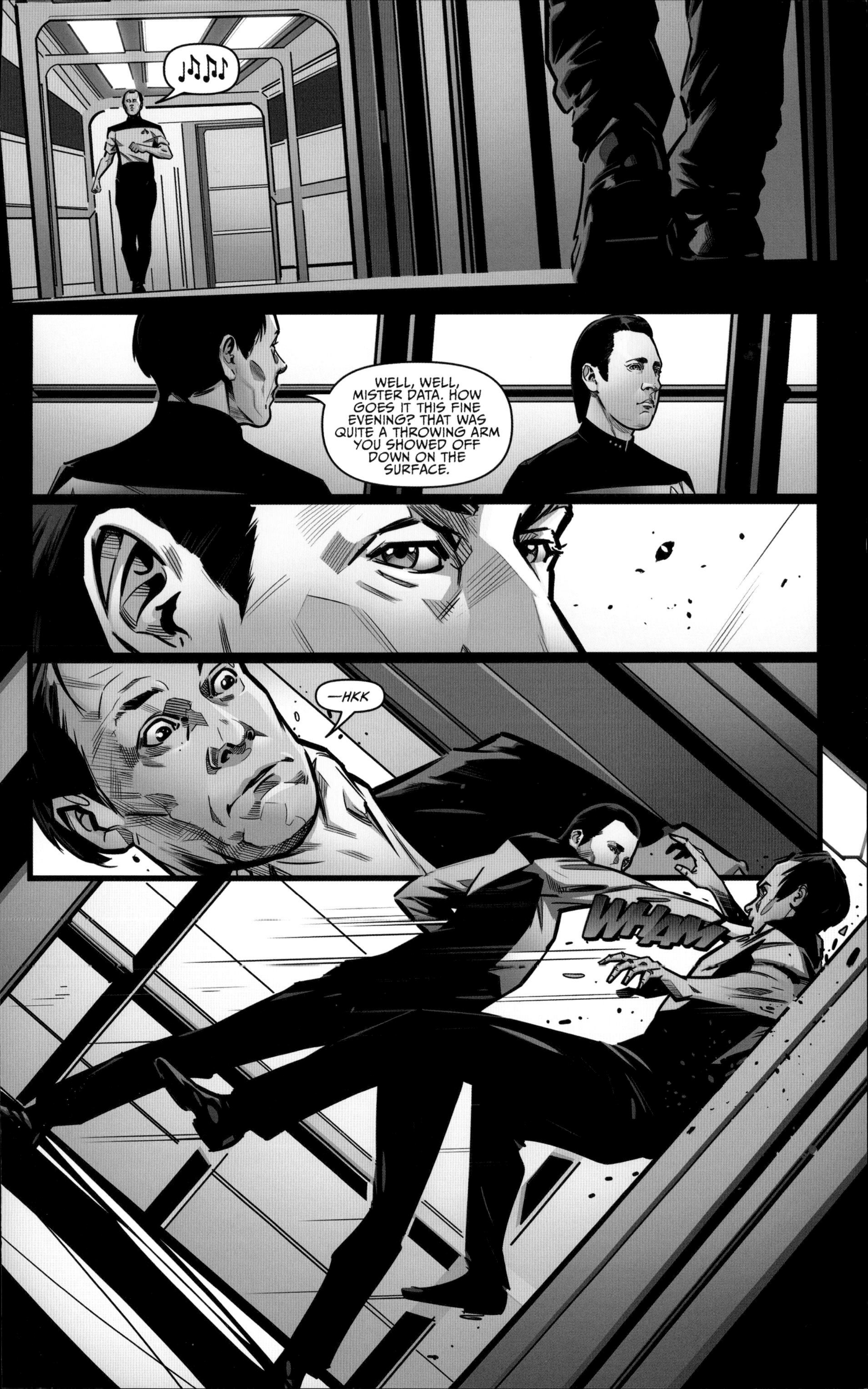
♪♫♪♪
WELL, WELL, MISTER DATA. HOW GOES IT THIS FINE EVENING? THAT WAS QUITE A THROWING ARM YOU SHOWED OFF DOWN ON THE SURFACE.
—HKK
WHAM

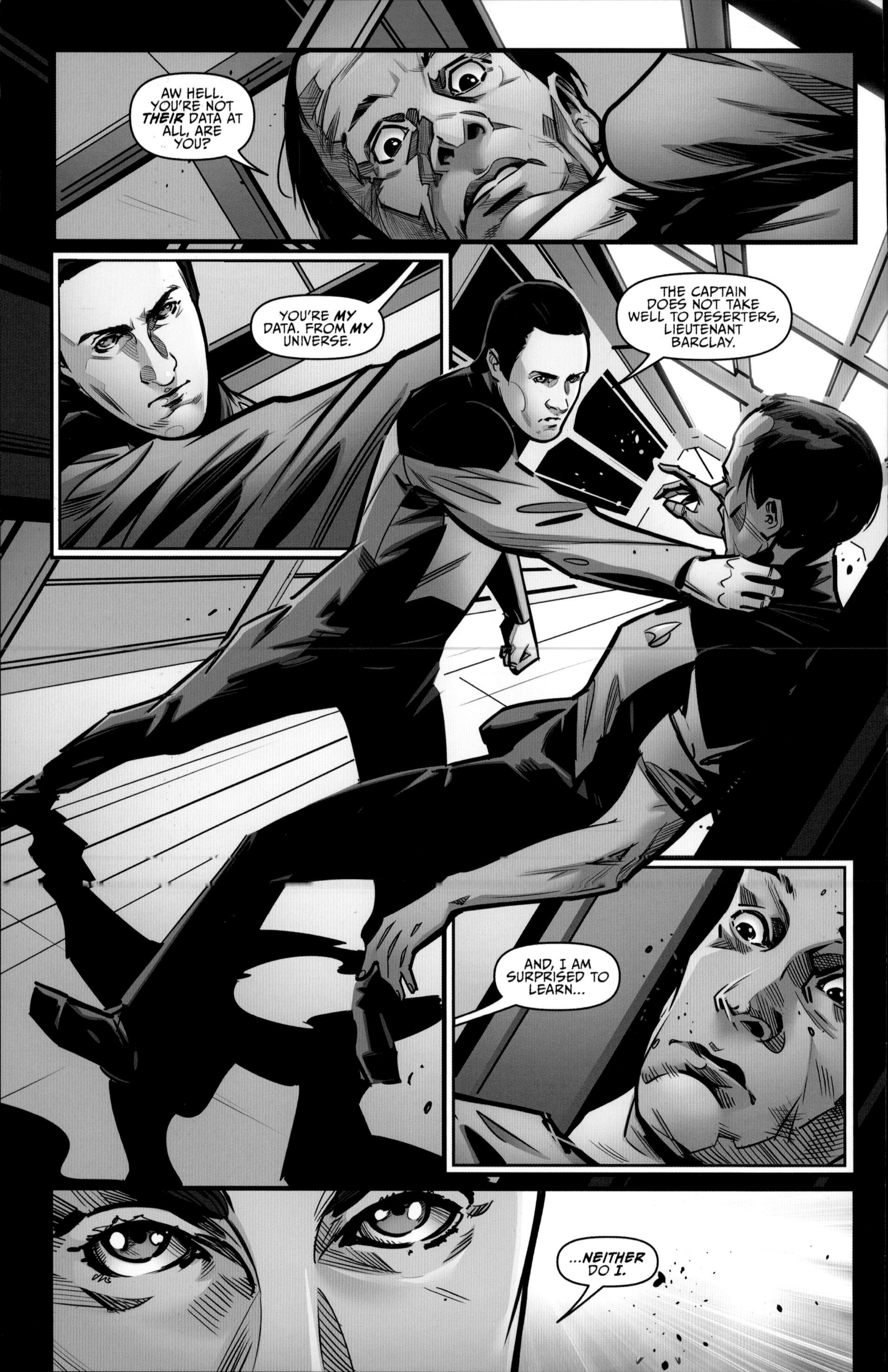
AW HELL. YOU'RE NOT THEIR DATA AT ALL, ARE YOU?
YOU'RE MY DATA. FROM MY UNIVERSE.
THE CAPTAIN DOES NOT TAKE WELL TO DESERTERS, LIEUTENANT BARCLAY.
AND, I AM SURPRISED TO LEARN...
...NEITHER DO I.

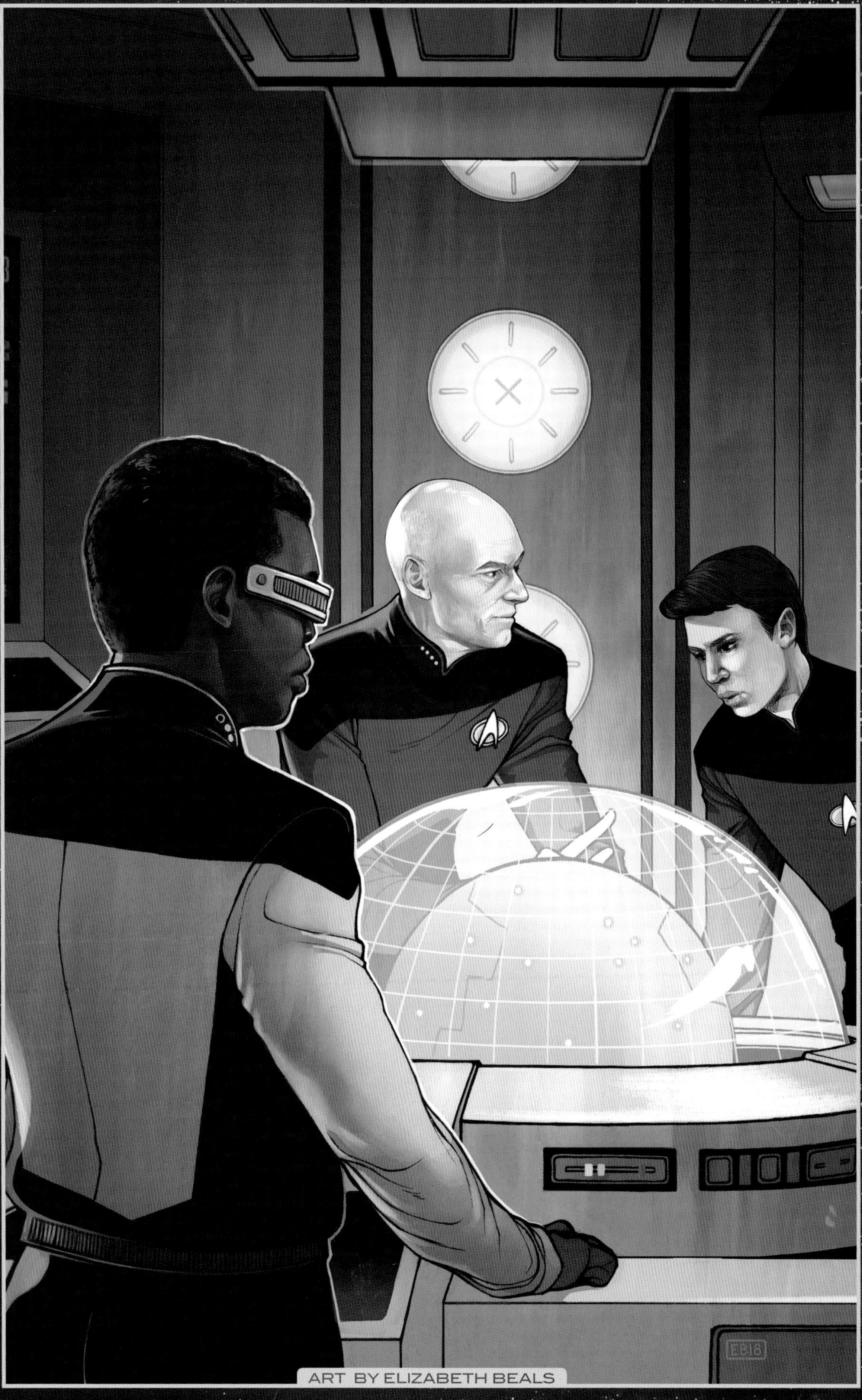
EB18

ART BY ELIZABETH BEALS

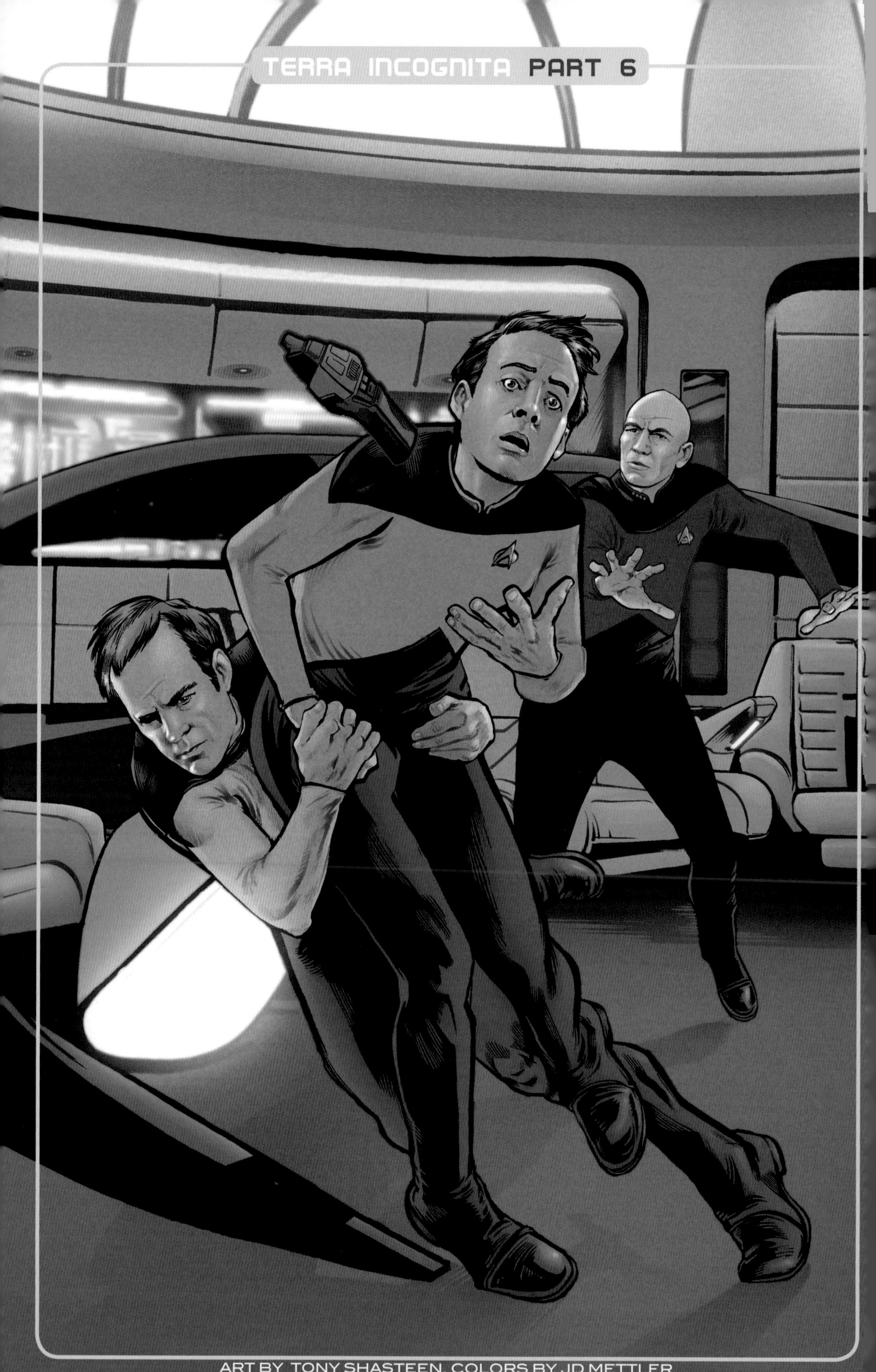
TERRA INCOGNITA PART 6

ART BY TONY SHASTEEN, COLORS BY JD METTLER

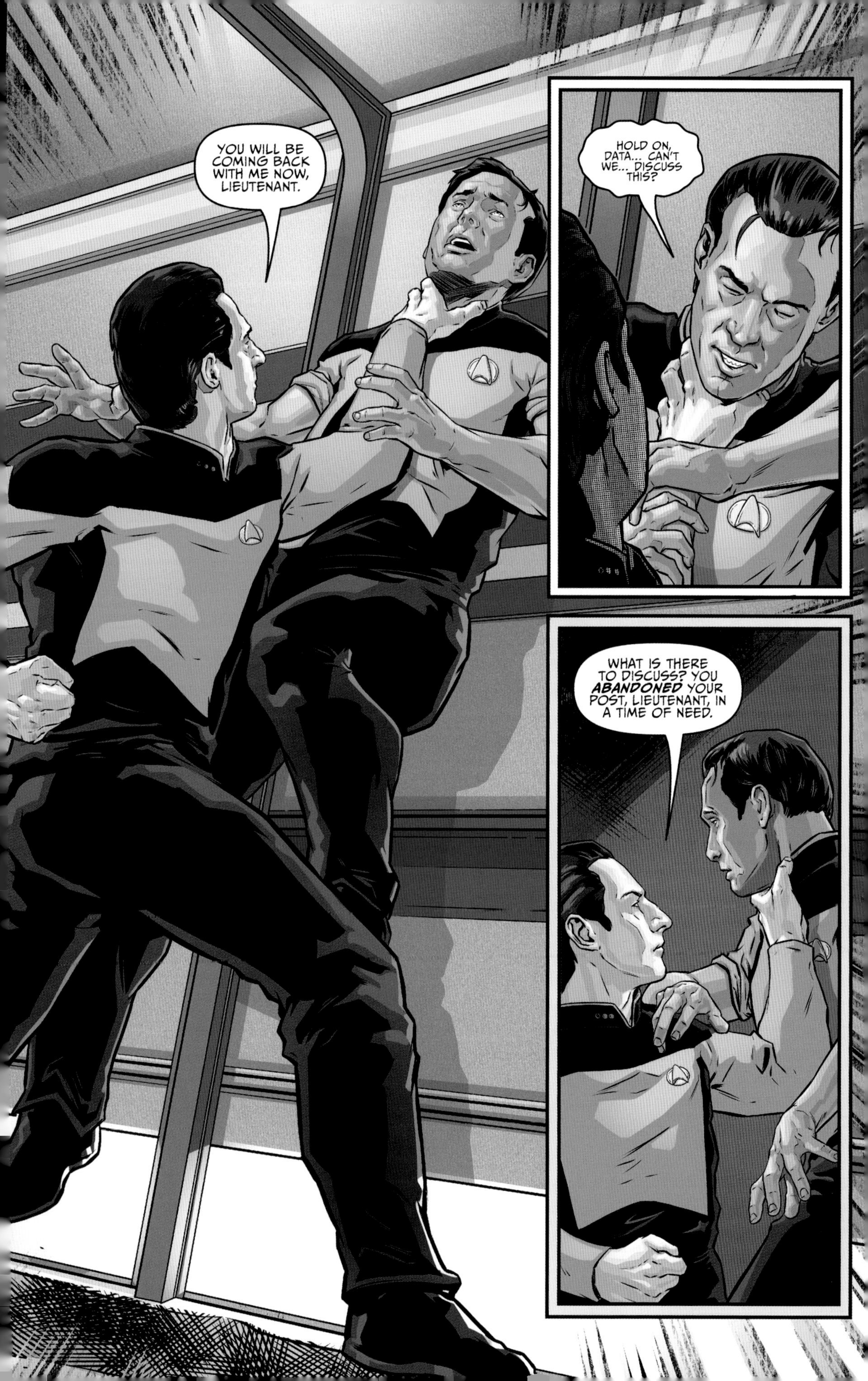
YOU WILL BE COMING BACK WITH ME NOW, LIEUTENANT.
HOLD ON, DATA... CAN'T WE... DISCUSS THIS?
WHAT IS THERE TO DISCUSS? YOU ABANDONED YOUR POST, LIEUTENANT, IN A TIME OF NEED.

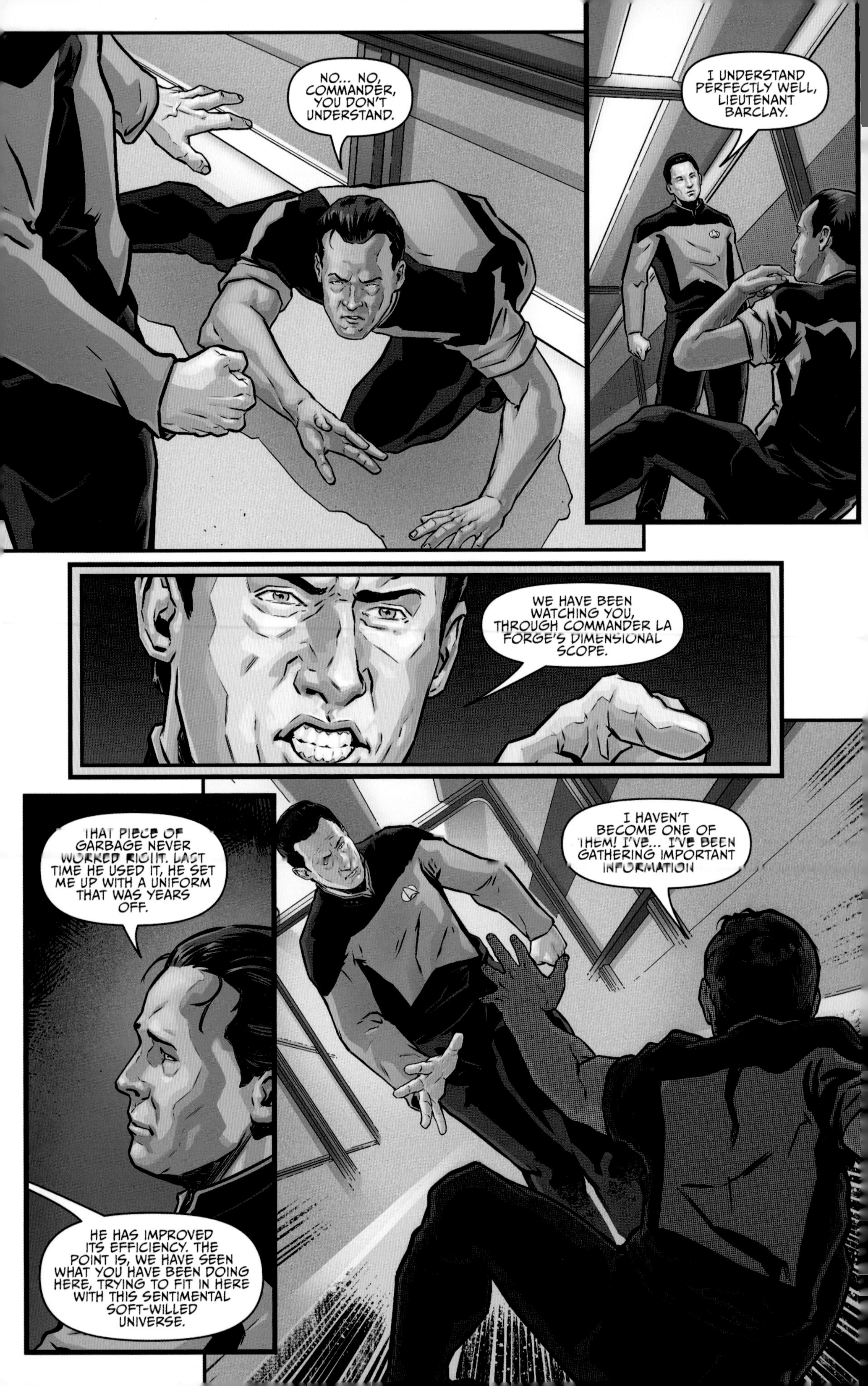
NO... NO, COMMANDER, YOU DON'T UNDERSTAND.
I UNDERSTAND PERFECTLY WELL, LIEUTENANT BARCLAY.
WE HAVE BEEN WATCHING YOU, THROUGH COMMANDER LA FORGE'S DIMENSIONAL SCOPE.
THAT PIECE OF GARBAGE NEVER WORKED RIGHT. LAST TIME HE USED IT, HE SET ME UP WITH A UNIFORM THAT WAS YEARS OFF.
HE HAS IMPROVED ITS EFFICIENCY. THE POINT IS, WE HAVE SEEN WHAT YOU HAVE BEEN DOING HERE, TRYING TO FIT IN HERE WITH THIS SENTIMENTAL SOFT-WILLED UNIVERSE.
I HAVEN'T BECOME ONE OF THEM! I'VE... I'VE BEEN GATHERING IMPORTANT INFORMATION

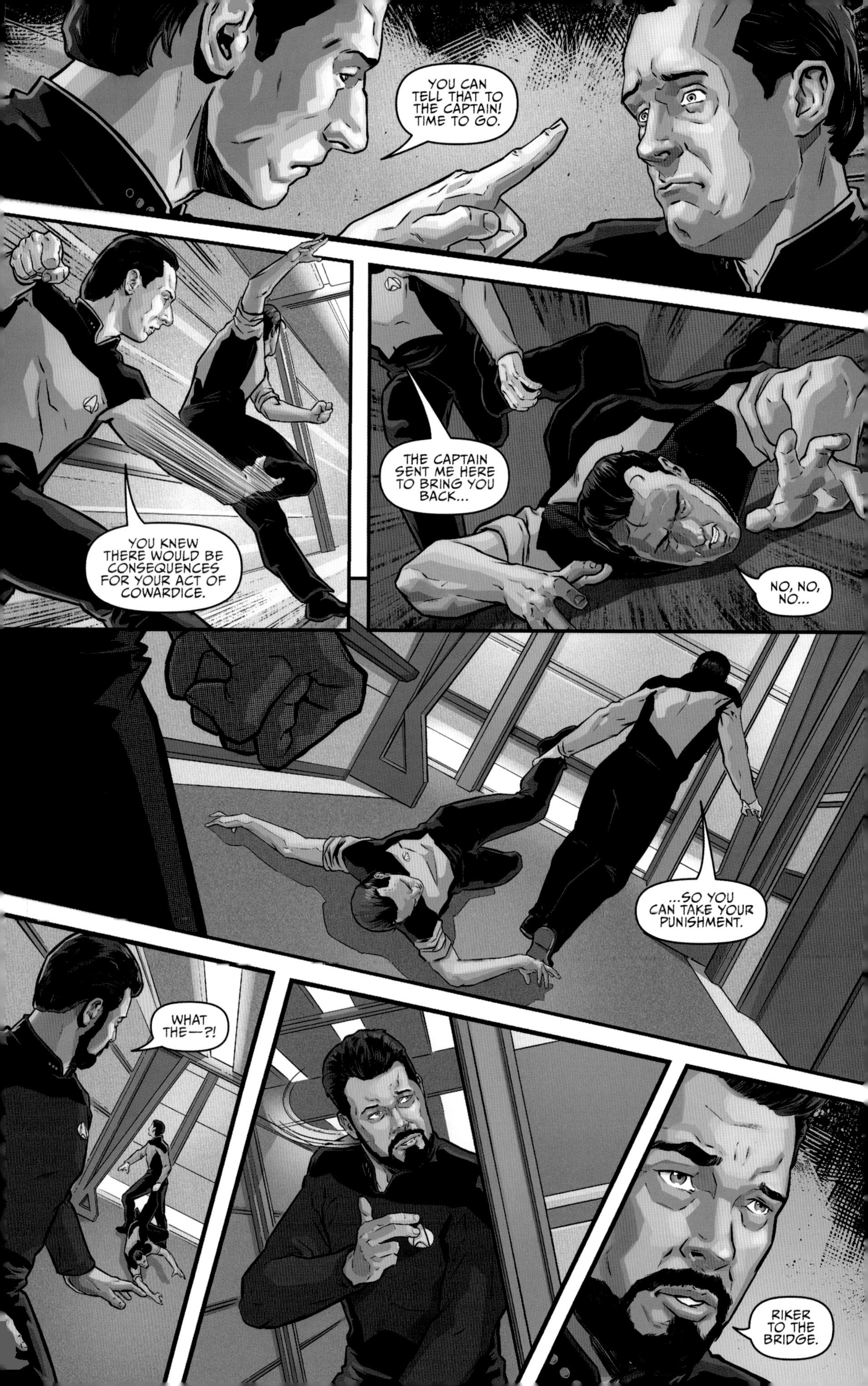
YOU CAN TELL THAT TO THE CAPTAIN! TIME TO GO.
YOU KNEW THERE WOULD BE CONSEQUENCES FOR YOUR ACT OF COWARDICE.
THE CAPTAIN SENT ME HERE TO BRING YOU BACK...
NO, NO, NO...
...SO YOU CAN TAKE YOUR PUNISHMENT.
WHAT THE—?!
RIKER TO THE BRIDGE.

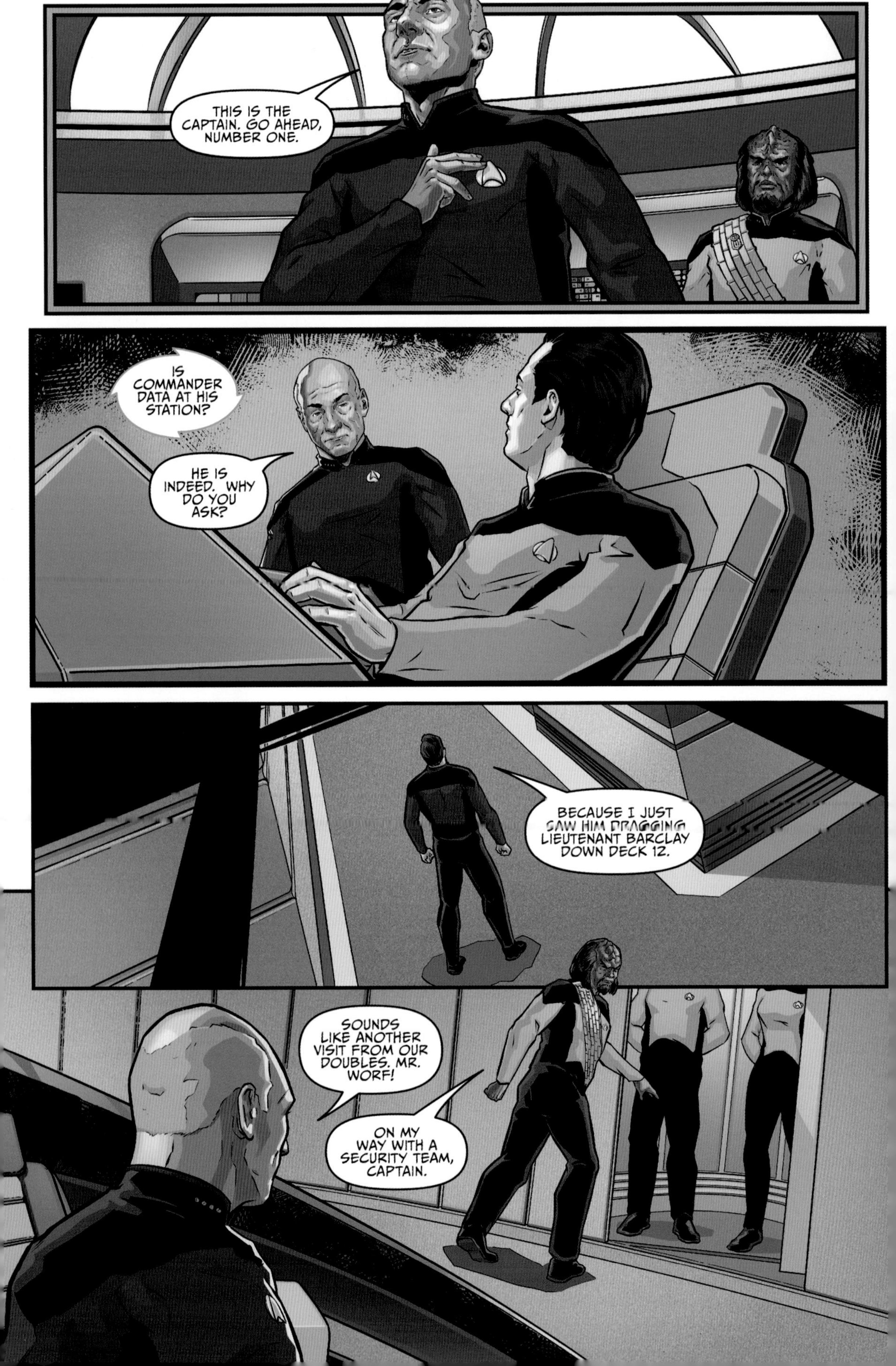
THIS IS THE CAPTAIN. GO AHEAD, NUMBER ONE.
IS COMMANDER DATA AT HIS STATION?
HE IS INDEED. WHY DO YOU ASK?
BECAUSE I JUST SAW HIM DRAGGING LIEUTENANT BARCLAY DOWN DECK 12.
SOUNDS LIKE ANOTHER VISIT FROM OUR DOUBLES. MR. WORF!
ON MY WAY WITH A SECURITY TEAM, CAPTAIN.

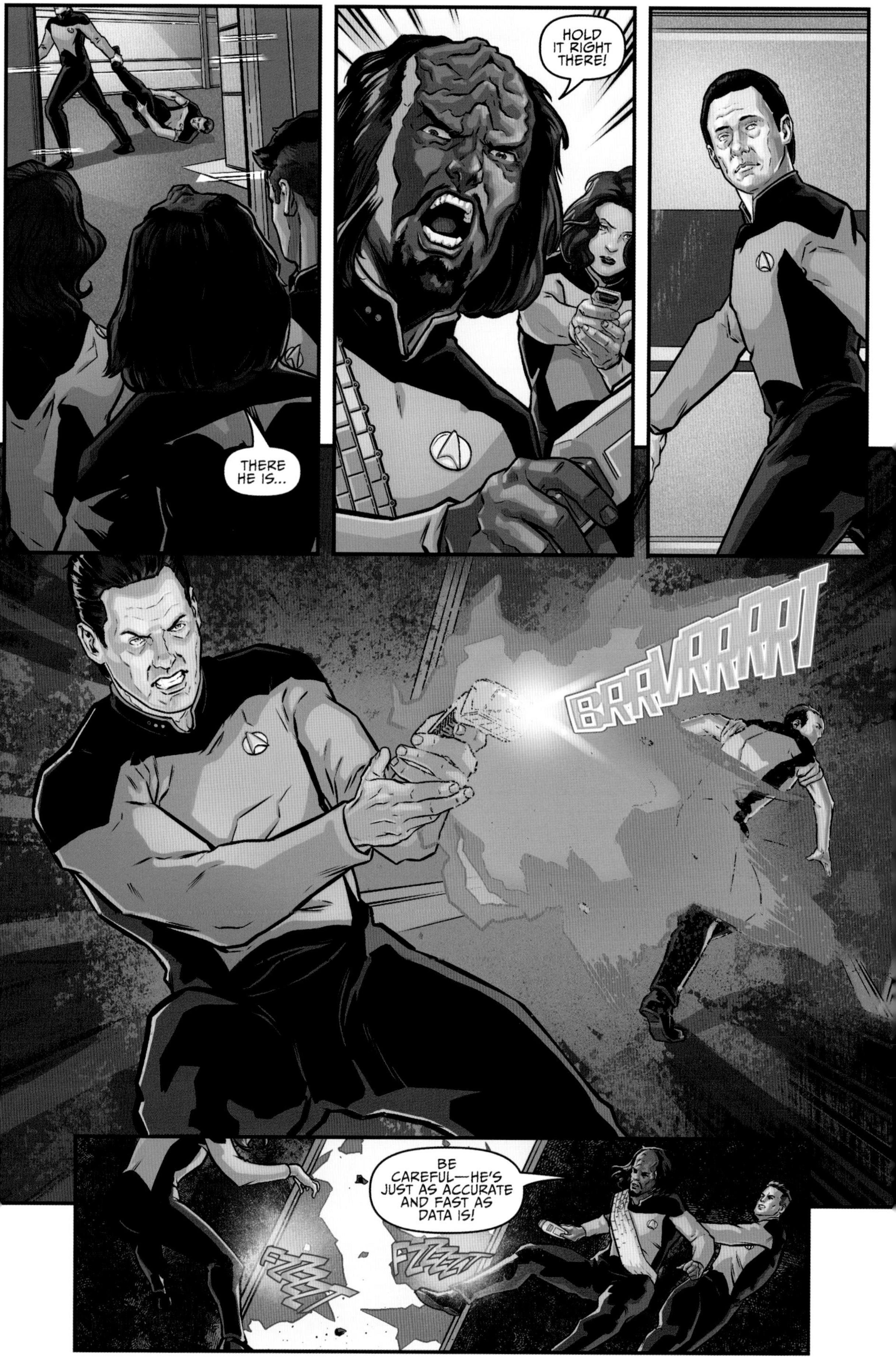
THERE HE IS...
HOLD IT RIGHT THERE!
BRRVRRRRT
BE CAREFUL—HE'S JUST AS ACCURATE AND FAST AS DATA IS!
FZZZT
FZZZT

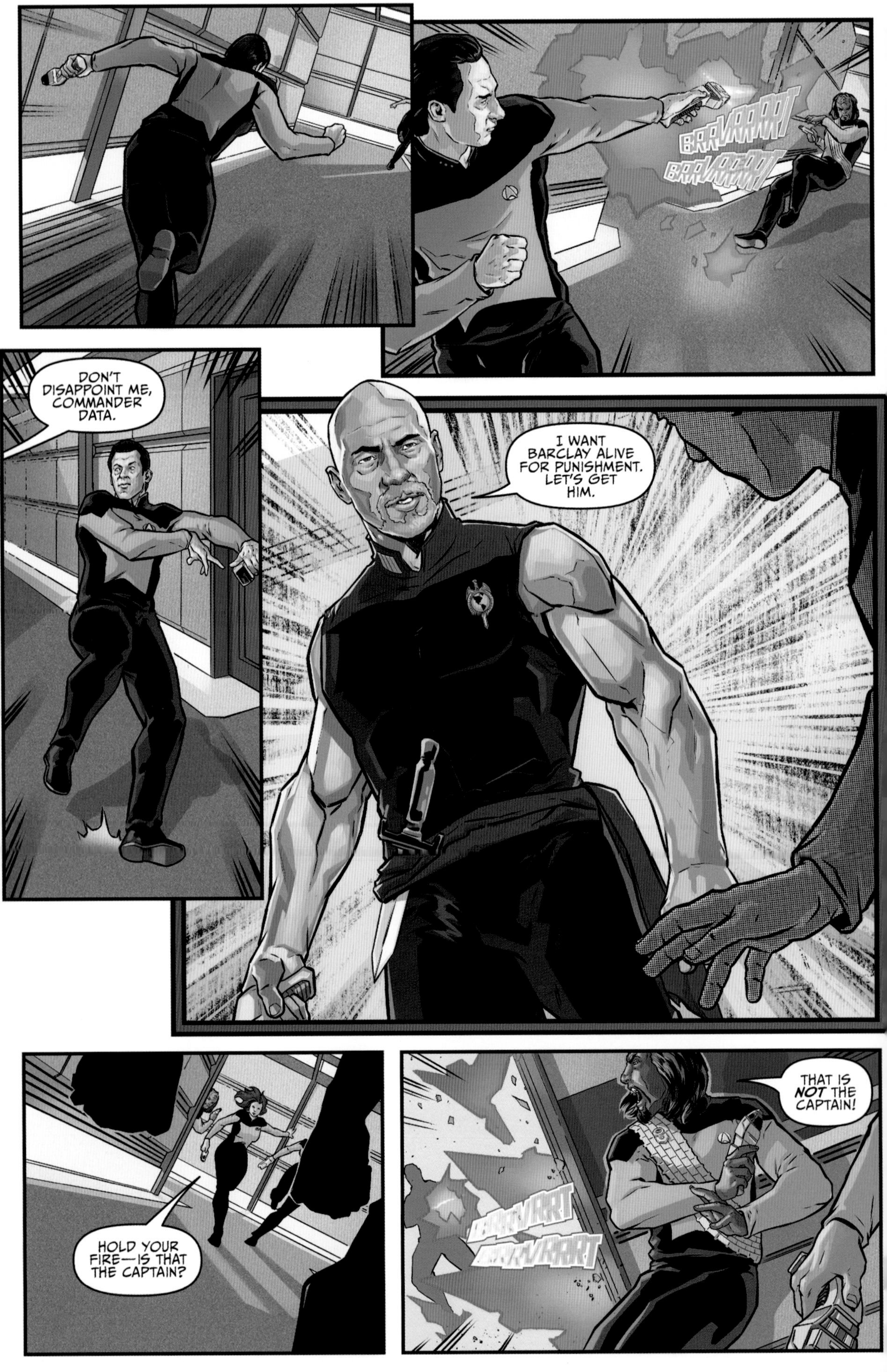
BRRVRRRRT
BRRVRRRRT
DON'T DISAPPOINT ME, COMMANDER DATA.
I WANT BARCLAY ALIVE FOR PUNISHMENT. LET'S GET HIM.
HOLD YOUR FIRE—IS THAT THE CAPTAIN?
THAT IS *NOT* THE CAPTAIN!
BRRRVRRRT
BRRRVRRRT

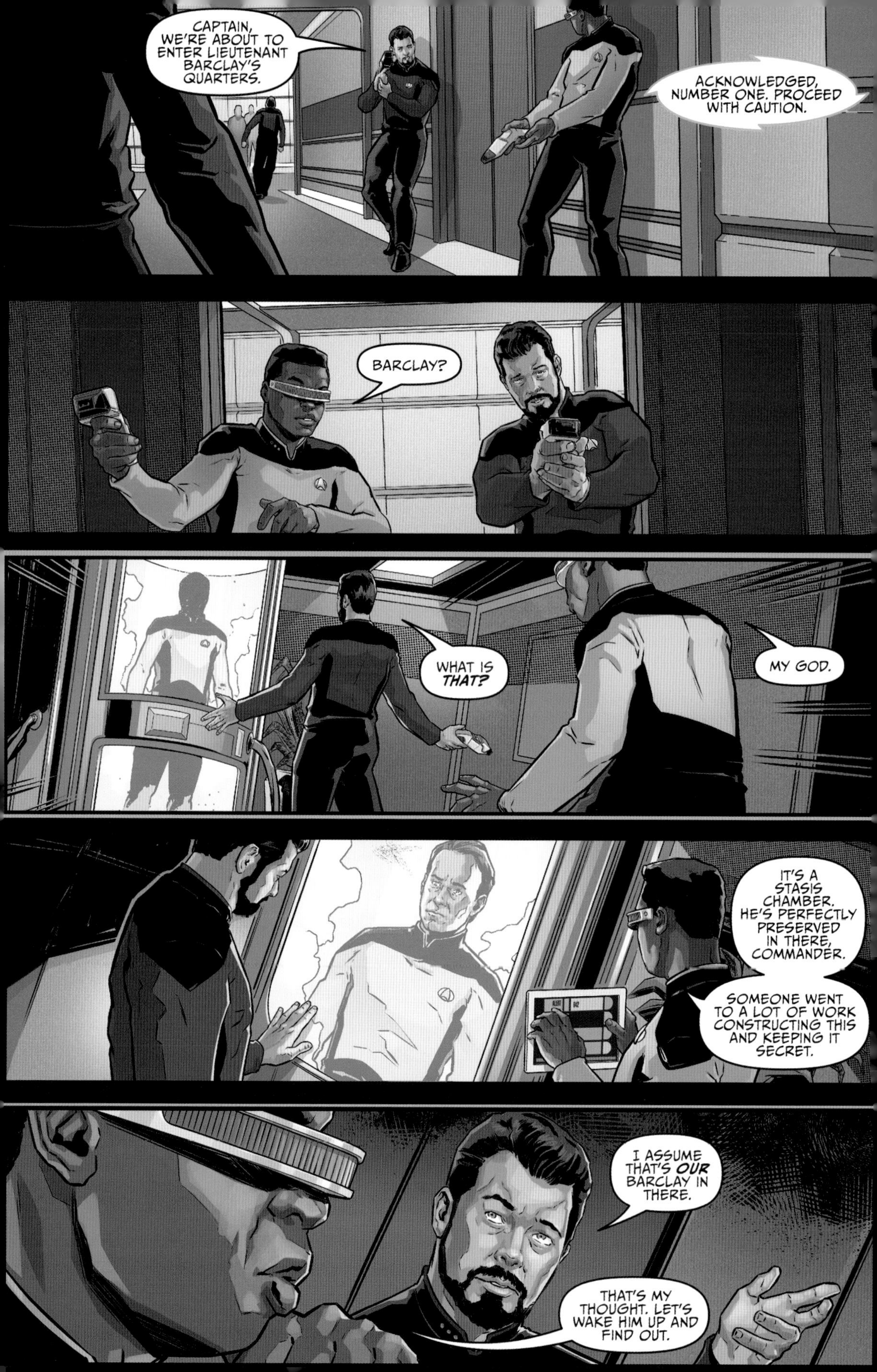
CAPTAIN, WE'RE ABOUT TO ENTER LIEUTENANT BARCLAY'S QUARTERS.
ACKNOWLEDGED, NUMBER ONE. PROCEED WITH CAUTION.
BARCLAY?
WHAT IS THAT?
MY GOD.
IT'S A STASIS CHAMBER. HE'S PERFECTLY PRESERVED IN THERE, COMMANDER.
SOMEONE WENT TO A LOT OF WORK CONSTRUCTING THIS AND KEEPING IT SECRET.
I ASSUME THAT'S OUR BARCLAY IN THERE.
THAT'S MY THOUGHT. LET'S WAKE HIM UP AND FIND OUT.

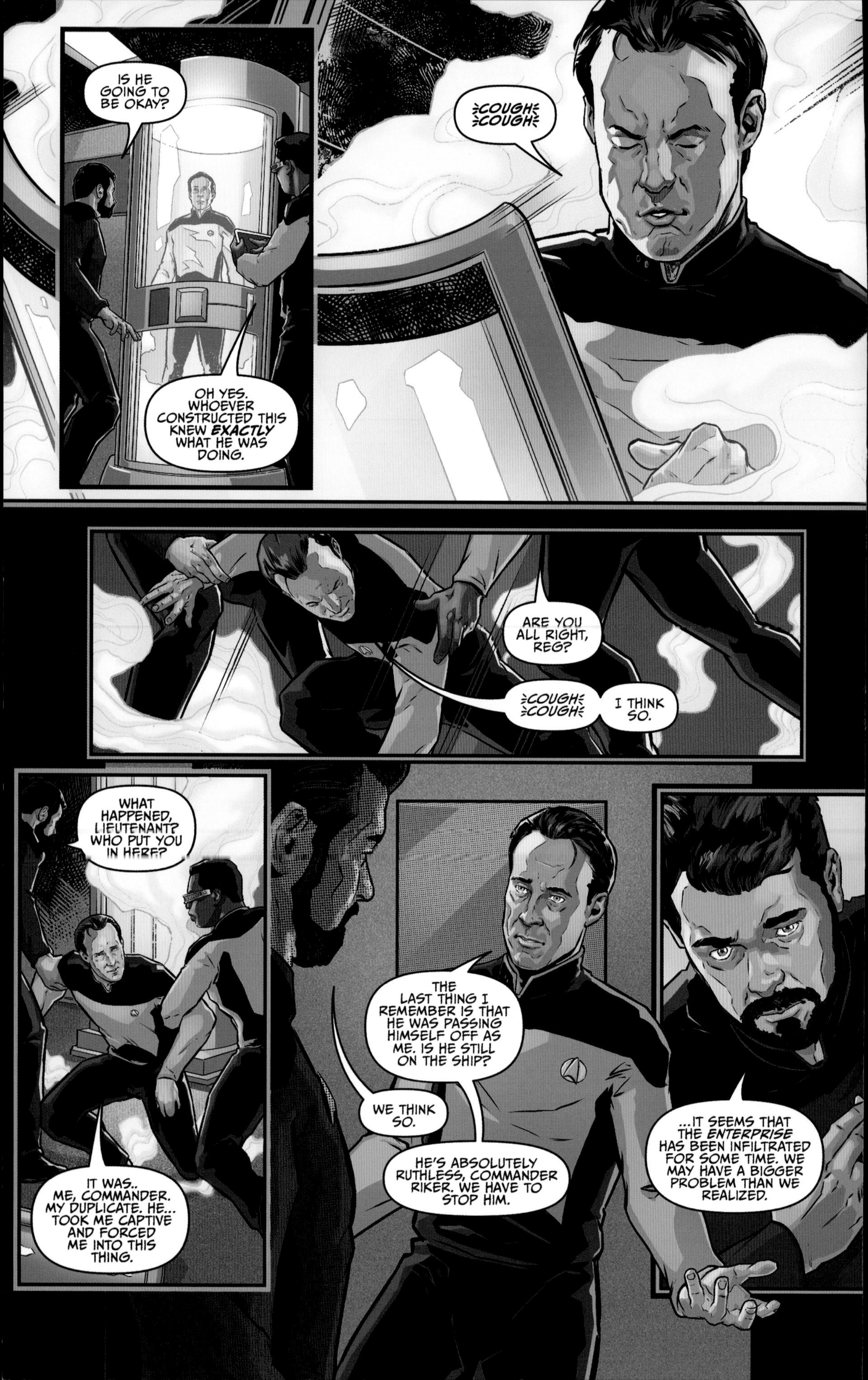
IS HE GOING TO BE OKAY?
OH YES. WHOEVER CONSTRUCTED THIS KNEW EXACTLY WHAT HE WAS DOING.
COUGH COUGH
ARE YOU ALL RIGHT, REG?
COUGH COUGH
I THINK SO.
WHAT HAPPENED, LIEUTENANT? WHO PUT YOU IN HERE?
IT WAS.. ME, COMMANDER. MY DUPLICATE. HE... TOOK ME CAPTIVE AND FORCED ME INTO THIS THING.
THE LAST THING I REMEMBER IS THAT HE WAS PASSING HIMSELF OFF AS ME. IS HE STILL ON THE SHIP?
WE THINK SO.
HE'S ABSOLUTELY RUTHLESS, COMMANDER RIKER. WE HAVE TO STOP HIM.
...IT SEEMS THAT THE ENTERPRISE HAS BEEN INFILTRATED FOR SOME TIME. WE MAY HAVE A BIGGER PROBLEM THAN WE REALIZED.

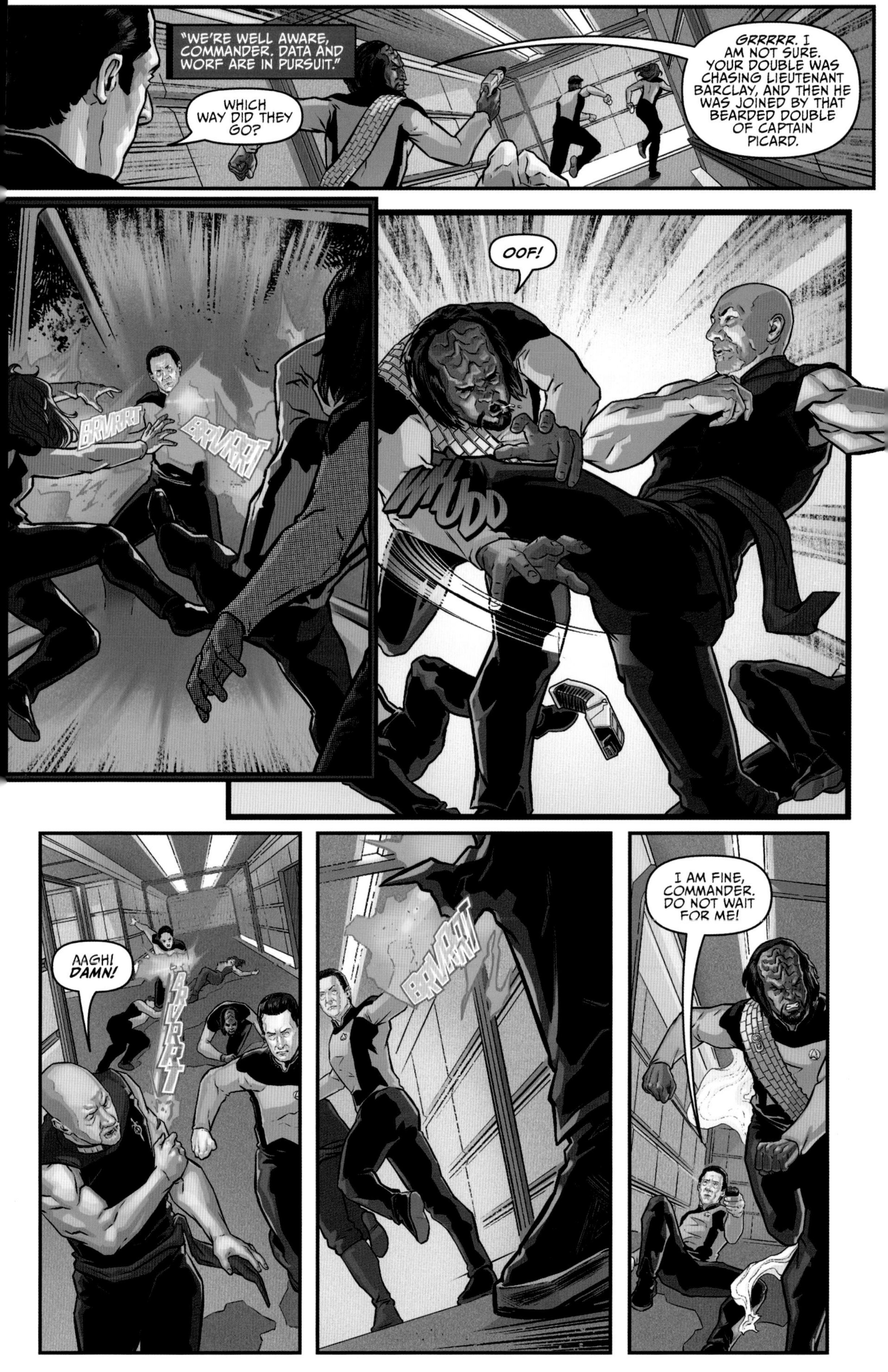

"WE'RE WELL AWARE, COMMANDER. DATA AND WORF ARE IN PURSUIT."
WHICH WAY DID THEY GO?
GRRRRR. I AM NOT SURE. YOUR DOUBLE WAS CHASING LIEUTENANT BARCLAY, AND THEN HE WAS JOINED BY THAT BEARDED DOUBLE OF CAPTAIN PICARD.
BRVRRT
BRVRRT
OOF!
WHUDD
AAGH! DAMN!
BRVRRT
BRVRRT
I AM FINE, COMMANDER. DO NOT WAIT FOR ME!

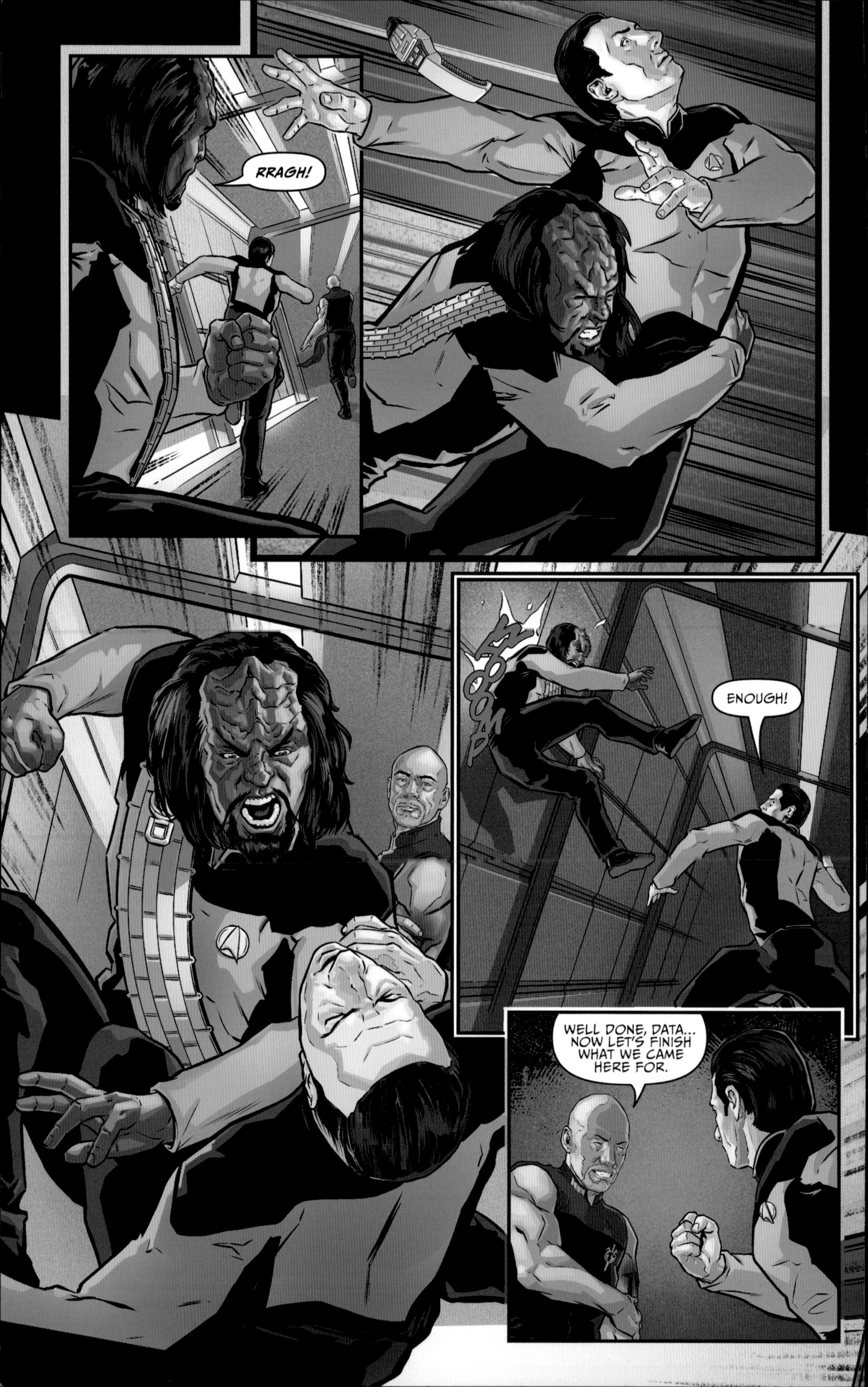
RRAGH!
ENOUGH!
WELL DONE, DATA... NOW LET'S FINISH WHAT WE CAME HERE FOR.

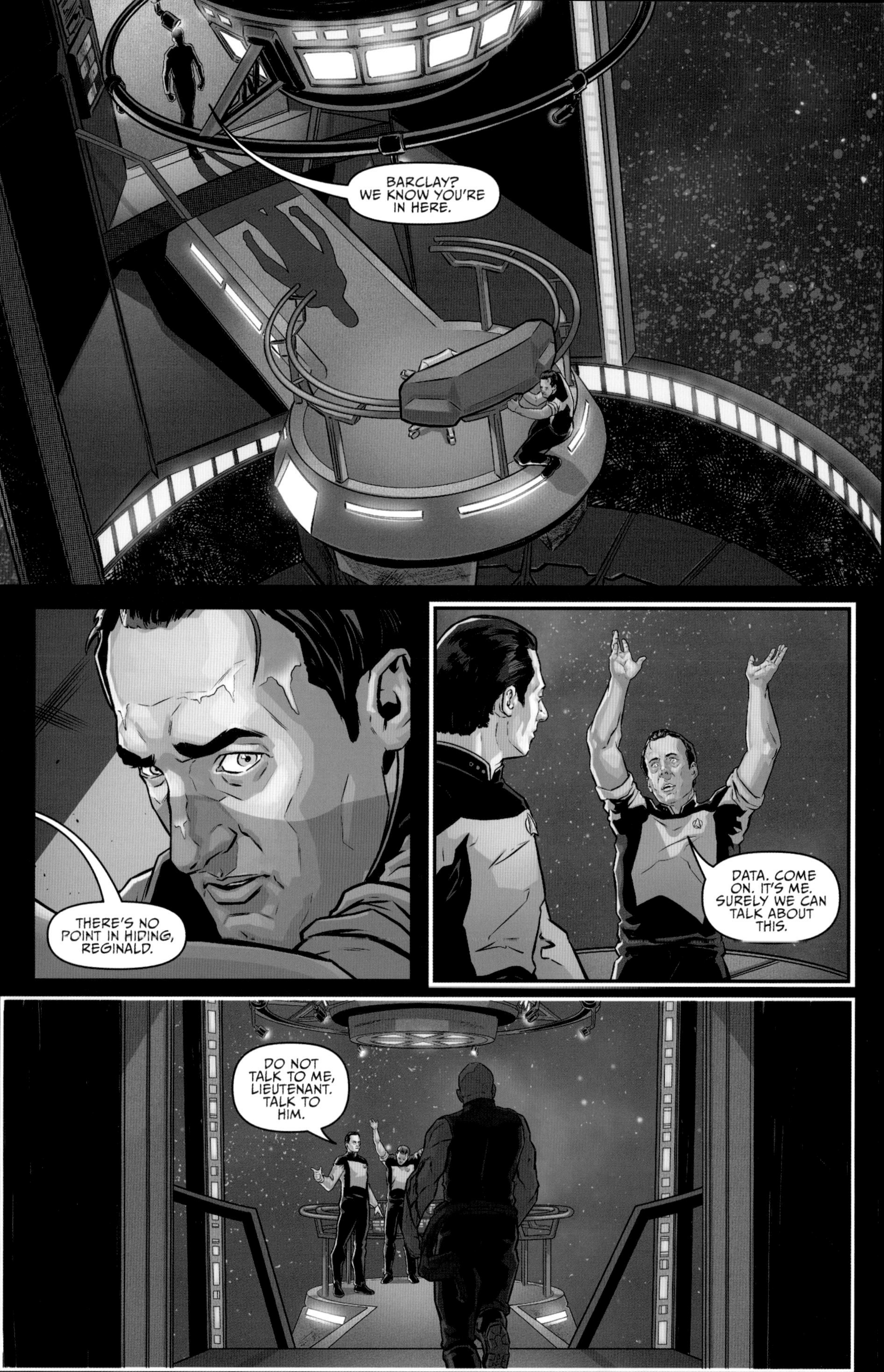
BARCLAY? WE KNOW YOU'RE IN HERE.
THERE'S NO POINT IN HIDING, REGINALD.
DATA. COME ON. IT'S ME. SURELY WE CAN TALK ABOUT THIS.
DO NOT TALK TO ME, LIEUTENANT. TALK TO HIM.

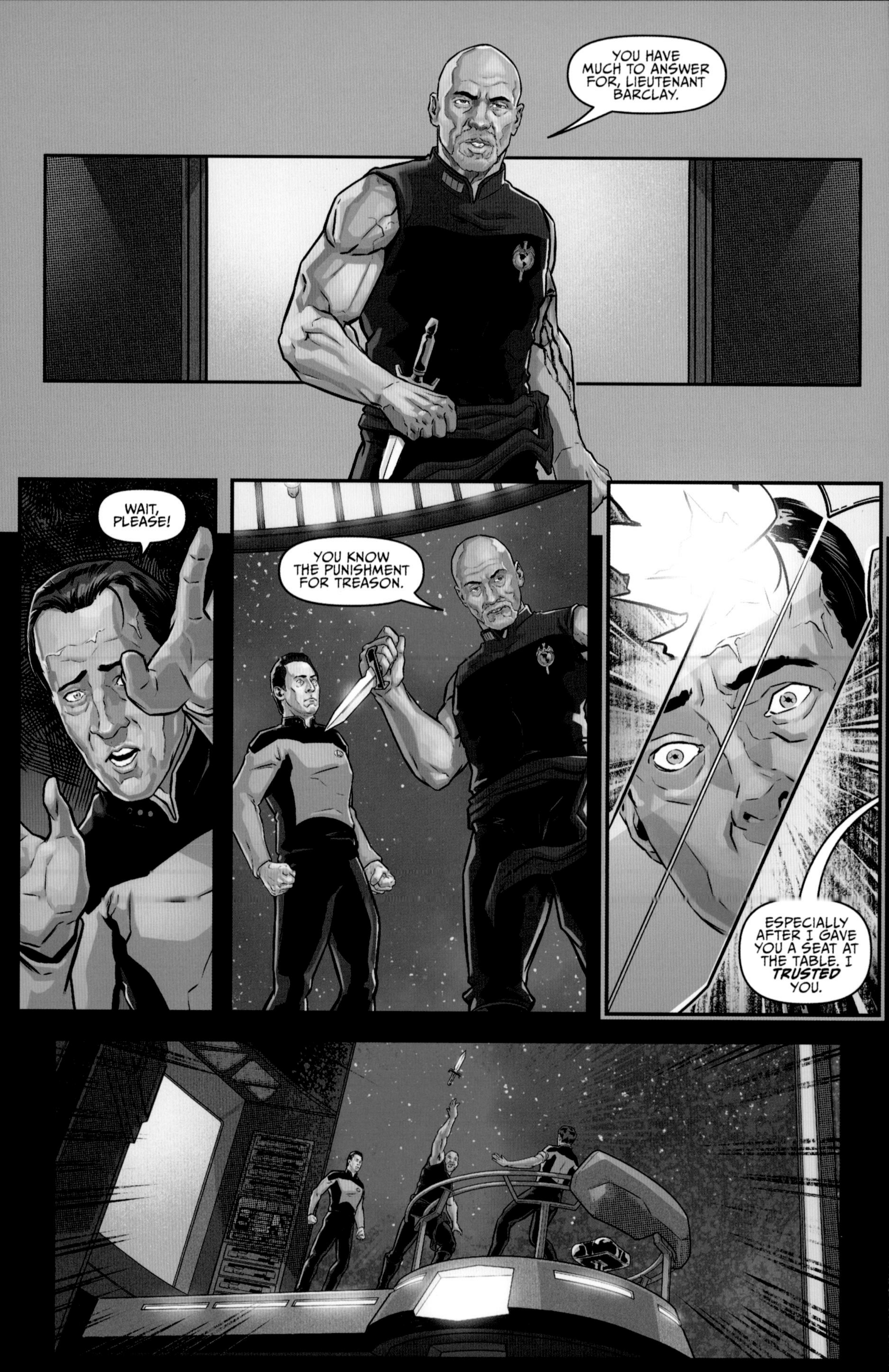
YOU HAVE MUCH TO ANSWER FOR, LIEUTENANT BARCLAY.
WAIT, PLEASE!
YOU KNOW THE PUNISHMENT FOR TREASON.
ESPECIALLY AFTER I GAVE YOU A SEAT AT THE TABLE. I *TRUSTED* YOU.

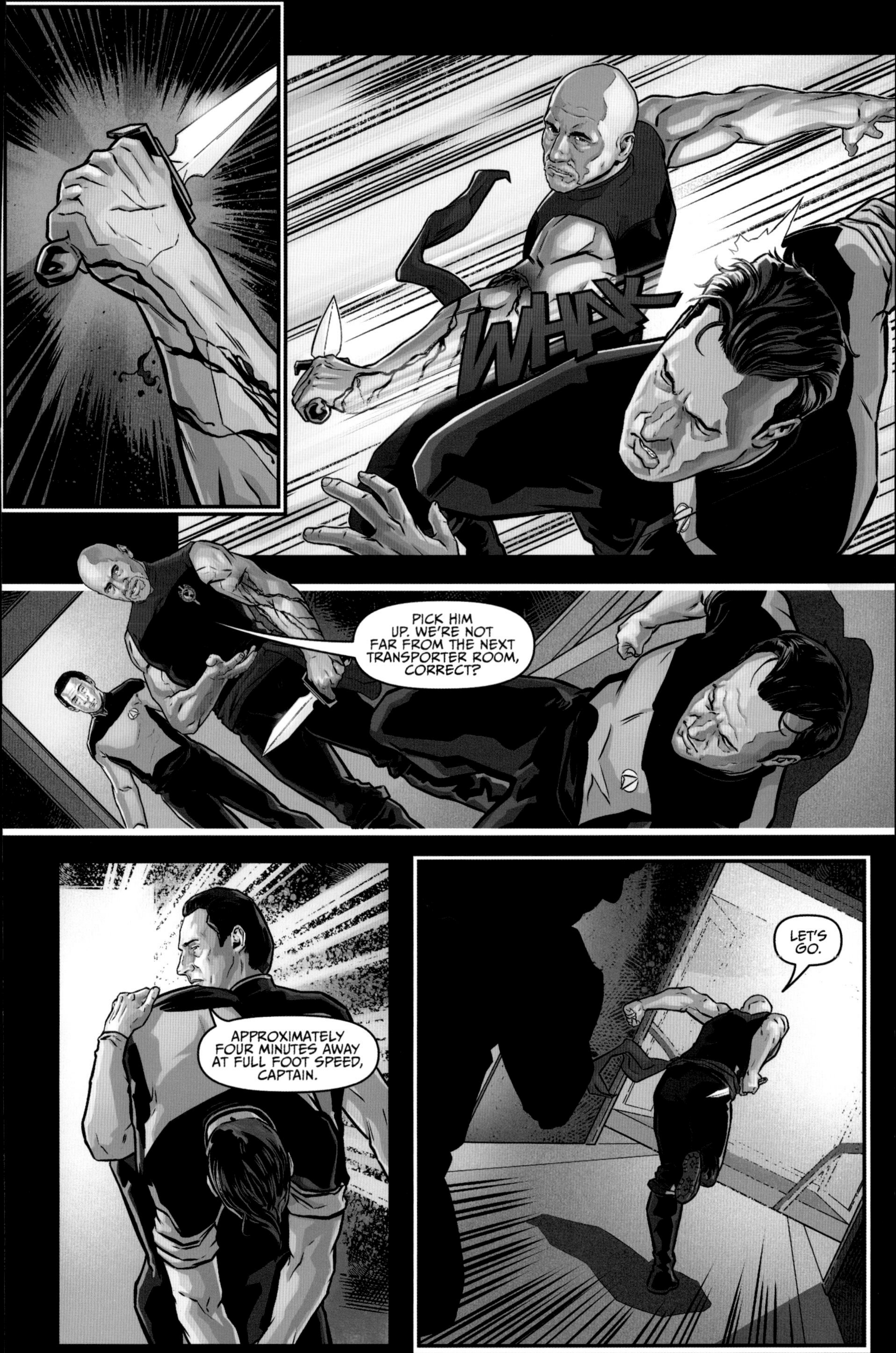
WHAK
PICK HIM UP. WE'RE NOT FAR FROM THE NEXT TRANSPORTER ROOM, CORRECT?
APPROXIMATELY FOUR MINUTES AWAY AT FULL FOOT SPEED, CAPTAIN.
LET'S GO.

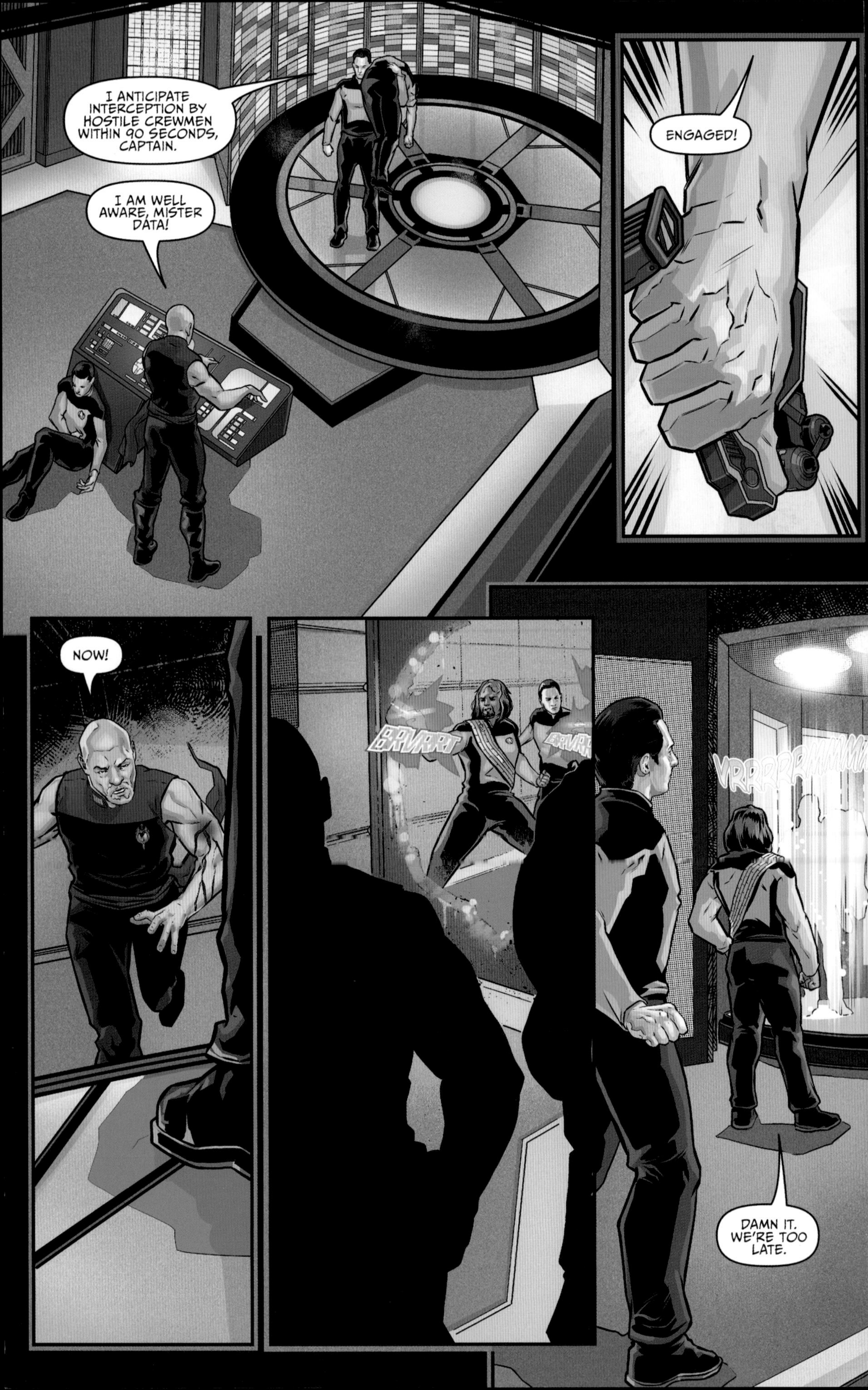
I ANTICIPATE INTERCEPTION BY HOSTILE CREWMEN WITHIN 90 SECONDS, CAPTAIN.
I AM WELL AWARE, MISTER DATA!
ENGAGED!
NOW!
BRVRRRT
DAMN IT. WE'RE TOO LATE.

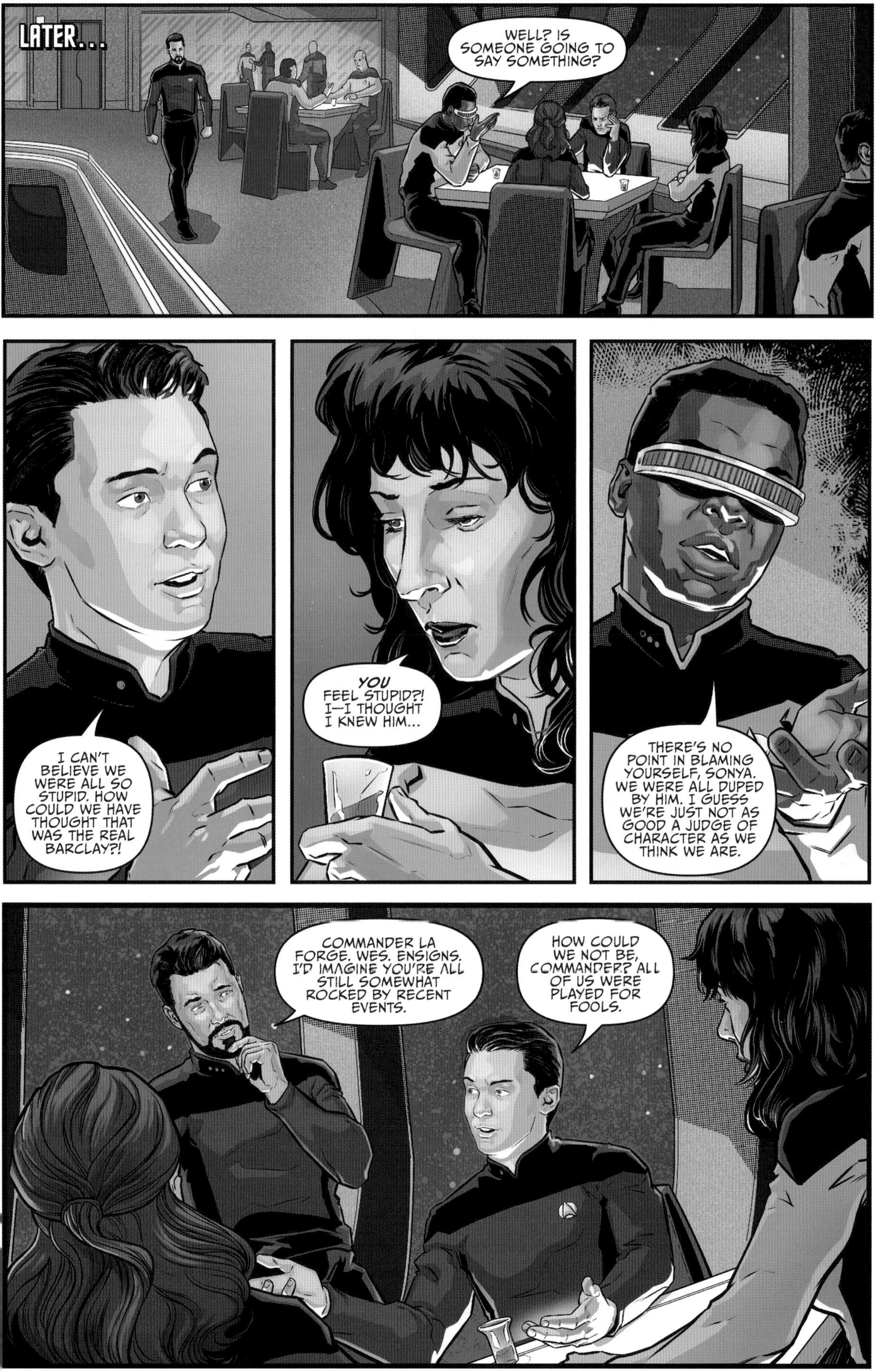
LATER...
WELL? IS SOMEONE GOING TO SAY SOMETHING?
I CAN'T BELIEVE WE WERE ALL SO STUPID. HOW COULD WE HAVE THOUGHT THAT WAS THE REAL BARCLAY?!
YOU FEEL STUPID?! I--I THOUGHT I KNEW HIM...
THERE'S NO POINT IN BLAMING YOURSELF, SONYA. WE WERE ALL DUPED BY HIM. I GUESS WE'RE JUST NOT AS GOOD A JUDGE OF CHARACTER AS WE THINK WE ARE.
COMMANDER LA FORGE. WES. ENSIGNS. I'D IMAGINE YOU'RE ALL STILL SOMEWHAT ROCKED BY RECENT EVENTS.
HOW COULD WE NOT BE, COMMANDER? ALL OF US WERE PLAYED FOR FOOLS.

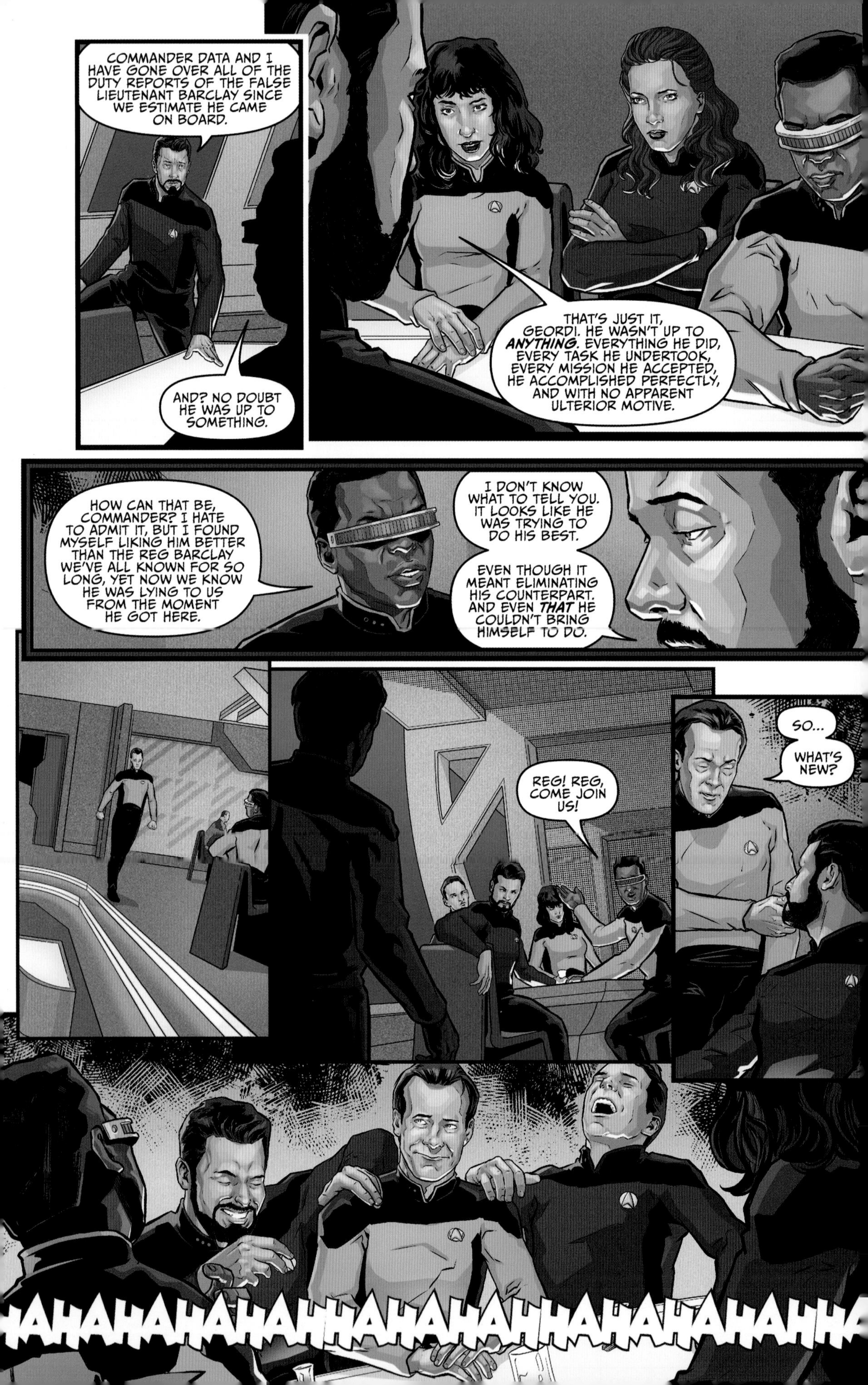
COMMANDER DATA AND I HAVE GONE OVER ALL OF THE DUTY REPORTS OF THE FALSE LIEUTENANT BARCLAY SINCE WE ESTIMATE HE CAME ON BOARD.
AND? NO DOUBT HE WAS UP TO SOMETHING.
THAT'S JUST IT, GEORDI. HE WASN'T UP TO ANYTHING. EVERYTHING HE DID, EVERY TASK HE UNDERTOOK, EVERY MISSION HE ACCEPTED, HE ACCOMPLISHED PERFECTLY, AND WITH NO APPARENT ULTERIOR MOTIVE.
HOW CAN THAT BE, COMMANDER? I HATE TO ADMIT IT, BUT I FOUND MYSELF LIKING HIM BETTER THAN THE REG BARCLAY WE'VE ALL KNOWN FOR SO LONG, YET NOW WE KNOW HE WAS LYING TO US FROM THE MOMENT HE GOT HERE.
I DON'T KNOW WHAT TO TELL YOU. IT LOOKS LIKE HE WAS TRYING TO DO HIS BEST.
EVEN THOUGH IT MEANT ELIMINATING HIS COUNTERPART. AND EVEN THAT HE COULDN'T BRING HIMSELF TO DO.
REG! REG, COME JOIN US!
SO...
WHAT'S NEW?
HAHAHAHAHAHHAHAHAHHAHAHAHAHHA

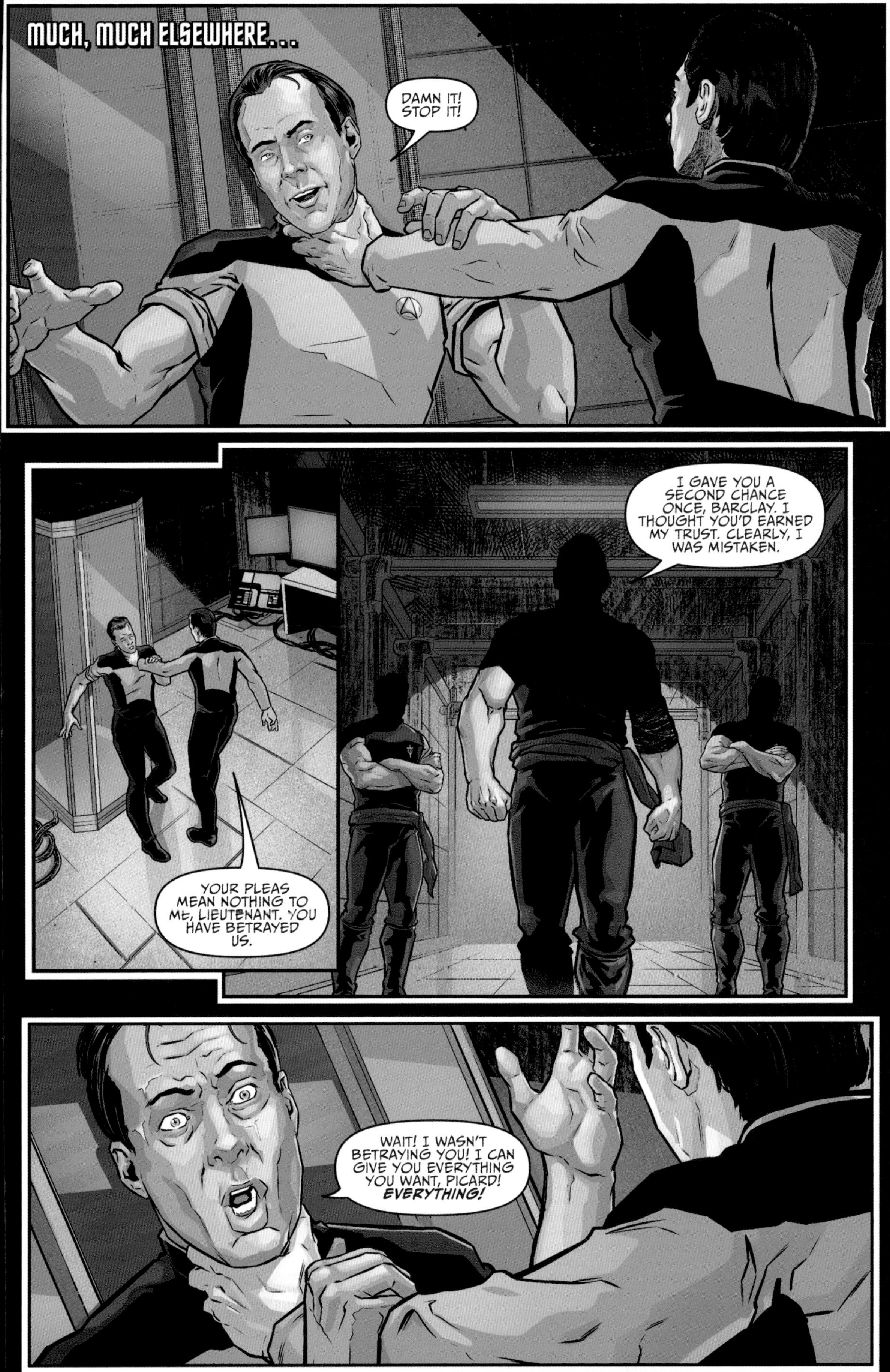
MUCH, MUCH ELSEWHERE...
DAMN IT! STOP IT!
I GAVE YOU A SECOND CHANCE ONCE, BARCLAY. I THOUGHT YOU'D EARNED MY TRUST. CLEARLY, I WAS MISTAKEN.
YOUR PLEAS MEAN NOTHING TO ME, LIEUTENANT. YOU HAVE BETRAYED US.
WAIT! I WASN'T BETRAYING YOU! I CAN GIVE YOU EVERYTHING YOU WANT, PICARD! *EVERYTHING!*

WHAT COULD YOU POSSIBLY GIVE ME, MR. BARCLAY? YOU'VE SHOWN ME WHERE YOUR LOYALTIES LIE.

THE THING YOU WANT MOST! POWER! IT'S WITHIN YOUR GRASP, IF YOU DON'T KILL ME NOW!

YOU HAVE MY ATTENTION, REGINALD. DO NOT DISAPPOINT ME.

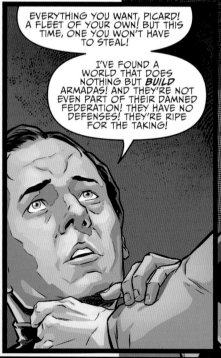

EVERYTHING YOU WANT, PICARD! A FLEET OF YOUR OWN! BUT THIS TIME, ONE YOU WON'T HAVE TO STEAL!

I'VE FOUND A WORLD THAT DOES NOTHING BUT *BUILD* ARMADAS! AND THEY'RE NOT EVEN PART OF THEIR DAMNED FEDERATION! THEY HAVE NO DEFENSES! THEY'RE RIPE FOR THE TAKING!

MR. LA FORGE? DO YOU THINK YOU CAN SUBSTANTIATE MR. BARCLAY'S CLAIM?

I'D BE HAPPY TO TRY, CAPTAIN.

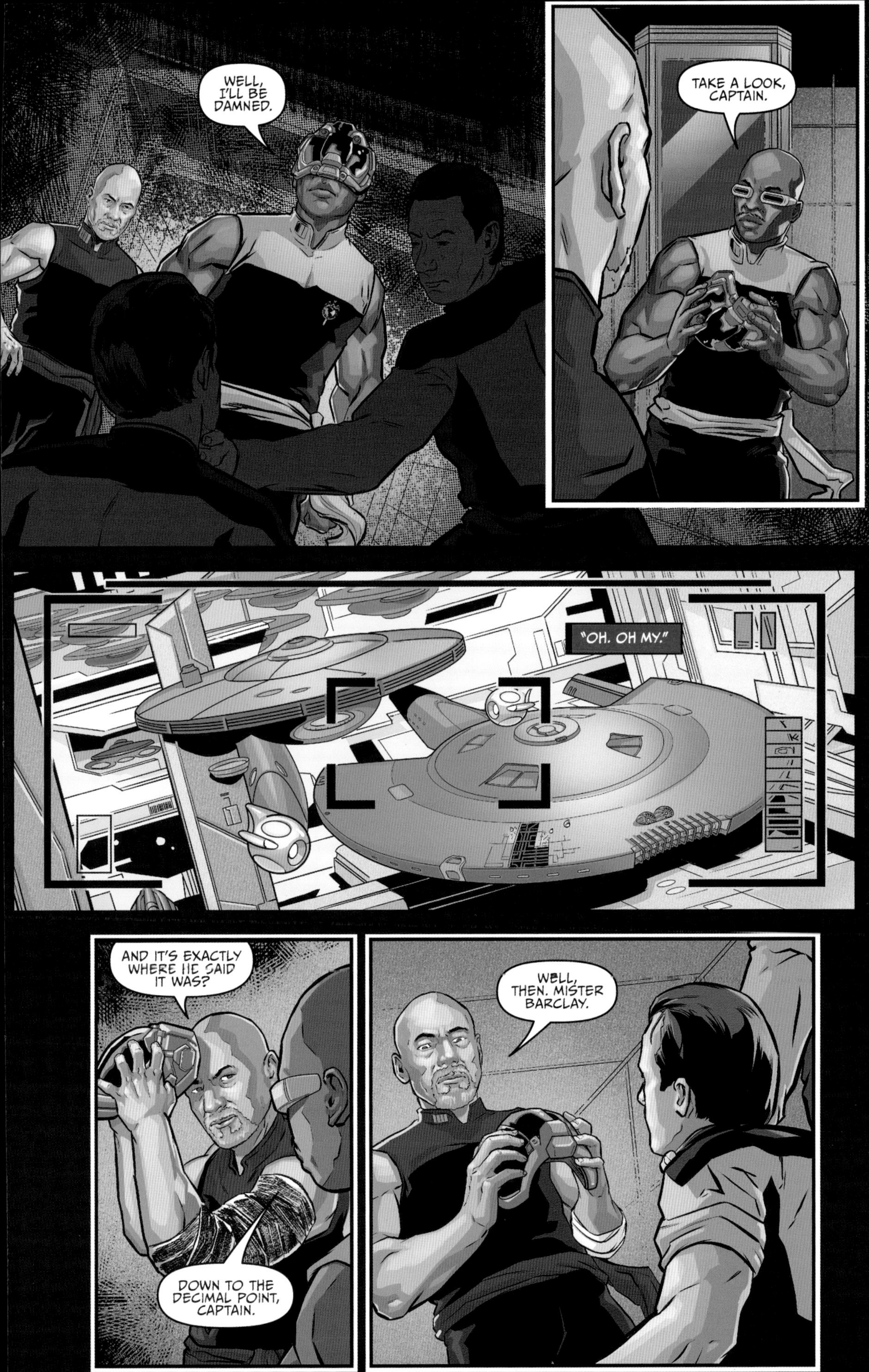
WELL, I'LL BE DAMNED.
TAKE A LOOK, CAPTAIN.
"OH. OH MY."
AND IT'S EXACTLY WHERE HE SAID IT WAS?
DOWN TO THE DECIMAL POINT, CAPTAIN.
WELL, THEN. MISTER BARCLAY.

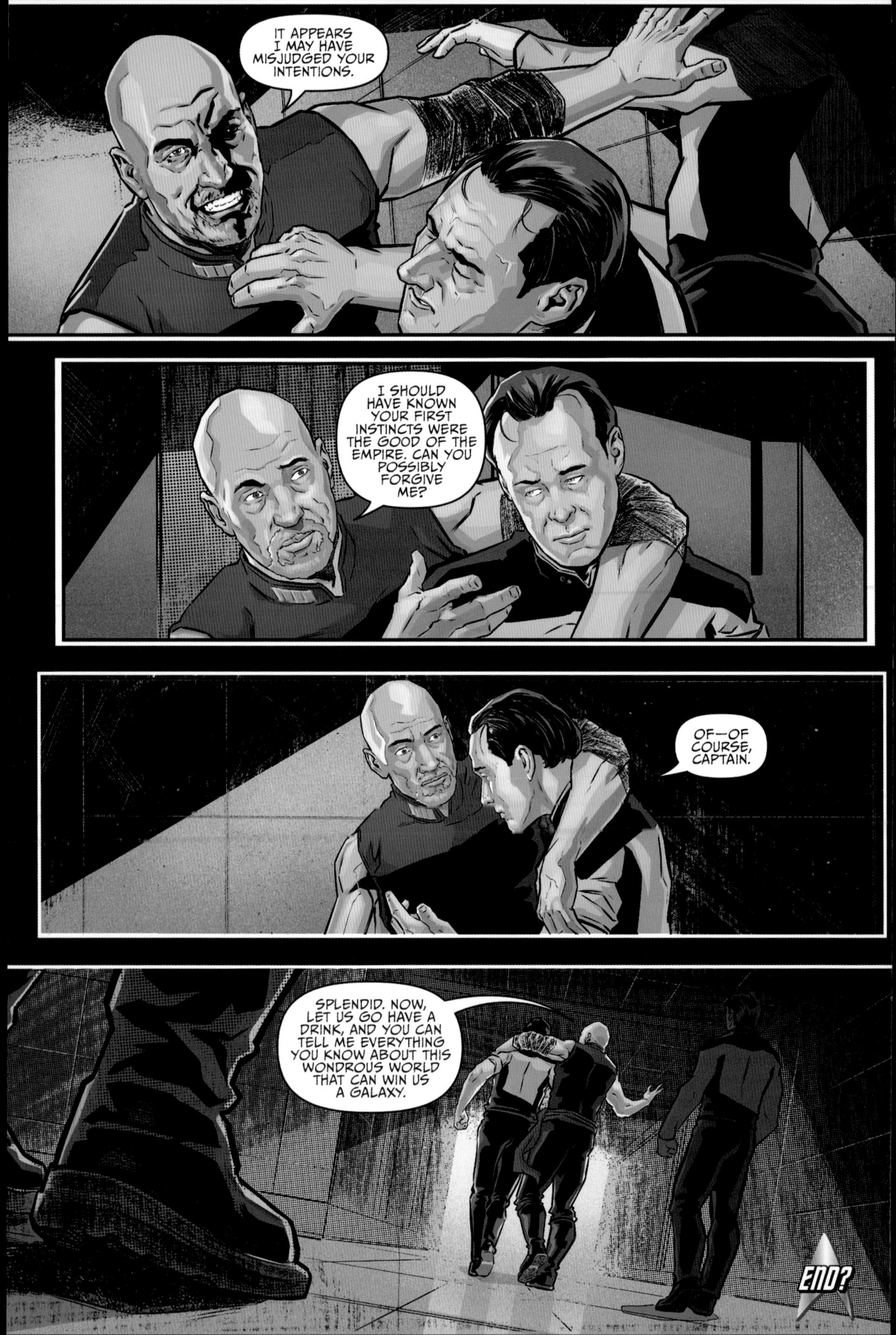
IT APPEARS I MAY HAVE MISJUDGED YOUR INTENTIONS.
I SHOULD HAVE KNOWN YOUR FIRST INSTINCTS WERE THE GOOD OF THE EMPIRE. CAN YOU POSSIBLY FORGIVE ME?
OF—OF COURSE, CAPTAIN.
SPLENDID. NOW, LET US GO HAVE A DRINK, AND YOU CAN TELL ME EVERYTHING YOU KNOW ABOUT THIS WONDROUS WORLD THAT CAN WIN US A GALAXY.
END?

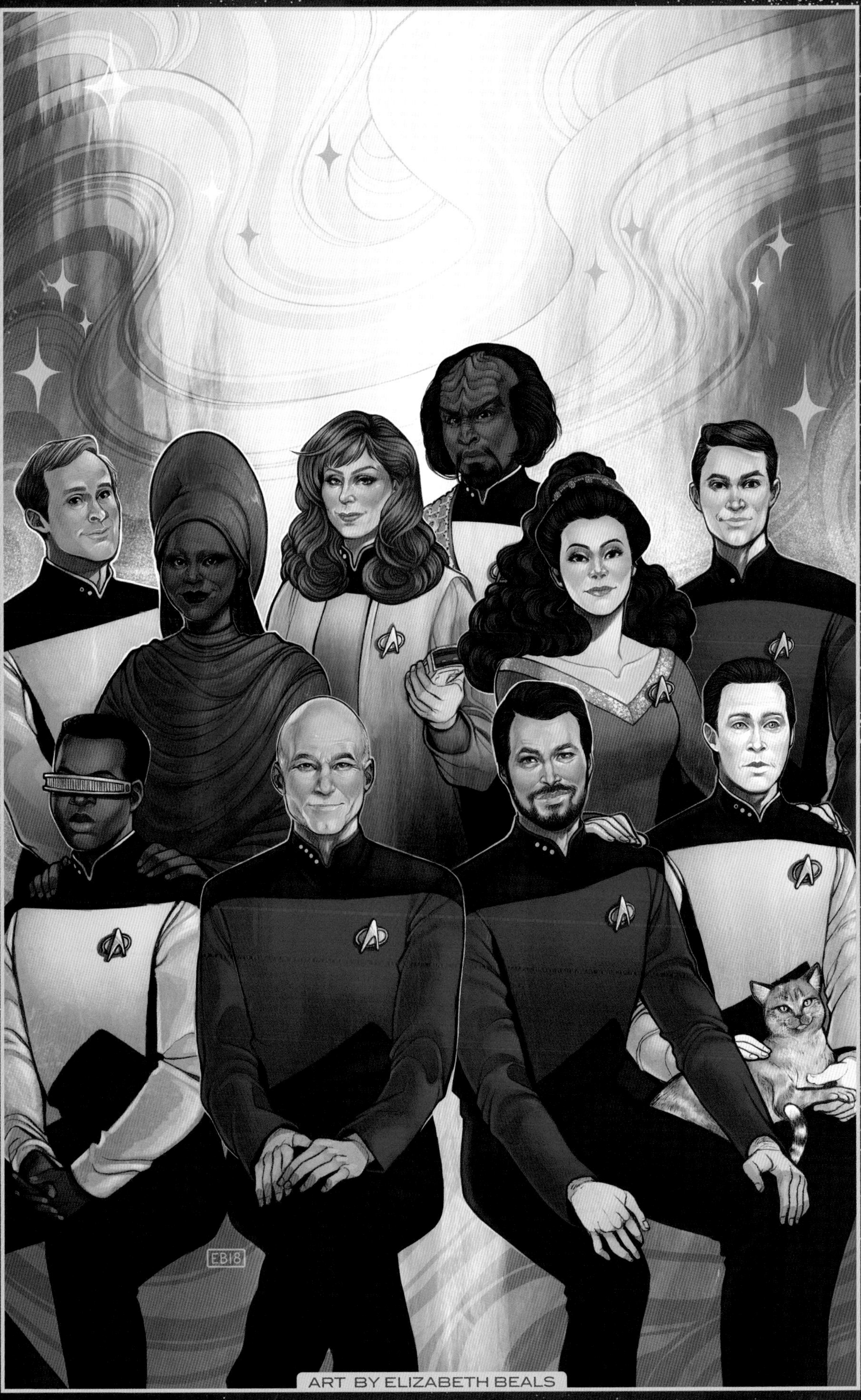
EB18

ART BY ELIZABETH BEALS

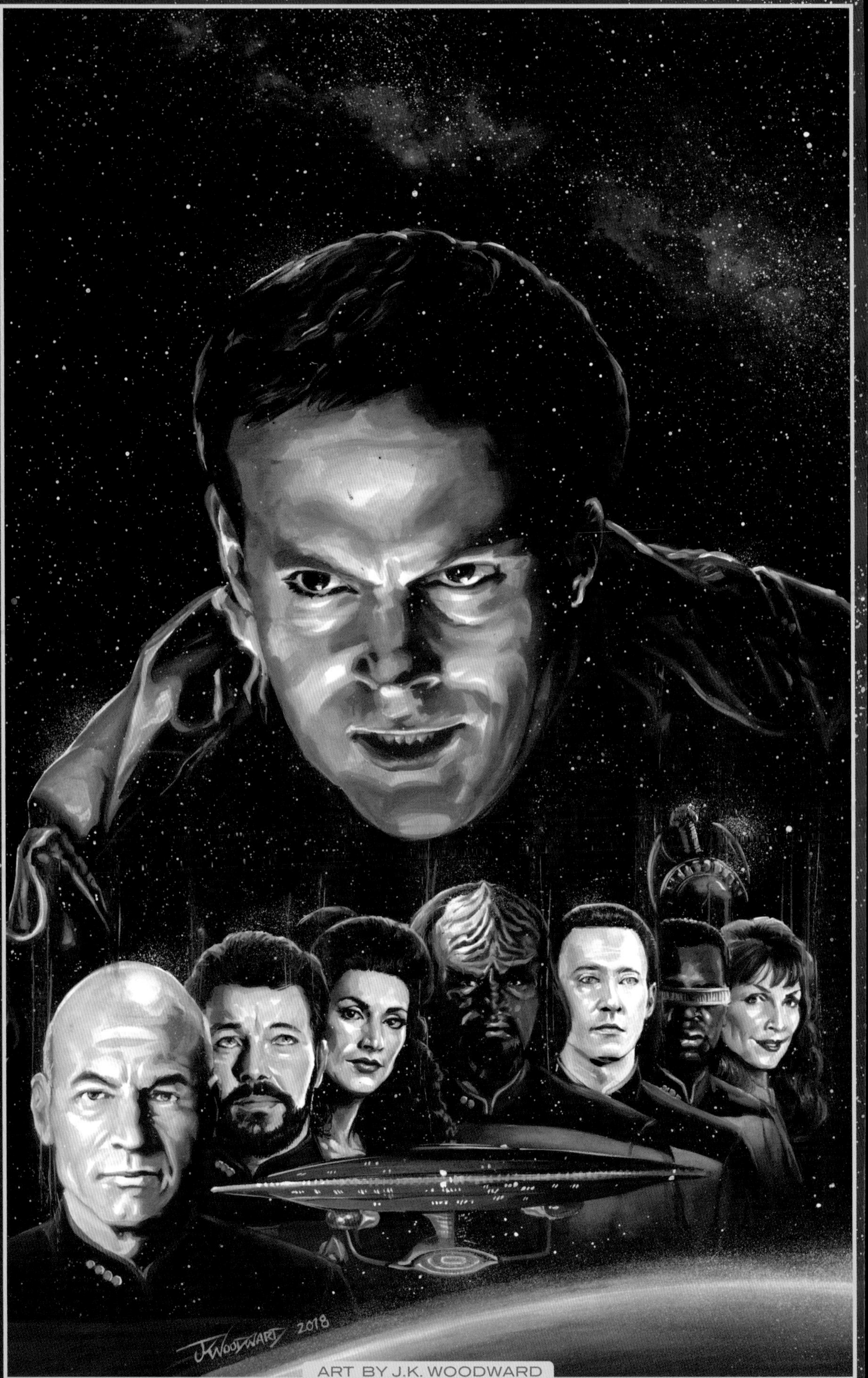

ART BY J.K. WOODWARD

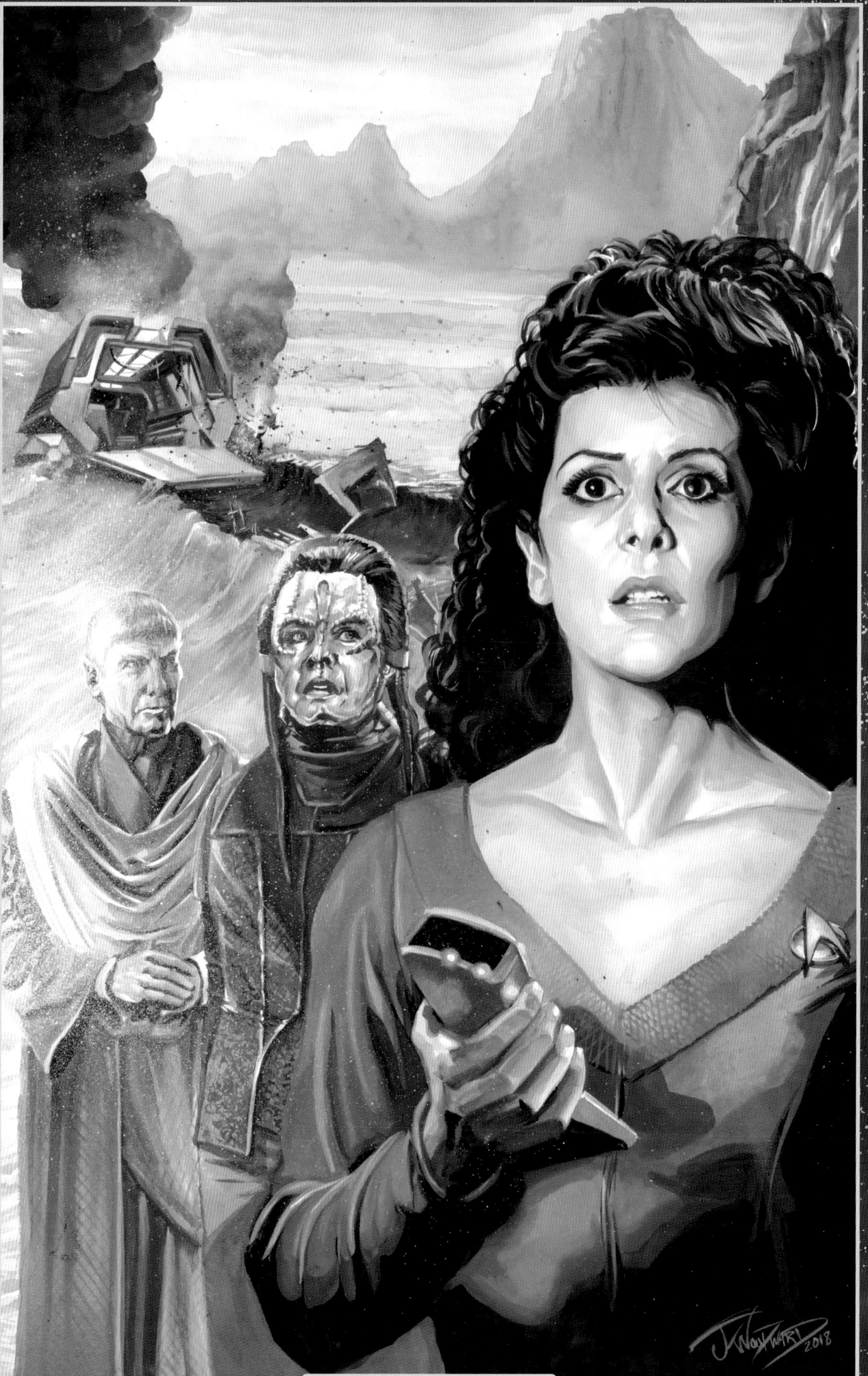

ART BY J.K. WOODWARD

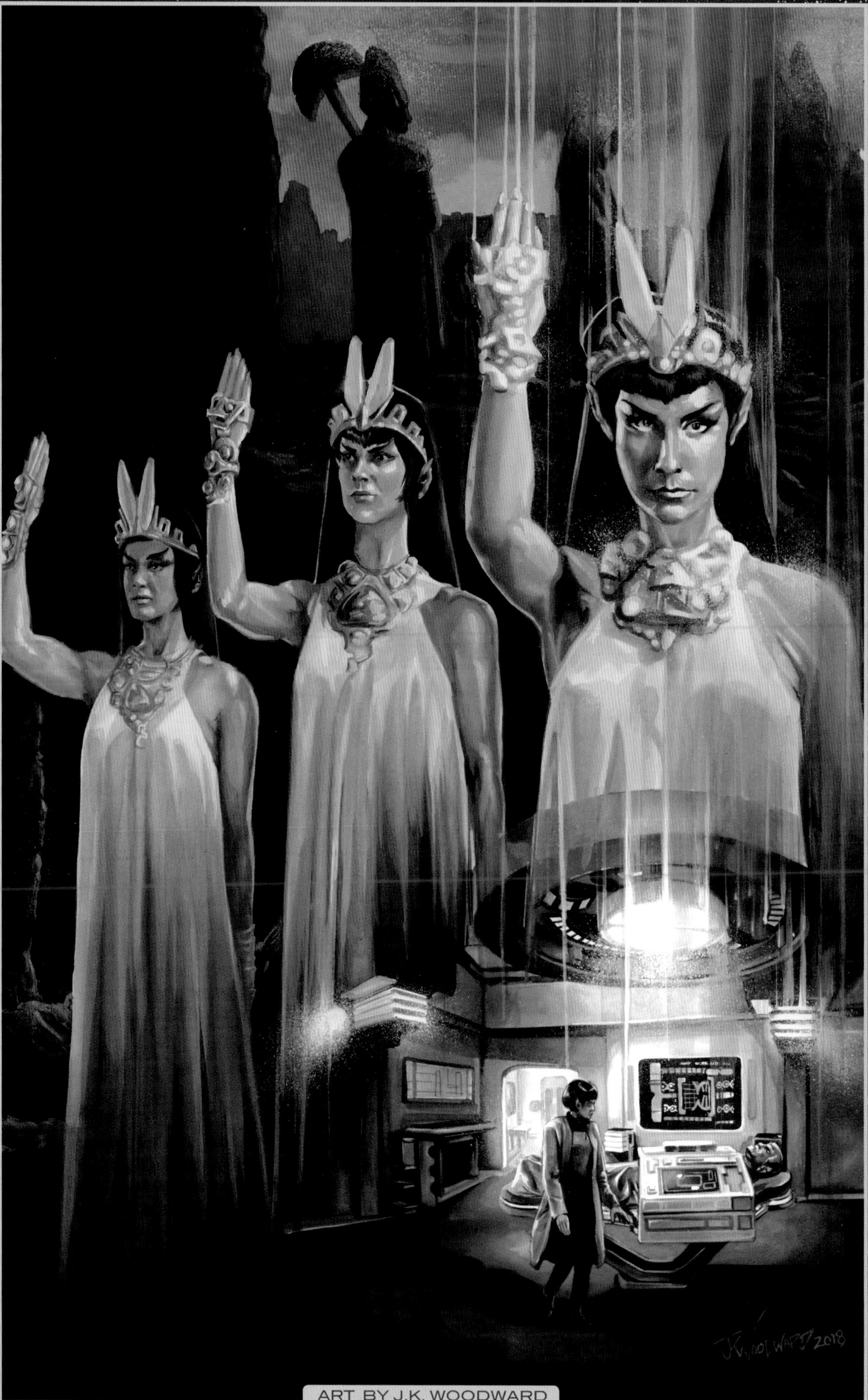
JK WOODWARD 2018

ART BY J.K. WOODWARD

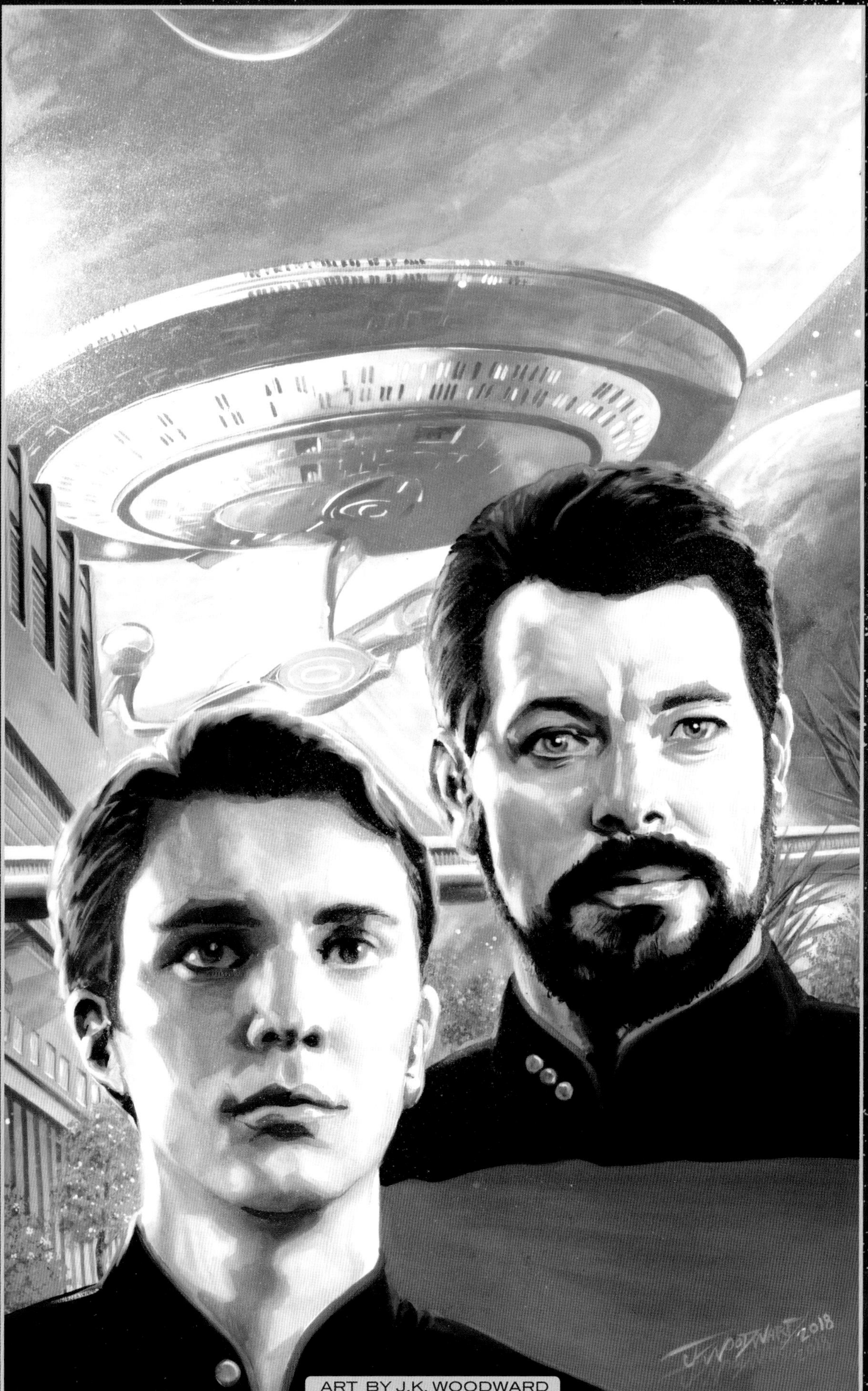
2018

ART BY J.K. WOODWARD

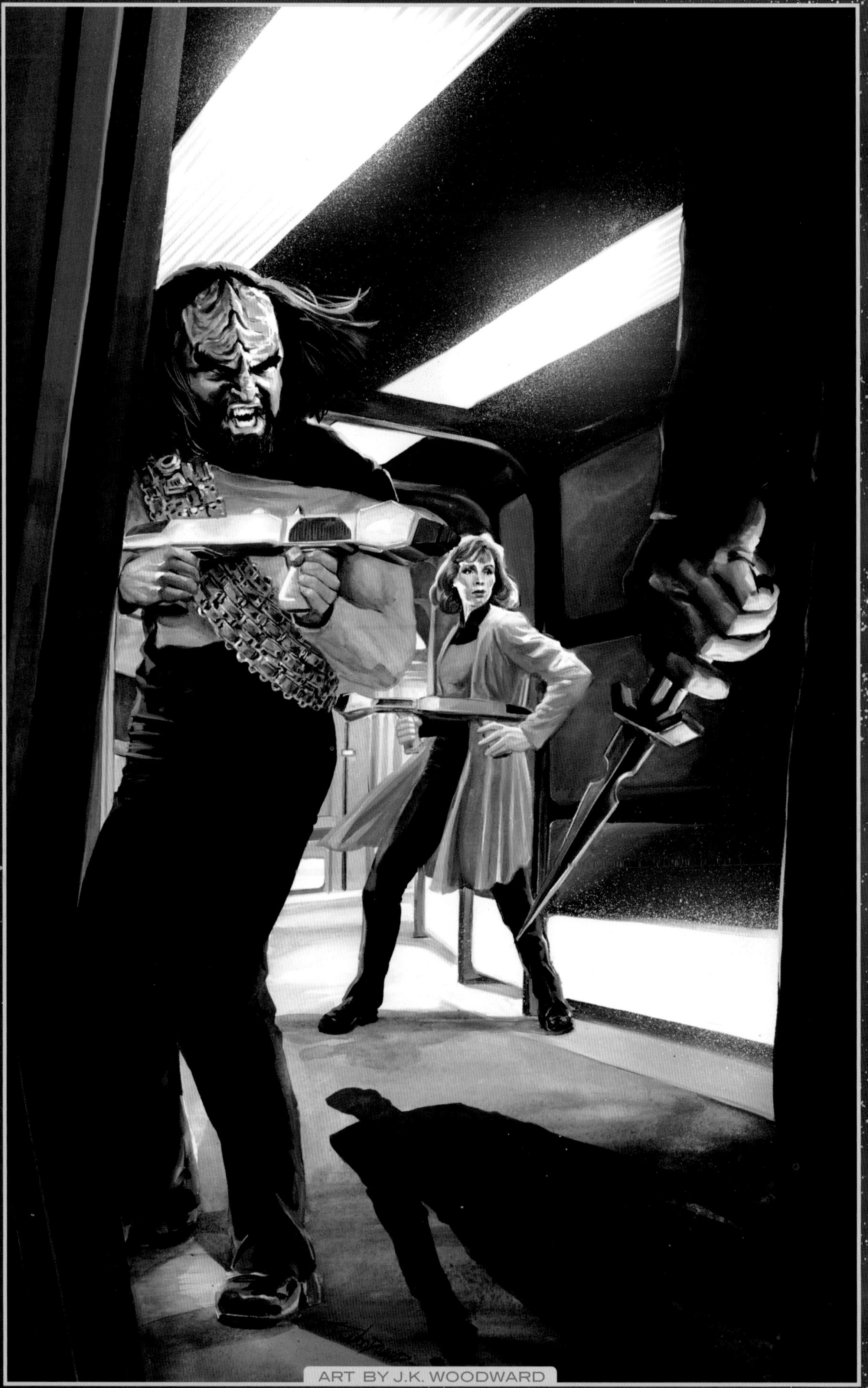

ART BY J.K. WOODWARD

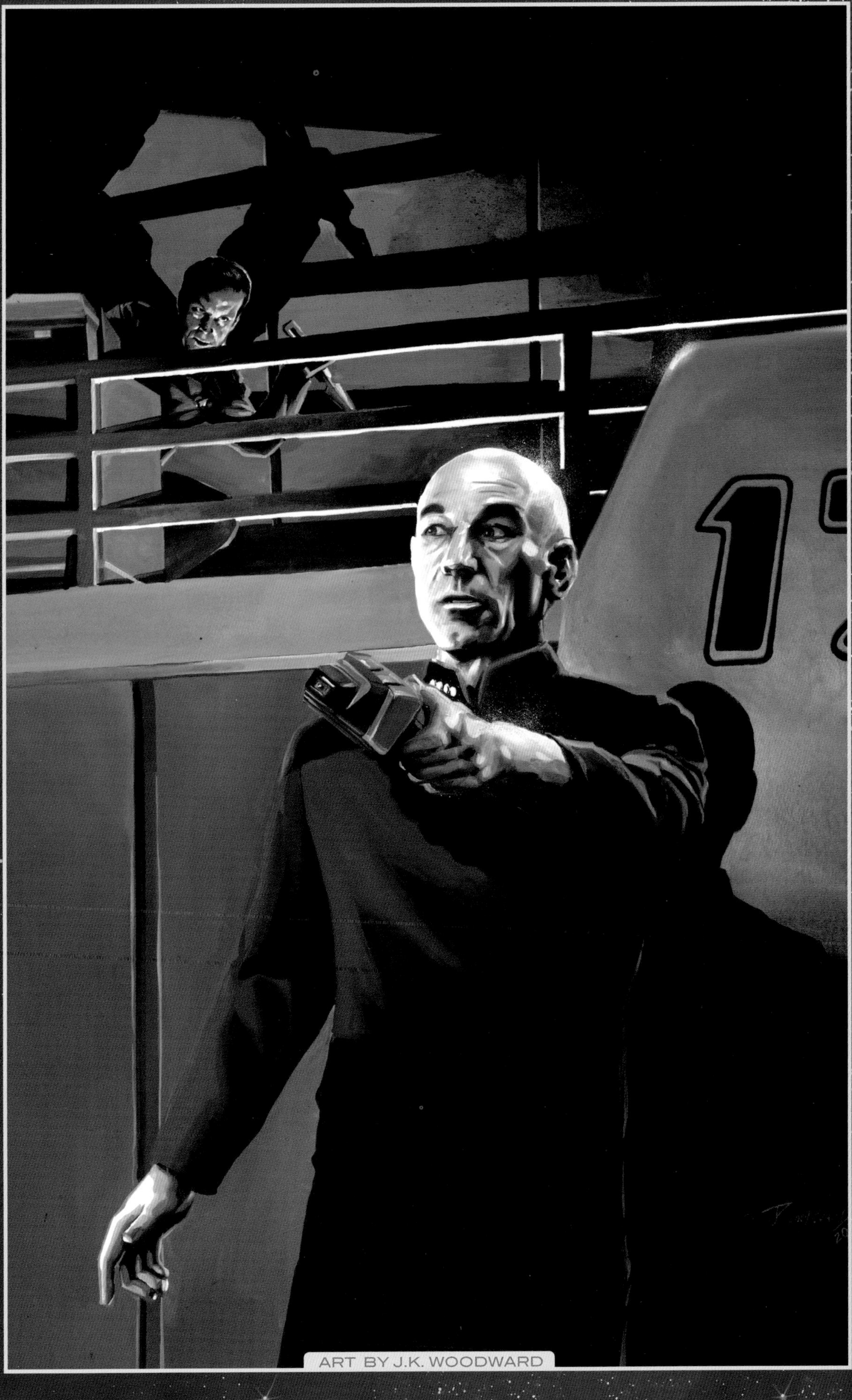
17
ART BY J.K. WOODWARD

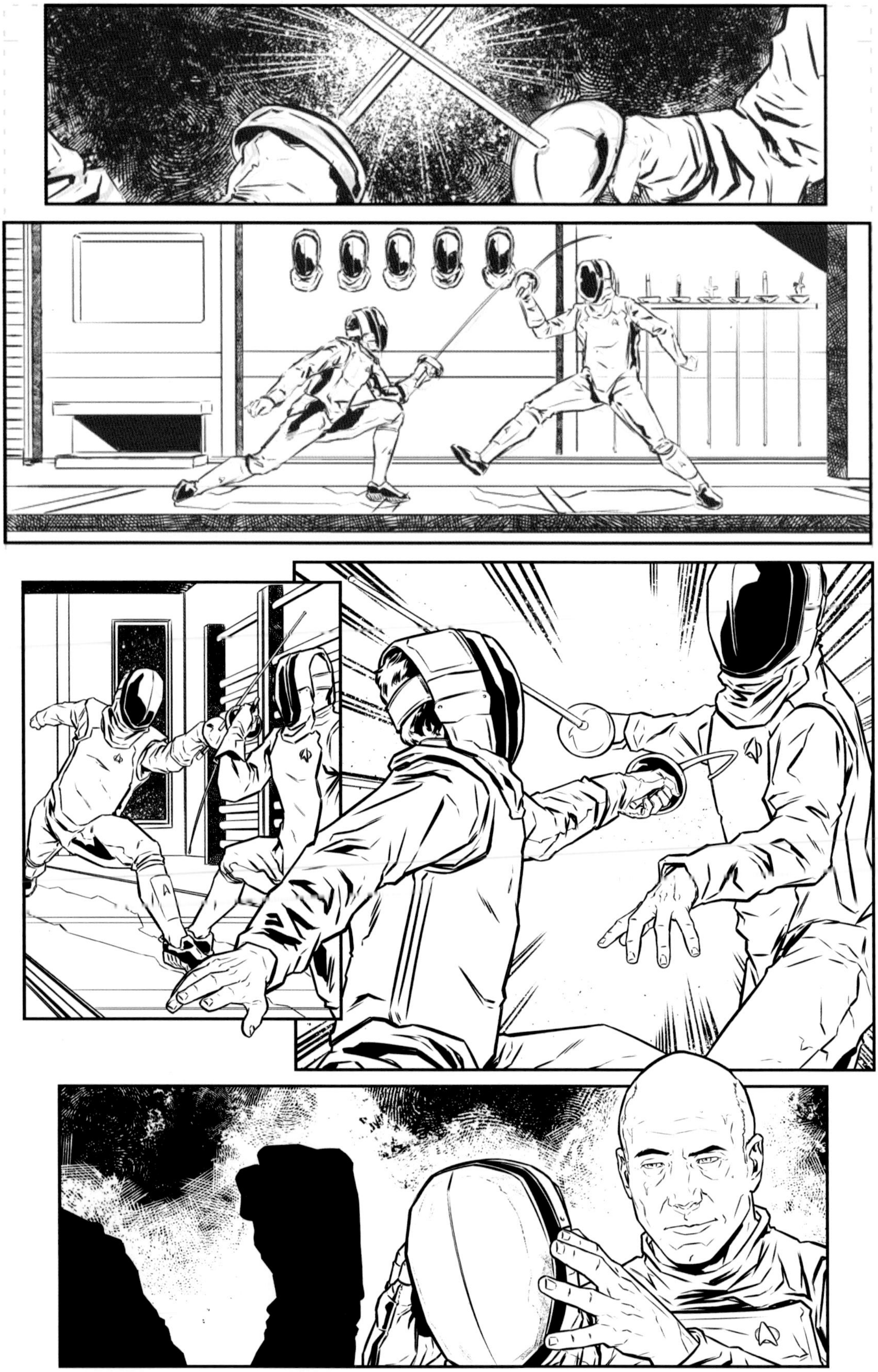

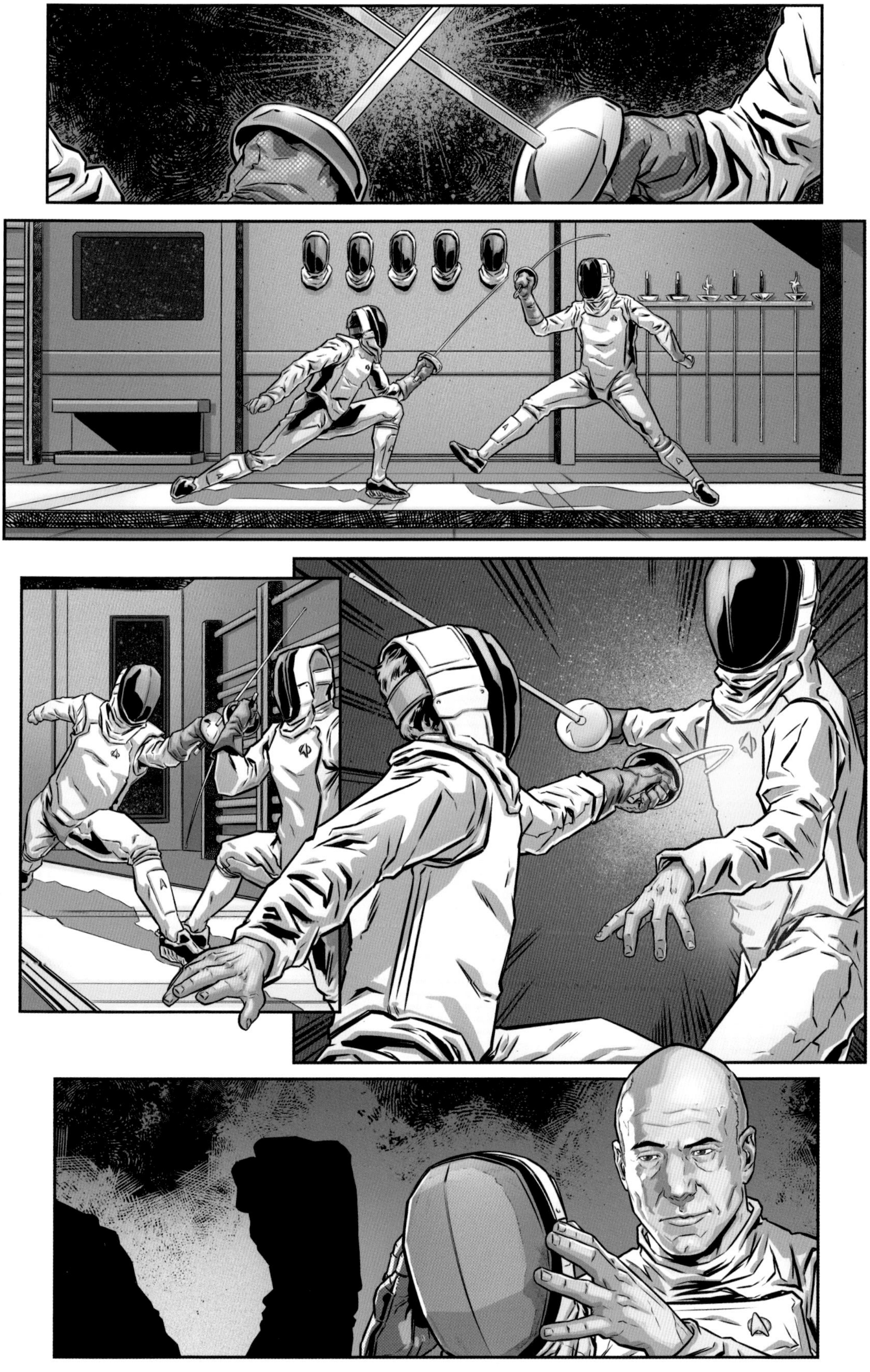

STAR TREK
THE NEXT GENERATION
TERRA INCOGNITA